I0831941

THE DRUGTECH TRILOGY

Book 1:
SPELLBOUND - THE WORKINGS OF DRUGTECH

Book 2:
DRUGTECH - THE DEEP STATE DEEPENS

Book 3:
DRUGTECH – THE FINAL DOSE

The DrugTech Trilogy
ISBN: 978-0-646-85255-3

Marcel Victor Sahade

Contents:

Book 1

SPELLBOUND

THE WORKINGS OF DRUGTECH

Book 1:

To my father-in-law,
Emeritus Professor Philip Kuchel,
whose unwavering dedication to
science provided most of the
inspiration for this book;

...even though he doesn't know it;

...or care to admit it;

...or wish he hadn't.

Chapter 1

Spellbound

Jake was trudging to the bus stop on the way home from school in the usual way. He had his hands in his pockets and his school bag slung over his shoulder. Occasionally he would kick a stone that appeared in front of him. He had made this journey countless times and now he had just completed year eight at his high school. Being the last day of school for the year, he decided to buy himself a chocolate bar for his long bus journey home. He turned right at Milson's Corner instead of heading straight to the bus stop and trudged towards the convenience store on the other side of the park.

Jake entered the park and wondered what he would do during the holidays. He decided he would buy a pair of running shoes and train every morning by running around the block. This way he could return to school in year nine and beat the other kids at running. Jake had always enjoyed running and as he thought about these plans, he hastened his pace towards the convenience store. Jake would go home, collect his money and buy the best pair of running shoes he could. He had been told that the newer kind of shoes not only comfortably gripped the feet, but felt as if you could run on air. As he considered this, he gazed down at his own school shoes. The toes were scratched and his left shoelace was undone. Jake bent down to tie his shoelace up before continuing. He was now only about 200 metres from the convenience store. When Jake had finished tying his shoelace, something golden glittered from beneath the bushes about 20 metres to his left.

Jake tilted his head to catch another glimpse. It was difficult to make out. He started to head towards it. There were several bushes in and around the park and this particular one was quite large. Jake needed to bend down and place his hands under the bushes to feel around for anything that could have caused the glittering that he had observed. After moving his hands around, Jake hit upon something hard and certainly not part of the bush. He put his hand around it and grabbed it. Jake slid out a rather large book.

The book was white with glittering gold edges. It was quite heavy for Jake and he needed both hands to hold it. It was as thick as the phone book but larger. On the front, in beautiful gold letters were emblazoned the words, "Book of Spells". He could have sworn the book had a slight hum but as he held it towards his ear, it was no louder. Perhaps it was because he was in an open park and the wind was playing tricks on him. As he flipped through the pages, he noticed that each page contained a beautifully coloured picture with a heading and smaller writing underneath. Jake was fascinated as he read things like "How to run faster than a Cheetah". Jake knew that the Cheetah was the fastest land animal on earth and that it was impossible for a human to run this fast. The picture showed a creature with the body of a Cheetah but the head of a boy. His hair was blown backwards as the creature sprinted through the woods.

Jake flipped over some pages and read, "How to breathe underwater." The picture was that of a young boy swimming underwater with a school of fish to his left and a dolphin to his right. Air bubbles had come out of the boy's mouth but the boy seemed to be very deep under water.

Jake flipped all around the book and was even more fascinated to read, "How to make yourself invisible." The picture showed an empty field made up of rich green grass. Towards the centre of the picture, the grass was depressed in two small footprints as if a boy was standing there, but there was no sign of him.

Jake looked around to see if the owner of this book could be found. No one took much notice of him. Jake knew the book really couldn't work. These so-called 'spells' were impossible. But the book was very majestic and the pictures and the writing were extremely beautiful. It was exactly how he'd imagine a wizard's book to be. He decided to read the book on the bus on his way home and put the book in his bag in the meantime. The bag was now bulky and heavy and Jake didn't really feel like buying himself a chocolate bar anymore.

Jake wished to catch the bus as soon as possible so he could read through the book more thoroughly. He was dying to try a spell. "Surely they couldn't work," he thought to himself, but that didn't stop the niggling feeling that was growing inside Jake as he made for the bus stop. "At least try one, see if it worked. Imagine if it did work. Could I really be invisible?" he thought to himself, "Could I really run as fast as a Cheetah or breathe underwater? What were the other spells? Was there one for flying?" Jake hastened his pace till he was running as fast as he could.

Jake arrived at the bus stop huffing and puffing. His bag was now extremely heavy and his shoulder was aching. He was sweating heavily and his heart was pounding both from the run and his excitement. He wouldn't dare pull the book out on the bus stop. Too many people about. It was quite awkward and heavy and too many stray eyes would be curious about the lovely pictures in the book. No, the only way was to wait for the bus to arrive. He would find himself a seat in the back corner of the bus and pull the book out on his lap. Finally, after what seemed like an eternity, the bus arrived and Jake waited for the others to board the bus as they hustled towards the narrow doors. "Hurry," Jake was saying to himself, "These people are taking forever." Eventually, he made his way onto the bus. Yes, everyone had now sat towards the front of the bus and Jake wandered towards the back of the bus and enjoyed his privacy. He settled down in the back corner and placing his bag on his lap, he pulled the book out of it.

He opened it again somewhere in the middle and read, "How to talk to the animals." The picture showed that of a boy talking to a bird perched on a fence in front of him. Excitedly he decided to read the book from the beginning. He noticed that each page was quite thick, thicker than cardboard which probably made the book as heavy as it was. He closed the book and examined the cover once more. He then opened the cover to reveal the first page. Funny, no introduction, no prologue, no preface, no instructions. The first page was like the rest. A spell with a picture. The first spell was, "How to always know the time." The picture showed a boy sitting at his desk with his elbows on the desk and his fingers crossed in the usual crisscross fashion. A pendulum clock was ticking on the wall behind him. The skin of his left wrist was clearly whiter than his surrounding skin showing where a watch must have been. Jake looked at his own watch. It was four o'clock and he pulled the watch away from his skin to observe a similar mark.

Jake read beneath the heading, "Place your watch on the picture and smash the watch with a hammer. You will then always know the time." Jake thought to himself, "I'm not going to do that. I would probably just wreck my watch. Perhaps I would try another spell first."

He flipped the page over and read, "How to learn all that is knowable." The picture was a scene from a library. Hundreds of books lined the shelves from floor to ceiling and several were open and strewn across a table.

Jake read on, "Peel the picture off the page, roll it in a ball, and swallow it." Jake took another look at the picture. This one was different. It was like a sticker. This picture could be peeled off the page. "Would I do it now?" he thought to himself. Jake decided he would keep the book intact for the moment. He would go home to his bedroom, lie on his bed and read the book some more. Then he could peel the picture off, roll it into a ball, and swallow it in due course. Jake was extremely fascinated by now and the book he was studying was quite mesmerising. "Surely there is a spell I could try right now on the bus just to see if the book was for real?" he thought to himself.

Jake was almost disappointed at the prospect. What if the spells didn't work? Would he be that upset? What if they did? Would he be too powerful? No, he would use the spells properly and carefully if they did work. If the spells worked, he decided he would keep them secret and never reveal to anybody how he was able to do what he did. Yes, he would keep it secret and harness the power in a good and proper way. He would think carefully before doing any spell and not make any mistakes, always proceeding with caution. But of course, only if the spells worked. He looked again at the book. The book contained hundreds of pages, with a different spell on each page.

The next page was the one he saw in the park, "How to make yourself invisible." He looked once more at the depressions in the grassy field.

He read beneath, "Illuminate this page with candlelight at night and say the passage below. You will be invisible for 24 hours:

With cloak and dagger and night time here

shroud me with darkness till I disappear."

Jake recalled where his mother kept the candles in the kitchen drawer. He could get one tonight and illuminate the page with it in the quiet of his bedroom.

Jake turned the page again. "How to remove magic spells". The picture showed a girl asleep in a bed. She must have been asleep for quite a while as cobwebs had begun to form on the blankets and the walls. Obviously, the girl was in a magical trance. A boy stood in front of the bed with an outstretched hand over the girl's head.

Jake read on. "Stretch out your hand to that which is spellbound and say the word 'Shaharazam'". Jake enunciated the word to himself. Jake wondered whether this spell was really useful. He thought to himself, if he was invisible from the spell before, instead of it lasting for 24 hours, he could remove the spell with this one. He then thought that the spell could perhaps be used to undo all the other spells. Maybe he could return the knowledge of all those books out of his head or he could give back the power of running as fast as a Cheetah or breathing underwater. Indeed, this was quite a useful spell after all. Perhaps he could not only undo his own spells but some other person's spell as well. What if other people had done spells? What if he was under a spell right now and didn't know it? Then Jake had a chilling thought.

What if the owner of the book was invisible and had followed him on the bus? What if someone invisible was sitting right next to him? This was, at last, a spell he could do on the bus. Jake looked all around him. He carefully held his hand up next to his chest. He faced the front of the bus and suddenly felt solemn and a bit frightened. He then muttered the word "Shaharazam" very quietly so no one on the bus could hear him. Jake looked around and no one had become visible. Either the spell didn't work or there were no invisible people next to him. Jake was slightly relieved but also slightly disappointed. He decided to continue reading. He gazed back down at the book. Jake was horrified and he immediately broke out into goosebumps all over his body. The pages of the book were blank.

Chapter 2

The Lost Treasure of Count De Jager

Samuel was the Captain of the pirate ship Douglas. The Douglas had sailed all week through stormy weather and rough seas. Its Captain and crew of 14 were exhausted and hungry. It was now late afternoon and the storm had finally passed. The setting sun had become visible through patches of clouds towards the horizon. Samuel stood on deck bathed in the red warm glow of the setting sun. His crew were preparing for the evening meal. Several of them were rolling newly acquired iron barrels onto the deck and stuffing them with wood and coal for the fire. Tonight, the crew of the Douglas were looking forward to a warm meal and rum. The ship was due to put down anchor in the morning where Samuel had promised the crew a week's shore leave on Mount Yearning.

The red glow from the setting sun made way to the glow from the blazing barrels on board. Samuel observed several of the crew gathering around them to warm themselves. Slowly the exhausted crew commenced speaking with each other as they became warmer from the blazing fires and the large quantities of rum they consumed. It wasn't long before the crew engaged in the usual revelry that preceded a well-deserved hot meal. The Captain had requested Sebastian, the chief cook of the Douglas to prepare a meal for himself and Terrence in the Captain's quarters. Terrence was the First Mate of the Douglas and tonight Samuel had planned to speak with him.

Captain Samuel commanded the respect and admiration of his crew. He had been Captain of the Douglas now for ten years and served as the First Mate to the former Captain for five. Samuel gave the former Captain a burial at sea and had always spoken fondly of his most beloved Captain. The crew often referred to the spirit of the former Captain of the Douglas possessing Captain Samuel.

Samuel did not engage in the crew's revelry tonight. By now the sun had set and the flames of the burning logs and hot coals had died down as the crew each held out their portion of meat over the coals. Sebastian signalled to the Captain that all had been prepared and Samuel motioned Terrence into his cabin. The Captain's cabin had been prepared for a meal. Sebastian, the now elderly cook of the Douglas knew quite well his Captain's desires for civilised meals. He had prepared the table with a fine linen cloth and set burning several candles for light.

Terrence knew the features of his Captain's face as they took their places at table. The Captain appeared concerned and slightly troubled. He was obviously fixated on an idea which he had been considering for quite some time.

Samuel began, "Terrence, tomorrow morning we should be dropping anchor and going ashore for shore leave. I expect this should last for seven days."

"I was surprised that you chose Mount Yearning for shore leave," replied Terrence, "Several other islands along the way would have done quite well."

Mount Yearning was an isolated island only used occasionally by pirates to effect repairs on their damaged ship after battle or to evade a naval search. The Douglas had made its way unnecessarily through stormy weather to head for this island.

Samuel stared at Terrence. "Have you heard of the lost treasure of Count De Jager?" Terrence knew the question was rhetorical and waited for his Captain to continue. "I have been in search of this all my life."

The lost treasure of Count De Jager was reputed to be the greatest fortune on earth. It was said to consist of rubies, diamonds, sapphires and countless other precious stones as well as gold and silver.

"I know that Count De Jager lived in the 13th century," said Terrence. "He had persuaded kings and princes and other rich people to invest with him and promised them large returns. He hoarded the finest jewellery, precious stones and gold. Then one night, the Count and his treasure had disappeared. It was rumoured he smuggled the treasure out of the country and had a map drawn up and that a trusted servant of his killed him and took the map. Neither the Count nor the servant had been seen since."

The Captain had always admired Terrence's historical knowledge. Samuel listened to the sound of the waves breaking under the ship as the crew outside broke into song. He gazed at Terrence and said slowly, "I have the map." As he said this, the Captain's voice became softer but the expression on his face hardened. Terrence was captivated.

Terrence wished to respond but Sebastian entered the room to serve the main course. The Captain and First Mate were being served roasted quail and bread tonight. The sound of the waves and the revelry of the crew were muffled once more when Sebastian closed the door upon leaving. In a voice not much louder, Terrence questioned his Captain, "How did you get it?"

"It's a long story," replied Samuel. "The treasure is located on the Island of Mount Yearning."

Terrence knew how serious the Captain was. Captain Samuel was extremely meticulous. He had thought out plans all his life and had never failed in a mission.

Samuel waited for Terrence to take it all in, then setting his meal to one side, he produced a scroll from inside his shirt which he unfolded on the table.

"It is important the crew do not hear of this for the moment," whispered Samuel.

"I understand," said Terrence. His eyes grew as he studied the map his Captain had laid out.

The map was clearly old and rugged. Illuminated by candlelight and shrouded by legend it appeared quite mysterious. It was jagged around the edges and seemed to be a leather parchment. There were several coloured pigments on the map which had faded over the years.

"Here is Mount Yearning," the Captain whispered as he pointed to a place on the map. "Over here begins a path up the mountain but beyond this ridge is the entrance to the caves." Samuel moved his finger over the map as he spoke. He had memorised every inch of this map by now and could reproduce it in its finest detail. "The entrance to the caves is the key."

Samuel looked at Terrence through squinting eyes. "The map shows where the treasure is hidden in these caves. When the crew goes ashore, we shall stay aboard and wait for night. Then under cover of darkness we shall enter the caves and take the treasure aboard. We shall place it under these floor boards." Terrence presumed the floor boards upon which they were sitting concealed a hidden area. He waited for his Captain to continue.

"I have planned this for the past ten years," said Samuel taking a deep breath. Samuel paused as Sebastian returned with some ale. Samuel waited for the elderly servant to fill both glasses and leave before he continued. "I have foreseen every possible contingency."

"What do we do once we get it aboard?" said Terrence.

"We sail home," said Samuel. "We shall unload the treasure there and both of us can retire from this life. We shall leave some money for the crew to take over, then you and I can return to civilisation as wealthy gentlemen. We will each take a wife and employ servants to take care of us. It's time both of us ended our career on board the Douglas and settled down."

Terrence smiled at the prospect. He had always known his Captain would take care of his crew and after faithful years of service, the Captain was providing him not only with early retirement but a wealthy one at that.

"To the treasure," said the Captain as he held up his glass and drank the ale. Samuel's plan was a simple one. He would recover the treasure with the help of Terrence and then kill him. The Captain well knew that Terrence would sooner or later desire Samuel's death. Treasure and riches had always been the prime mover of the pirate and Samuel knew that his survival depended on careful planning and sharp wits. Captain Samuel had not risen to his state in life by taking risks and he was not willing to start. All had been planned now for some time and the Douglas was precisely where he had wished it to be. Terrence sat wide eyed and smiled as he thought of the treasure.

Samuel now relaxed and afforded himself a smile as he looked at Terrence. How pathetic his First Mate seemed to him sitting ignorantly across him from the table. Samuel had always seen Terrence as naïve in the ways of piracy, and Samuel, for one moment, thought he would almost regret Terrence's death. As Samuel smiled, he felt his mouth seize up. Foam bubbled out of his mouth and his head felt heavy. He rose suddenly from the table and snatched the map stumbling across the room. As Terrence approached, Samuel recalled how he had once pried the map from the hand of his own dead Captain.

Chapter 3

The Barrister

"Has the Jury reached a verdict?" asked the Clerk of Arraigns standing in front of the Judge. The crowded courtroom had become deathly silent.

"We have Your Honour," said the foreperson as she looked towards the other nodding members of the jury.

"How say you? Is the accused guilty or not guilty?"

"Not guilty," said the foreperson, and the Court erupted.

"The accused is discharged," said the Judge over the commotion of the gallery and hustle of the journalists, "Court will adjourn."

The law student sat quietly as she observed the cool features of her barrister who had just won the case for the accused. She was now into her third day of work experience with Mr Hunter Barrister-at-Law but she had well known of his reputation and unblemished record. Mr Hunter was the most unusual barrister she had ever observed.

The accused and his solicitor left to make a statement to the media. "Now when the media ask you how we did it Jennifer" said Mr Hunter to the law student, "remain poker faced and say nothing at all. We don't talk to the press. Come on, let's get back to Chambers."

Jennifer was almost disappointed. It was not that she wished the media attention in her new business suit and mini skirt that she bought for the occasion, but she really wanted to know just how Mr Hunter did win this 'doomed from the very beginning' case. In fact, Mr Hunter had never lost a case in the 15 years that he practised as a barrister. Jennifer vowed she would not relax until she discovered his secret.

"Remember," said Mr Hunter, "poker faced," and he gathered up the last of his papers and headed for the door.

"Right," said the law student as she jumped from her seat and grabbed her bag.

On the steps of the Court the barrister and the law student were mobbed by the surrounding media. Jennifer was dazzled by camera flashes, news cameras and tape recorders which were shoved in front of her face and Mr Hunter.

"Do you think justice was really done today?" screamed one reporter over the other. "Will your client return to acting Mr Hunter or has he given up?" jested another reporter.

Jennifer observed that Mr Hunter remained incredibly stone faced. In fact, his face seemed quite pale and his stone-cold cheeks were almost blue. He was unreadable as he steadfastly made his way through the media jungle. This was not arrogance. Mr Hunter had no need to show any arrogance with the unblemished reputation that already buzzed around him. Jennifer could see this reputation growing ever so more as the media were sure to continue this story for some time to come.

Finally, the crowds dispersed as Jennifer and Mr Hunter made their way into the lift of his barrister's Chambers. The lift stopped at the ninth floor and the barrister and Jennifer alighted into a huge foyer. It had a tremendous view over the harbour with several visitor seats arranged to capture it. It had a thick rich olive-green carpet so that when Jennifer and the barrister walked to his office past the reception desk, they made no sound.

"Shut the door," said Mr Hunter as he slumped in his chair behind his desk. He held his hands up to his face and rocked back in his chair. Jennifer did as she was told and settled into the chair in front of the desk. Jennifer thought now was the chance to get some answers.

"Mr Hunter, I think you are a brilliant man and an extraordinary barrister. You have such insight in the cases you run and yet you hardly open a book or take a piece of paper home with you. Can I ask you, how do you do it?"

Mr Hunter stared at Jennifer. She felt his look penetrate the depths of her soul and she feared him. Then his expression changed and she detected a slight quirky smile and she found herself captivated by his eyes.

"I read face," said the barrister.

Jennifer waited for him to continue but he didn't. "What do you mean?" she said, "I don't understand." Her eyebrows narrowed.

"When you read a word to yourself, do you spell out each letter to yourself before you know what it is?"

"No, not anymore. Not if I know the word. It is pattern recognition," Jennifer was trying hard to understand him.

"Yes. The Chinese have their own pattern recognition as do the Japanese and the Arabs. They can all look at their own patterns of letters and know what a word means on sight."

"Yes, I'm sure they do, I hadn't really thought of that. But what are you getting at, I don't understand?"

Mr Hunter continued, "And when you look at a clock. Do you recognise a pattern in the hands of the clock which tells you the time?"

"Yes, I suppose I do," Jennifer said looking quizzical.

"And when the deaf communicate through sign language, they have learnt to read the other person's hands and actions."

"Yes," Jennifer wished he would come to the point.

"But do you really appreciate the significance here? We are all well adept at recognising patterns. When you see a car in the street, do you look to see if there is a steering wheel with doors and wheels before you know that it is a car or are you just familiar with the general shape of a car allowing for slight differences between different makes?"

"I guess I just thought I knew a car when I saw one."

"Well, I read faces," said Mr Hunter. "There are quite a number of muscles on the face and each one can interact in a complicated language that tells me precisely what the person is thinking. As a person has thoughts, the face expression changes. To me it is like reading sign language or the pages of a book. The teeth, the cheeks, their colour, the eyebrows, eyes, even the angle of the head, all of these are the letters that make up the words of my language. You could say, I read face."

"You mean you know if a witness is frightened or happy or things like that?

"Everybody knows things like that," said the barrister, "From the obvious patterns we have been brought up to recognise but if you look closer at a person's face, you can know much more indeed. You can read all that the person is thinking. This is what gives me the advantage over the witnesses, the judge and the jury."

"If I am thinking of a number between one and ten, can you tell me what I am thinking?" suggested Jennifer.

"You are thinking of 25, your favourite number, the day of the month you were born. You are also wondering if what I am telling you is true or not."

Jennifer was amazed but tried to remain objective.

"Do you have a photograph on you, let me show you something," said the barrister.

Jennifer opened her handbag and pulled out a photograph of herself and four friends which was taken when she was last at the movies with them. The five of them were standing in a line smiling at the camera.

"This person's name is Allison," said the barrister as he pointed to the second person in the photo.

"Yes, how did you know that, do you know her?" asked Jennifer.

"No, I have never met her at all," said the barrister, "but the boy's face here is telling me that he is thinking whether he could ask Allison out to dinner and he is waiting for the best time to ask her."

Jennifer found it difficult to believe. She recalled that Brad and Allison did go out to dinner last weekend. "How can you tell that detail?" she asked.

"To me it's like reading a book." The barrister continued pointing at the second person in the photo, "Allison is wondering if her hair looks OK for the photo. She also wishes to get home to take her washing off the line."

Jennifer was dumbfounded as she watched him continue.

"The third person is hungry. He wishes to eat before the movie but is too embarrassed to ask you all because he knows it is only four o'clock and he would seem foolish." The barrister continued, "The fourth person is Steven. He is very tired and wants to go to sleep. He was at his friend Melissa's party all night last night and still has the sound of the loud music in his ears."

"What about me, what does my face show?" Jennifer was slightly embarrassed but too excited to stop.

"You want Pamela to give the camera to Steven so he can take a photo of you with Pamela." Jennifer was astonished. He was exactly right. She could not believe how he was doing this. "What am I thinking about right now?" Her eyes were wide with excitement.

The barrister looked at her and smiled. "You are thinking of sun baking by a beach. You also believe what I am telling you but you are scared also that I may know everything about you, well relax Jennifer," the barrister paused, "I know everything about everyone."

Jennifer believed him. "Can you teach me to read face Mr Hunter?" asked Jennifer.

"Of course I could teach you, but you don't know what you are asking," he replied.

"What do you mean?" she inquired. She really wanted to learn to read face for herself.

The barrister peered at her with those penetrating eyes and looked quite serious. It frightened her but she admired him and wanted to be like him.

"You know how when you see a word, you cannot help but read it? Have you ever tried not to read it?" he asked without removing his stare, "You will always fail."

"Once I played a game with my sister where we tried to see words without reading them," she whispered.

"I know" he said. "You will know every thought a person is thinking. I mean every single person. You will not be able to look at a person without reading them. Your life will never be the same again. Your own thoughts will frighten you and you will never be able to look at yourself in a mirror again. Are you really prepared for that? Your life will change forever."

Jennifer was certain, "Yes please. I really want to be like you. Please."

His stare at her did not subside and she felt a chill up her spine but she was determined.

"Then stand up and close your eyes."

Jennifer willingly complied.

"Now wipe your mind of all thoughts."

As she stood still with her eyes closed, she wiped all thoughts from her mind. She felt paralysed and felt her life energy drain from her body. She had not seen the vampire rise from his desk and approach her.

Chapter 4

The Cure

Charlie left his lab for the day and headed to the university campus for the usual Friday night drinks. Tonight, Charlie had much to celebrate; he had found a cure for cancer.

For the past ten years, Charlie had analysed cancer in all its forms. Charlie had long known that every cell of a person (with the exception of red blood cells) contained the genetic make-up of the human being called DNA. The DNA contains the building block instructions of the human such as eye colour, height, sex and the like. Also encoded within the DNA is the life span of the cell. When a cell reaches the end of its life, it dies to make way for a fresh new cell to take its place.

Now occasionally the DNA of a person's cell can be altered by various means whether it be by a virus or radiation or even sunlight. Sometimes a cell's DNA is altered so that the life span of the cell is changed and the cell fails to die. This is called a cancerous cell. Eventually, the cancerous cell multiplies itself into several cancerous cells which crowds out the other healthy cells and results in death of the human being.

Charlie had been employed for the past ten years as a biochemist in research at DrugTech, which manufactures and sells various drugs to pharmaceutical stores and hospitals. DrugTech adjoined the university and tonight Charlie gleefully headed towards the bar where he saw Philip, an old university friend.

"Philip, I haven't seen you in years," Charlie said as he approached him.

Philip was the Professor of biochemistry at the university who once worked for DrugTech himself. Charlie knew of Philip's reputation as a biochemist. After several years as a research scientist at DrugTech, Philip's love of teaching prompted him to return to the university to lecture to students. Philip looked at Charlie as he approached him and said, "Charlie, pull up a seat. How are things going?"

"Great Philip." Charlie knew that as an employee of DrugTech he was bound by a secrecy agreement. But this did not apply to Philip, a former employee and lecturer in biochemistry at the university. Charlie could hardly contain himself. "I have a cure for cancer."

"Really," said Philip with notable lack of excitement. "Congratulations."

Charlie did not understand Philip's attitude. It must be the depressive effects of the alcohol he had consumed.

Philip took a deep breath and looked at Charlie. "Tell me all about it."

That was more like it. Charlie began. "You know how a cancerous cell has its DNA altered so that it doesn't know when to die?"

"Yes," said Philip. "The immune system fails to recognise it as a foreign cell because most of the DNA is the same. So the immune system does not attack it and leaves it to multiply."

"Well, I have found a way to get the body to kill off cancerous cells," exclaimed Charlie as he nudged Philip in the ribs.

"Go on," said Philip.

"At DrugTech I have developed a machine which analyses the body samples of a patient and finds their normal DNA. It then produces a specific serum for the person, which attacks all cells except those made up of the normal DNA. Of course, it is important to provide healthy normal samples to the machine, but there are safeguards put in place to ensure this. The serum then effectively kills off all the cancerous cells." Charlie felt elated.

"What's the catch?" said Philip. "There is always a catch."

"The catch is that the serum blinds the patient. I have not yet found a way to stop the serum from blinding the patient, but this is a small price to pay given that I have just managed to prevent a human being from dying." Charlie's enthusiasm failed to excite Philip.

"I will take my research into the Managing Director's office at DrugTech tomorrow and put my serums on the market." Charlie started munching on some nuts that were on the table. "That should get me a promotion and save heaps of lives."

"I would work out a way to fix that blindness side effect before you march into the MD's office if I were you."

"What are you talking about Philip? Being blind is much better than dying. And besides, it could take years before we cure that."

"Do you think the MD will buy it?"

"Why do you question that?" Charlie asked as his enthusiasm started to give way to scepticism.

"Because at DrugTech, they are interested in profits, not cures. DrugTech makes a fortune on products that it sells right now to dying patients of cancer not to mention the money it gets from research grants and various charitable donations. The company will fear that if it sells your serum, some other biotech company will analyse it, cure the side effect of blindness and sell their own cure for cancer. This will put DrugTech out of business and they are not prepared to go under based on your whim." Charlie could see Philip was quite serious. "So do you really think the MD will risk all that?"

"But it is a cure for cancer, people will be saved. Surely, they will be interested in that. In any event, I should at least get a Nobel Prize."

"You can't get a Nobel Prize because your contract with DrugTech requires your secrecy which can be enforced by an injunction of the Supreme Court. And if DrugTech decides to keep the serum secret until they work out the most financial way to introduce it, you can't stop them. Have another read of your employment contract."

"How do you know anyway Philip? You really are a wet blanket tonight," Charlie exclaimed almost resentfully. Charlie was not expecting an answer.

"Because Charlie, ten years ago I developed a pill which prevented cancerous cells from multiplying. When the cancerous cell is left alone long enough without being able to replicate itself, it does eventually die. The only thing was it made a patient deaf. When I presented this to the Managing Director, he gave me a lesson in economics. It was in the best interests of the shareholders that my research be refined and I was fired. DrugTech has had a cure for cancer for the past ten years."

Chapter 5

The Atlantis

Astronaut Dr Helouise Dawson settled into her command chair on board the spaceship Atlantis. It was now less than one hour before her launch at the Cape Canaveral Space Centre. Helouise looked around her at her crew of three and received the thumbs up. All systems checked out. It was now a matter of waiting for Ground Control to finalise the preparations and await the countdown.

Helouise smiled at herself as she sat comfortably in the shuttle. It had been a long journey to arrive at where she was. She had graduated at the top of her class in Michigan State. She had always had a dream of blasting off into space and convinced her family to move to Boston where she attended the Massachusetts Institute of Technology. Helouise had made a study of space science her whole life and it was no surprise to her friends when she graduated with the Institute's highest medal. Helouise had kept her fitness up as well in anticipation of one day becoming an astronaut. Upon graduation from MIT, she applied to the National Aeronautics and Space Administration.

She recalled how she arrived at the NASA base ten years ago wondering where her new career would take her. She was disappointed to be assigned to a work station at Mission Control where she worked the radar station for 12 months. Whilst at her station one day, she came across Lieutenant David Johnson, Mission Commander and pilot. A new concept had emerged at NASA and David was commissioned to conduct a feasibility study. It was proposed to build the spaceship Atlantis for the first human landing on Mars. David was putting together a research team for some of the finer points and had various questions to pose to the radar specialists.

Helouise had embraced the concept eagerly and assisted David in reporting back to Dr Jamieson's research committee various ways in which the mission could be successful. Dr Jamieson was head of NASA and oversaw all projects. He reported directly to the Pentagon and at times to the President.

After another 18 months from Helouise's first contact with David, Dr Jamieson gave the go ahead for the Atlantis mission. The mission was to land on Mars, conduct certain tests, and bring back some of the various rocks and minerals on the surface of the planet. The mission also involved the effective hand delivery of a probe on the surface of Mars designed to report back various data over the course of the years and of course, for ceremonial reasons, the raising of the American flag. Not since the Apollo moon landing had a space mission attracted such public attention as this one.

Dr Jamieson had chosen Helouise to be the Mission Commander on board the Atlantis. It was to be piloted by David and co-piloted by Lt. Andrew Watkins. Dr Brian Jenkins was the other scientific crewmember to assist Helouise in the mission.

As Helouise sat strapped in her seat, she thought back to her days at the radar station at Mission Control and pictured what must be happening there right now. The radar station occupied the front corner of Mission Control. It received data from powerful radars around the world and would track the spaceship for as long as possible. Next to this was the communications station whose staff always had a close affiliation with the radar staff.

Mission Control was effectively a large room full of computers each with their own task to perform at various stages of the mission. All of the computers were linked in to the terminals in the Upper Room. The "Upper Room" as it was called, was the headquarters of Mission Control. It was situated at the back of the room and elevated to a mezzanine level where its front large windowed wall allowed its occupants a full view of the staff at work in Mission Control.

Helouise had only once seen the inside of the Upper Room which was off limits to the regular staff. She had expected the room to be laid out in a similar fashion as the room it overlooked but instead saw only four computer terminals, one for each of four places around a board room table. To Helouise, these were the bigwigs of NASA who made all the important decisions. Today Dr Jamieson himself was present in the Upper Room overlooking the mission that the whole world was watching.

Helouise thought of how proud her family would be as she would make history as the first woman to walk on Mars. She waited for the final countdown. She heard the tremendous blast of the rockets, then felt her body thrown back to her seat. Her feelings of nausea and the blood in her eyes did not lessen her excitement. This was what she had been trained for.

All systems were go. Dr Jamieson stood at the window of the Upper Room and smiled to himself as the ship lifted off. He observed the well-trained staff at Mission Control coordinate the launch beneath him. All was running well. Two other members of the Upper Room were present seated around the board room table, their heads buried in their computer terminals.

Shortly after the successful lift-off, Dr Jamieson picked himself up a cup of coffee from the side table and settled into his seat around the table.

The fourth member of the Upper Room now entered. He ensured the doors closed behind him, sat down at his place and looked at Dr Jamieson.

"Sir, we have a problem."

"What is it?" Dr Jamieson had been accustomed to dealing with all sorts of crises and emergencies in the Upper Room.

"Tony McGrath was killed in a car accident two weeks ago. He was an engineer who worked in D garage here at NASA. He was directly responsible for the landing system of the Atlantis as it touches down on Mars. He had reported all was well and filled out the customary logs and reports which Ground Control goes through as part of the pre-launch checks. All was reported as well."

Dr Jamieson knew not to interrupt. He sat silently at his desk waiting for him to continue as the other members of the Upper Room listened intently.

"Then apparently Tony McGrath removed the landing system from the Atlantis two weeks ago. He had intended to run a series of tests and log the removal of the landing system that night or early next morning. But as he left the base that afternoon, he was killed in a car accident. The removal of the landing system was never logged. Another engineer from Houston was called in to replace him to ensure all would be well for the lift off. He noted the log books showed all was well and was assured by the other mechanics that the log books were strictly kept. He then moved on to other duties. It turns out the landing system of the Atlantis has been left behind. It's sitting on the shelf in D garage. The ship will not be able to land safely on Mars. It will crash on impact and the astronauts could not possibly survive it let alone lift off again." As he relayed this information to the other persons, his sweat visibly ran from his face down his shirt.

Dr Jamieson slowly placed his cup of coffee down and paused before speaking. "If we turn the Atlantis around and land on earth, how soon would the next launch window be?"

"Ten years," he said nervously.

Dr Jamieson frowned at the others. "The President is expecting a call within the hour. There are a thousand journalists outside reporting this launch all around the world just dying for a press conference, and now we find out the damned space ship can't land on the planet. We will be the laughing stock of the world. And what am I supposed to say to the astronauts and their families. Sorry people, we left the landing system off the shuttle?"

The member to Jamieson's right spoke out. "There would be an inquiry. And the billions of dollars promised to NASA for research on this mission would be frozen. The launch expected to occur in six months' time would be indefinitely postponed."

"It was bad enough swimming through the Hubble Telescope fiasco," said Jamieson. "The media reported that NASA was off in its calculations by a country mile. They would have a field day with this one."

The fourth member shuffled in his seat, "Sir, it seems as if we have to abort the mission."

The room became silent at these words as all eyes were on Jamieson. Jamieson looked at the member to his left, "What do you think?"

"No question Sir, it seems to be the only way."

"And you?" said Jamieson as he looked at the final member.

"Abort Sir, no option." The Upper Room had become deathly silent.

Jamieson felt tired and weak. His hand flipped open the clear plastic cover located above a red button to the right of his terminal. As he gently pressed the destruct button, he looked at the other members present and said under his breath, "Not again."

Chapter 6

The Deceived

Robert was jogging through the Botanical Gardens. He had much to be happy about. Tomorrow he was to be wed to Kathleen. It seemed like only yesterday when he had proposed to her over dinner. She had been the one and only love of his life and he felt a very special attachment to her. Robert was the shy and bashful type when it came to women and he had always found it difficult to express his emotions. Kathleen had made Robert feel easy. He was captivated by her and knew he could not live another day without her.

Before Robert had met Kathleen, he had long since felt he would never marry. Yet all had changed when Kathleen came into his life. She was lively and vivacious. She had made him feel wanted. To Robert, Kathleen had been his saviour.

The Botanical Gardens consisted of large trees and beautiful shrubbery. It was always a popular place for couples who would sit on the grass and take in the scenery with their loved ones. Robert had often jogged through the gardens and only too vividly recalled how lonely he once was in his life. As he jogged, he breathed deeply. He took in the beauty of the scenery and smiled to himself when he saw couples walk through the gardens.

Robert followed the path through the rose bushes. As he rounded the corner, he observed a couple arm in arm sit down on the grass at the base of a hill. As he looked closer, he felt a jolt to his body and stopped himself immediately. It was Kathleen and another man. They had sat down on the grass together. Robert was stunned and shocked. He felt immobilised. Robert attempted to rationalise the situation. He recalled how Kathleen had said to him that her family was flying in from Ireland for the wedding. He had never met her family and wondered if the man could be her brother.

Robert was not consoled. The man was much taller and darker than Kathleen. From where Robert stood, he could hear her giggles and laughs as they played with each other in the distance. Robert ducked down on the grass to remain out of sight as he watched on with horror. The man put his hand behind Kathleen's neck and kissed her on the lips. Robert was devastated as he saw Kathleen move to lie on top of him.

Robert felt betrayed and deceived. His own family were so excited that he had finally met the right girl for him. How proud they were of him that he would be wed tomorrow to a young and beautiful girl. Robert felt the tears well up in his eyes. He placed the inside of his elbow to his eyes and he sobbed into his arm.

Kathleen had sat up and the man had commenced tickling her. It was too much for Robert. He wished to remain out of sight and crept his way up to the top of the hill. The top of the hill was a car park. Robert ducked behind each parked car till he made his way to a truck that was parked directly atop of them. Robert continued to observe the couple as he thought of how his life had been ruined. He could not understand how Kathleen could turn from him like this. Robert felt that Kathleen had been making fun of him and would leave him at the altar tomorrow. Robert felt his life was a failure. He had been teased at school all his life. Now the girl he thought was most special was mocking him in adulthood. He commenced sobbing once more and felt dizzy. His life was a disgrace and he did not wish to go on.

Robert gazed at the couple as he stood beside the truck. He observed Kathleen's slender body and milky white arms. Her giggles had always been distinctive and rang out like a pounding bell in his head. Robert wished to go home and take his own life but as he observed how happy Kathleen was beneath him, his feelings turned to rage and anger. As he stood beside the door of the truck, he noticed it was unlocked. He looked back down at the couple and observed the man was now on top of Kathleen. This was the last straw. Robert opened the door, placed the truck in neutral and released the hand break. The truck moved slowly at first as it rolled down the hill towards them.

Robert turned his back and walked away. He was grief stricken and despondent. He walked for hours before he finally returned home. His house reminded him of the final wedding preparations he was to arrange and it sickened him. He disconnected the garden hose and picked it up off the front lawn. He entered his garage and closed the door behind him.

Robert tore up some old newspapers that were sitting beside his car and stuffed them in his exhaust with the hose. He sat in the driver's seat and closed the window on the other end of the hose. Robert started the engine and revved the car. He then climbed through the middle of the front seats and lay down on the back. Robert did not wish to face the world again.

As he lay down, he felt the fumes rising in the car. His dizziness increased and he became breathless. As he lay, his mobile telephone commenced ringing. Not wishing to answer it, he pulled it out of his pocket and was startled to see the call came from Kathleen's mobile phone.

Robert could not think straight. In a trance like state, he answered the phone and choked out a quiet "Hello?"

"Robert, can you come over quickly?" It was Kathleen and she was sobbing heavily. "My twin sister and her husband flew in from Ireland this morning for the wedding and..." Robert fainted.

Chapter 7

The Market Trader

Simon was busy at work in his garage. It was a Saturday morning and his brother Evan had come to visit him.

"What are you doing?" asked Evan as he walked into the open garage.

"Oh, just setting up this camera for a front door intercom system. I am going to have the camera beam the signal to the reception box inside the house instead of having to run wires everywhere. Hand me that screwdriver, will you?" Simon hardly looked up to acknowledge his brother.

Simon had always been gifted in electronics. He worked as a video repair man at Video Electronics but on Saturdays he would be busy at his hobby putting together all sorts of various electronic equipment.

Evan handed his brother the screwdriver and looked around at all the various electronic components displayed throughout the garage which he had obviously transformed into a workshop. "Where do you get all this stuff?"

"Well Video Electronics has a large supply of stuff that doesn't work. Occasionally I borrow a few items here and there. They don't seem to miss them. How's the market going?"

"Oh great," Evan replied. Evan was a stockbroker. Each day he would analyse charts and financial reports. He would advise his clients of his best guess as to which stocks to buy and sell and all too often he was wrong. "A major telecommunications company is going to report its financial situation to the market tomorrow. Gee I wish I could be a fly on the wall of the board of directors of that company."

"What do you mean?" asked Simon. Simon knew very little about market trading. He had always occupied himself with electronic problems and had very little time to study the financial markets.

"Well, the directors would have discussed their financial situation and are due to make a public report on Monday. Depending on how the company went, their share price will either take off or plummet. Several analysts are betting they have done better than expected, but many are sceptical. Those who guess right will probably make a fortune."

Simon made one further adjustment then flicked a switch on. "Ahh, take a look at that," said Simon visibly excited.

Simon moved a small box which obviously housed a miniature camera. On the television screen behind him, the images seen by the camera were being displayed.

"Hey that's pretty neat," said Evan as he observed that there were no wires between the camera and the television. "What's the range on that thing?"

"Well, this is only a couple of metres. But you could boost it with an aerial to transmit the signal."

Evan tilted his head to one side as an idea started to dawn within him. "What kind of aerial. Do you mean a television antenna on the house?"

"Well, that would work, but any aerial would do."

Evan looked at the television and the camera once more. "Could you install one of those inside a video player? You could use the coaxial connection on the back of the video player to get access to the television antenna that plugs into it."

"Sure", said Simon. "I hadn't thought of that. What would you want to do that for anyway?"

Evan smiled. "Inside the board rooms of every major corporation, they would probably have a television and video player to play videos to the directors. But most of the time it would be off doing nothing but keeping time. If there was a camera and a microphone in there, it could act like a bug. It could transmit sound and images outside the room through the antenna. I would be able to know exactly what directors are talking about and what the financial situations of companies would be before the information gets released to the market. We could make a fortune. Something's going on at DrugTech for example, and I want to know about it."

"Watch this." Simon pulled a video player off the shelf and undid the lid. He then undid the box and removed the camera and transmitter from the box. The camera was small and Simon mounted it just behind the remote-control sensor on the video. He connected the power supply to the power cord and the aerial to the 'video in' plug. This was the wire that had access to the outside antenna which would be used to transmit the signal.

When all was done, Simon switched the video player on. The television showed whatever the video player was facing.

"That's great," exclaimed Evan. "What about sound, can you transmit sound also?"

Simon turned up the sound on the television set which winced with feedback. Turning it down slightly, he said, "There already is a microphone here," and his voice reverberated through the television set.

"If we mount several of these things inside video players, all we would have to do is somehow get them to the board rooms of these major corporations."

"Oh, that's easy," said Simon. "All you would have to do is probably get to the toilet closest to the board room. Once you were there, you could plug a device into the power point that does nothing but join the positive and negative terminals together. This would blow a fuse in the place and if you were close enough to the board room, it would probably blow the video also if it was on the same circuit. Then you could replace their blown video with our bugged video. Shouldn't be too much trouble at all."

Evan was quite excited. "Could you start up a production line of these things fast?"

"Shouldn't be any problem at all. I could probably rig you up ten of these by tonight."

"And the range, what would be the range of them?" asked Evan as he licked his lips.

"I reckon we could get around 50 metres out of it. You would have to be in a van around 50 metres away which could pick up the signal where you could watch what was going on inside the board room."

"This is great. Let's do it," said Evan. "I'll go blow a few fuses tomorrow."

50 metres away, the occupant of a van dialled a number on his mobile phone. Holding it to his ear he said quietly, "Hey Serge, you know that guy we planted a listening device on for suspected theft of video equipment from Video Electronics? Well, you're not going to believe the conspiracy that I've got on tape."

Chapter 8

The Rescue

The prison cell door opened and two Federal Police officers approached Alfonso binding him in handcuffs.

"The extradition papers have been finalised and you are getting a one-way trip back to America," said one of the officers. "I suppose Australia didn't want to try you for drug smuggling because we don't have the electric chair."

"You are both dead men," Alfonso muttered as the handcuffs clicked into place.

"Sorry Alfonso, I'm a little bit deaf in this ear," the officer retorted as he swung his closed fist into Alfonso's ear. Alfonso seemed shaken and kept his head low. "Next time speak up," the other officer said as he struck Alfonso with an uppercut to the jaw.

Alfonso fell backwards. When he composed himself, he looked at both of the officers and gently smiled at them. This annoyed them more than any violent retaliation. The Australian Federal Police knew what kind of man Alfonso was and dreaded any rescue his colleagues were bound to attempt. Alfonso was one of the leaders of an organised syndicate to smuggle drugs around the world and was one of the most wanted men in America. The United States was closely watching the formal hand over of the prisoner which was being broadcast around the world.

Alfonso was marched out to the yard where he boarded the prison van bound for the airport. The two Federal Police officers were ordered to escort Alfonso out of Australia to the United States. The last two rows of a Qantas Bowing 747 jet had been booked by the police for the occasion. There Alfonso would sit constantly handcuffed and guarded by two Federal officers until the handing over in the United States where he was due to stand trial. Should Alfonso make any trouble on board the commercial jet and disrupt any of the passengers, the officers were to administer an injection to subdue him.

The van made its way to the airport surrounded by police cars and motorbikes. A police helicopter circled overhead watching for anything suspicious as they approached the airport. Several media vehicles followed filming the van and its entourage.

Alfonso and the two guards were the first passengers on board the jet. They settled into the back row and kept a low profile as the other passengers shuffled in. Alfonso settled into his seat, closed his eyes, and thought about the lounge room of one of his colleagues where doubtless several of them were sitting, planning a rescue operation thousands of miles away.

“Security in Australia and the US is too tight,” said one of the group as he lit himself a cigar and leaned back in the lounge chair.

“I have organised it to occur in East Timor,” said another of the group.

“What have you done?” the first man asked.

“One of the ground crew in Australia owes us a favour,” he said, “We once got the police off his back.”

The rest of the group sat silently as they listened.

“He’s a grease monkey working under the jet that Alfonso is to board. He is replacing one of the fuel gaskets with a faulty one sealed with silicon. By the time the jet gets as far as East Timor, it should be losing fuel fast. This will cause an alarm to go off in the cockpit and the pilot will be forced to make for the first available runway in East Timor to set the jet down. Otherwise, it will crash from lack of fuel.”

Several of the group nodded in approval as they listened to the plans. The man continued. “We have several of our people waiting at East Timor for the jet to set down. They will storm the jet there to rescue Alfonso and we have arranged transportation from East Timor through Indonesia before the Australians will know anything.”

“Good, good,” the others said as they considered this.

“It’s only a question of time now before the jet starts to lose fuel.”

The jet took off and the Captain welcomed all aboard. As he switched off the "seatbelt" sign, Alfonso held his handcuffs out to the guard to be removed. The guard responded by elbowing him in the ribs.

The jet passed Cape York and continued north towards East Timor when a soft tone started to sound in the cockpit.

"What's that?" the Captain asked his co-pilot.

The co-pilot looked over the dashboard where he observed a small light flashing over the fuel indicator. "The instrument says we are short of fuel."

"That's impossible," the Captain said, "This jet was refuelled at the airport. Not only did we check that off but I saw the tanker myself."

"Yes I did too," the co-pilot said. "It must be a faulty instrument."

"Switch the alarm off. We'll have it looked into when we land."

The co-pilot flicked a switch turning off the alarm tone.

"Now let's get some tea in here," the Captain said leaving the jet in autopilot mode.

Chapter 9

The Statement

The policewoman barely looked up from the counter as Angela mentioned her appearance. "Just take a seat and we'll be with you in a minute," the policewoman said as she rummaged around the papers on her desk.

Angela had never been in a police station before. She turned around and saw various people sitting on chairs reading magazines and newspapers. She saw an empty seat near a rather handsome man and headed towards it.

"What are you in for?" the man said as Angela settled in.

"Nothing, I am just making a statement because I was a witness at the bank holdup last week," Angela said as she looked at him.

"Me too actually, I was a bank teller there and the police told me to come down and make a statement, were you a customer?"

"Yes, I was," replied Angela, "I was standing in the line when the men stormed in."

"My name's Jeremy, what's your name?" the man asked as he smiled at her.

"I'm Angela," she said.

"I wonder how much longer they'll keep us waiting to take a statement off us," Jeremy said not wanting the conversation to die down.

"Have you been waiting long?" Angela was in her lunch break and needed to be back at work by two.

"About 20 minutes already," Jeremy said.

"So, I guess we just go and tell the police what we saw, three men with balaclavas and guns rob the bank. I suppose it will be pretty difficult to catch anyone," Angela said as she reached for a magazine on the table.

"One of the robbers came around the counter to get some money out of the draw and when his glove came away from his hand as he bent his wrist, I noticed he had a tattoo of a scorpion on the back of his hand."

"Well, that's something," said Angela as she considered this. "If they have criminal records, they probably record whether they have distinctive tattoos like that. Make sure you mention that to the police when you go in."

"I will," said Jeremy pleased with himself. He leaned back thinking he had much to contribute to the investigation.

"Jeremy Andersen?" the female police officer called out. Angela noticed a familiar looking female bank teller walk from behind the counter as she folded up what appeared to be her statement. She placed the statement in her handbag and left the station.

"Wish me luck," said Jeremy to Angela as he stood up and approached the desk.

"Good luck," she said. Angela admired his physique as he approached the counter. Before disappearing from sight, he turned around and raised his eyebrows at Angela smiling.

Angela turned to her magazine for something interesting. After a few minutes of flicking through various pages and reading the odd article, she stretched back, looked at the time and let out a slight sigh. About 20 minutes later she heard some distant thumps from behind the counter and a young police officer came running in.

"Quick call an ambulance," the young officer screamed.

As the female officer at the counter picked up the phone she inquired, "What happened?"

The young police officer answered her, "The witness had some kind of epileptic seizure and fell down the stairs. Seems pretty bad."

The police station became busy with the bustling of several police officers moving to and fro. Angela hoped all was OK with Jeremy. The other people in the waiting room looked at each other with concerned expressions, but none of them said anything.

Within seconds, a siren sounded in the distance. Angela turned around to peer through the glass windows of the station for any sign of the ambulance. The ambulance came and stopped at the front of the station. Two ambulance personnel alighted carrying medical kits as they burst into the station.

"Over here," screamed one police officer catching their attention.

Several confused minutes went by as Angela considered how serious the injury may be. Soon after, another ambulance arrived and this time, the ambulance personnel carried in a stretcher.

Angela was now late for work but she decided to stay a little while longer to see what would happen. Before long, the stretcher was carried out and Angela was shocked to see the blanket pulled up over the head of the body. Angela sprung up and walked to the counter.

She overheard an ambulance officer talking into his radio as he left the station "... yes completely broken. It was a pretty bad fall...".

"Is he OK?" Angela asked the female officer at the counter.

"It looks as if he broke his neck," she answered.

Angela was visibly shocked.

"You had better sit down," the female police said, "You are looking pale."

"No, I'm all right" Angela said, "Do you mind if I come back tomorrow, I have to get to work, I'm running late?"

"No that's all right, we probably couldn't get to you today anyway."

"OK see you tomorrow then," Angela said. She turned and walked out of the station.

Angela felt quite upset for Jeremy as she returned to work. Tomorrow was Saturday and she decided to give her statement first thing in the morning.

She returned at 9:00am. The station seemed much calmer now with no trace of the commotion that occurred Friday afternoon. Angela mentioned she was a witness to the bank hold-up and was taken behind the counter. She followed an officer between several desks to the door at the back of the room. The door led into a narrow corridor which proceeded up a flight of stairs to the interview room.

"Watch your step," the police officer said. "The stairs are actually quite dangerous." Angela noticed the light above the stairs was not on and the corridor was quite poorly lit.

Angela entered the interview room. She was met by two friendly looking police officers. They were each around 50 years of age and seemed quite fatherly to her.

"Would you like some tea or coffee ma'am?" one of the police officers said pointing to a table with the appropriate tea making facilities.

"No thanks" Angela said.

"Please take a seat," the officer said. "My name is Sergeant Adam Michaels, and this is Senior Constable Greg Davis. The Constable will take your statement down on the typewriter."

Angela felt at ease as she told of how the men in balaclavas burst into the bank. She spoke of how the men had guns and forced the customers to lie on the ground. The officers seemed quite friendly with her but insisted on knowing whether she had seen anything which could identify any of the robbers.

Eventually the interview came to a close and the Sergeant walked to the table to fix himself a cup of tea. He took it back to his desk and moving the cup to his lips he asked, "Is there anything else you can tell us or would like to say about the incident?"

Angela decided now was the time to ask about Jeremy. She looked at the Sergeant and as he drank the tea, she noticed a red scorpion on the back of his hand. "No nothing, I'm fine," Angela said smiling sweetly.

Chapter 10

The Jailbird

Maxamillian Jones was sweeping the upper deck of the mezzanine level of the prison complex. He was to be released at midday and the morning hours had proceeded too slowly. Maxamillian had been imprisoned three years ago for being in possession of drugs that he had always maintained had been planted in his house by the police. Of course, all people maintained their innocence in jail, but Maxamillian was not the jailbird type. He was known as the meek and mild one and probably more so by the screws than the inmates.

Geoffrey Coleson was a prison guard that enjoyed making an example of Maxamillian in front of the other inmates. Mr Coleson was well aware of Maxamillian's departure today and as a final torment to him, he required Maxamillian to sweep the upper deck. Maxamillian had long despised Geoffrey Coleson and the other inmates had wondered how long it would be before Maxamillian was pushed to breaking point. Inmates at Long Bay all had a particular breaking point. At some point they either lash back out at the prison guards who torment them even at the risk of losing all privileges, or they collapse into a fit of mental anguish and despair becoming a prison recluse.

Some had bet that Maxamillian would lash out at Mr Coleson whilst others had seen him as a recluse. Maxamillian at times showed signs of going either way but today he saw himself as grateful for leaving the godforsaken hole he had lived in. He peered over the handrail at the floor beneath him seeing inmates and screws occasionally walk beneath him. Mr Coleson was walking in a new inmate to the cell downstairs and stopped directly beneath the handrails to instruct the inmate on some form of prison etiquette.

Maxamillian smirked as he saw Geoffrey Coleson standing directly beneath him. Maxamillian had never avenged himself on Coleson for the injustices that Coleson showered on him. Today Maxamillian was leaving and couldn't help but smile at the prospect of allowing a mouth full of saliva to fall onto Coleson beneath him. The saliva welled in his mouth at the thought. If for nothing else, Maxamillian could perhaps feel somewhat better at having the last say, or at least the last spit, when it came to Coleson. Maxamillian leaned over the railing and gently let fall from his mouth. The aim seemed right and as it headed for Coleson's back, Maxamillian ducked away and out of sight.

The hours seemed to pass quicker for Maxamillian from that point on. He was discharged from the jail without incident and walked out of the complex.

Since Maxamillian's arrest, he had not returned home. Maxamillian kicked open the door to his house. He had often thought of this moment. Apart from the dust, all was as he left it. He was home again. He stripped his bed from the old sheets and threw them in the washing machine along with his own clothes. After changing into something more comfortable, he took an empty cardboard box and emptied the contents of the fridge into it. He loaded up the washing machine and made for his local supermarket to stock up.

Maxamillian returned and unpacked his shopping. He had planned to make himself a nice quiet dinner at home before telephoning any of his outside friends. Tonight was his own and he wished to contemplate his life alone. When he had finished dinner, he nestled into the couch and thought back on his arrest. He recalled how he had come home to see the police in his house. He remembered being presented with some sort of search warrant and watching the police marching out small sachets of white powder that he had never seen before.

Maxamillian had often been plagued by these thoughts. He thought on his time in jail and how it had been made worse by Coleson. Coleson had introduced himself to Maxamillian with a stinging blow to the ribs, accusing Maxamillian of sneaking up behind him. From that point on Maxamillian feared Coleson and tried to avoid him at every turn. Coleson of course had made this impossible for Maxamillian. Now on the outside, Maxamillian wished to put the whole story behind him and begin life anew.

Maxamillian awoke the next morning to a loud pounding on the door. He opened the door and was greeted by two police officers. Maxamillian instinctively froze as the police officers turned him around and placed handcuffs on him.

Ten minutes later, Maxamillian was walked into the interview room at the local police station. The police officers turned on the video recording machine and sat calmly around the table.

The first police officer began.

"Maxamillian Jones, we are making enquiries about an alleged incident between yourself and Mr Geoffrey Coleson yesterday. You have the right to remain silent however any questions you do answer will be recorded and may be used against you, do you understand that?"

"Yes," Maxamillian said wondering what it was all about.

The second police officer jumped in immediately, "Mr Jones, did you spit on Mr Coleson within the last 48 hours?"

Maxamillian felt puzzled. He was sure that no one had seen him spit on him in prison. Surely if he had been seen, he would have been dealt with there and then. Perhaps this was Coleson's way of getting back at him after he was let out. Maxamillian wondered if Coleson wanted him charged with an assault over the incident so that he could meet him again in prison. Maxamillian felt sick but decided to resolutely deny the accusation.

"No absolutely not. Of course not." Maxamillian looked defiant as the video recorded his every movement.

"Are you absolutely sure about that Mr Jones, you positively deny it?" the first police officer questioned.

"Of course I am sure. I have never ever spat on Mr Coleson at all. Who says that I did anyway?"

"Mr Jones, please just let us ask the questions. I shall ask you once more and warn you that your answer is being videotaped to be used in evidence in a Court of law if necessary. As before, you do not have to answer any questions if you do not want to. Mr Jones, did you within the past 48 hours ever spit on Mr Coleson?"

Maxamillian took a deep breath. He looked at the police officers then said into the video camera, "I have never in my life ever spat on Mr Coleson, I swear on my mother's grave and I don't wish to answer any more questions or go on with this stupid interview."

"Are you sure about that Mr Jones?" the first police officer calmly asked.

"Yes, I am sure, now turn off the camera, you're just wasting your time." Maxamillian responded.

"Very well, turn it off," the first police officer said.

The second police officer turned off the camera and removed the videotape sealing it in a yellow envelope.

"Mr Jones, you are charged with the murder of Mr Coleson who was stabbed to death last night outside his home. Several of the inmates at Long Bay Jail say you had a grudge against him, and the lab reports have positively identified your DNA in saliva that was found on his back. You have denied it on the tape that will be played to the jury in your murder case. You are a liar and you are a murderer and you will rot in prison for the rest of your life."

Chapter 11

Family Business

Dorothy Wilcox was an obsessive-compulsive woman. Her days were now quite routine. After breakfast when her husband would leave for work, she would commence by mopping the kitchen and bathroom floors. They were of course impeccable from yesterday's mopping, but Mrs Wilcox felt better watching the midday movie knowing that they had been freshly mopped. In anticipation of the midday movie, she would boil herself a mug of coffee and remove a chocolate biscuit from the biscuit jar. Everything had to be perfect. Whilst the water boiled, Mrs Wilcox would give the lounge room the usual once over with the vacuum. After washing her hands, she would settle herself into the lounge with her coffee and biscuit on the side table. The midday movie never made much of an impression on Mrs Wilcox. This was because she would spend it worrying about not spilling her coffee or staining the lounge with the chocolate biscuit or letting any crumbs fall outside of the saucer. When she wasn't involved in such negative thoughts, she would spend the rest of the movie puffing up the cushions that were nestled behind her and keeping them in place.

In the evenings when her husband returned from work, she insisted on him having a shower. Whilst he would shower, Mrs Wilcox would take the clothes he left for her on the bed and put them in the washing basket. This was all second nature by now, except tonight, something was not quite right. When Mrs Wilcox picked up her husband's shirt, she believed it smelt slightly of perfume. Actually, this wasn't right at all but it was a thought that occurred to Mrs Wilcox. Mrs Wilcox had always regarded her husband as a mild-mannered gentleman and quite incapable of having an extra-marital affair, but the more she tried to put this thought out of her mind, the more it nagged her.

By the next morning when her husband had left for work, Mrs Wilcox had resolved to do something about it. For one day in her 23 years of marriage, the kitchen and bathroom floors would not be mopped. Nor would the lounge room be vacuumed or the usual cup of coffee consumed. While Mr Wilcox worked busily at his office desk, Mrs Wilcox took a seat in the reception area of Wilfred Banks & Son Private Detectives.

"Mr Banks will be right with you," the receptionist said.

Mrs Wilcox responded with a smile as she considered how un-puffed the cushion behind her was. She noticed several small bits of fluff on the carpet and when she spotted some white bits of paper in the corner, she felt all together uncomfortable.

"Please come in Mrs Wilcox," said a gentleman in a three-piece suit. Mrs Wilcox walked into the adjoining office as the gentleman held opened the door. "Please take a seat," he said as he politely pointed to the chair opposite his desk. Mrs Wilcox did as she was told.

The office was rather cramped and contained no pictures. There was an office desk, which she sat facing, with a high-back chair on the other side. Above this, on the wall, was a small certificate, which she presumed, was the person's qualifications as a private detective.

"My name is Wilfred Banks and this is my nephew, Darren. He is apprenticed with us to become a private detective. If you have no objection, I have asked him to sit in on your case and he promises to assist us in every way he can."

"Oh, yes that's all right," Mrs Wilcox said as she acknowledged his presence.

Darren took a seat on the sofa just off to the side as Mr Banks sat behind the desk.

"What can we do for you Mrs Wilcox?"

Mrs Wilcox had her response planned from the night before. "I would like you to follow my husband and tell me whether he is having an affair or not. Are you able to do this and can you tell me how much this would cost because I would have to pay you in cash?"

Mr Banks responded. "Yes of course we can do this for you Mrs Wilcox, this is quite a usual request. But we don't encourage our clients to find out this way because we charge $330 an hour, and such a way of finding out whether your husband is a cheat or not is too expensive and unnecessary."

Mrs Wilcox seemed surprised, "What do you suggest then?"

"For an all-up fee of just a thousand dollars plus five hundred dollars expenses, we can arrange for your husband to win a one-night stay in a luxury hotel. We put it on the basis of a one-off promotional thing for the hotel and manipulate it so that it is limited to one person only. You of course insist that your husband goes while you stay home and do some housework."

Mrs Wilcox considered that she could withdraw 15-hundred dollars from her savings account and waited to hear more of Mr Banks' plan. Mr Banks continued.

"While your husband enjoys his complimentary dinner, we organise for him to be joined by a beautiful girl that we have an arrangement with. At the end of the evening, she will ask your husband to walk her to her room. Now if your husband is a good and honest man, nothing should eventuate, and we will tell you all about it. But if your husband is a cheat, he will naturally fall for her. You will know all about it even before he comes home. You can then do what you want. You can see if he lies about it or you can be out of there even before he shows up. That is entirely up to you."

Mrs Wilcox seemed horrified at the suggestion of Mr Banks. Surely such an approach was unethical – but so was hiring a private investigator in the first place. Mrs Wilcox knew enough about her personality to know that if she refused this offer, she would nag herself to death with curiosity in the days to come. She sat thinking only for a second, and then attempting to hide her enthusiasm she said, "Yes that sounds like a good idea Mr Banks. Can I organise for that to happen now?"

"Yes of course, but we will require payment up front," responded Mr Banks.

"Oh, that's not a problem, can I just leave for a few minutes so I can withdraw some money and come back?"

"We shall wait for you Mrs Wilcox," Mr Banks said as he smiled and rose from his chair to see Mrs Wilcox out.

Mr Banks shut the door behind her and resumed his seat behind his desk. "What do you think of our Mrs Wilcox, Darren?" he asked as he looked at his nephew.

"Oh, I think she is very excited about the idea. Will you organise for her husband to go to your sister's hotel?"

"Of course, Darren. The idea is to keep the business in the family. Your aunty offers rooms at $250- a night and I on-sell them in this way for $500- a night."

"What about this winning a one-night stay? How do you organise that?"

"Oh, the wording and the prize was worked out a long time ago with your father." Darren's father was a solicitor and was Mr Banks' brother. "It has always been useful having a solicitor in the family. We will organise for this winning ticket and terms to be sent to Mrs Wilcox through the mail and she will simply show it to her husband." As Mr Banks said this, he pulled out an envelope from his office draw and held it up to his nephew.

"You have it all worked out," Darren said. "But what about the girl, how do you arrange for that and how much does it cost?"

His uncle smiled as he made a humph sound blowing heavily out of his nostrils.

"We don't arrange for a girl Darren. That's way too expensive. Mrs Wilcox will get a report that her husband cheated on her. Oh, he can deny it all he likes of course, but in the end, she will believe us. They always do. She is not going to take the word of a cheating husband over a private investigator's firm that she paid 15-hundred dollars for. All our clients have communication problems in the first place anyway. And when she gets quite upset about it all, we shall refer her on to your father, the divorce lawyer." Mr Banks looked at his nephew. "You see, it's all about keeping the business in the family."

Chapter 12

The Medusa Curse

Dr Smedley was eager to make a good first impression on his patient and his staff. This was his first working day at the Mary Immaculate Psychiatric Hospital. He had eagerly studied the file of Cain Todd which had been handed to him the night before. The file indicated that Mr Todd, a 42-year-old man, was diagnosed as suffering from a chronic paranoid schizophrenia which had been exacerbated over the death of his wife in a motor car accident five years previously. Mr Todd had never come to terms with the loss of his wife and especially with the fact that the perpetrator of the crime had never been brought to justice. The file indicated that as a result of his delusions, Mr Todd commenced blaming himself for every motorcar accident that involved the driver proceeding through a red light. The file indicated that Mr Todd's delusions were so manifest that he even claimed responsibility for the deaths when he was himself physically incarcerated in the hospital. His most recent claim was that he was responsible for the death of his former psychiatrist Dr Watson, who was tragically killed in a motor accident at Milsons Corner two months ago. Cain Todd was admitted to the hospital when he was found attempting to commit suicide by hanging himself in his garage. The file also indicated that Cain Todd was completely unaware of his delusions, completely refusing to accept that he had them.

Dr Smedley entered the psychiatric room and observed his patient sitting on the bed.

"Go away," were the first words spoken by the patient to the doctor.

"I am here to help you," said Dr Smedley as he pulled up a chair next to his bed.

Dr Smedley tried to use his knowledge that he had obtained from the patient's file. "Mr Todd, if you really feel responsible for the death of all those people involving motorists going through red lights, why don't you tell me and maybe we can do something about it?"

The patient looked as if he was about to answer but made no response.

"Why don't you explain it to me and help me understand the situation and in return, maybe I can help you?"

The patient looked directly at the doctor. He saw that the doctor was not planning to leave without an explanation. The patient took a deep breath and began.

"It all started 20 years ago. I was about 22 back then and I had gone to stay the week on my dad's farm out in the country. I was very interested in the stars, so one night I decided to go for a walk. I wanted to get to a place which was as dark as possible so that I could lie down and look up at the stars. I set out with my dog Rex who loved a night time walk."

The patient saw that the doctor had a pleasant disposition and seemed to be listening. He found he was quite relaxed in talking with him and he continued.

"I hadn't gone far when I noticed an eerie green glow coming out of a rock a couple of yards ahead of me. It was about as big as a brief case and was cracked open right down the middle from which the glow emanated. I pointed to it saying to my dog in a loud whisper, 'What's that Rex? Check it out!' This excited Rex so he ran on ahead to the rock but the moment I saw him put his nose over the rock," the patient paused, "He fell down dead."

"Was anybody else with you?" the doctor asked trying to encourage the patient to go on.

"No, I was all alone," he continued. "I only took a few more steps and realised what had happened. The cracked open rock looked as if it was made of iron and contained many craters. It was clearly a meteorite. The green glow I reckoned was radioactivity that was emanating from the meteorite. It was obviously deadly and killed Rex instantly. I decided not to get any closer. I went back to the farm wondering what to do."

"Why didn't you inform the authorities?" the doctor enquired.

"Well, it's like this. My father wasn't supposed to be earning any money from his farm and he certainly wasn't declaring anything in his tax returns. It might not seem like a big deal to you but back then my father was getting on in years and I didn't want all these federal cops crawling all over the farm seeing that it was actually a thriving business."

The doctor seemed to accept this explanation for the moment and waited for the patient to continue.

"Anyway," the patient said, "I decided to return the next night, but I had a plan. Under the house my dad kept a whole lot of disused lead pipes. I took these with me in a bucket and some matches. I returned to that same place with that eerie green glow and got as far as I did last time. I wanted to go at night in case I couldn't see the green glow in the light of day. I was also scared that I might accidentally stumble across the deadly radiation and be killed. When I saw it, I lit a small fire and melted the lead in the bucket that I brought with me. When the lead melted into a liquid, I used thick mittens, and crawled on my stomach towards the meteorite carrying the bucket of molten lead in front of me. As I lay there on my chest, I raised the bucket over my head and poured it into the open meteorite. Almost immediately the green glow subsided. I knew that radiation could not penetrate lead, so I knew that I had successfully contained it."

The doctor had become quite interested in the patient's story and moved his chair closer to the patient. "Go on Mr Todd, what happened next?"

"Well, I had to wait for the lead to cool down, didn't I? So, I returned the next day in the sunlight. Poor old Rex had started to decay by now but I ignored him. I looked into the meteorite for any sign of what caused the green glow. I saw it. It was about the size of a small pea. Of course, now it was completely covered by the molten lead from the night before. Most of the lead had stuck to the iron meteorite, but this small pea thing broke off easily. It must have been a radioactive substance from outer space. I carried it back home and kept it secret. At least for a while."

The doctor was quite inquisitive by now and wanted to hear more. The story told by the patient was incredible, but it didn't sound delusional. The doctor wished to get to the bottom of it. "What did you do with it Mr Todd?" the doctor asked.

"Well for a long time I didn't know what to do with it. I knew that if I scratched the lead off, it would expose an extremely deadly radiation which could kill instantly. At least it killed Rex that way. I wanted to be able to harness that power and direct it. The ideal way would be to keep it covered but expose it for a flash when needed. Then it came to me. I ripped open an old camera of mine and painted molten lead on the insides. I glued the pea just behind the camera aperture. I made myself a small tool. I hammered a nail into a ruler. Then working in my bathroom mirror so as not to face the pea directly, I scratched off a bit of the lead with the nail by moving the ruler."

"Did you see the green glow?" the doctor asked becoming more and more interested by the moment.

"I didn't really wait to look. As soon as I knew it was scratched, I immediately closed the camera. Then if my theory was right, all I had to do was point the camera at a living thing and click. This would open the aperture for a fraction of a second and release a burst of radiation."

"Did you hold it close to your face and look through the camera?"

The doctor asked this wondering if the patient may have exposed himself to a mild dose of radiation. He still believed the patient was delusional and was wondering if the radiation could possibly be a cause.

"Yes, I did and when you looked through it you could see the cross-hairs in the camera. This helped me aim it. The first thing I photographed was a sparrow on some power lines about ten metres up. As soon as I clicked, the sparrow fell down dead on the ground. It was awesome power. I came to call it the 'Medusa Stone' because any living thing that was exposed to it, was instantly killed. It worked extremely well but I never told anyone about it, except," the patient paused, "A few years later when I married, I told my wife."

The doctor noticed a sorrowful expression on the patient's face as he remembered his late wife. The doctor recalled the information contained in the patient's file regarding his wife dying in a motorcar accident and wished to hear more.

"At first my wife abhorred the idea and wanted me to get rid of the deadly camera. But then she started flashing the kitchen floors at night-time and killing all the cockroaches in one instant. In fact, it worked so well, that once a month my wife would even zap the mould right off the bath room tiles."

The doctor was quite intrigued by the story but the patient still did not seem delusional to him. "What happened next?"

"Well, that's when I had my first accident. One day when I was in my garage, I noticed a big hairy spider on the door so I zapped it. As soon as I pressed the button, I heard a crash outside. Apparently, the postman was delivering my mail. The radiation penetrated through my garage door and killed him instantly. Naturally I was shocked and terrified but the man was dead and it was an accident. I didn't mean to kill him. When I enquired after the postman who died outside my house, I was told that they believed he died of a heart attack."

"Perhaps it was just a heart attack," the doctor suggested sceptically.

"Heart attack my foot," the patient retorted in disbelief. "It's just that the doctors didn't know what to make of it. I reckon it was some kind of cellular disruption as the radiation passed through him. Anyway, by now I knew that the Medusa Stone worked on animals, insects, bacteria, fungi and now a human. I always felt that absolute power corrupts absolutely. I started to refer to it as the Medusa Curse."

"So, what did you do?" the doctor asked.

"For a long time after that I just put it away. I refused to let my wife even use it on the cockroaches. Then it happened." The patient began to cry.

"What happened?" the doctor asked gently.

"I got the news that my wife was killed in a car accident. Some bastard went through a red light and ran straight over her. The driver didn't even stop to help. All I ever got from the police was a photograph from the red-light camera of a stolen car. The driver was never caught."

The doctor remained silent as the patient paused to catch his breath.

"I became extremely depressed and then it occurred to me. Just as the postman was killed by my accident, so too was my wife. It was the Medusa Curse come back to haunt me. This was the price I was paying. I loved my wife more than life itself, so the Medusa Curse came back on me and took her away. Don't you see doctor?"

The patient became quite emotional and the doctor rose from his chair calming him down with a hand on his shoulder. "Calm down, calm down," the doctor said gently, "What happened then?"

"Well, I was angry that I couldn't get revenge on the driver of the stolen car who killed my wife. I thought it was extremely unfair that a driver could go through a red light and get away with it. As far as I was concerned, anybody who blatantly disregarded the traffic signals endangered the lives of other motorists and pedestrians and so, like self-defence, one would be justified in killing those drivers. The law was just not working. All I got from the law was a photograph of a car that went through a red light. I now had the means to instantly kill a driver who goes through a red light. That way I would avenge my wife's death – and I would avenge myself on the Medusa Curse."

"What did you do?" the doctor asked as he looked at him quizzically.

"I went to Milson's Corner where my wife was killed and I tampered with the red-light camera. I broke it open and painted the inside with molten lead. I put the Medusa Stone in the camera and pointed the crack in the stone at the camera aperture. I positioned it so the green glow would shine through the aperture and not interfere with the film."

"Did it work?" the doctor asked.

"Oh, it worked all right," the patient said. "From that moment on, every driver who went through the red light there was killed instantly. I have killed hundreds of drivers at Milson's Corner. I even heard that the late Dr Watson from this hospital died there."

The doctor was astounded but became sceptical. "If that is true, why did you attempt to commit suicide?"

The patient looked distressed as he squeezed his eyes shut.

"Because my conscience is killing me," he said. "It's the Medusa Curse. It wants revenge for every death that I have extracted. It wants me to dismantle the camera and make reparations for the victims. But I won't. I won't!" The patient began to shout.

Then the patient stared at the doctor. "The Medusa Curse. It wants you to do it doctor. Are you going to dismantle it? Don't you dare." The patient stood up and walked towards the doctor staring at his eyes.

"Calm down, calm down" the doctor said. It was no use; the patient would not be calmed. The doctor backed off out of the room and slammed the door shut.

The doctor was rattled and thought to himself, "Do I investigate this fantastic story of Mr Todd or is the man delusional?" The patient did have an intriguing story. But the doctor reasoned it was surely the product of a delusional imagination. If the doctor recorded his belief that the patient's ridiculous story was actually true, the doctor would be the laughing stock of the hospital. The patient's so-called memories were hallucinations. For one thing, there was no such thing as the Medusa Curse. The doctor had settled it in his own mind. The man was clearly psychotic. "Nurse, quick, prepare five milligrams of Haloperidol for Mr Todd."

The doctor commenced documenting the delusions of the patient in his notes. That was when the phone rang.

"Oh my God," the nurse said as she hung up the phone. "Doctor, your father has had a heart attack at Milson's Corner."

Chapter 13

The Science Ball

"What do you want to do when you leave school?"

This was the question that Benjamin Jones was often asked, and he would always give the same answer. "I want to do Science at Sydney Uni."

After a few expressions of pretended interest and discussions of possible subjects that he may enrol in, the questioner realised the answer to the first question was not adequately given. Benjamin Jones always waited for the questioner to try again.

"So, what do you want to be?"

The truthful answer to the question was "I wish to be happy. I want to find myself a girl and get married and have a great family." But Benjamin knew that that answer sounded corny. Guys could not admit that sort of thing. "I'll probably become a research scientist or something like that," Ben would respond. This always satisfied the questioner.

Benjamin Jones enrolled in Science at the University of Sydney. He was pretty much an average guy with one slight exception. He stuttered horribly when he was nervous. And the one thing that made him extremely nervous was when he had to speak with an attractive girl. Above all things, Ben wished to be really good friends and very close to a girl that he found attractive.

At certain times in an average guy's life, he needs to choose words to describe himself. With Ben it was always, "student" or "scientist". But the truth was Ben was lonely. It was not that Ben couldn't admit this to himself. In fact, he knew it all too well. He just couldn't admit it to others. But when he was alone, Ben knew that his heart was yearning.

When the first semester of university had passed, Benjamin would look back and could only really describe it to himself as average. He had completed the average science courses, physics, chemistry, mathematics and computer science. He had obtained average marks and he had the average prospects of completing them.

As a science student, he liked chemistry the least. But as lectures in chemistry went, he enjoyed being there the most. Benjamin had set his sights on Pamela. Every lecture, Pamela would sit in the same place. This was three rows back from the centre and slightly off to the left. She was the first-person Ben would look at as he would enter the lecture theatre. He had decided to position himself two rows behind her and would occasionally observe her beauty. He had overheard her introduce herself to someone once as "Pamela" but Ben was too shy to formally make her acquaintance.

Ben knew that if he ever introduced himself to someone like Pamela, he would stutter so horribly he would barely get the words out. Pamela would think he was some kind of freak or perhaps even worse, an idiot. A freak was always better than an idiot because a freak was just an average guy with un-average peculiarities. But an idiot was a guy that was not worth knowing. And Ben knew that if he spoke to Pamela, he would risk being characterised as an idiot.

Every night Benjamin would come home from university feeling somewhat unsatisfied and discontented. When his parents would ask him how his day had been, he would always reply "Good". This was now a lie. To Ben, the day would be good when he finally managed to speak with Pamela. But how to break the ice? Ben did not have any other friends in chemistry to have himself introduced to her. The only real way was to simply go up to her and start a conversation. And this was what terrified him. Even if he managed to pluck up the courage to attempt it, Benjamin knew he would get tongue-tied.

As the second semester of university was drawing to a close, Benjamin knew that all would end the way it started if he did not at least try to make an attempt. At least if Pamela thought that he was an idiot, she couldn't tell anyone because they had no mutual friends. But Ben refused to let the year go by without at least making one serious attempt at trying to talk with her. The truth was that he would dream of being married to her and living happily ever after. She always had a pleasant gentle attitude about her and seemed to have a perfect personality. He had observed her for almost a year and believed he knew so much about her. And now every chemistry lecture was simple sweet torture.

It was now the last chemistry lecture for the year. Benjamin had known for some time that the Science Ball was next week and that he would just love to take Pamela. Even if for some reason it didn't work out, Ben thought that it would be just so nice to take her out. He could be the perfect gentleman and learn all about her.

Ben saw Pamela take up her usual seat. It was five minutes before the lecturer would walk in and start the lecture. This was his moment of opportunity and it was going fast. Ben's heart started pounding. How he wished he could just go and take up his usual seat. All of a sudden, sitting behind her in the usual way, was more appealing than making Pamela's acquaintance. Ben knew that he had to speak with her. As he approached her, his legs felt like jelly. His heart was beating so hard and fast that he felt others could hear it. His face was now blushing so hard that he felt an immediate headache. Ben knew that even if he managed to stumble out the words, she would know in an instant that he was terrified, and this was almost worse than being an idiot.

For a moment Ben thought that he would abort the plan. This was more than he could bear. But he thought about feeling miserable in his room tonight and continued to head towards her. This was closer than he had ever been to her. She looked so lovely. Her hair was blonde, her eyes were blue, her face was sweet. And now she smelt great.

Benjamin Jones took a deep breath and Pamela smiled at him as he approached her. This meant a lot to Ben. Her smile gave him courage and he felt his second wind. His heart subsided slightly and he felt that he could manage to speak to her. He smiled back to her as he commenced to speak.

"Would you like to go to the Science Ball with me?"

Each word was as clear as a bell. Benjamin surprised himself. Perhaps it was all the times he had practised these words in his head. In recent times, he had imagined saying them to Pamela almost at every moment. Benjamin continued to smile hopelessly as he waited for an answer.

"Oh," Pamela said visibly surprised, "I would have to ask my boyfriend".

Chapter 14

The Charlatan

Madam Kizana was seated at the table when the two police officers arrived. The room was darkened to give the impression of gloominess. In the centre of the table was a crystal ball on a plain tablecloth. The other side of the table consisted of two empty chairs where her customers would sit awaiting their fortunes to be told to them. Madam Kizana wore a dark gown with several dark colours worked into the cloth. She had overly sufficient quantities of makeup applied to her plumpish face and resembled more of a fantasy witch than a suburban charlatan.

The silent air conditioner was always set to chill. This added to the goose bumps her customers would feel when their fortunes were told to them. The side tables of the room contained burning candles giving off the eerie glow of candlelight and casting moveable shadows across Madam Kizana's ever changing face.

The two police officers felt uncomfortable in this environment and did not take well to Madam Kizana remaining seated gazing into the crystal ball as they entered.

"Madam Kizana is it?" began the first officer, "We would like to ask you some questions about a Miss Charity Jenkins who has been coming to see you."

Madam Kizana made no response to the police officer's invitation. She commenced to move her hands slowly over the crystal ball in a circular motion.

The discomfort of the police officers increased feeling their superiority was compromised. The first police officer removed his notebook from his top pocket and started his note taking.

"You're not of course obliged to speak with us but anything you do say will be taken down and may be used in evidence."

The police officer looked more closely at Madam Kizana as she swirled her hands over the crystal. He then looked at his partner with raised eyebrows. Madam Kizana seemed to be ignoring them.

"Charity Jenkins says she has paid you over ten thousand dollars to read her fortune. She complains that you have ripped her off. We are concerned that an offence has been committed. It is against the law to obtain a financial benefit by deception."

At this Madam Kizana made a response. "It is not a deception to tell the truth gentleman. The crystal never lies."

Madam Kizana raised her eyes ever so slightly from the crystal as her swirling motion slowed. This was enough to allow the candlelight to dance across the makeup on her face.

The police officer commenced taking notes of her response. He immediately found the gloomy lighting difficult to write in.

"Why don't you take a seat gentleman and we can discuss it," was her next response.

The police officer found the table appealing for his note taking and looked at his partner. He cocked his head towards the table indicating that his partner should go first. They both took their seats and gazed at Madam Kizana. The speaking police officer put his notebook on the table and continued his notes. He found the chair he was sitting on was too low for his comfort, the table coming up to his chest.

"Do you say you told the truth to Miss Jenkins Madam?" the police officer continued.

"All that I told her came from the crystal. The crystal never lies," was the response.

The police officer wrote this response in his notebook. This would be an easy conviction he thought, his discomfort was worth it. Now he would try and get her to admit to taking the sum of money from the girl. Then if she could sign the book, it would be over. Her arrest would be soon in any event. The police officer relaxed into the environment and smiled to himself. A few more convictions up his belt and he would get promoted. He started thinking of his parents being so proud of him when he told them he would be promoted to a Sergeant.

"Constable Harris, how is your mother Sally? I see she suffered a stroke last year?"

Constable Harris looked confused. How did she know that? Was he that obvious with his face expressions? The Constable thought he would shrug it off and continue. "Did you take money from Miss Jenkins Madam?"

"Not as much as you took from that drug dealer," Madam Kizana paused as she squinted into the ball, "what was his name? Oh yes, Mr Dyson."

"I beg your pardon?" the Constable said feeling a little scared and embarrassed. This was a little more than the police officer had expected.

"You received five thousand dollars from Mr Dyson yesterday." Madam Kizana paused while she gazed into the ball for maximum effect. "I see you stored it in your police locker... let me see... number 438 back at the station."

Madam Kizana looked up at the Constable, the candlelight now illuminating her face from beneath. "You had better remove it Constable Harris. Quickly. Sergeant Gillcrist back at the station suspects you and is going to open that locker in the next 25 minutes." The Constable seemed embarrassed and lost for words. "You had better get down there fast Constable," Madam Kizana said in an almost motherly voice concerned over the actions of her dishonest son.

The police officer stopped taking notes of the conversation.

"You are making this all up," the Constable responded visibly agitated. The redness in his face brightened.

Madam Kizana ignored the interruption and methodically gazed back into the crystal.

"You keep a picture of your wife and children in the glove box of the police car I see…" Madam Kizana began again. "I see it burning in a car accident in your haste back to the station." Madam Kizana feigned her fear. It had its desired effect. "You had better drive slowly when you leave Constable Harris."

The Constable looked at the crystal in an attempt to see what she claimed. He believed it started to glow red.

"And you Constable Willis," Madam Kizana shifted her attention to his partner. "I see you have become distrustful of your partner over the last week. What's this?" Madam Kizana faked her surprise as she appeared to look with immense curiosity into the crystal. "You have complained to your superiors about what your partner has done. You don't trust him."

Constable Willis was stunned at the accuracy of her accusation. "How on earth?" he commenced to think to himself.

"What's this?" Madam Kizana said raising her voice slightly. The crystal appeared to turn bright blue. "It is the voice of a young aborigine child. He is crying from being beaten up." Madam Kizana gazed into Constable Willis' eyes. "You bashed him to a pulp. You did it at the station."

"You are lying," the Constable said as he rose from his chair. Constable Harris also stood up.

Madam Kizana seemed unperturbed as she continued. "You had better go talk with him soon Constable. He is about to lodge a formal complaint and you will be investigated."

"She's crazy" Constable Willis said to Constable Harris. "She must be having delusions."

"The woman's got a screw loose" Constable Harris said wanting to get back to the station as soon as possible. "She'll probably just make a section 32 application under the *Mental Health Act* if we arrest her. Waste of time and money really."

"That's what I was thinking," Constable Willis responded quickly. "Let's get out of here."

The two police officers scurried out of the room the way they came.

Madam Kizana did not rise from her seat. Seeing the two police officers leave, she retrieved her cordless telephone from under the table and dialled a well-used number by heart.

"Oh, hello Sergeant. They just left," she said, "Thanks for all the information. I owe you one."

Chapter 15

The Inducer

It was ten years to the day when the letter arrived. Thomas recalled how his best friend Bruce had promised he would contact him in ten years' time. At school Thomas had always seen Bruce as an eccentric scientist. His ideas were the most radical and unique he had heard of. Bruce would often spar with his physics and chemistry teachers and challenge their way of teaching. Bruce was a red-haired freckled boy with a fiery personality who didn't often get on with anybody. Thomas was the exception. Bruce's parents had died whilst he was young. He had been raised by his uncle and aunty but confided in Thomas that he couldn't wait till he was 18 so that he could take his inheritance and set himself up somewhere in the country where he would build his laboratory.

Bruce had done very well at school but he did not attempt to enrol at university. Bruce believed that university would hold him up. He would often tell Thomas how all he needed was a few years of solitude when he would emerge once more and shock the world with his discoveries. Thomas who had enrolled in physics at university often encouraged his friend to enrol also. But Bruce would not have a bar of it.

On the last day of school, Bruce approached Thomas and told him that he would be turning 18 in two weeks' time. He confided in Thomas that his plan to build himself a laboratory somewhere out in the country was on track and that he would contact him in ten years' time to the day.

Thomas felt such a move was totally unnecessary and a waste of his excellent talent. Nevertheless, Thomas had not heard of Bruce for ten years. He opened the letter that he received with immense curiosity. Sure enough, the letter was from his friend Bruce. It enclosed a map showing the way to his laboratory out in the country. Thomas was invited to attend this weekend and see for himself the "Trans Warp Inducer". Thomas smiled to himself at the name of Bruce's invention but felt he owed it to his friend to at least treat him seriously until he could see for himself what he had been up to all this time.

As Thomas made his way out into the country, he thought back on what he had done in the ten years since he parted Bruce's company. Thomas had completed his science degree in three years and spent another year completing his honours degree in physics. He had spent the next three years completing his doctorate in physics. He had remained at the university as a lecturer in physics. He would often think of Bruce and wondered what he could have accomplished if he had attended university with him ten years ago. Thomas had anticipated this event for some time.

After several hours of driving, he found the dirt track that the map indicated. He proceeded along this road for approximately 20 minutes when he arrived at what appeared to be a shack in the middle of nowhere. He recognised his friend immediately.

Bruce was holding a shovel when Thomas' car arrived. Thomas observed that Bruce had just finished shovelling around a thorny rose bush.

"That you Bruce?" Thomas began with an uncontained smile on his face and hand outstretched.

"Knew you would come," Bruce said as he approached his friend dropping the shovel. The handshake never proceeded and the two hugged each other with much backslapping.

"What are you doing?" Thomas said looking at the roses.

"Oh, just burying some compost," Bruce said as he picked up his shovel. "Come on in, I have much to show you."

Bruce ushered Thomas into the shack. The front half was obviously the living section. It appeared run-down with the bare living essentials. The two didn't waste time here as Bruce led Thomas into the back section.

"Welcome to my laboratory," said Bruce as he placed the shovel against the wall and opened the door. This was not what Thomas had expected. Thomas had expected the laboratory to be something out of a science fiction movie. At the very least he expected the room to be clean. This room however looked like a dingy oversized barn. Wooden floorboards had been carelessly strewn across the floor and a musty stench was evident. There were two parallel series of tables that contained the odd electronic equipment. A standard computer was on the front table with several coloured wires heading from it into a fridge-like object by the corner. Next to this was an empty walkway with electrical tape stuck on the floor in the shape of an X inside a square in the other corner of the room.

"What's all this?" Thomas asked as he looked around.

Bruce wasted no time walking towards the fridge-like object. "This is the Trans Warp Inducer," Bruce said sliding his hand over the door. "I am currently finishing the computer program to fully drive it."

"So, what is a Trans Warp Inducer exactly?" Thomas asked trying to see the differences between that and a common kitchen appliance.

"It's the next step in Einstein's theory of relativity," Bruce began. "You know how Einstein postulated that time is dependent on the relative position of one thing against another?"

Bruce did not wait for an answer, he had become excited. "This takes the experiment one further step."

"How so?" Thomas asked as he sat himself down on the table watching his eccentric friend.

"Consider this," Bruce said taking a breath. "Suppose we are standing by the side of the road and we see that a car is traveling in a straight line at a certain speed down the highway. Suppose the car passes a truck which is traveling in the opposite direction at another speed."

Thomas tried to imagine it and waited for his friend to go on.

"Well, we find ourselves are stationary and the cars are moving at certain speeds in different directions right?" Bruce asked.

Thomas saw nothing profound in the question. "Of course," he said waiting for him to come to the point.

"But from the sun's point of view for example, the earth is spinning and rotating around the sun. The sun sees the car and truck move quite differently than we do, doesn't it?" Bruce looked quizzically at Thomas.

"Are you saying it depends on your frame of reference?"

"Exactly, that's right," Bruce said with much enthusiasm. "Consider the position from the driver of the car. He would see himself and his car remaining absolutely still. He would see the rest of the world wiz by behind him and he would see the truck move at a much faster speed behind him than the world itself. Do you see how it depends on your point of view?"

Bruce waited for Thomas to respond. "Yes, to the driver of the car, I guess you could say he sees the road and the world ahead of him move toward him and he would see the world go by in his rear vision mirror."

"Good. That's right. Also now, the truck driver, he would also see himself as stationary but he would see the world move in the other direction, right? Do you see what I mean?" Bruce again looked at his friend with much enthusiasm.

"Yes, the same would apply for the truck driver, but I don't quite see the point," Thomas replied waiting for Bruce to go on.

"Ahh well consider this for the moment," Bruce said as he took another deep breath. "The car driver sees himself as being stationary and the truck driver also sees himself as being stationary, and yet the person by the side of the road sees them both moving in opposite directions. Isn't that extraordinary?"

Thomas didn't really see anything extraordinary in such a mundane event but waited for his friend to go on.

"The point is, that whatever we consider moving, whether it be a car or a truck or whatever, when we place ourselves at that moving object, we find ourselves at rest and everything else moves instead. Do you see how we can effectively stop a thing from moving by our relative point of view and instead consider that other things are moving relative to us?"

"Yes, I see what you mean," Thomas said, "Where do we go from here?"

"Let's first give this a name," Bruce said. "Let's call this the doctrine of 'relative stillness'."

Thomas interrupted, "Hang on, I don't quite follow. What do you mean by 'relative stillness'?"

"The phenomenon that whatever we consider moving, when considered from the moving object's point of view, it can be considered to be absolutely still and instead other things are moving in different ways – that is what I mean by 'relative stillness'. Do you follow me now, movement is relative?" Bruce said waiting for an acknowledgment.

"Yep, I follow you so far," Thomas said wanting to hear more.

"OK good. Now consider this." Bruce looked madly around for a sheet of paper. He grabbed one from a bundle on a table and walked towards Thomas. "Suppose an ant had to crawl from point A to point B on this piece of paper." Bruce scribbled a dot toward the left of the paper which he labelled A and a dot toward the right of the paper which he labelled B. "What would be the quickest way?"

"A straight line," Thomas answered. "The quickest way would be for the ant to crawl from A to B in a straight line."

"Wrong," Bruce barked at his friend. "That's the old way of thinking. That is what I have been working on all these years with the Trans Warp Inducer."

Thomas was puzzled as he looked at his friend.

Bruce continued, "I can fold the piece of paper inside itself so that A touches B. Then the ant who was at A is now also at B." Bruce folded the area of the paper between the dots towards his chest so that A touched B.

"Well, you tricked me," Thomas said, "I didn't think you could fold the paper."

"That's the whole point," beamed Bruce. "You don't have to see the paper as being folded. You can consider the paper is absolutely still and doesn't move by our doctrine of 'relative stillness'."

"Hang on I don't quite follow," Thomas said looking puzzled again.

"It's simple," Bruce said. "From the piece of paper's point of view, it hasn't moved. It has remained absolutely still just like the driver of the car or the truck. All that happened is that the ant trans-warped from point A to point B. And for the last ten years, I have made the Trans Warp Inducer which can effectively transport anything from one place into here." At this, Bruce pointed at the fridge-like object.

"I don't believe it," Thomas said sceptically.

"Hand me your wrist watch," Bruce said pointing at it. "Let me show you how it works."

Thomas removed his wrist watch and gave it to Bruce. "I have programmed the Inducer with the co-ordinates of that X over there." Bruce positioned the wrist watch at the centre of the marked X on the floor. He then went to the computer and started typing.

"Keep your eyes on the watch," Bruce said as he typed.

Thomas stared at the watch. At first nothing happened. Then the colours of the watch faded and it appeared slightly darker. The watch then appeared translucent and the X could be seen through the watch. The watch then disappeared.

"Did you see that?" Bruce piped in.

"Yeah, where did it go?" Thomas asked.

"In here." Bruce walked over to the Inducer and opened the door. The interior even looked like the inside of a fridge but without shelves. On the floor, a similar X was marked in tape and Bruce removed the watch from the centre of the X.

"That can't be," Thomas thought to himself. He said out aloud, "It is some kind of trick."

Bruce grinned at the suggestion. "It's not a trick at all. You saw it with your own eyes."

"Do something else," Thomas said. "Can you get something from outside?"

"I haven't finished the computer program yet which links in co-ordinates from other places, but I did do one. Do you remember the bank that's just outside our old school?" Bruce inquired.

"Yes, I do" Thomas said wondering what Bruce had in mind.

"I have managed to program the computer with the co-ordinates of one of the teller's cash drawers." Bruce moved over to the computer keyboard. "Watch this."

Bruce started typing into the keyboard. "That ought to do it," Bruce said as he hit the enter key. Bruce opened the Inducer and removed a wad of cash from the floor.

"Satisfied now?" Bruce asked.

Thomas was convinced it was a trick. "No, I am not so sure," Thomas said walking over to the Inducer. He looked inside. Nothing. Just a plain empty space with a bit of electrical tape on the floor.

"Let me see you transport me". Thomas walked over to the X.

"You will have to bend down and grab your knees, it's a little cramped in there." Bruce knew the circumstances were too much for his friend and he had been induced to request this.

Thomas complied with Bruce's instructions. Bruce commenced typing into the computer once more.

Thomas faded from sight in a similar fashion to the watch. Bruce then heard a familiar thud. "Damn," Bruce muttered to himself. Retrieving the shovel from the entrance to the room he said to himself, "Always goes wrong with humans."

Chapter 16

The Traitor

The olive trees were bathed in the pale light of the near full moon and swayed gently in the heat wave. Daniel made his way through the olive grove towards the house of Barshimon.

Daniel had always respected Barshimon as a wise and benevolent leader of the people just under the chief elder. Barshimon had always been the right-hand man of the chief and could be prevailed upon to keep a level head in times of crises. Daniel was his close friend and wished to follow in his footsteps.

It was now approaching midnight as Daniel lightly tapped on the door of Barshimon. He was greeted by the fat servant who ushered him into the living room. The servant automatically made for the kettle of warm water to wash the feet of his master's expected visitor.

"My master will be with you shortly," the servant said as he knelt by the side of Daniel and washed the dust from off his feet.

It was customary for a man of Daniel's rank not to respond directly to the servant. Daniel waited in silence. He did not wait long.

"Ahh my good friend Daniel," Barshimon said as he entered the room. Daniel immediately rose from his seat and kissed the ring on Barshimon's hand with much affection. "Please have a seat we have much to discuss," Barshimon said as he pulled up a seat next to his friend.

"For some time now, we have ruled the people in peace and solitude from any who would threaten the peace. Even from external forces who do not believe as we believe. We have met all challenges and responded appropriately to all dangers." Barshimon looked at his friend as he spoke these words. Daniel noticed a sense of deep concern, almost panic, in the eyes of his friend which he had never noticed before.

"But now we live in very different times and the greatest threat to our people comes from within. A band of revolutionaries are attempting to overthrow the government of our people and install their own king." Barshimon continued, "This cannot be tolerated."

"We should just set an ambush for them," Daniel interjected.

"I agree in times gone by this was the usual way of dealing with these sorts of troublemakers," Barshimon replied. "But this group is a lot more cunning. They are trying to work from within and turn the people against the government. An ambush could backfire and make the government look like cowards."

"Are you saying we need to expose them?" Daniel asked. "Perhaps we could show the people that the ringleaders are speaking lies. We could bring them up before a Court of law and let justice deal with them in public."

"That is exactly what I have in mind, but first we have to get them into custody," Barshimon cautioned. "And that is not going to be easy."

"No, it won't," Daniel added. "They have a large following already and any sign of violent force or resistance against them will arouse bloody protests and cause more damage to the government."

"Daniel," Barshimon began as he pulled his seat closer to his friend. "Yesterday I asked you to personally see if you could plant a spy amongst them to report on all their movements. Have you had any success?"

"Yes and no," Daniel replied. "They are a close-knit group and it is difficult to put one of our own kind amongst them. He would be too easily recognised and exposed. But I have managed to make some progress with one of their number. I think he is willing to turn if the price is right."

"Good, excellent," Barshimon exclaimed. "Then perhaps we can get the best of both worlds."

"What do you mean?" Daniel asked. Daniel knew that Barshimon was a perfect tactician. He had pre-empted the moves of many enemies in the past and had always taken appropriate countermeasures. It was this quality that Daniel most admired in his friend.

"We *will* ambush them tomorrow night," Barshimon said as he rose from his seat. He commenced pacing around the room in deep thought.

"I thought you had decided against that," Daniel piped in.

"But it will not look like an ambush," Barshimon quickly added. "We will set upon their leaders tomorrow night. We will then announce the following morning that they have been taken into lawful custody and put them on public trial before the rest of them can regroup." Barshimon muttered these words under his breath as he spoke attempting to visualise how it would all proceed.

Daniel had learnt not to interrupt his friend at moments like these. He watched his friend continue.

"Somehow we need to set the cat among the pigeons. They are not yet expecting us to strike." Barshimon turned towards his friend, "Daniel," he said looking at him, "Can you arrange for a squadron of our men to be ready tomorrow night and keep it secret?"

"Yes, that shouldn't be a problem. Where do you want them to ambush?" Daniel asked.

"That we don't know yet. That is where your spy will come in handy," Barshimon said. "Do you think your spy could give us some notice of where the leaders of the group will be tomorrow night? Our squadron would have to assemble beforehand in secret and be ready at a moment's notice."

"That shouldn't be too difficult," Daniel answered. "I have arranged for some small amount of money to be paid to our spy."

"But don't you think ambushing them at night will cause the violent protests that you fear, even if we do call it an arrest?" Daniel asked wondering what Barshimon was thinking of.

"That is why I will speak to the judge tonight and arrange for the trial of the men to be held immediately." Barshimon commenced smiling as he saw his plan unfold to the last detail. "Their followers will be taken by such surprise and many of them will be more interested in the outcome of the trial and what it will unfold than the mere intricacies of a night time arrest."

"Are we ready to proceed with a trial so hastily?" Daniel asked.

"We have to be, the whole plan depends upon it," replied Barshimon. "Tomorrow after you make arrangements with the spy, start collating the statements we have obtained from our witnesses and have them also on standby to testify at a moment's notice. I will clear it with the judge."

"OK," Daniel said smiling. "It looks as if it might work."

"But remember Daniel. It is not enough that the ringleaders be convicted. The people have to know why they were convicted. They have to be discredited in public. If we can strike the head of this movement tomorrow night, then the rest of their following should collapse soon after. So, make sure the witnesses are ready and get onto securing that spy." Barshimon looked at his friend awaiting an acknowledgment.

"Understood," Daniel said. "I will get right on it." Daniel rose from his seat and made for the door. He had much to prepare.

Opening the door and stepping out, Barshimon touched his friend on the shoulder and asked, "Who is the spy you are liaising with anyway, do you know his name?"

Daniel turned to answer him. "Judas," he said, "Judas Iscariot."

Chapter 17

The Last Resort

The sound of howling wind and roaring waves were only drowned by the frequent crash of thunder, as the clouds burst forth a torrential rain. The lightning-lit sky illuminated the black ocean as it rose and buckled. The fishing trawler fell downwards only to be whisked up high again as another wave moved beneath it.

The hull was now compromised and its only crewmember had no option but to scramble for a life vest. Pedro had never known a storm like this. He had been a fisherman for 30 years and now started to fear for his life. The emergency life raft inflated on the deck of his ship. Pedro knew that this would disappear with the next wave if he did not jump into it. But with the speed of lightning, Pedro frantically turned his back on the life raft and made one last dash for the bridge of his doomed trawler. Underneath the helm lay a silver casket which had never been opened. Pedro snatched it up and leapt for the life raft.

The following morning showed no trace of the storm. The sun beat down on the life raft through the clear blue sky. Pedro lay exhausted on his back propped up by his life vest. Cramped tightly under one arm was the silver casket. He had kicked off his shoes exposing his feet to the sunlight. He had lost his trawler and was lost at sea. He had no food on board but currently of significantly more importance, he had no shade. Pedro toyed with the idea of submerging himself into the ocean by the side of the life raft for shade but he was still exhausted from last night's rough ride.

The silver casket was about the size of a shoebox. It had two twist locks on the front. Nothing moved about inside when it was shaken and Pedro had no idea of the contents of the container.

As Pedro lay grasping the casket, he recalled his father lying upon his deathbed 25 years ago. He was frail and the cancer was much advanced. Pedro was present with other family friends when his father asked them all to leave so that he could be alone with his son. Pedro's eyes were full of tears and his chest felt heavy but when the others had left the room, his father seemed to chirp up and a gleam fell upon his face.

"My son," his father said, "I won't be with you much longer, but I must tell you something."

"What is it?" Pedro asked looking somewhat surprised.

"At home, in my bedroom. Go to my cupboard and look in my sock drawer."

"I don't understand father," the young Pedro said wondering if delirium had set in.

"Listen to me," his father continued, "Go to my sock drawer and find the key. It is hidden in a pair of socks towards the back of the drawer."

"What key father?" Pedro asked. His father perched himself up on his elbow and in much pain, he lifted his head from his pillow to look his son in the eye.

"There is a key there, you must find it," his father said.

"Yes father, what will I do with it?" Pedro said wanting to relax his father.

His father swallowed and continued in obvious pain. "It unlocks a safe that is in the attic of the house."

Pedro recalled as a child he would play in the attic until his father made him promise never to go up there. Since then, he concluded a ghost was up there and had always avoided the attic.

"You must unlock the safe and recover the casket," his father said leaning towards his son.

"What is it father, what is it for?" Pedro asked trying to take in his father's directions.

"Listen, it is very important," his father said coughing as he spoke. "You must recover the casket from the safe but you must not open it. Do you understand me? You must not open it. Promise me. Pedro?"

Pedro could not deny his father anything especially in a state such as this. "Of course, father, I will do as you say. But tell me what it is for."

"It is the last resort," his father said lying back on his bed and muttering to himself, "...the last resort."

Pedro leaned forward in his chair waiting for his father to continue. His father swallowed once more and looked at his son directly. "Listen to me my son, you may open the silver casket only as a last resort. Everything else must be hopeless. Absolutely hopeless."

Pedro was confused. His father had been making sense up to this point but now his son was losing him. "I don't understand father," Pedro said, "What is it, what's in it, what does it do?"

"It is for you my son, it will save your life one day," his father said, "But you must promise me you will only open the silver casket as a last resort when everything else has been tried and failed. Promise me this before I die my son," his father in agonizing pain sat up from his bed as he enjoined his son, "promise me this now my son so I can rest in peace."

"I promise father," Pedro said as the tears fell down his cheeks.

"Come here my son."

Pedro moved into the outstretched hands of his father and put his head on his chest.

"Never forget this promise," his father said as he kissed his forehead. With this, he breathed his last.

Pedro left the hospital in a dazed state. He had never known his mother who died giving birth to him. His father had raised him in the only way he knew how, as a fisherman. He had inherited his father's fishing trawler and carried on his father's trade when his father became too sick. But he had never known of the silver casket.

Pedro returned home and went to his father's bedroom. In the corner of the room was the sock drawer. It cracked open and Pedro squeezed every pair of socks for something solid. There was no sign of it so Pedro commenced opening every pair and laying them out on the floor. Pedro's heart sank as he opened the last pair of socks and did not find the safe key. He frantically looked again in each pair. Not finding it he sat on his father's bed and thought to himself.

Pedro gazed at the open sock drawer with the pairs of socks laid out on the floor in front of it. The open drawer was the top in a series of five. Pedro jumped up and opened the second drawer. He was relieved to find that it was also full of socks. The drawer under that only contained underwear and the remaining drawers did not contain clothing. Pedro again commenced squeezing every sock and found the one towards the back containing the key.

Pedro took the key and headed for the attic. He had not been into the attic for years and had come to believe in the ghost that haunted it. Pedro did not feel comfortable and decided to be as quick as possible. He raced into the attic without caring to look around. He found the safe and pushed the key in it. Clicking it open he found the silver casket. He grabbed it and made for the stairs wishing never to return to the room.

Pedro made for his own room where he had always felt at ease. He sat with the casket on his bed and examined it.

It was surely made of silver. It looked like a typical pirate's treasure chest but much smaller. The base was rectangular but the lid was a rounded arch with curved edges. There were beautiful and exotic carvings on every surface including the base.

Remembering what he had promised his dying father, Pedro did not open the casket. There were two twist locks on the front and two hinges on the back. Clearly the lid could flip up revealing the contents within. Pedro started to become frustrated. The adventure seemed to have come to an abrupt halt. He had not expected this.

Pedro decided to do a little more experimenting. The casket weighed exactly 4.98kg according to the bathroom scales. It did not stick to a magnet. Shaking the casket did not produce a rattle. No smell emanated from the casket.

Pedro thought back on the promise he made his father. He wondered if the promise extended towards having someone else open the casket. For a moment he thought this would be a way around his father's injunction but Pedro knew it wasn't. If another person opened the casket for Pedro, he reasoned that this person would in reality be Pedro's instrument and he would really be guilty of breaching his father's death wish. Pedro had no desire to do this.

Pedro decided to leave the casket in his room, and open it as he promised his father, as a last resort only.

For many days the casket nagged at him and he thought of having the casket x-rayed at the airport security station. He dreamed of putting it in his backpack and throwing it onto the x-ray machine. He reasoned however that this would only result in the security personnel ordering him to open the casket and this would certainly breach his solemn vow. In the end Pedro decided no other thing was open to him. The casket must sit around until the last resort – if ever that occur.

It was not long before Pedro realised why his father had kept it in the safe in the attic. Sitting on the shelf in his bedroom was far too much a temptation. Pedro decided to keep it on board his fishing trawler. For one thing, there would be no point waiting to open it until the last resort, if one did not have it ready to open at the last resort – and to Pedro's reasoning, this was more likely on board the fishing trawler.

After several days Pedro wondered how the casket came into the possession of his father. He scoured his bedroom for his father's diaries and when he found them, he sat madly on the floor of his father's bedroom scanning every page for mention of the silver casket. But the diaries contained no entries regarding the silver casket at all.

It started to become too much for Pedro and feeling angry with himself for not asking his father more questions about the casket, he felt justified in taking more risks than ever in his fishing expeditions. There was no rule against manufacturing the last resort.

It was with the silver casket in mind that Pedro set out last night in the fishing trawler. The weather had been threatening all day. He now lay in the life raft with the sun beating down on him. He estimated he could only last a further 24 hours at the most. The sunlight was extreme and his throat was parched. Pedro's situation was desperate. Ordinarily one would have become extremely cross with oneself for venturing out on a fishing trip in the reckless disregard of a pending storm but Pedro had been wanting to know the contents of the silver casket now for a quarter of a century. On the contrary, Pedro lay back in the life raft feeling proud with himself for never having breached his father's injunction. For 25 years Pedro had wondered what the contents contained. The last resort would soon be upon him. Even if the contents of the casket could not save his life, he would nevertheless die knowing what the casket contained. This would be satisfaction enough.

Pedro sat thinking of the one torment of his life as the sun started to set. The temperature dropped and Pedro started to shiver. Pedro believed he could last the night – but no longer. That would be it. Exposure to the sunlight all day, the cold air at night. No food, no water, no prospects. Amidst the discomfort of the night, Pedro felt comforted in the knowledge his curiosity would finally be satisfied.

Daylight came and Pedro could not take it any longer. He was certain he could not last. This was not wishful thinking. This was the last resort. The casket had made its way down to his feet during the night. Were it not for the stiffness of his body, Pedro would have snatched it up. Opening his eyes, he used all his effort to sit up. His feet were frozen and his neck was stiff. His back was extremely sore and Pedro felt his muscles were weak. He stretched his hands out towards the casket and leaned towards it. He was about to touch the casket when he heard it. About a nautical mile away was the unmistakable sound of a foghorn from a passing freighter.

Chapter 18

DrugTech

Philip headed into the university bar for the usual Friday night drinks. It was a quiet night tonight as most of the usual Friday night revellers were preparing for the Science Ball this evening. Being the Professor of biochemistry at the university, Philip chose not to attend the ball not wishing to fraternize on a social level with his students.

His usual chair was available with the regular assortment of nuts to which he helped himself. Surveying the room, he noticed a gaunt unshaven man settle into a chair in the corner. Philip was sure he had seen this man before but couldn't quite place him. Studying his features, Philip tried hard to place him. The man sat with his head resting in his hands and seemed somewhat despondent. He was alone and seemed as if he wished to drown his sorrows. The man lifted his head and scanning the room caught a glimpse of Philip.

The man stood up and made his way over to Philip's table. "Hello Philip," the man said, "How is the university treating you my young friend?"

Philip instantly recalled the man. There had only been one acquaintance in Philip's life who had referred to him as his young friend. Ten years ago, when Philip was employed as a research scientist at DrugTech he had come to know Martin. Martin was a senior scientist at DrugTech in another classified research department. Their paths had often crossed and Philip would often discuss his work with him. Philip's security clearance however was less than that of Martin's and so Martin could not discuss his work at DrugTech with Philip. This had always been somewhat of a mystery to Philip.

Philip's observation of Martin was certainly not as he expected. For one thing many of the senior research scientists at DrugTech would retire extremely wealthy. But Martin appeared as a worn-down man in the despair of poverty.

"Hello Martin," Philip said, "Life isn't bad, please have a seat."

"Thanks," Martin said as he sat down, "Made any more breakthroughs in the laboratory since DrugTech?"

"A few things here and there," Philip said, "What about you?"

"I am out of the research business Philip," Martin said, "I am looking for something else these days."

"What do you mean?" Philip asked curiously.

"Well, Philip, since my days at DrugTech I have been looking to redeem myself with others and the world in general. I never did tell you what I was working on at DrugTech did I?"

"No, Martin," Philip said wanting to know. He knew not to ask directly.

"Many research departments were working on various things. Some were trying to cure the common cold but others like yourself were trying to cure cancer," Martin began. "As one of the senior research scientists at DrugTech, I decided to research the most noble of all cures. The cure for man's mortality. I wished to make someone immortal."

Philip listened intently to Martin who seemed quite content to disclose it to him.

"At first I worked on an antioxidant organ. This was a device that I wished to implant in a human being just before the human heart. It would release various antioxidants into the body at various stages in an attempt to slow down cellular aging." Martin seemed to raise his eyes to heaven before continuing. "Eventually one thing led to another and the project moved on to attempt to transplant a human brain from a dying elderly person into that of a young healthy body. This was one way it was thought to achieve a certain form of immortality."

Philip recalled how various white-coated scientists would move about in the upper levels of DrugTech, which had always been off bounds to him.

"At first the hardest thing to do was to keep the brain and body alive when we separated them," Martin continued. "We tried for years on animals and eventually solved the problem. We found a way to actually do it." Martin's voice dropped to a whisper, "several years later we refined the operation so much that we felt comfortable with working on humans as well as animals."

"We did a range of experiments and that's when the most astonishing thing happened," Martin said looking directly at Philip. "For example, our first human to human transplant was between a man and a woman."

Philip found himself captivated by Martin's story and waited patiently for him to continue. "We actually transplanted the man's brain into the woman's body and vice versa. Two weeks later they came out of their coma and I was the first to speak to them."

"What happened?" Philip asked wanting to know more, "Did it work?"

"Well, the operation was a success, but it was not what was expected," Martin replied.

"I don't understand," Philip whispered.

"I had expected the memory and thoughts of the man to be in the woman's body and similarly I expected the woman's body to house the very consciousness of the man," Martin said as he stared through Philip recalling the incident. "But it wasn't that way at all."

Philip eagerly awaited an explanation. "The memory and thoughts of the man were still present in the man, and the memory and thoughts of the woman were still present in the woman," Martin said, "Yet we had swapped their brains. I had done the operation myself."

"That's impossible," Philip volunteered.

"That's what I had thought," Martin replied. "I tried desperately to come up with an explanation. I left the labs that night but I didn't go home. I wandered all around the streets that night until I came up with an explanation and it finally hit me."

"What was that?" Philip asked.

"Our consciousness, what makes us an actual person, our very thoughts and memories, our human intellect," Martin said as he looked directly at Philip, "It cannot be contained in the brain. I had discovered by scientific experimentation that our intellect was not the operation of a corporeal organ. It had to be something else."

Martin seemed depressed as he continued. "My whole life I had thought that our brains were what made us human, but now I realised that the brain just processed the sensory perceptions. Our intellect must be immaterial, it must be the operation of an immaterial soul. Then the real significance hit me."

Philip seemed perplexed and waited for Martin to continue.

"I had been searching all this time for a cure to man's mortality. But if man's intellect is itself immaterial, then it could not decay like the material body. It was already immortal. I was trying to find a cure for something that was unnecessary."

"What do you mean?" Philip asked looking confused.

"My experiment had proved that man's intellect is contained in an immaterial and therefore immortal soul independent of the brain. Through my science I had discovered that God exists and had made us immortal. Then something else hit me," Martin said frowning at Philip. "If it really was from God, then our very immortality was put at risk from our very own immorality. And my career at DrugTech had been quite immoral. I had supervised operations on human beings as unwitting guinea pigs. I had authorised the suppression of cures for cancer for economic reasons. I had worked on the destruction of several thousand human embryos all of which must have contained their own immortal soul. I decided things had to change at DrugTech."

"What did you do?" Philip asked.

"The next day I went into the Managing Director's office and explained to him the implications of my research. He told me to take the rest of the day off and let him think about it." Martin took a deep breath. "But the next day I was told a fire had broken out in my lab which had destroyed my research. The Managing Director advised that DrugTech was not going to fund my project again and I found I was out of a job. From that time on I have been looking to redeem myself with the world in search of putting straight my own plans for immortality."

"But come on Martin," Philip said, "Surely you could be mistaken?" Philip searched for the most diplomatic way of expressing his scepticism. "You must admit your story sounds a little fantastic," Philip said as he reached for some nuts.

Martin seemed unperturbed. "Don't you remember twelve years ago waking up one day in the hospital adjoining DrugTech and being told that you fell asleep at the steering wheel of your car? Surely you must have observed that peculiar scar at the base of your skull by now?"

"What are you saying?" Philip said remembering a scar he had observed on the back of his neck at the barber one day.

"My young friend," Martin said looking depressed, "For the past twelve years, you have carried on with your own life and your own research in biochemistry with a genetically engineered monkey brain."

Chapter 19

Project X23

Benjamin Jones adjusted his bowtie.

"Table for one?" the surprised receptionist asked at the entrance to the Science Ball.

"Yes please," Ben stammered as he nervously paid his money.

"We have a spare seat at table eight," the receptionist said without looking up. She wrote the seat number on the ticket and gave it to Ben.

Ben had arrived late to the Science Ball on purpose. The last of dinner was being served and Benjamin had no desire to partake in pre-dinner conversation with strangers who would each be paired off to their own dates. Benjamin settled into his seat and signalled the waiter to bring him dinner. The rest of the table like the other tables were either finishing their dinner or heading to the dance floor. The music was starting to get louder and faster and the lights were becoming dimmer.

As Ben commenced eating, he scanned the room for any potential girls that may afford him a dance when the time was right. He had expected most to be paired with their boyfriends but was well aware that several wallflowers attended balls with other girls and these may afford him the first dance.

Across the dance floor, Ben caught a glimpse of Pamela with her boyfriend. Ben had always wished to make an impression on her and even asked her to the Ball. Her boyfriend seemed tall and handsome. Benjamin knew he would appear the nerdy geek in comparison but tonight Benjamin touched his shirt pocket and smiled to himself.

As he neared the end of dinner, Benjamin found himself the last one at table eight. With the lights on dim and he being so late, the waiters didn't bother to collect his plate. Benjamin pushed it to one side and grabbing his glass of water, he nervously removed the contents of his shirt pocket and examined it closely.

In all respects, it looked like a standard antibiotic capsule except that it was slightly smaller and quite iridescently red in colour. Benjamin wondered if it glowed in the dark or perhaps the ultra violet lights of the dance floor caused it to phosphoresce. It was a lone tablet in the centre of the packet surrounded by the usual transparent plastic on the front and silver lining on the back. For only one tablet, the packet seemed unnecessarily large. This was probably done to allow for the wording on the back of the packet.

Benjamin flipped it over and studied it carefully making sure that his actions were unobserved by all others. In the centre of the packet read the words "CLASSIFIED Project X23." The word "DrugTech" appeared beneath.

Benjamin recalled his father's instructions. "The tablet is only good for one hour and must be taken on a full stomach." Benjamin looked at his watch. Ten to eleven. The Ball was scheduled to finish at midnight. Benjamin recalled how several hours earlier he had settled into his bed with the latest computer magazine when his father entered the room. Benjamin rarely had a father-to-son conversation about his university and social life but what happened next was quite unexpected.

At first his father had seemed concerned that his son was simply missing out in not attending the Science Ball and his father was merely giving him parental encouragement. Benjamin had always stuttered and was shy among girls. This fact had not escaped his parents' observations who had hoped that such a boyish manner would change over time. His father shut the door, sat on his bed and started talking to him in a whisper. Benjamin recalled how his father said he had worked at DrugTech as a counsellor. Occasionally some research scientists he would speak to would give him some things. One of these things was the capsule of Project X23.

His father had explained to him that one department at DrugTech was working on a pill that increased the body's production of natural pheromones for men. It had been studied that in nature the male of the species was usually grander than the female. For example, the lion possessed the magnificent mane as opposed to the relatively scrawny female. Similarly, the male peacock possessed the beautiful tail of colourful feathers whereas the female peacock was a single brown colour. In both such cases the males with the superior male characteristics were generally more successful in attracting the female of the species. Yet in the human species, females had for years been placing makeup and perfume on themselves. They had grown their hair longer and constantly attended to it. Human fashions developed such that the female clothes were colourful and varied whereas the male clothes conformed to the general tie and suit and most especially at formal social occasions where males are expected to all dress alike with a black tie.

Whilst social customs and habits have their place in all the human species and such must be conformed with, the general attraction between male and female is essentially animalistic. His father explained that even when humans married each other in what would be the most outward social expression of human monogamy, on a more basic level, married people still observed the animalistic characteristics of other humans. Project X23 had been innovated to essentially encapsulate the very essence of woman's attraction to man at the most basic animalistic level. Such was the success at DrugTech that several of the scientists were fighting amongst themselves as to who would be credited with the research and inform the Managing Director.

Benjamin Jones recalled how his father handed him the pill looking him in the eye and exclaiming most emphatically, "The pill is guaranteed to work. Go to the Science Ball, you won't be disappointed." And as his father knew, anything short of a miracle contained within the molecular structure of the capsule headed Project X23 would disappoint Benjamin Jones.

Benjamin popped the packet open. His heart began beating extremely hard and fast from his mere expectations. He swallowed it. He waited. He tried to calm himself and let the capsule do its job. He noticed his heart actually sped up but his chest seemed sterner and tighter. Though his heart rate increased, he felt its beat decrease in pitch to that of a bass drum. It felt more efficient and grandiose. Then his body broke out in such a sweat that his clothes became uncomfortable. Within moments however the sweat seemed to evaporate from his body to the extent that a noticeable updraft from his shirt collar could be felt around his neck. Indeed, he felt his hair take on a rugged windswept look.

Things seemed to look different to Ben. The room seemed redder. At first, he thought this was the blood welling behind his eyes. But the darker parts of the room seemed more illuminated to him and he believed he could see in the dark. Then he noticed a most astonishing effect. The skin of the females seemed luminescent. It was almost as if they were transparent with a bright light source that shone from inside. The female clothes, as with the men in the room and most other objects seemed relatively dark and ordinary, but the skin of the females attracted his eyes in what he felt was a lion stalking its prey.

He stood up and felt as if he could run as fast as a lion. His chest and arms seemed bigger and all his nervousness left him. He felt that such strong animal hormones had been released through his blood that he could not feel nervous if he tried to. The effects became more pronounced with every second and soon he found it difficult to differentiate between different girls and the men seemed insignificant.

He walked over to who he believed was Pamela with the words, "Would you like to dance?" Benjamin's body had taken over his thoughts. It was neither arrogance nor presumption that prompted him to move his hand towards her and take her up without waiting for a response. He felt his heightened sense and instincts had simply guided him to expect her to respond favourably as a matter of course. Pamela responded favourably and melted into his hand. To Ben, it was a hungry dog responding to a luscious piece of meat. Her boyfriend was of no significance to the situation.

Ben started dancing with Pamela on the dance floor. The redness in his vision continued to increase and with it the skin of all other girls on the dance floor started to shine brightly. As he danced with Pamela, he gazed at the brightly illuminated bodies of the other girls. As he looked at them, they smiled and approached him. It started with one flinging her arms around his waist and urging him to form a train with others. He grabbed Pamela. Within seconds Benjamin found himself the centre of ten girls gyrating in a dragon's tail-like motion around the dance floor. When he released his grip from Pamela's waist, the others did so also and commenced dancing around him in a circle, all competing to the best of their ability to gain his attention. As the music played, he felt his dance movements improve to such an extent that the other girls commenced clapping and cheering. They were all smiling at him and looking incredibly desirous for him.

It was not long before the slow dance songs started and several of the girls commenced tugging at him. By now he couldn't differentiate one from the other and he was not disposed to mind. Anyone would do. As he danced, he saw another approach him and put a note in his shirt pocket. He took it out to read it but as with other things, it appeared too blood red. He was unable to distinguish the letters on the page nor could he determine which girl was dancing with him. With each new song a different girl would fling her arms around his neck and dance slowly with him.

As midnight approached, he felt his heart rise in pitch and the deep red colour in his eyes subside. As his vision returned to normal so did his nerves increase. He found his way to the toilet and hid in a cubicle. He started to shiver and his sweat had completely evaporated. He took another look in his pocket. It was Pamela's name and phone number. He couldn't believe it. He couldn't recall if he had asked for it or if she volunteered it. The past hour seemed as misty as a dream and his muscles were aching. He felt too scared to walk out of the toilet and be seen like this. He decided to wait until all had left. He would go home and find out how he could get some more of Project X23. He would not take no for an answer.

After shivering for nearly an hour, he alighted from the cubicle. The students had dispersed. He made his way to the car and with his head down for fear that he would be recognised, he clung to the shadows. It was not long before he found himself at home again with his father in his bedroom.

"Dad, I need some more of Project X23. It was brilliant, it worked perfectly. I have to have some," he pleaded.

His father shut the door and approached him in a fatherly way. "Son, I think you had better sit down," he began.

Benjamin sensed he would be met with a rejection and braced himself for the response.

"Ben, when your mother and I worked as counsellors at DrugTech, we found that many of our counselling techniques did not work on scientists. They were too used to having mathematical formulas for everything and expecting psychological answers to problems in pill form. Eventually in almost a fit of desperation, your mother and I hit upon Project X23."

"I thought you said it had been researched by a pheromone department at DrugTech," Ben cried.

"Project X23 is nothing more than a piece of red gelatine. Your standard placebo in a so-called classified packet. It does nothing more than fool the recipient into thinking that his problem would be solved by a pill so that he or she would find the courage they needed to continue," his father exclaimed. "To other scientists at DrugTech, Project X23 was an intellect pill, a sleeping pill, sex-drive pill, you name it, we passed it off as such. The departments at DrugTech were so classified anyway that no one could even think to dispute us."

"But it worked, the pill caused physical changes in me. All sorts of things happened that couldn't otherwise be explained," his son cried in desperation.

"Son one thing I learned about counselling at DrugTech was this. The human mind is a powerful instrument and is quite capable of deceiving itself. If one wanted to believe he was Superman and someone told him that Project X23 would make him Superman, you would quite probably find him dead the next morning splattered at the base of the Empire State Building," the father exclaimed. "You can be anything in your life that you want to be son. All you need to do is put your mind to it. Why don't you ring Pamela up tomorrow?"

"I am scared that I would stutter and look like an idiot?" Benjamin said almost sobbing.

"Just be yourself," his father said as he was leaving the room. "After all, that's all you were tonight. Just be yourself."

With that his father left the room and headed upstairs to his bedroom. His wife was already in bed when he closed the door.

"Think he bought it?" she asked in a whisper. He removed his slippers and shrugged his shoulders.

"Dunno," he replied, "Probably."

Chapter 20

The Rich Man and the Priest

It only happens once in a while when an administrative error occurs of such a magnitude that disastrous consequences are sure to follow. Some are more or less devastating than others but they are always unwanted and unexpected. Usually in smoothly flowing operations such as commercial businesses and hospitals, which have been set up with fairly rigorous safeguards in place, they are kept to a minimum, but as with all things, the interaction of human beings brings human error. The one such administrative error, which we are concerned with here, involves the incorrect MRI scan results of a rich man by the name of Carlton McBride.

Carlton McBride was a stockbroker and had complained of regular headaches whence he was referred to hospital for a standard MRI scan. The results were expected to come back negative and the examination was ordered merely for more abundant caution to rule out any suggestion of a brain abnormality. The test results were sent for analysis at the same time as a Carl Michael Brady who had a developing brain tumour and was not expected to live. Ordinarily such a mistake would never occur, but things not being perfect on this particular day, Carlton McBride was unexpectedly informed of terrible news.

It was barely midday when Carlton had entered the hospital for the routine scan. He had now cleared his diary for the rest of the day and was doing his best to settle into a private hospital ward. He was now not expecting to return home again.

Carlton was a single man who had dedicated his life to his success. He was at most times calm and had been described as having a moderate temperament. He usually worked well under pressure but found himself mystified and nervous at the results. Carlton, had never come to terms with the inevitable fact that people, at one time or another, die. Carlton had considered himself an entrepreneur. After finishing university with an economics degree, he went into business for himself borrowing and lending money to others. His keen business sense quickly ensured his success and soon he found himself investing and trading his money on the stock exchange. This quickly became his full-time job and with every successful trade, more money was traded the next time. Carlton had never decided when enough money would be made to pull out of the market and retire early. Until a change of life had been forced on him, he was content, for the moment at least, to continue to double his money.

As Carlton undressed and settled into the hospital bed, he started to feel alone. He had not spoken with his sister in years and had always wanted to contact her after the death of his parents. Being faced with the immanent prospect of death causes one to look back on one's life and re-assess what are considered successes and failures. Suddenly the emptiness of his moneymaking ideas started to pervade his thoughts.

Carlton pulled the blankets up to his neck and started to shiver. It was at this point when he heard a knock on the door followed by a rather small and plumpish Catholic priest enter.

"I am Father John Delaney," he began, "And I was wondering if you wanted to talk with me at all."

At first Carlton shuddered at the thought that he had got to the stage of needing to see a priest in his life. He had expected to live out today like every other day when suddenly his life turned upside down. Whilst considering whether he would ask the priest to leave, he found himself asking, "If you were told you were going to die, would you look back on your life and be happy?"

The priest took this as his invitation and closed the door. He pulled up a chair and sat by his bed. "Why are you asking this my son?" he asked looking concerned.

"My whole life, I had studied economics and made a lot of money," Carlton continued. "The more I made, the more I wanted to make. I just felt like I never had enough time to really put my life in order, and I don't think I am prepared to die."

"No one is ever really prepared to die unless one is at peace with God my son," the priest volunteered.

"I never really had much time for God," answered Carlton. "I just never really thought about it."

"When a man is told he is about to meet his maker, the only things that seem important to him is how he will be judged for them," the priest responded. "Why don't you tell me about your life?"

"You know Father, I have always wanted to ring my sister and tell her I love her. This was something always important to me but I just never got around to it," Carlton said. "I was always wanting to get my career off to a flying start and before I knew it, I just got bogged down in it."

"What would you do if you could start all over?" the priest asked.

"Well for one thing, I wouldn't worry so much about my business. The first thing I would do is ring my sister and see what she was up to."

"It's not too late to ring her now," the priest advised.

"I just feel funny ringing her on my death bed," Carlton sighed. A tear started to glisten in his eye and run down his cheek. "I just wish God could give me some more time."

"Well, if you're too uncomfortable to ring your sister in this situation, why don't you start talking to God in prayer?" the priest enquired. "It's never uncomfortable to pray."

Carlton seemed to consider this. "Do you think God could give me more time?" he asked.

The priest seemed to smile a calming smile. "One way or another, God listens to your prayers and looks after his beloved. Would you like to reconcile yourself with God?" the priest asked.

After only a slight pause, the man leant up on his elbows and responded, "Yes Father."

We will never know what transpired between the priest and the rich man at this point, but it ended with the priest leaving him with a smile and the words, "never stop praying to God. He is the only one who can work miracles for you."

The priest left the room and headed down the corridor. He was passed by a nurse and a doctor who seemed flustered and in a hurry. They both had flushed red faces. The doctor was carrying a file in his hand with the results of an MRI scan. They came to the room that the priest had just left and didn't wait to knock.

"Mr McBride," the doctor said as he burst the door open. "We have just been advised of an awful mix up. Your MRI scans are quite normal," the doctor said gasping for air in-between sentences.

"Apparently your results were mixed up with somebody else," the nurse said smiling nervously. "You can actually get dressed and go home, there is nothing wrong with you," she said trying to look pleasant.

Carlton lay back on his bed not being one to get worked up on hearing surprising news. He thought back on his life before responding. "May I please have a telephone, I wish to make a call," he said.

"Yes of course," the nurse said, I shall bring you in one.

She left the room and returned with a portable telephone. As Carlton commenced dialling, she smiled at the doctor and they turned to leave the room evidently relieved that the news had been taken well.

"Don't forget to call if you need anything," the nurse whispered looking over her shoulder at her patient out of habit.

Carlton acknowledged with a wave of his hand, then spoke into the phone. "Hello Susan," he said, "I want to buy some shares I've been thinking about, quick!"

Chapter 21

Piratical Contract

The pirate ship Douglas dropped anchor off the shore of Mount Yearning and the wearisome crew disembarked for a long-awaited shore leave. The ship's former captain was given a burial at sea and its First Mate Terrence ascended to the Captaincy. The crew had already spent a day on Mount Yearning but was under strict orders from its new Captain to remain in sight of the ship until an announcement was made. The Captain remained on board after having writing materials brought to his quarters. Apart from the ship's cook Sebastian, all other crewmembers had taken shore leave.

As the daylight hours faded, the crew commenced gathering firewood for the nightly bonfire on the beach. However, the usual rum was denied the party as the Captain requested that all crewmembers were to remain sober and alert pending his announcement. This was met with both disappointment and surprise but the crew were well accustomed to following orders. At the conclusion of the meeting, all crewmembers were promised a 'belly full of rum.'

The Chief-of-the-Boat sat by himself on a log facing the bonfire. He was a burly unshaven man and had served the most part of his life on board the Douglas under its former Captain, Samuel. Captain Terrence had passed over the Chief-of-the-Boat as its new First Mate and had instead appointed Lawrence, a relatively younger person with much less experience. This came as a surprise to the crew who had more than expected the Chief to become the First Mate. Lawrence had understandably avoided coming face-to-face with the Chief. Rank always had its privileges on board the Douglas and tonight Lawrence found himself befriended by several of the crew who had previously remained relatively indifferent to his presence.

As midnight approached with no sign of the Captain, the crew started to become restless. The Chief was in no mood for anybody, and the new First Mate found himself assuring others that he knew nothing of the reason why the Captain had concealed himself so secretly from the crew.

In a further hour, the crew would be pushed to breaking point. Captain Terrence knew the personalities of his crewmembers well. He chose this moment to disembark and the crew soon found him standing knee deep in water facing the bonfire on the beach. With a swirl of his finger, the Captain commanded the remaining pile of firewood to be thrown onto the fire. This was promptly obeyed and the bonfire blazed high casting a red glow over the Captain's features as he stood in front of his crew with a parchment in his right hand. The murmur of the crew gave way to the crackling of the burning logs as they examined their new Captain and awaited the announcement. The crew had separated into two lots, one on each side of the bonfire. On the right of the Captain was Lawrence with seven of the crew. On the left was the Chief-of-the-Boat with Sebastian and another four. The Captain waited for all to settle down on the sand before he began. Without so much as a rumour amongst the crew concerning the Captain's address, it had become the most anticipated announcement in the history of the Douglas.

"My friends," he began. "On this island lies the lost treasure of Count De Jager. Our former Captain left behind a map showing the exact location of the treasure."

The Captain waited for the news to settle in. He did not have to wait long. His crew was mystified and sat gaping at the announcement.

"The map has been destroyed; however, I have memorised the precise co-ordinates of the treasure right down to the finest details." The Captain did not wait long before continuing, knowing that the crew's digestion of this news alone would leave them all with a sour stomach. With a wry smile and without undue haste he added, "We shall gather the treasure tomorrow at dawn but first we must come to some sort of arrangement." At these words he raised the parchment he was holding high above his head to be observed by his crew.

The crew was obviously troubled at these words and the Chief broke the silence. "Is this some kind of trick to get the treasure yourself my Captain?" the Chief blurted out. The Chief-of-the-Boat had been obviously depressed and clearly resented the Captain's decision in choosing Lawrence as the new First Mate of the Douglas.

In any event, the Captain, knowing his crew quite well, was aware that every other crewmember had started to think the same thing. The Chief's outburst merely voiced the inner murmurings of the Crew. The outburst had its desired effect and the crew commenced speaking openly to each other regarding the motives of the new Captain. But as the location of the treasure remained a secret to all bar the Captain, and as he was promising to share it with his crew at dawn, he commanded their full attention – for the moment at least.

The Captain continued, "The lost treasure of Count De Jager is reputed to be the grandest fortune in the world. It will more than satisfy each one of us. There would surely be enough for everybody, but we need some kind of order among us before it is retrieved."

"So, what is the plan Captain?" questioned Lawrence wishing to assert himself and demonstrate some of his newly acquired privileges in front of the Chief and the crew.

"Simple," the Captain responded. "One third of the treasure will be skimmed off and will go towards the upkeep of the Douglas or a new ship."

While the crew listened intently waiting to hear what each crewmember's share would be, the Captain looked intently at each crewmember before continuing, constantly assessing the situation. He had their perfect attention. This was the language of the crew. As the red glow of the blazing fire danced across the Captain's face, the greed of a pending fortune dripped from the mouths of the crewmembers.

"Another third will be split equally amongst us and distributed immediately to each crewmember upon the treasure's return to the Douglas." Several of the high-ranking crewmembers were looking forward to a higher cut but decided to bide their time for the moment.

"The other third will be kept here hidden on the island," the Captain announced. The crew was evidently dissatisfied at this and started arguing amongst themselves. This effectively meant that service to the Douglas would cut each member out of a full two thirds of the treasure which seemed unreasonable. Each crewmember however was content to let the Captain know of his dissatisfaction through his murmurings with his neighbouring crewmembers and each avoided expressing any concerns direct to the Captain.

"Hear me," the Captain shouted as the crew settled down once more. "As each crewmember reaches retirement age and leaves us to go back to civilization, he will be given his share of the last third of the treasure then, but only then. Anyway, you should all have enough treasure dispensed to you tomorrow when we separate out the first one third, but as Captain of the Douglas, it is my obligation to concern myself with the retirement prospects of each of my crew and concern myself with your future." The Captain continued after a brief pause, "but, if any crewmember wishes to leave us early, he will forfeit his retirement share of the treasure to the rest of us."

This arrangement seemed to appease the high-ranking crewmembers who were generally older and closer to retirement. This gave the Captain a working majority amongst the crew and ultimately assured the crew's agreement to the plan. But the Chief seemed dissatisfied. Spitting into the fire, he walked to the back of the gathering. The Captain would obviously have to deal with the Chief later, but for the moment at least, he was no threat to the Captain's plans.

"Besides," said the Captain obviously directing his attention to the back of the gathering, "if the treasure is as much as it is reputed to be, we are all going to be so rich it won't be worth arguing about."

The Captain observed that excitement started to spread amongst the crewmembers and several of them commenced smiling and laughing. The crewmembers were now on their feet rubbing their hands together and licking their lips.

"But first," the Captain shouted once more silencing his crew. "We must all agree on this contract before the treasure is retrieved. Here it is written down," the Captain said holding up the parchment once more. "Let this be a solemn vow between us. I want no backstabbing. No treacherous plots or underhandedness. Everyone must work for the benefit of the crew according to this agreement and not just himself. Let it be known that if anyone breathes a word to another crewmember about breaking this contract, it will be considered a crime of high treason. Such a crewmember will be given nothing short of the plank. Do we understand each other?"

The Captain's remark had its desired effect of subduing the greedy crew. "I expect full co-operation and agreement." With this the Captain pulled a dagger from his sleeve and held it up in front of the crew. Walking to the back of the gathering, he solemnly placed the parchment on the sand. The ritual had been performed once before under the former Captain Samuel.

As the crew stared silently at the Captain, he grabbed the blade of the dagger with his left hand and pulled the dagger through with his right. Within seconds his hand was covered in blood. Throwing the dagger to the ground, he spat on his bloodied hand and stamped a handprint on the parchment. "Let us all sign it in our blood," the Captain said staring at his silent crew.

Several of the crew swallowed hard. Ritually the First Mate was required to sign the contract next but the Captain clearly looked at the Chief-of-the-Boat for any sign of resistance. This did not come and Lawrence grabbed the dagger. Turning to face the crew, the First Mate cut his hand in a similar fashion, spat, and stamped the parchment with his bloodied hand. The mood of the crew changed instantly and the silence was replaced with cheering and whistling. As the parchment was handed to each crewmember in turn, the Captain ordered the rum to be brought ashore. Drinking with his crewmembers, the Captain commenced explaining to all precisely where the treasure was and making a plan for its retrieval at dawn.

Being only a few hours before dawn, the Captain suggested that the crew sleep all they could before they set out in the daylight. It was agreed that the Captain would leave the First Mate, Lawrence, in charge of the crew from this moment on. As expected, the Captain ordered the Chief-of-the-Boat to return to the Douglas to 'sort out some matters.' Any differences the Chief may have with the Captain's handling of recent events was best settled in private away from the crew. With the prospect of treasure at dawn, a settled piratical contract and thrilling retirement prospects, the crew had already thrown their support behind the Captain and the First Mate.

On board the Douglas, the Chief-of-the-Boat stood on deck looking out at the now dying bonfire. The crew was now quite drunk and several of them lay strewn upon the sand looking up at the stars or sleeping. As he raised the anchor, he steered the ship out to sea. "I don't think they suspect anything," he said as he walked into the dining room seeing the Captain and Sebastian counting out the treasure.

Chapter 22

The Perfect Crime

Mr Justin Winston was a thief. He was not the ordinary, run of the mill, garden-variety type of thief. No, Mr Winston was far lower and far more cunning. Like many of his criminal contemporaries, Mr Winston possessed no discernible conscience. However, unlike many who wish to embark upon a career of criminality, only the few with a great intellect seem to manage their affairs well enough to make crime pay. And Mr Winston possessed an extraordinary intellect.

From his earliest school days, Justin coveted things that were not his own. If things seemed desirable in one way or another, Justin wished to assert some proprietary interest over it. The taking of such goods by Justin was never accompanied by feelings of remorse or regret. To him, such was his birth right. When told he could use his mind creatively, only one thing seemed to satisfy his appetite – the thought of one day, pulling off the perfect crime.

In his university days, Mr Winston was no petty thief. He did not trifle with mere cat burglary and he never involved himself in robbery. His intellect was too precious to be put at risk by the use of physical violence. Cheating and deception on the other hand were always fair game so long as he was never caught. He possessed the charming smiling knock about kind of personality that could relate well to his neighbour and in turn, his neighbours never knew who it was that stabbed them in the back.

It was only at the conclusion of his university days however that Mr Winston seriously thought about putting his lifelong ambition into play and actually planning and pulling off the perfect crime. The prize of course had to involve millions of dollars, billions in fact. Money was always the purest form of coveted good and a class one thief with a great intellect ought not to aim too low.

In respect of money, Mr Winston considered that the genus of thievery was effectively divided into four species. Firstly, there was simple larceny. This was the mere taking of another person's money without that person's consent and with the intention of permanently depriving the person of the money. The problem with simple larceny however was that the opportunity to make off with millions or billions of dollars in one crime rarely if ever presented itself, at least not without more. This species of thievery on its own was therefore considered manifestly imperfect and could not make out the perfect crime.

Secondly there was robbery. This involves the use of threats, intimidation and force to require persons to hand over their money. As no one person goes around carrying so much money however (and it would be evidently impractical to rob so many) a robbery involving so much money would have to be limited to banks and casinos. The problem with this species however is that it usually requires other persons, is way too dangerous and is never guaranteed to succeed, not to mention that banks and casinos have their own kind of built-in security to thwart the attempt.

A third kind was fraud. At first glance, this species seems like the one real opportunity of committing the perfect crime. Especially when computers of today allowed one to carry out all sorts of fraud over the internet without having to leave home. Mr Winston well knew of cases where through computer hacking, people have managed to transfer a mere cent from every single bank account in the country into their own. These days a mere cent is hardly worth worrying about especially since the cent has physically gone out of circulation and people are so used to rounding to the nearest five cents. What is not realised by the unintelligent however is that fraudulent activity is in fact the worst kind of crime for getting caught. This is because the actual system that sets up the opportunity of committing a fraud, whether it be through a computer or otherwise, at the same time is the very thing that leaves behind a trail of documents or files that leads right to the mastermind. Mr Winston was not about to be caught in this way. It wasn't much use taking an insignificant cent from every account only to be nabbed when one presents to withdraw the amassed fortune at some time in the future.

The fourth kind of thievery was misleading and deceptive conduct. This effectively involves the use of a trick in some fashion or another. Like larceny however, the problem with this species is the rare opportunity if ever one could get to trick one out of such a large fortune. Of course, one could prey on the elderly and the vulnerable in society and trick them out of their life savings, but this would usually only be a couple of hundred thousand dollars, a few million tops. Mr Winston was of course lower and bolder than this.

Then of course there are combinations of these species in various forms. Each of the pure species taken simply had its advantages in some way or another over the others but most importantly, each had their own disadvantages. It was treading through this web that the unintelligent thief at one time or another demonstrates to the world time and time again why crime doesn't pay. Such was the dilemma that Mr Winston once found himself in.

The intelligent Justin Winston realised that the perfect crime involving millions if not billions of dollars would have to be comprised of combinations of all of the species of thievery in various fashions, all designed to extract what was perfect from all of them. This is because like the computer fraud case, the perfect crime would have to be subjected on several victims in order to amass such a large fortune. One person would never be enough. So naturally the taking without consent would also be an ingredient because not everyone could be tricked into just handing over one's life savings. And as a last resort, the use of force would be needed at least as a backup with the difficult few that still refused. Such was the reasoning and planning of Mr Winston, but at the same time, he realised that the complex and elaborate act would have to be unleashed in one simple and effective way. The perfect crime may well be planned for years, but it would be doomed to failure if it took too long to be carried out once it started.

Such was the secret planning and work of Mr Winston now for several years. It was only natural that such a difficult dilemma could be solved by such an intellect. Unlike many other intellectuals however, Mr Winston had no pangs of conscience to wrestle with. These were long buried if they ever existed. After careful consideration and years of work, Mr Winston was only a few minutes away from pulling off the perfect crime. And I should mention from the outset that he will succeed in pulling it off. For such a man as this does not spend several years of his life planning the perfect crime without foreseeing every possible contingency. As he sat behind his desk, he thought back on his lifelong ambition and finally allowed himself a quirky smile. Everything was now prepared. It was minutes away. The Prime Minister rose from his desk, gathered the papers of his second reading speech and made for the House of Representatives with the tax bill under his arm.

Chapter 23

The Wanderer

Gary felt trapped. He came home from work to another night of problems and monotony. His wife was the monotony. She was a constant incessant nag. It was not just that she would nag him about hanging his clothes up, vacuuming the house or cleaning the bathroom, moreover it was the fact that his marriage had become loveless. There had been no excitement in his life since his university years, and he wasn't getting any younger. Gary was now middle aged and he felt he was a man of no achievements. He had left nothing and done nothing to be remembered by. His wife and her friends did not respect him, and worse still, he started to lose respect for himself.

His wife now lived for herself and she didn't try to hide the fact. When she wasn't on the phone to her friends, or fixing herself something to eat, she would be flicking through the latest in vogue magazines. This was always accompanied with comments on just how eligible the newest and youngest males in Hollywood were.

Gary settled into his lounge and tried to read the evening paper. His wife must have been expecting her friends over tomorrow as she was busy cleaning the kitchen. That of course meant he couldn't fix a meal for himself – not without facing a barrage of complaints from his wife about making a mess.

As Gary pretended to read the paper, he reflected on his own life. What he really wanted at the moment was a pizza and a can of beer in front of the television. But this was just out of the question. It wasn't just the money; it was the price of being lectured about getting fat, eating in the lounge room and being a lazy oaf. No, he would just have to wait for his wife to finish, and then heat himself up a plate of boring leftovers that, no doubt, his wife had chosen for him.

Then there were the problems. His work hadn't been going so well. His boss expected a detailed report by next week on something he never understood in the first place. And as the workplace became more and more modern with computers, mobile telephones, email, Gary felt more and more out of date. And every day brought new bills. Telephone, electricity, gas, groceries, petrol, mortgage – they were endless.

"Can you take the rubbish out please?" he heard his wife bellow from the kitchen.

This was spoken and phrased like a question. But it was understood as it was meant to be – a superior order from his commanding officer. It just had to be complied with. In fact, he would probably only get one warning. If the order hadn't then been carried out, his wife would feel compelled to take the garbage out herself. Gary knew he could never live that one down. Obediently, like a well-trained puppy, he folded his newspaper and put it neatly on the side table, and proceeded to collect the rubbish bags from the kitchen.

"Of course, dear," he would respond to his wife. The translation was an obsequious "yes sir." Walking to the kitchen, he saw the leftover pumpkin soup sitting there, waiting to be microwaved for his dinner on an impeccably clean kitchen bench.

"Oh joy," Gary thought to himself.

Wrapping the bag around his hand, he headed for the front door. It was cold outside and Gary grabbed his jacket from the bedroom and the keys to let himself back in. There was no point in ringing the bell – this would only inconvenience the wife.

Gary closed the door and headed for the bins. "I'm taking the rubbish out," he thought about himself.

Things just had to change. This life was not liveable. Throwing the rubbish out, Gary did not head back inside. He pulled his keys out of his jacket and made for the garage. It was not well thought out, but it brought him some relief. His plan was conceived on the spot and simple. Just drive away. He wished to turn his back on everything and drive as far away as possible.

He didn't bother shutting the garage door behind him. He drove out into the cold night and headed out of the city. For the first time in many years, his old car felt cosy. With each passing kilometre, he felt he was seizing some control over his life. He would drive through the night, drive straight and drive onward. Or perhaps he would find himself a hotel room on the outskirts of town and buy himself a cold beer. Then he would continue his journey in the morning. It didn't matter, the choice was his. At last, he was breaking free.

Gary turned the radio on and tuned it to his own station. He hadn't felt this free in years. He smiled to himself and had no regrets.

"Good riddance to it all," he thought, and it was not worth another thought.

Gary hadn't smiled in a long time. The last time he enjoyed driving so much was as a teenager with a new licence looking to impress some teenage girl. Now he felt like a real man, and it was time to be a man.

After driving for several hours, Gary saw a hotel sign in the distance and headed straight for it. He parked the car and walked up the porch. The hotel had the olden saloon type doors, which he gladly swung open.

In front of him was the check-in counter, presently unattended. To the right of him was a saloon with a jukebox playing light music. There were about a dozen patrons in all going about their own lives – smoking, drinking, laughing.

"Perfect," he thought to himself.

"Can I help you?" a young woman enquired from the direction of the counter.

"Oh," he said, "A room for the night please."

"Just passing through?" the woman asked smiling at him.

Gary didn't take long to think about the question. "Yes, that's right," he said.

It had been a long time since a woman had smiled at him and the counter girl was very beautiful. He smiled back at her feeling young and excited.

After checking in, he made his way into the saloon and sat at a table.

Gary stretched his feet and his arms. Then placing them in his lap he rotated his shoulders in circles. "It's good to be free," he thought to himself.

"Just a Four X please" he asked the waitress.

Gary sipped his beer quietly and tried not to think on the past. He would return to his room and see about ordering in some pizza. Then he would sleep the night after having watched some sport on television, then head out again in the morning. He would drive forever onward.

Gary soon found himself lost in his dreams. He could do anything he wanted to. He was in control. Maybe he would find himself a country job and start a new life. Maybe he would drive to the edge of the country and then by sea or by air continue his quest. He was now a wanderer and he was happy. For the moment he would roam on by, see what happens.

Finishing his beer, he ordered another, then another. Gazing up from his table, he noticed a pair of sparkling blue eyes. She was sitting at a table on her own and rummaging through her handbag. Gary estimated her age at around 21. She was blonde and gorgeous, extremely cute to say the least, gentle-looking, long hair, good-figure, all that. She seemed sweet.

Taking another sip of beer, Gary remembered his university days. Picking up girls was part of the campus life. Gary reminisced about his time at uni and felt young and invigorated. He surveyed the room and saw that nothing much had changed, and then settled his eyes once more on the beautiful blonde stranger in front of him. She had put her bag down and patted a tissue to her eyes a few times before screwing it up in a ball.

With the same impromptu planning that began his wandering quest by the rubbish bins earlier, Gary stood up and walked to the girl's table. "May I?" he asked pulling a chair out and sitting himself down at her table. She didn't have time to refuse him. She seemed a little nervous and turned her head away from him desperately trying to hide the fact that she had been crying.

Gary remembered the rules he had learned at university and realised he had to keep talking before it became too awkward. "You just looked like you could do with a drink, and I figured I could do with some company, so I wandered on over here." As he said this, he raised his hand and signalled the waitress for two beers. He thought the action looked so cool, and with a smirk on his face he chirped out, "you could say...I'm a wanderer."

This caused the girl to chuckle slightly. "Excellent," Gary thought to himself, "I've still got it." The rules had been long established. If the girl doesn't laugh within five minutes, you may as well give up.

Gary hadn't made love in years. Back home, he didn't really have a sex drive and though he slept in the same bed as his wife, it just didn't really seem like an option any more. But times had changed and Gary was getting with it.

The waitress dropped two beers on the table. "Thanks," the blonde said to the waitress.

"Oh look, she speaks too," and this brought another smile from his beautiful stranger. "So, what do you do when you are not chasing every guy in the town off you?" Gary asked. Flattery was the second rule. If ever in doubt, flatter. Works every time.

"You're just full of confidence tonight," the stranger said to him meeting his gaze.

"Ahh well you see, when you're not moving, you're rotting. Recently I figured I needed more movement in my life. I could either wallow or wander," Gary felt he was on a roll, "I chose the latter."

"And that's the best advice you can offer a stranger?" she said starting to take more of an interest in her male acquaintance.

"Young lady," he beamed back, "It's the best advice there is – except maybe that of your hairdresser, whoever it is, he's done a wonderful job." He didn't care how corny it sounded. Touching the girl was always the last step. Gary well knew the little-known secret in courting – touch the girl. With those words he twirled her hair around his finger, then pulled it behind her ear.

He continued, "I just drove in this town, and tomorrow I drive out. I haven't even seen the room they've given me yet. Are they any good in this place?" Gary was not asking for the sake of asking.

"Are you asking me up to your room?" she enquired directly.

"No of course not," he said shaking his head. "Ok yes," he said before long, "But you can't stay in this place, gotta keep moving remember." Gary clicked the fingers on both of his hands a few times and swayed his torso. This brought another laugh from the stranger. He smiled and blushed and he didn't care. He just wanted her to say "Yes".

She finished her beer and stood up. "Let me freshen up a bit, and I'll meet you at the counter." With this she moved off to the lady's room.

Gary observed her slender waist in her somewhat skimpy black cocktail dress. "Yes" he thought to himself as he slung his head backwards. "Should have done this years ago."

Gary fixed up his bill and meandered on over to the counter. With his hands in his pockets and whistling like a teenage idiot, he waited for his date. As she approached, he turned and met her stride. They headed for the stairs and checked out his new room.

The next morning Gary sat once more in the driver's seat of his car. Fastening his seat belt, he thought back on the last 24 hours. Everything had finally started to go well for him. He had been paroled from his home prison. He sat and smiled at how much control he had seized of his life. Forget the wife, forget the job, forget the home. He had a new lease on life now and he was larger than it. Today he would make decisions for himself. He would drive where he wanted to and live how he wanted to. Gary sat in his car with a smile of ultimate relief and satisfaction on his face. At last, he felt contented.

"Quite a nice town," he thought to himself, "I learned a lot here," he mused to himself, "just like university."

"I'll teach you to muck around with my wife!" somebody shouted. As Gary looked around, he saw the baseball bat smash through his window.

Chapter 24

Mr Solitary

Maxamillian Jones waited in the cells under the Taylor Square Supreme Court Complex for his arraignment. He had just had a conference with his solicitor through the usual Perspex screen. She had explained to him that he would be formally charged in Court for the murder of Geoffrey Coleson and he would be asked how he pleads to the charge brought against him. At this point he would simply say "Not Guilty," and then a date would be set for the trial of the matter before a jury. There was no point applying for bail pending the hearing.

Maxamillian had given strict instructions to his solicitor to find him the best Queen's Counsel in Australia. This was one case he could not afford to lose. He hated every minute of jail and he was perfectly innocent of the charge. He had told his solicitor in no uncertain terms that he wished to sell his house if he had to, to pay for his legal costs.

There were several cells under the Court complex. The cells contained nothing more than a bench to sit on and a small toilet in the corner. Maxamillian was thankful that he was placed in a cell with another person. Some company was better than none and some of the other cells contained prisoners on their own. This was virtual solitary confinement.

The prisoner sharing the cell with Maxamillian seemed content to sit on the bench with his back dead straight and his eyes closed. Maxamillian wished he could feel as relaxed. He found himself nervously pacing the cell back and forth wondering just how strong the prosecution case against him would be.

Occasionally he would cast another glance at the person asleep on the bench. Maxamillian could not quite place it, but there was something peculiar about him. He was about 55 years old and seemed quite fatherly. Whilst the other inmates had gone to some lengths at least to look respectable for their court appearance, this prisoner had seemed to go out of his way to make himself look scruffy. His clothes looked deliberately torn and his hair was messed up. Yet he seemed to just sit there with an inner glow and seemed perfectly content with his surroundings.

"All right Mr Solitary," the guard blurted out through the bars. "It's your turn."

Maxamillian Jones watched the prisoner open his eyes. He looked at Maxamillian as if almost surprised that there was another person in his cell. The prisoner stood up and winked at Maxamillian. Then brushing past him, he muttered in his ear, "Here we go again."

The guard marched him down the corridor and handed him over to the waiting Court guards for his Court appearance.

Maxamillian hated being alone. Even a sleeping prisoner was better than solitary confinement. He recalled the solitary confinement he served several times previously at the Long Bay Jail. The room in solitary confinement, like this cell, contained nothing more than a bed and a toilet. No television, no books and no clock. Every minute would go by like a year. Maxamillian knew if he was convicted of the charge of murdering a prison guard, he would be confined to solitary confinement more often than not. This had to be avoided at all costs.

After about 20 minutes, the prisoner was brought back to the cell.

"Well, that was painless," he mused to the guard. "Can I get back to my solitude now?" he asked as the door clanged shut. The guard did not answer.

Giving a broad smile to Maxamillian, he settled back into the same place he was in before and closed his eyes.

Maxamillian felt bored to breaking point. Now was the time to at least strike up a conversation with the guy to help pass the time away. Maxamillian knew he could be waiting for another five hours. Something had to give.

"My name is Maxamillian Jones," he began, "And you are Mr Solitary I take it?"

The man slowly opened his eyes and turned to look at his questioner. "Actually, my name is Peter McKinnon," he said, "But you can call me Mr Solitary if you like."

"I don't understand," Maxamillian said, "Is that a nickname?"

"Yep," he replied. "I am called Mr Solitary because I have done more solitary confinement that any other inmate. In fact, I enjoy solitary confinement more than anything else in the world."

"That's amazing," Maxamillian said wishing he could share his enthusiasm. "I hate it. Want to teach me how to enjoy it?" he asked not really expecting an answer.

"Sure," Peter replied, "If you really want to."

"I think I will be doing a lot of solitary confinement if I am convicted," Maxamillian said pleadingly, "I am charged with murdering a prison guard."

"Fancy that," Peter replied. "I wish we could swap places. I find that being outside of solitary confinement presents me with too many distractions. I like to be on my own for as long as possible," Peter looked as if he was searching for the right words, "gives me time to collect my thoughts."

Maxamillian was not expecting that response and felt quite confused.

Sensing his puzzlement, Peter looked at Maxamillian and continued. "On the outside, I was a lecturer in the philosophy department at the University of Sydney. I haven't taught in several years, but if you would like, I can share with you one of the biggest secrets since Aladdin's wonderful lamp! But I must warn you," he continued, "it's not for the small minded. It is guaranteed to change your life forever."

"Please do," Maxamillian said taking a seat on the bench, "I want to learn."

"Very well," Peter said rising from his seat. "Let's begin then."

Maxamillian never attended university. He had always felt he was lacking an education. At the opportunity of having his own private lecturer in jail, and to relieve the boredom of solitary confinement, Maxamillian didn't care if Peter spoke forever. Anything was better than being ignored.

"Tell me," Peter began, "We have five senses – hearing, seeing, touching, smelling and tasting. Which one of these do you value the most?"

Maxamillian tried hard to think about the question. "I guess seeing," he volunteered.

"That's right," Peter said getting a little excited. "We value our sense of sight more than the others but have you ever stopped to ask yourself why we value this sense more than the others?"

Maxamillian tried hard to follow the lecturer's train of thought.

"All of the senses are instruments for our intellect. They are used to receive information in certain forms so that we can then think about it. You know all knowledge is obtained through the senses. We value sight the most because it is the most capable of informing the intellect about things."

"I guess I had never seen it that way before," Maxamillian thought aloud.

"Indeed," Peter responded. "Did you even notice in the way our language has evolved; we speak about 'seeing' things even when we are speaking about invisible ideas? Just now you said you had never 'seen' it that way before. This is because we recognise that the sense of sight informs the intellect the most."

Maxamillian tried hard to understand what the lecturer was getting at and let him continue. He felt that having his own private tutor giving him a university education was something worth paying attention to.

"But on the other hand," Peter continued, "When we shut our eyes and stop seeing visible things, we don't at the same time stop understanding them right? This is because our eyes and ears and all the other senses are not actually the intellect or the mind, but only the instruments or agents to get things into our mind. Our very consciousness, I mean our persona, the actual thing that makes us what we are, our inner voice you could say, this is something quite independent of our external senses."

"Well, I have always thought that," Maxamillian said, "That is, I think I am with you so far, please go on."

"Take this door for example," Peter said rubbing his hand over the steel door at the entrance to their cell. "We see it's colour and know that it is there. We can hear it clang; touch its coldness and the like. But after all that, we can turn our back on it and still know that it is there by the very form of the door received into our minds. The information has already gone into our intellect and we are certain of its presence even when we no longer look at it or hear it or touch it."

"I think I understand what you are saying but I just don't see where you are going with this," Maxamillian said feeling a little perplexed.

"Well don't you see?" Peter said beaming, "It's not a thing's colour or sound or smell or touch or any of its perceived external accidents that makes a thing be real for us, it's our knowledge of it. It is something internal, it is the mind, and it is not the senses itself. Otherwise, we would stop knowing something when we no longer perceived it with our senses."

"I guess so," Maxamillian said really wanting him to come to the point.

"Well, the point is," he continued, "We don't need our senses to enjoy our intellect. Our minds are the things that perceive reality as real not our senses. They can imprison our bodies, but they cannot imprison our minds because our minds are essentially immaterial." Peter came close to his pupil to whisper in his ear as if he was teaching him valuable wisdom not meant for any unintentional third party. "We can think! And by virtue of our thinking, we can go beyond the prison walls. We can go anywhere, do anything. We can live life to the fullest. We can imagine!"

"That's it?" Maxamillian enquired, "That's the big secret?"

"Don't underestimate what I have just given you," the lecturer said. "Let me give you some examples."

"Please do," Maxamillian said hoping for something more.

"Last night, while the prison guards thought I was in solitary confinement, I was flying a fighter jet over Iraq."

"What do you mean?" Maxamillian asked, "You just imagined it?"

"I didn't just imagine it," Peter answered. "I lived it. I was the pilot in the cockpit. I had enemy aircraft on my radar. I nose-dived to 300 feet and increased my speed. My wingman and I then shot a volley of air-to-air missiles and blew up our attackers. It was one of the most exciting and thrilling things that I have ever done in my life."

Maxamillian was wondering if he was serious or joking. Peter however was speaking with such enthusiasm and excitement that it obviously didn't matter to him.

"While you're trying to work out the philosophical difference between something actually happening and something being merely imagined," Peter said, "You will soon come to realise the difference to us is only academic. As far as practical difference is concerned, there is none. Both are memories. Both are perceived and beheld in the intellect. Both are experienced. What difference does it make to us if the forms of fighter planes and enemy missiles exist in the outside world and are perceived through a real pilot's eyes or just perceived by our intellects without going through the senses? Don't forget that your whole life experiences up to this point are now nothing more than memories to you. I have developed my mind to such an efficacious point that I can experience virtual reality as well as you experience actual reality. I know things by my mind, not my senses. And after the event, both are real memories with no real practical difference."

Maxamillian squinted his eyes as he started to appreciate where his new friend was coming from.

"The night before for example," his friend continued, "I sailed around the Greek Islands on my 30-foot yacht."

Peter crouched before his seated listener and continued, "And earlier this morning in this cell whilst my body was seated where you are now, I was a starship captain. My crew and I were exploring the far reaches of the galaxy before I had to beam back into this cell to get my stupid Court appearance over and done with. I still can't wait to get back to my crew, they are waiting for me now, we have a mission to complete."

Maxamillian smiled at the idea.

"And a couple of nights back," Peter continued, "I was sweeping the deck of a pirate ship after a glorious battle for gold. The pirate captain had given me strict orders to get the deck clean before he returned – it was both horrible and fascinating. And the night before, I actually managed to rescue the beautiful princess from the witch's castle in the thick of the forest. I had to defeat her dragon with my limited wizardry skills and magical diamond encrusted sword that the king had given me for the occasion!"

Peter took a breath as he reminisced about his exciting past. "And tonight, let me tell you about tonight," Peter said with still more enthusiasm. His eyes started to glow and he almost began salivating. "While my gorgeous wife watches eagerly as a spectator from the public gallery, I get to race a Ferrari cross-country against some of the best drivers in the world. Don't you see?" Peter said looking at his new protégé, "It all depends on me getting solitary confinement again. Otherwise, I can look forward to another boring night of playing cards with the other inmates. And if I were on the outside, if it wasn't the telephone, it would be the job or the neighbours or the neighbour's cat, whatever. There were always too many distractions. Give me solitary confinement any day. The truth is, on the outside, we only yearn to do the things that I already experience here on the inside."

"Yes, I see what you mean," Maxamillian said, "I had always wanted to take a trip to Hawaii. I guess there was nothing really stopping me, right?"

"That's the ticket mate," Peter said lightly slapping him on the shoulder, "Why sit and wish you were on the outside where you probably couldn't even afford to go, when tomorrow you could wake up with the memory of having stayed first class at the best hotel in all of Hawaii? And you could go as the rich businessman, the undercover spy, or the guy on his honeymoon – it's all up to you. You decide. I tell you, it's the greatest of secrets not taught in schools or universities."

"So that is why you are Mr Solitary? Because you want solitary confinement to actually get your liberty?" Maxamillian enquired.

"You got it," he said, "All I need is some peace and quiet, and off I go again on my next wonderfully full adventure. And I tell you, the more you do it, the better you get at it. It won't be long before you can choose to see your prison food as a meal fit for a king. I can even interpret being flogged as having a lovely invigorating back massage. It's all in the mind, and I have learnt to control it, to live it, to take it out for a spin every so often!"

"You're incredible," Maxamillian confessed. "I guess I just ignored this aspect of my mind all of my life."

"Now if you will excuse me," Peter said winking at him, "I have a crew on the edge of the galaxy waiting for their captain to beam on up. Catch you later."

Maxamillian smiled a friendly smile to his newfound friend as Peter resumed his usual seat on the bench and gently closed his eyes.

Maxamillian had much to think about. As he paced once more in the cell, he felt Hawaii start to beckon him. The sun was beating down, the water was crystal blue, and the hotel foyer was nothing short of magnificent. There was a tremendous chandelier hanging over a beautifully plush rich blue carpet on his way to the grandiose check-in counter. Maxamillian was dying to see the presidential suite where the manager had told him his new wife was waiting for him.

Maxamillian opened his eyes in the dock as the clerk of arraigns patiently waited to hear how he pleaded to the charge brought against him. As he wondered how his friend was going on board the spaceship at the edge of the galaxy, the answer was now a foregone conclusion.

Chapter 25

The Rise and Rise of Dr Jamieson

It was now six months after the spaceship Atlantis exploded. The head of the National Aeronautics and Space Administration was concluding the official press conference on the matter.

"We have had a full internal inquiry," Dr Jamieson announced. "From all the evidence available to us, we have determined that the explosion was caused by fuel leakage in the starboard nacelle."

Dr Jamieson knew the journalists wanted to hold someone responsible and he paused before continuing.

"NASA has found that responsibility for the accident rests with two ground personnel whose job it was to service the part." This was the sensation the journalists were waiting for.

"Their names have been suppressed pending an investigation by the State District Attorney into possible criminal charges." The room hummed like a frenzied beehive, as the journalists desire to print the names and photographs of the persons responsible on the front page of the morning newspaper evaporated. They would therefore have to be content with a photograph of Dr Jamieson instead. Amidst the flashing and clicking of cameras, Dr Jamieson continued, "The personnel have been stood down and NASA will be assisting the District Attorney in all of his enquiries."

Jamieson and his colleagues knew that the announcement shifted the blame away from NASA and onto the shoulders of two unfortunate individuals. The story would be followed up for many months to come. Dr Jamieson was an expert at playing the media. The purpose of the press conference was not to make something clear, but to put NASA in the clear.

"Pending the outcome of the investigation by the District Attorney," Jamieson continued, "NASA has no further official comment, except to express once again our deepest and sincerest sympathies to the families and friends of the crew of the Atlantis."

Dr Jamieson then parried and ducked several probing questions. A journalist at the back of the room then asked, “Sir, is it true that you are planning to retire at the end of the year and can you comment on the rumour that you are being sounded out for the next Nobel Prize for your past work in biochemistry?”

As the room hummed in amazement, Jamieson feigned surprise at the question. The leak had come from Jamieson’s office earlier this morning. “Yes, I am planning to retire from NASA at the end of the year and shall apply for a position in private enterprise in Australia.”

“And the Nobel Prize sir?” the journalist pressed.

“Yes,” Jamieson paused for effect, “It is true that it is rumoured.” This response and Jamieson’s pretended embarrassment had its desired effect of eliciting peals of laughter from the audience.

“What position shall you apply for Dr Jamieson?” a young female reporter towards the front questioned.

“I have been asked to apply for the CEO’s position in DrugTech, a relatively small pharmaceutical company in Sydney.” Dr Jamieson gestured with a nod to his staff to bring the press conference to a close.

“Sir, before you go, do you have any final comments on NASA?” another journalist piped in.

“Well,” Jamieson answered. “It’s not the custom of NASA officials to make political statements, but I feel I should say before I go, how deeply indebted this organization is to the President. It has been his vision and support, which has encouraged the organization and has ultimately led to many of its greatest and finest achievements. I should say that the pursuit of science in this great nation has had no finer patron than the President of the United States. Thank you, ladies and gentlemen.” With that, Jamieson closed the press conference.

~~~
~~~

It was only in the rare emergencies that the board members of DrugTech would meet on a Sunday. This particular Sunday morning was cold, windy and wet. When the rain wasn't falling steadily, it was ever present in the drizzle. The wind made umbrellas unworkable. While most people slept in their beds, the big six members of DrugTech sat around the boardroom table on the 42nd floor at six o'clock in the morning.

It was still dark outside. The warm air conditioning caused the windows to mist up. The vertical blinds had been drawn closed but this did not drown the sound of the occasional gush of rain, splash against the window with each howl of the wind. The room had no paintings on the walls. The boardroom table was mahogany but otherwise lacked any distinction. Six high leather back chairs surrounded it. In the corner of the room was a smaller side table with several unused cups for tea and coffee. With no secretary present to assist with the tea and coffee, these remained unused. Apart from the absence of computer terminals on the boardroom table, the room looked remarkably similar to the Upper Room at Mission Control where Dr Jamieson would supervise a shuttle launch at Cape Canaveral.

"DrugTech is in a bad way," Jamieson commenced. There was no need to begin by welcoming the members for attending so early. "Apart from the eight percent hike in the share price when the company announced to the market that I would be joining the board, the share price has still fallen 20% in the past six months."

This was not news to the board members who did little but concern themselves with the share price each trading day. It merely served as a springboard for Jamieson to commence outlining his plan for reform. "For the past three years we have funded several areas of research and have had little if nothing to show for it," Jamieson continued. "At this rate, and given the plummet in blood plasma prices, we will have to announce to the market that DrugTech will not meet current profit expectations by around 300 million dollars. I expect that this will cause the share price to crash."

Nothing turned the stomach of board members more than a falling share price. It was not just the fact that they each were 'incentivised' with share options when they joined the board, all of which became worthless when the share price fell, but it made them more accountable to the shareholders who could demand investigations, the removal of the board members, or worse still, external enquiries.

The board members sat silently, some with their heads buried in their chest to avoid being looked at, others waiting nervously to hear Jamieson's plan for survival.

"You asked me to join the board for a reason," Jamieson said, "And now it's time to start making some radical changes."

Jamieson knew that a falling share price and a failure to meet financial expectations gave him the leeway he needed. "All research which is not funded from external government grants or other private sources outside DrugTech will be suspended for two years," Jamieson said as he surveyed the room. "The research which is funded externally, such as cures for cancer and AIDS and the like shall continue but at a scaled back rate of 80%. Many of the staff will unfortunately have to be laid off."

All the board members knew that this was just the beginning and Jamieson continued. "For the past month I have worked closely with the biochemical division and it is now time to release a serum onto the market. The serum is an inoculation for six known biological hazards and two known chemical hazards."

"I don't understand," the member to Jamieson's right interrupted. "What hazards are we talking about, and who do we propose to sell this serum to?"

Jamieson expected the question. "The hazards are currently classified by the US Central Intelligence Agency. They are believed to be potential biological and chemical hazards that may result from a stockpile of weapons of mass destruction by enemy countries of the United States." Jamieson read the confusion on the faces of the board members and continued his explanation. "Our customers will be the United States military personnel. All of them."

"How do you propose to market to them?" the board member further enquired from Jamieson.

"I don't," Jamieson replied. "Let's just say the Commander-in-Chief of the United States Military owes me a few favours. I am calling in on one of them. It's a sure thing."

There was evident relief on the faces of the board members. Jamieson knew that they had not yet appreciated the significance of his announcement and spelled it out to them. "I intend to sell the serum at $500US a pop. They will also require a further booster injection in twelve months' time which will be sold at $300US."

Jamieson saw the members doing the mathematics and he continued. "DrugTech must cease manufacturing all other pharmaceutical products for the next two years – we can rely solely on our stocked supply for our customers during this time. All departments will be required to dedicate their energies into manufacturing enough of this serum to go around." This was the radical step that required board member approval and the reason for the Sunday morning meeting. "If everything goes according to plan," Jamieson continued, "and I don't see why it shouldn't, the earnings of DrugTech for the next two years, before income tax, depreciation and amortisation, is expected to be around six billion Australian dollars."

Jamieson was speaking their language. The frustrated looks were replaced with evident relief and satisfaction. "I expect DrugTech will jump from being number 25 to being the third largest company on the Australian Stock Exchange just behind the National Australia Bank and Telstra," Jamieson added.

"When will we get the US signed up?" a board member asked.

"Just as soon as we have enough stock supply of the serum to start going around," Jamieson answered. "In fact, we had better get a move on with it. As soon as we have the US signed up we can put an official announcement out to the market. This will cause the share price to skyrocket. I estimate it will quadruple in price almost immediately and continue on when the rest of the market actually appreciates what the figures mean." Jamieson knew that this was dynamite. As Jamieson expected, the board room members started wondering what was in it for them.

The board member to Jamieson's right voiced the others concerns. "Third below NAB and Telstra, eh?" he began, "We should increase our fees." The other board members eyed off Jamieson to see what he was thinking.

"On the contrary," Jamieson answered, "We need to take a pay cut." Jamieson waited until he had their complete attention once more. The board had faith in Jamieson and they waited to hear more.

"We will have to announce on Monday our expectation that we will not be able to meet this year's financial expectations." The board members remembered the anxiety that they were feeling earlier and waited for Jamieson to continue. "At the same time the board should issue a statement that it proposes to change the focus of the company slightly to concentrate on its vaccination division. Undoubtedly the scare will force the price down further." Jamieson had their complete attention.

"In this same statement, we should express how all board members are united behind the decision and have agreed to forego a significant amount of their salary. Now we have received legal advice from Mr Hunter Barrister-at-law," Jamieson continued taking up a piece of paper, "To the effect that when a company issues or proposes to issue several statements to the market, the board members should not trade in the company's shares for fear that it may be interpreted as insider trading. Therefore, none of you should be buying or selling shares in DrugTech. However, there is nothing illegal with having stock options issued to the board members as a means of providing incentives to them in lieu of salary. Given that the share price is about to be dirt cheap when we take up these stock options, I don't expect that the shareholders will complain too much when their directors agree to take a pay cut only to be issued with currently valueless stock options."

"Not at all," the furthest board member piped in. "It shows that the board members are committed to their company and have faith in it."

The other board members sat nodding their approval and smiling under their breath. Jamieson's plan was now fully understood. The bottom line was that in two years' time, each of them would be multi-millionaires. When the share price quadrupled, the stock options would increase forty-fold. The only thing left to do was to have all board members sign off unanimously on the strategy. This was eagerly consented to.

Upon signing the documents that Jamieson had prepared for them, the board members left the room.

Jamieson returned to his office and sat behind his desk. The meeting had gone well and he afforded himself some time to relax. After a few minutes, there was a knock on the door. "Enter," Jamieson yelled as the board member who sat to the right of him during the meeting entered his office.

"May I?" the board member said pointing to the chair in front of Jamieson's desk.

"Please do," Jamieson said gesturing with his open palm towards the seat.

"I don't understand one thing," the board member said leaning forward in his seat with his hands in his lap. "How did the lab demonstrate that the serum was beneficial if the hazards are classified by the CIA?"

"As discussed with the President, it was conclusively demonstrated in three simple ways," Jamieson replied. "Firstly, the serum will increase the morale of the US soldiers, secondly it will increase the fear of its enemies and thirdly it will make us very rich. Besides," Jamieson said grinning at the board member opposite him, "If anyone were to publicly suggest that the serum was only as effective as a simple saline solution whilst the CIA files remain top secret, they would be hit with a Supreme Court defamation suit before they could say 'six-billion-dollar placebo!'"

Chapter 26

The Problem with Submarines

The USS Clinton was the most advanced attack submarine in the United States fleet. Her captain, one named Captain Jackson, was the most senior and experienced in the Navy.

The USS Clinton was one of three submarines each sent to patrol their own pre-assigned section of the South China Sea. Together, their mission was to covertly interdict a cruiser suspected of carrying nuclear weapons to North Korea.

The crew had been warned that several Chinese submarines might be in the vicinity patrolling the passageway and it was common knowledge, that the Chinese did not appreciate US submarines around their territorial waters. The orders of the USS Clinton were quite clear. It was to remain undetected and to sink the suspected cruiser. If fired upon by hostile forces, it would protect itself at all costs.

Apart from various training simulations, which were never the real thing, the crew had never seen battle before.

The Clinton had been sailing now for three days and was cautiously approaching hostile waters.

"Towed array fully deployed Sir," the sonar operator announced.

"Slow to one third helmsman and take us to 400 feet," the Captain ordered.

The helmsman responded efficiently. For the Clinton to remain undetected by other submarines, it would have to proceed slowly and quietly. An air of silent trepidation descended upon the crew as it advanced into enemy territory.

Captain Jackson remained seated at the command console in the centre of the control room. His sonar officer was to his left. Directly in front of him were the weapons and navigation stations. To his right were the communications and radar stations.

The first officer stood to the Captain's right. "Report all contacts," the first officer said looking at the sonar officer.

"Currently none Sir," was the reply.

The sonar officer sat, nervously listening for any new sounds.

"They've improved the engines on these submarines," the first officer whispered into the ear of the Captain more to relieve his own nerves than the Captain's.

"Intelligence reports indicate that the latest Chinese submarines are based on US technology," the Captain playfully retorted.

The first officer did not have an opportunity to respond. "Torpedo in the water!" the sonar officer shouted, "Bearing 237 degrees, direction...interception course Captain!"

"Helmsman, stop all forward momentum and dive to 900 feet," the Captain ordered immediately.

The helmsman responded swiftly. The crew was thrust forward as the nose of the Clinton pointed downwards and the submarine descended.

This was not normal battle tactics. For a torpedo to be on an interception course, a hostile force must have detected the boat. The usual tactic was to turn the boat at right angles to the incoming torpedo and proceed to full flank in the hope of evading the torpedo. This would mean cutting and losing the towed array for extra speed. The towed array of the USS Clinton, being now fully deployed, was about two nautical miles of sensitive microphones at the rear of the vessel. This would normally be abandoned in a crisis situation for the sake of the boat.

"Distance of the torpedo?" the first officer asked as he strode nervously to the sonar station.

"One nautical mile and closing Sir," the sonar officer yelled back. A loud ping, almost deafening, and then repeating every second rang out over the speakers. "Torpedo has gone active and is attempting to acquire a lock," the sonar officer announced.

"Keep descending," the Captain said.

"Weapons officer, standby countermeasures bearing 237 degrees," the first officer barked nervously.

"But do not fire until my command," the Captain yelled sternly at the weapons officer.

The first officer had been trained never to question his captain in front of the crew, but he turned rapidly and threw him a nervous glance. The Captain responded by giving him an assuring nod as if to say, "everything will be all right."

"900 feet Sir," the helmsman announced.

"Full stop," the Captain responded.

"Torpedo now 400 yards from previous co-ordinates and closing," the sonar officer yelled. He, like many of the crew, had broken into a severe sweat that protruded quite visibly through his uniform.

"Has the torpedo changed altitude?" the Captain asked.

The sonar officer looked at a screen to his left. "No Sir," he responded. The sound of the pinging grew louder still. "Torpedo closing to 300 yards, 200 yards."

"Sound the collision alarm," the Captain ordered. The Captain flicked a switch on his command console, which put him on speakers all over the boat. "All decks brace for possible impact," he said. The wailing sound of the collision alarm broke out over the boat. If the submarine was hit, it would almost certainly be crippled beyond repair, if not destroyed. The Captain had not exercised the standard evasive manoeuvres, he had not cut the towed array and he had not deployed the countermeasures.

"100 yards," the sonar officer announced. Each successive ping of the torpedo was louder. The crew squeezed themselves to the chairs they were sitting on. Several of them commenced praying.

"Torpedo has passed us by Sir" the sonar officer announced.

The crew was too nervous to express their relief immediately. The pinging of the torpedo now grew softer and the Captain disabled the collision alarm.

"Torpedo has entered standard search pattern Sir," the sonar officer said as he touched his earpiece.

"Bearing and altitude?" the Captain asked.

"Bearing 057 degrees, altitude 450 feet," the sonar officer responded consulting his computer terminals.

"Helmsman, take her down to 1050 feet and come to a full stop."

"Torpedo has run out of fuel Sir," the sonar officer announced.

"Full stop," the helmsman said as the boat reached 1050 feet.

"Now, shut down the engines," the Captain ordered.

The first officer stared at his captain. This was an unorthodox and extremely dangerous move. If another torpedo was aimed at the boat with engines shut down, it would not be able to power-up fast enough to move out of the way.

The helmsman nervously complied. "Engines shut down Sir."

"Everyone quiet," the Captain said. There was now deathly silence in the control room as the crew froze. The crew had never been in battle before let alone evading an incoming torpedo. The stress and anxiety were starting to display on the faces of each of the crew. They sat in silence for a full five minutes, each crewmember hoping that the boat was now undetected.

The Captain broke the silence. "Any contacts?" he enquired.

"No Sir," the sonar officer replied.

"The attacker may have turned and run whilst the torpedo was incoming," the first officer suggested to the Captain.

"Or she may have shut down her engines as well," the Captain argued.

After a further five minutes the first officer asked the Captain, "What do we do now?"

"There are two possibilities," the Captain answered. "Either the attacker turned and ran when it fired its torpedo," the Captain said, "Or it has done what we have done and shut down its engines waiting for us to make the next move."

The crew fixed their eyes on their captain waiting to hear more. The Captain continued. "The torpedo was fired at us from a long distance away," he said. "Ordinarily a submarine would have gone to full flank and outrun or out-dodged the incoming torpedo. But this would give away our precise location to the attacking vessel and most of all confirm our actual presence. Luckily we didn't have to do that." The Captain took a deep breath before continuing. "Since the attacker fired before we even managed to detect them, I am guessing that the attacker isn't actually that sure that we are an enemy submarine. The contact that it fired upon could have equally been a biologic signature. Hopefully they think they were just shooting fish because we made no noise."

The Captain stared into nothing as if placing himself in the mind of the enemy commander. "No doubt its captain is now waiting patiently to make sure one way or the other and then he will ultimately decide to move on. When he does," the Captain said looking at his first officer, "We've got him."

The crew now understood the Captain's plan. "But for the moment," the Captain continued staring at his crew, "Whoever powers-up first is dead. That's because the moment a contact is detected from a stationary submarine, all that is needed to hit the boat is to fire a torpedo at that bearing. No submarine could power-up quick enough to get out of the way. So, for now, we just sit tight and get ready to fire."

The plan seemed simple enough. The crew sat silently in the belly of the USS Clinton with engines powered-down. After two hours, the Captain asked for some tea to be brought to the control room. All crew had a drink and stayed manning their stations. It was a dangerous game of cat and mouse and the Captain was not about to get sprung.

Six hours had now transpired and there was still no sign of the attacking vessel. It was negative on all contacts. Several of the crew started to wonder if the attacking vessel had turned and run upon firing its torpedo. The loud signature of the incoming torpedo would have drowned out any sound from the engines of the running attacker. But this was not something the Captain was planning to risk.

After another six hours the crew started to look visibly weak. "Get some more food and coffee into the crew," the Captain ordered the chef through the intercom. "I want everyone as alert as possible in the control room to react at a moment's notice." The Captain broke with protocol and allowed, in fact insisted, that each of the crew eat at their stations. If the Captain was in doubt as to whether the attacker turned and ran or whether it was sitting out there, the Captain certainly wasn't showing it to the crew. "Keep monitoring," the Captain would occasionally say, "Standby."

It was now about 21 hours since the torpedo was fired. The crew still manned their stations full of caffeine and food. Sleep was out of the question. Toilet breaks were allowed but only one at a time and only after a replacement officer arrived to man the station. The first officer came and stood next to the Captain.

"How long do you think they'll wait?" he whispered.

"Unknown," the Captain responded defiantly. "We have a shrewd Asian commander stalking us," he said turning to look at his first officer, "And the Asian mind is inscrutable." The Captain was obviously obsessed with his theory.

"Stay alert," the Captain would occasionally announce to the crew, "Be lively." The crew was not even allowed to look tired. This was not like the training exercises. They had been fun for the crew and had always lacked a sense of realism. Every battle simulation was over in about 20 minutes, 40 tops. No battle had gone on for several hours, let alone more than 20.

Several of the crew started to think that if the attacking vessel was really out there and had waited this long; surely its captain would start to think that the USS Clinton's signature was a false alarm. It started to seem fanciful and far-fetched to some of the crew that the attacking vessel would sit around for so long playing the waiting game. In any event, the USS Clinton was now effectively crippled. Being so deep underwater, it could not send a message through to headquarters and report on the battle, nor could it continue with its mission and interdict any cruiser suspected of carrying nuclear weapons. But its orders to protect itself in battle were paramount, and the Captain seemed to be in no doubt. And Captain Jackson's belief was all that mattered.

It was around 30 hours and 23 minutes when the sonar officer detected a faint signal. "New contact Sir," the sonar officer whispered. The crew snapped to attention as the Captain stiffened in his chair.

Any sensation of drowsiness immediately left the crew. Each crewmember had a burst of adrenalin at the words. "Bearing and altitude?" the Captain demanded.

"358 degrees," the sonar officer responded, "at 850 feet."

The Captain wasted no time. "Weapons station, flood tubes three and four. Set torpedoes at bearing 358 degrees altitude 850 feet. Let them go active immediately. Fire!"

The Captain did not wait to listen to the whoosh of the torpedoes escape from the boat. "Helmsman, power up the engines and ascend to periscope depth. Sonar station, retrieve the towed array."

The crew reacted efficiently. This was what they had been trained for. Indeed, this was what the Captain kept them 'caffeinated' for.

"Sir," the sonar officer yelled, "Enemy is ascending fast. He must have hit the 'emergency surface' and blown his tanks."

The Captain had him right where he wanted him. An 'emergency surface' on a submarine is usually used as a last resort. As the attacking vessel had powered its engines down, it was unable to run out of the way of the incoming torpedoes. The immediate surfacing of the boat would probably evade the incoming torpedoes, which were set at an altitude of 850 feet, but the submarine would then be a sitting duck on the surface of the water.

"Weapons officer, standby harpoon at bearing 358 degrees," the Captain ordered, "Fire immediately the boat reaches periscope depth."

The harpoon was a ship-to-ship missile. Unlike the torpedo, the harpoon missile was launched at periscope depth and immediately became airborne. It used radar instead of sonar to hone in on its target. Unlike torpedoes, which swam through the water, the flying missile travelled faster than the speed of sound and could not be outrun. The only defence a ship could have to an incoming missile was by the use of its phalanx system. The phalanx effectively produced a screen of bullets that it sprayed into the air in the hope of shooting down an incoming missile. But no submarine had a phalanx system on board, as it is principally designed for underwater activities.

"Direct hit," the sonar officer announced.

The crew immediately burst into cheering and applause. The waiting had finally paid off.

"Any further contacts?" the first officer asked.

"No Sir," was the reply.

"Let's make sure," the Captain said looking at his sonar officer, "activate sonar ping."

The sonar officer flicked open a clear plastic cover and pressed a red button. The boat rattled as a thunderous ping emanated in all directions. The sonar officer listened intently for any echoes. "No further contacts Sir," the sonar officer said.

The Captain looked proudly at his first officer. "Inform headquarters," the Captain ordered, "I'll be in my cabin. You have the control room."

It had been a long two days and the Captain felt relieved and vindicated. "This battle would surely be reported in the textbooks," he thought to himself. "If not a Congressional Medal of Honor, then at the very least, it deserved a promotion and a Gold Star," he thought to himself smiling.

As the Captain headed towards the exit, he froze at the first officer's announcement as he peered through the periscope.

"Captain," he said horrified, "It's one of ours!"

Chapter 27

Occupational Discord

I don't like to speak ill of truck drivers, generally. But let me tell you about one named Michael Baker. Actually, Mr Baker was quite an intelligent man, and were it not for just a few vices, I am sure that he could have been a brain surgeon. But Michael Baker had a few problems, not the least of which was undertaking the appropriate planning to arrive for an appointment on time. What I mean by this is that Michael Baker was notoriously late for everything he did. He also had a bad temper, lacked patience, temperance, prudence and wisdom but then many of us get by in this world without possessing these virtues in any great abundance. It should perhaps be said at the outset though that Michael Baker's temper wasn't exactly ordinary and had long been foreseen as the instrument for his ultimate downfall. As it was, Michael Baker was a truck drlver.

He lived outside of town deep in the Australian bush land. His trek to work each day, which he would do in his Ute, meant traveling down a dirt road from his shack, then onto the southbound highway for a 20-minute drive to work. On this particular day, Michael awoke late as usual. He plodded around the kitchen believing himself to have more time than was available, then after fixing himself a truck driver's breakfast, he grabbed his backpack and mobile telephone and made for his ute in the garage.

The drive out on the dirt track was always rough and bumpy. Not being the richest of people, Michael had felt the pinch when he purchased his second-hand ute from his cousin. Accordingly, the drive on the dirt track each day was undertaken with extreme caution and usually in second gear. Damaging the ute would just not be worth it.

The highway however, was always a different story. Normally a person would take around 40 to 45 minutes to arrive at his place of work from his entry onto the highway, but to Michael, the highway afforded him his catch-up time.

Now perhaps truck drivers are generally more experienced drivers than most others, and when they are driving Utilities, which are much more manoeuvrable than the regular articulated vehicles that they usually drive, they are able to handle it with precision. Perhaps it had something to do with the fact that Michael Baker had the intelligence of a surgeon after all, but one way or another, he never seemed to have an accident – at least none caused by him.

Living so far out in the bush land, or the 'scrubs', as his workmates would call it, usually meant that he was met with little if any opposing traffic. In fact, it was a rare case indeed when a police officer just happened to be patrolling the highway that Michael was commuting. But such was his luck on this particular day. Speeding southbound on the highway to work, Michael passed a police officer on his motorbike heading northbound.

The police officer was a highway patrolman looking for the usual motorists that would place members of the public in jeopardy by their manner of driving. And passing Mr Baker in this instance left the police officer in no doubt that this was the sort of driver he was looking for. Activating the police siren, the police officer executed a U-turn with his motorbike and sped southbound in pursuit of the speeding ute.

Now I mentioned earlier that one of Michael's vices was his bad temper. It could only be fair to say that a police officer with a siren blaring in pursuit of him was not the most relaxing of things that Michael had come across.

Reluctantly, Michael Baker slowed his Utility to a stop and waited for the police officer to approach him. He had thought about speeding off as the police officer dismounted his motorcycle, but his intelligence told him that this would only put him in more trouble than he was in. He decided, for the moment anyway, to wait this one out, but on the other hand, he declined to turn off his engine.

The police officer dismounted his bike at the rear of his Ute, and leaving his helmet on, he approached Michael's side window. Michael had nothing but contempt for the police officer, and when the police officer ordered him to open his window by rapping his knuckles across them, Michael started to see red.

"What seems to be the problem officer?" Michael asked almost in a rage.

"This is a highway to the city mate," the police officer responded, "Not a runway to the airport. What's all the hurry for?"

Michael was angry enough that the police officer had stopped him, let alone sit calmly by while a police officer ask him such a stupid question – the answer to which would no doubt be taken as an admission of guilt.

"Don't know what you're talking about," Michael said through clenched teeth, "You must be dreaming."

It is also true that Michael Baker did not possess a monopoly on intemperance, and this particular remark was sufficient to annoy the police officer.

"Well, if that's your attitude mate," the police officer retorted angrily, "You've got yourself a $500 ticket. I was gonna let you off with a caution, but you obviously need a lesson. Wait right there!"

These were just the right words to cause Michael Baker to blow a gasket. It's one thing to be stopped and to get a simple ticket for speeding, but to be told that one's attitude, as opposed to the speeding, was the essential cause of a speeding ticket, and which would otherwise have merely been a caution, was just too much. But more importantly, to Michael Baker, $500 was simply far too much money to part with. It had been hard enough for Michael when he was out of work and finding employment as a truck driver was virtually impossible, but 500 big ones was like working three and a half days for free for the government. This could just not be borne.

Michael watched in the rear vision mirror as the police officer plodded back to his bike to get his book out of the saddle bags. At this point, Michael shoved the car into reverse and floored the Ute. The ute jumped backwards slamming the police officer into the rear and with a tremendous crash, the bike was crushed under the Ute. The police officer was surely dead.

It's at moments like these that Michael Baker's intelligence powers up. "Well, that takes care of the $500 ticket," he thought to himself, "Now, how to get out of this mess?"

Michael considered abandoning the ute on the road where it was and leaving the scene. He could then report the ute as stolen from his garage at home and catch a taxi to work. After some more thinking however, Michael quickly discarded the plan. For one thing, taxis in this part of the bush were very rare, and using his mobile telephone to ring for one would record his position on his phone bill. This, he thought, may implicate him by placing him at or around the scene of the crime – not to mention the fact that the damage to his ute and the taxi fare would add up to much more than just accepting the $500- ticket in the first place.

Michael Baker thought some more. Then it occurred to him. Ringing the emergency number on his mobile telephone, he asked to speak to the police.

"Police emergency," was the response, "Can I help you?"

"Yes please," Michael began. "As I was driving to work just now, this police officer on his motor bike rode up so fast behind me, and when I slowed suddenly to give way to a kangaroo that hopped in front of my Ute, he slammed into the back of me."

Michael paused for effect, and then feigning nervousness in his voice, he continued, "I think he's dead!"

"Calm down Sir," the police officer responded, "Just tell us where you are."

Michael then provided the police officer with his locality and was told to wait around half an hour for the accident investigation team and for an ambulance to arrive. "This is brilliant," he thought to himself, "Not only do I not get a ticket for speeding, but I'm gonna make the police insurance pay for the damage to my Ute!"

Going over his story several times to get it straight and smiling smugly to himself, Michael Baker waited patiently by the side of his Ute. "This is too easy," he thought to himself as he looked at the bloodied corpse on the road, "There's no way that that bastard is going to cause me to be out of pocket."

Then his mobile telephone rang. "Hello, Michael Baker here," he said answering it.

"Mr Baker," someone shouted. He recognised the voice as his boss.

"You're late for the third time this week. You promised me yesterday that you would be on time today even if your life depended on it," his boss continued shouting. The phone call was terminated with the words, "If you're not here in the next ten minutes, then don't bother coming back at all!"

Chapter 28

The Cheater

Quentin Banks was a divorce lawyer. Much of his work was referral work from his brother's private detective firm Wilfred Banks & Son. The business relationship had been quite successful to this point and Quentin Banks had become quite a wealthy man. He had also developed a reputation as an extremely competent solicitor, and his uncanny ability to find loopholes in the legislation earned him the reputation amongst his peers as 'the loophole kid.' He had been married now for 18 years to Claudia, a beautiful 36-year-old and together they had had one son named Darren.

Last night, Quentin had stayed back in his solicitor's office for the Friday night drinks with the usual colleagues. This was when one of his associates had told him to keep an eye on his wife Claudia who had been spotted holding hands with a younger man at the local shopping centre during business hours. Claudia was a housewife, and until this news had come to Quentin last night, he had thought that he was a happily married man with no problems in his life.

It had never occurred to Quentin that Claudia could be having an affair and the more he thought about it, the more he believed how possible it could be. When Quentin returned home, his wife had already retired for the night. His meal had been left out for him, which he re-heated. He ate quickly and silently. Then stepping into the shower, he remained deep in thought. He decided that it would not be appropriate to confront his wife directly, at least not yet, with the allegation. He thought about contacting his brother and employing his private detective services to follow his wife, but he regarded this as an embarrassment that he could not bear.

As he climbed into bed next to his wife, he lay awake on his back attempting to decide on a firm course of action. His wife lay on her side with her back to him. She lay asleep oblivious to her husband's concerns. Quentin thought some more. Now that Darren had moved out of home, there weren't that many home duties for his wife to do. Quentin remembered though that his wife would always stay home on Mondays, and that on one particular Monday when he rang home, she answered the phone with a giggle and then snapped to seriousness when Quentin had spoken.

Quentin was not one to jump immediately to conclusions, and as a lawyer, he was not in the habit of filling in holes in the evidence with mere speculation or suspicion. But this only meant that the holes in the evidence only needed to be filled in; it was just a question of how. As he lay back on his bed, he gazed around the room waiting for some inspiration.

The bedroom contained a queen-sized double bed with drawers on either side. There were matching 'his and her' wardrobes on each side of the room. The door to her wardrobe had been broken for some time and it hung slightly to one side. But his wardrobe door was in perfect working order. Gazing at the wardrobe, a simple plan started to hatch inside Quentin.

The wardrobe had pull-out drawers on the left-hand side and hanging inside the main body of the cupboard were a few of his old suits. Quentin considered that the interior of the wardrobe was actually quite large and that he could easily hide inside it. Indeed, a small plastic chair that he usually kept in his study as a footstool could easily fit inside the wardrobe and thus allow him to eavesdrop on his wife's Monday activities in relative comfort.

Quentin now resolved to put off his Monday work activities and spy on his wife. He would carry on with the weekend as usual without confronting his wife directly about the accusation, though of course he would watch carefully if anything slipped out. Nothing did.

During the weekend he carefully studied the lock on his wardrobe. It seemed to him to have enough room to slip his finger under the latch and pull it back, thus enabling him to open the wardrobe from the inside. As Sunday night came to an end, he decided to have a dress rehearsal. Waiting for his wife to enter the shower, he went to his study and picked up the small plastic chair in the study carrying it to his bedroom. Then opening his wardrobe, he pushed all his suits to one side and placed the chair inside. It seemed to fit with more than adequate room for himself. Then checking once more to make sure that his wife was still in the shower, he then sat down on the chair and pulled the wardrobe shut.

The interior seemed much bigger than Quentin had expected. More than that, a slight crack between the door and the frame enabled Quentin to strategically position a pupil in order to peer out giving him a more than expected view of the room. Checking that he was comfortable, and knowing that he would be spending most of Monday in the confined space, he exited the wardrobe and closed it as usual. All was now set.

Quentin made sure that he did not have much to drink that night and often went to the toilet during the night. There was not much point going to so much effort to stake out the bedroom, if a busting bladder caused him to blow his cover.

Monday morning came around, and Quentin awoke as usual. His wife had prepared breakfast in the kitchen and Quentin showered and put on a suit as if to make out that he was going to work in the usual way.

"I might be late coming home tonight darling," he said to her, "I have a client who can only come in after hours."

"That's OK dear," his wife said smiling.

"Can I leave you to clean all this up, I had better get going?" he said as he stood from his breakfast barstool.

"Sure," his wife said as he approached her giving her the usual kiss goodbye.

Quentin then made for the front door leaving his wife behind in the kitchen to clean up his more than usual mess. All was going according to plan. He opened and closed the front door deliberately closing it louder than usual. He then tiptoed into the bedroom and quietly opened the wardrobe. Ripping his coat and tie off and throwing it into the corner of the wardrobe, he settled into his chair and closed the wardrobe. Now that the sunlight had lit-up the bedroom, he was quite surprised at how much he could see through the crack. In fact, he was able to gaze into the mirror of his wife's wardrobe that faced him and see his closed-up wardrobe that he was hiding in. He was invisible, the proverbial fly on the wall. All had gone according to plan. Quentin tried to make himself comfortable and waited to see if anything would happen.

After about half an hour, his wife returned to the bedroom and made the bed. Surprisingly, she changed into a mini skirt and blouse. Then spraying on some perfume around her neck, Quentin knew that something was up, definitely. The knock on the door came after another 15 minutes. Claudia adjusted her hair and clothes in the mirror, and then opened the door.

Almost immediately, Claudia screamed and giggled as the man at the door picked her up and carried her into the bedroom kicking the front door closed. The stranger placed her down on the bed and gently climbed on top of her kissing her. Claudia was obviously enjoying it with her hands affixed tightly around his neck.

Quentin was horrified. This was now not only evidence, but proof beyond reasonable doubt. Quentin knew that the normal manly thing to do would be to swing the wardrobe open and "punch the guy's lights out" as his clients would put it. But this was not his style. Quentin was dumbfounded and couldn't understand why his wife would turn like this. A thousand questions sprung up in his mind. He wondered how long the affair had been going on for, he wondered if there were any others, he wondered how many of her friends knew; it was becoming unbearable.

His wife was now on top. He wondered if it was simply that he was a lousy lover. His wife had always seemed uninterested in sex when he was around. Quentin then thought to himself that while he may be a lousy lover, he was still a brilliant lawyer. He started scouring the law in his mind for the kind of loophole that made him famous amongst the courts and his clients. He thought and he thought. Being married for 18 years meant that a property settlement in the Family Law Courts would almost guarantee her half the marital assets – and Quentin didn't want to give her a cent.

As his wife and her lover moved around on the bed, Quentin considered various strategies until it finally occurred to him. His plan seemed simple enough to him. He needed to dispossess himself of his marital assets but he also needed to have access to them for himself and deny his wife access. This meant putting the assets in a legal relationship that could not be upset by the Court in her Family Law suit, but on the contrary, enforced by the Court. It had to be an arrangement, which gave him no actual legal right to the property, which his wife could therefore exercise through him. Then it occurred to him – a discretionary trust. Tomorrow morning, he would execute a trust deed nominating his father as the trustee to his house and of all his bank accounts, shares, cars and jewellery – all of his assets that he had worked so hard for. He would then nominate himself, his wife and his son as well as two charities to be discretionary beneficiaries to the trust. Then every year, and at any other time the trustee considered appropriate in his absolute discretion, the trustee could apply any of the income or assets of the trust to any of the beneficiaries that the trustee desired. And this of course, with his father's cooperation, would always favour him and would never favour his wife.

Then being dispossessed of all his legal assets and having no rights under the discretionary trust, he would then declare himself a bankrupt and have a trustee in bankruptcy appointed to administer his estate. This would leave his wife with absolutely nothing. Quentin knew that the trustee would not be able to set-aside the discretionary trust, so long as it was up and running for at least six months – as this would frustrate the provisions of section 115 of the Federal Bankruptcy Act. As Quentin thought about it, the plan seemed more and more feasible. It was dependent of course on having the discretionary trust set up tomorrow morning, and then not upsetting the applecart for at least six months. His wife must not know that he suspected anything and he would have to continue on with the ruse of his so-called marriage in this time. If his wife found out or suspected that he was planning a divorce, she would appoint a lawyer and have the marital assets frozen by the Court. This would nullify the plan.

As his wife and her lover continued their lovemaking, Quentin felt somewhat relieved that he would have the last laugh. His plan for finding out that she was a cheater was simple enough. And his legal plan to him seemed even simpler. It was time for him to now cheat her out of her share of the marital assets – only to Quentin's mind; she deserved nothing and would get nothing. The cheated would become the cheater.

When his wife and her lover had finished, Quentin listened carefully to see if he could make out any conversation between them.

"Do you think your husband suspects anything?" the lover asked.

"No, I don't," she said, "He is too pre-occupied with his work. That's fine with me, it gives me time to see you and it also pays the bills."

"Why don't you divorce him and have a property settlement?" he asked.

Quentin held his breath – if she divorced him now, he would not be able to put his plan into place fast enough.

"I think I will next year when my son finishes his apprenticeship. I don't want my son to be distracted by any domestic issues, and I don't think my husband would just go quietly."

Quentin thought to himself, "Darren finishes his apprenticeship in eight months' time. Perfect!"

"When does Darren finish his apprenticeship?" the lover questioned pressing the issue.

"About eight months' time," she answered, "Let's wait until then and see what happens."

"Besides," she said getting up from the bed, "As long as my husband doesn't suspect anything, I don't mind waiting. He mentioned that in about eight months' time he would be receiving a big cash settlement in a case that he is finishing. Why not wait until then and get more money?"

Quentin recalled mentioning the Dorothy Wilcox divorce settlement that was due to settle around then. This was going to land them with a couple of hundred thousand at least. He smiled to himself and knew that he would have the last laugh.

Then to everyone's surprise, there was a knock on the door.

"Quick," his wife whispered spotting the broken door on her wardrobe, "It could be my husband come back to collect some papers. He shouldn't be too long, just hide in his wardrobe!"

Chapter 29

The Beginning of the End

Benjamin Jones came home with a black eye and a bloodied nose from a fight with Pamela's boyfriend. The date with Pamela was a total failure. Without acknowledging his parents, who were waiting for him in the lounge room, Benjamin ran straight upstairs to his bedroom and slammed the door. His parents exchanged concerned looks, then walked upstairs after their son.

"Go away," Benjamin yelled through the closed door, "I don't want to talk about it."

Benjamin's parents had noticed that Benjamin had been depressed for most of the year. His parents were trained psychologists at DrugTech and they both knew that unless something was done, and soon, Benjamin's mental health could be in peril.

"Come downstairs son, into the basement," his father said through the closed door, "There is something we want to show you. It concerns Project X23."

Benjamin had always wanted more of the drug that gave him the confidence and ability to attract Pamela at the science ball. But his father had told him that it was nothing more than a placebo. Benjamin knew that it was useless to nag his father who had always been very secretive concerning his work at DrugTech. The invitation of his father was therefore irresistible, and Benjamin quickly opened the bedroom door.

His father and mother had already started walking to the basement of the house and Benjamin followed.

The basement had long been turned into a makeshift study for his father. There was a table and a filing cabinet. There was also a huge safe behind the desk. Benjamin's father was seated behind the desk and was going through his wallet, which he had pulled out of his pocket. His mother was seated on the other side of the desk and motioned to her son to occupy the other empty chair next to her.

Benjamin had rarely spent time in the basement and was extremely intrigued at what his parents had in mind for him. His father removed a key from his wallet and then returned the wallet to his pocket flicking the key around several times in his hands. He then looked at Benjamin and studied his son's features.

"Son, your mother and I are concerned that you haven't been happy this year," he said looking for a reaction. He observed that Benjamin was close to tears.

"At DrugTech, there were always two competing factions. On the one hand we had the big six board members who would make all the economic decisions. But on the other hand, we had the top ranking three scientists who were concerned with the power of scientific breakthroughs and the like."

Benjamin's eyebrows narrowed as he tried to follow his father.

"The scientific clan at DrugTech had a saying: 'Captain Terrence was more powerful possessing the lost treasure of Count De Jager, than if he were to spend it.'" His father breathed in deeply, "I never did tell you how the treasure of the pirate Captain Terrence managed to start up DrugTech years later did I?"

"No," his son answered knowing that his father had never discussed DrugTech. It had always been a forbidden topic and was just way too secretive for Benjamin's liking. He sat fascinated by his father's words though and wished to hear more.

"Well, that story will have to wait for some other time, but the point that we used to make was basically a philosophical one, son," his father said. "We scientists believed that it was better to understand the things that were beneath us and love the things that were above us. But the economists actually loved the things that were beneath them rather than fully understanding them and realizing their full potential."

"I don't understand," Benjamin said interrupting his father.

"Maybe you should start at the beginning for him," his mother volunteered.

"About 30 years ago at DrugTech, there were three scientists who were fascinated with the breakthroughs that had been made by the company. Many of these breakthroughs never hit the market or got into production because of economic reasons. The big six board members at DrugTech always had the last say in that regard. But these three scientists were not so much interested in money as they were in power." His father realised that he had his son's complete attention and he continued.

"Anyway, these three scientists secretly collected all the breakthroughs that the company had achieved and compiled them into three simple accessible caskets, each one for themselves." His father took the key he was holding and opened the big safe that was behind him. There was only one item inside it. His father picked up the item and placed it on the table in front of him. It was a silver casket about the size of a small television set.

"When this first came out, it was about the size of a shoebox," his father said. "We have been updating it every time since then when there has been a major breakthrough, but the new chief executive officer of DrugTech, Dr Jamieson, has currently suspended all research at DrugTech for economic reasons."

"What happened to the three scientists?" Benjamin asked curiously.

"Well, the oldest one died 25 years ago of cancer," his father answered. "He retired early because of his illness and lived as a fisherman in his last remaining years. Unfortunately, DrugTech was still some years away from finding a cure for cancer. Now we have two," his father said as he patted the casket.

"The other scientist, Bruce, was secretly set up by DrugTech in the country to work on a 'trans warp inducer'. This was a theoretical device designed to transport goods from one place to another. I'm told he is still a few years away from making a breakthrough."

Benjamin was more and more fascinated at the history lesson. "What about the other scientist?" he asked, "You said there were three."

His mother answered the question. "Your father is the other scientist Ben," she said. "When we married, he became a counsellor at DrugTech and he ended his research days."

Up to this point Benjamin Jones had had no idea of his parents' activities at DrugTech and he never knew of the existence of the silver casket before him on the table. The silver casket had two twist locks on the front. His father put his hands on these locks, but before twisting them he looked at his son and started to explain.

"Son you will shortly familiarise yourself with everything in here. You will also discover that the contents will give you all the power that you could possibly want in this world. You will be able to accomplish anything that you want to, but I should warn you," his father stared at his son straight in the eye, "In keeping with the philosophy of the scientific clan, it is for you to possess it, not for it to possess you. Do you understand what I am saying?" his father questioned. "You must use this only as a last resort – when all the other legitimate attempts have failed. This can then be used to open that door that won't open by any other means. Do I have your word on this son?"

"Yes father," he said as he keenly wished to know the contents of the silver casket. His mother sat smiling as she observed her son's composure change from a sulking adolescent to a noble expression of such resolute sternness that comes with awesome power and great responsibility.

"One other thing," his father said before opening it. "This casket, and its contents must remain absolutely secret – you must not speak of it to anyone, and you must take all necessary steps to prevent any person from knowing of it. Do you understand?"

"Yes father," Benjamin said solemnly.

"Let me demonstrate just how seriously DrugTech has kept this confidential Ben," his father said. "Do you remember my cousin Maxamillian?" his father asked in a new tone of voice.

"You mean the guy that killed the prison guard or something?" Benjamin replied.

"That guy," his father said. "A few years ago, he came over to visit me. I was busy discussing a few things with the managing director of DrugTech at the time in the kitchen so your mother asked him to wait for me in the lounge room."

Benjamin knew vaguely of his father's cousin Maxamillian Jones and knew that he was sentenced to imprisonment for life, but he did not know any of the circumstances.

"Unfortunately, Maxamillian took it upon himself to go snooping around in this basement," his father continued. "The managing director at the time was of the scientific clan and wanted to keep the silver casket and its contents absolutely secret. So, fearing that Maxamillian may have stumbled across it, he telephoned his friend, a Sergeant Adam Michaels to take care of him."

"Oh, Sergeant Adam Michaels," his mother said. "I knew of him; he was going out with Mandy Kizana's sister Beatrice. I heard that he got killed recently in a motorbike accident just outside of Sydney when he rear-ended a truck or something. I didn't know that he was involved with Maxamillian."

"Oh yes," Ben's father continued. "We used to refer to him at DrugTech as the leader of the red scorpion brigade because his folks all had a tattoo of a red scorpion on the back of their hands. He and his gang always protected DrugTech for us."

"So how did they fix up Maxamillian?" Ben's mother asked smiling curiously.

"Well apparently they had just arrested a drug dealer by the name of Alfonso and they were handing him over to the Federal Police for extradition to the United States," the father continued. "Acting on the managing director's instructions, he planted some of the drugs they got from Alfonso on Maxamillian and then had him put away for drug trafficking."

"What, all because he might have seen this?" Benjamin asked nervously.

"Of course," his father answered in a matter-of-fact tone as if almost irritated by the question. "The casket was on the table at the time, we didn't have the safe then," his father explained, "but since then, we have kept the casket locked in here." His father indicated the safe behind him.

"Now," his father continued, "Come closer and study this, Ben." As he said these words, he twisted the locks and flipped open the casket. Then standing up, he dug both his hands inside and pulled out a huge white leather-bound book. It was about A3 in size and as thick as two phone books.

"Each page here represents a particular scientific breakthrough that we had at DrugTech," his father said flipping through the book. He placed the empty casket behind him on the floor. From his handling of the book, it was obvious that he had memorised every page.

"For example," his father continued flipping over the pages to somewhere in the middle, "This one is Project X23 which you are familiar with."

The page had printed at the top in big black letters "Project X23" and immediately underneath was a beautiful coloured picture of a peacock with its tail fully fanned out. There were several other relatively scrawny female peacocks competing to get closer to the male peacock.

"Every page contains a picture summarizing what each project was about," his father explained pointing at the picture. "It was thought that this would help the reader memorise each page. Then underneath the picture, you will find the explanations on what it does, how it works, the dosage, its side effects and everything else you need to know. Some pages explain what happens in the event of an overdose and gives other specific information relevant to each project. Directly behind each printed page is a clear plastic envelope containing several finished samples of the product."

His father flipped the page over and Benjamin observed the familiar silver and plastic covered red gelatine capsules that he had seen the night of the science ball. They were outlaid one next to the other to minimise space inside the clear plastic envelope. It was obvious that one packet had been removed. Benjamin quickly counted about 15 remaining.

"That's incredible," Benjamin said as he stood up marvelling the majestic leather-bound book. "Show us another page."

"Well let's start from the beginning," his father said flipping over the pages to the start. "This was Project Gamma Alpha Kappa. Originally it was designed as a pain and trauma relieving medicine but it developed into a powerful hallucinogen and memory wiper."

The picture showed a man obviously confused with a typical comic strip balloon coming out of his mouth. The contents of the balloon contained gibberish.

"As you can see this is administered as a spray," his father said showing a small spray can about the size of a D cell battery in the clear plastic envelope behind the pictured page. "DrugTech has documented three such cases in which Project Gamma Alpha Kappa was used all with varying doses."

His father flipped the page back showing the picture and the writing but he clearly knew the information that was printed there off by heart. "It was first used on a teenage kid at Milson's Corner," he said. "We were going through this book on the counter of the convenience store there, which at the time was run by the wife of the managing director, when all of a sudden this kid spoke to us wanting to buy a chocolate bar and asking if there were any shoe shops around so that he could buy himself a pair of running shoes. We didn't even know that he was there until he spoke to us which took us all by surprise. As one of us took him outside and gave him directions to the nearest shoe shop, we laced his chocolate bar with a spray of Project Gamma Alpha Kappa."

His father smiled as he recalled the incident. "It was later reported that the kid saw a golden glittery effect but he had no recollection of purchasing the chocolate bar or asking about the shoes. Also, his recollection of the book was completely distorted."

"You will also see," his father said pointing towards the bottom of the page, "That this was also used on two other persons each with greater doses. It was used on a Mr Cain Todd who reported seeing an eerie green glow instead of the golden glow that the teenage kid reported seeing at a lesser dose. Cain Todd never recalled the incident when his food was laced with Project Gamma Alpha Kappa and his hallucinations continue today. He is presently incarcerated at the Mary Immaculate Psychiatric Hospital."

Benjamin was horrified at the information but his morbid curiosity urged him to hear more and more of his father's story. "Lastly it was used on a Dr Smedly who was Cain Todd's treating doctor at the hospital," his father continued. "At his high dosage level, he reported seeing a bright white flash, kind of like a camera flash, but he became brain damaged and very soon after died. As you can see though, Project Gamma Alpha Kappa is an excellent pain and trauma reliever when used in small doses and is also a powerful hallucinogen in spray form."

His father looked up at his son and said, "You can go through this book at your own leisure, but let me show you just a few more."

"Why don't you show him one which could help him when he gets in a fight," his mother piped in winking at her son.

Knowing the precise page to turn to, his father flipped over several pages to one headed, "Project Vat 00".

The picture illustrated a slender Asian man with his shirt off engaged in a martial-arts type fight with three relatively fat persons.

"This is something which needs to be strapped around your arm under your shirt," his father said showing him the small plastic armbands in the envelope over the page. "In an emergency, you slap the band that is strapped to your arm and it injects the formula directly into your arm. We tested this on a fellow named William Hunter and have now managed to find the correct dosage. Within seconds it will give you the agility of a cheetah allowing you to out manoeuvre, evade and attack up to three attackers at once – all going their hardest."

"What happens if you overdose?" Benjamin asked thinking of Pamela's boyfriend.

"Well William Hunter did," his father exclaimed. "We used him to test this project as well as Project Spectrum 77 and he overdosed."

"What happened to him?" Benjamin asked again quietly.

"Well, the formula uses much of the iron in the haemoglobin of the red blood cell," his father replied. "Effectively it means that you can't inject this stuff twice into you within seven days. If you do, your craving for the iron will become so severe, that you will end up drinking the blood of a human being in an attempt to satisfy an insatiable thirst. We called it the vampire drug."

Benjamin shuddered at the thought. "So, what does Project Spectrum 77 do?" he asked as he thought about William Hunter.

His father turned over several pages so that he was towards the end of the book. The picture showed a rainbow with colours numbered one through to seven, but when the colours stopped, the numbers continued on to 77.

"This object of this project was the eye," his father said," Which is all about colour." His father raised his eyebrow as he recalled an incident. "One day at DrugTech a group of counsellors tried to explain to a girl, who had been born blind, what the colour 'red' was. After hours of explanation, the best she could explain was that it was like the sound of a trumpet blast. It was then concluded that a person who was born blind had no concept of colour – it just has to be seen by the eye in order to know it. Then one of the scientists suggested that the only colours we could see were the seven in the spectrum and the race was then on to find a drug that could help us to see many other colours in the ultra violet and infra-red end of the spectrum that we would obviously have no concept of."

Benjamin could see that the following page contained an eyedropper for Project Spectrum 77 to be inserted directly into the eyes.

"William Hunter was used to test out Project Spectrum 77," his father continued. "He reported seeing many more colours than the seven that we have grown up with. In particular, he reported that the human face exhibited many more colours than anything else. After a time, he said he was able to 'read face' – meaning he could decipher immediately what a person was thinking by the pattern recognition of 77 distinct colours on the person's face. So effectively, the drug became a powerful mind reader."

"That's awesome," Benjamin said as he pulled the book towards him and studied it. "What about this one?" he asked as he grabbed a handful of pages towards the front of the book and turned them over.

"Ahh, this is one of your mother's favourites," his father said looking at Benjamin's smiling mother. She stood up and looked at the book.

"This is Project Hippos 90," she said with obvious enthusiasm.

The picture was that of a horse but with a human head.

"All you do is chew and swallow this gum," his mother said showing several packets of gum over the page. "It allows you to run at your absolute fastest speed for the next 90 minutes. In fact you are forced to do it or you will burn up." She was obviously speaking from experience.

"So, it provides an excellent work out," she continued. "You only need to do it about once a month really and you can keep your weight right down to a slim figure." At these words she indicated her own slim figure with her hands. "Apparently it makes your heart as fit as a horse's for a full 90 minutes and gets the blood pumping around the body. It also strengthens the muscles and lets you really power on. You could literally win an Olympic marathon on this."

"What about intelligence?" Benjamin asked, "Is there anything here which increases your intelligence?"

"Well, there was a problem there," his father answered. "At one stage one of our scientists, a guy named Martin, thought he came close, but then he started to prattle on about the immateriality of the intellect and immortality. His research was pulled and he left DrugTech a little disgruntled."

Benjamin Jones was overwhelmed and he looked wide-eyed at both his parents.

"Do you see now son, how this book will allow you to do anything in this world that you want to?" his father looked at him for an answer.

"Yes father," he said, "I see that now, I really do."

"Good lad," he replied. "So, tell me now son, what is your greatest ambition, what do you want to do in this life?"

Benjamin sat down and smiled his broadest smile at his father before answering.

Chapter 30

Loose Ends

It was now 50 years since Benjamin had had that talk with his parents. Benjamin was now in his retiring years. He had replaced Dr Jamieson as the managing director of DrugTech and had led the company through ever more scientific breakthroughs. I would like to say that he had married Pamela, but life rarely works out that way. He had in fact married Kathleen, a similarly somewhat despondent person as Benjamin, whose twin sister had died in a tragic accident at the Botanical Gardens. They had gone on to have three wonderful children who never valued an education and became happily estranged from their parents. Benjamin and Kathleen in their later years had become counsellors at DrugTech.

Scientist Bruce never quite perfected his Trans Warp Inducer, at least as he had originally planned. To him, it was never quite right until it could simply transport a human. Don't get me wrong, it actually managed to transport a human. But it came with consequences. Bruce had tried the experiment on many a volunteer. One day a wanderer by the name of Gary just, well, wandered on in. Gary was his first successful human transportation. And eventually Bruce himself plucked up the courage to step into the machine. He too was transported. But when Bruce confessed all to a priest by the name of Father John many years later, he said he had first transported back in time to the house of Barshimon and had lived a full life as a servant in a distant time where he had witnessed the crucifixion of Christ.

I mentioned Benjamin's wife Kathleen, but she also had a brother that I should give a quick mention to. He was a rich stockbroker by the name of Carlton McBride. He had invested heavily in the shares of DrugTech and had made a substantial profit but he later lost the lot in the global financial crisis. The loss was unbearable, and like many stockbrokers who had achieved and lost their life's goal, he drew comfort from the solace of alcohol before blowing his brains out with a colt 45.

Dr Jamieson never indulged in the scientific breakthroughs of DrugTech. His power came from powerful friends and money. He was the leader of the economist's guild par excellence. The modern-day Godfather if you like. And so, when one Captain Jackson was facing a Court-Martial for his dreadful performance as Captain of the USS Clinton, he leaned on his uncle by marriage, the great thief and former Prime Minister of Australia, to lean on Dr Jamieson, to lean on the President of the United States, to grant Captain Jackson a pardon. The Captain retired and lived in Australia where he married an obsessive-compulsive divorcee by the name of Dorothy Wilcox.

DrugTech continued its clandestine scientific works. It was always careful to choose who to experiment on and to make sure that at least in that respect, it always tied up any loose ends. Secrecy was always paramount. But one person did manage to escape its clutches, sort of. That person is me. Who am I? I am the person who has managed to collect these stories over time from many different sources. You know me as William Hunter, Barrister-at-Law. But unlike the other unfortunate souls who have been experimented upon by DrugTech, my side effects are quite unique. You have heard already how I can read face. But there are other changes in me. I drink blood to survive. I have the strength of ten men. But more importantly, I have ceased aging; I am eternally youthful. Every half generation or so I move on so as not to attract too much suspicion as to why I never age. I have assumed many more identities than William Hunter. I have lived many lives. I shall continue to live and stay close to DrugTech. DrugTech has both robbed me of a normal life but has also rewarded me with eternal youthfulness. And after all this time, I am still not sure whether I would do it all again or not. If knowledge is power, then I am all powerful. But at the same time there is a burning desire in me that can never be fulfilled, the desire to live a simple normal and happy life. One of these days I will explain it to DrugTech and write a sequel. But not today.

Book 2

DRUGTECH

THE DEEP STATE DEEPENS

Book 2:

Once again, though I have thought long
and hard about this, I absolutely
dedicate this book to my father-in-law,
Emeritus Professor Philip Kuchel;
whose philosophical approach to science;
and scientific approach to philosophy;
was the poem (if not the poet)
that inspired this second book,
and drove me quite mad in the process.

Chapter 1

The Stickler

Generally, the Bar Association governs the Bar. In other words, when barristers engage in morally questionable conduct, the Bar Association investigates and if it appears that a barrister has engaged in unprofessional conduct or even worse, professional misconduct, then the Bar Association institutes and prosecutes disciplinary proceedings seeking a remedy to rectify the wrongdoing in order to protect the public from such a barrister. Remedies can include fines; reprimands (both private and public); conditions placed on the barrister's practicing certificate; or ultimately, a strike-off.

The Bar Association is made up of volunteer barristers and, understandably, the public became somewhat suspicious of barristers checking up on barristers. So, one day, a publicly astute political party campaigned on cleaning up the perceived mess by introducing the Office of the Legal Services Commissioner and promptly enacted such legislation upon winning office.

But that Office did not disrupt the Bar Association's duties, rather it complimented it. The Office of the Legal Services Commissioner just became another body that also checked-up on barristers and worked hand-in-hand with the Bar Association.

This story is not concerned with the political ramifications of such a scheme, but rather with the reminiscence of a particular stickler for ethics, the impeccably honest Legal Services Investigator, Mr Watkins.

Watkins had long-retired from the Office of the Legal Services Commissioner and was speaking to his son about his time as an investigator of many questionable barristers.

"What were the first types of cases you investigated Dad?" his son asked as his father lit another cigar by the fireplace.

"The first lot were a group of bankrupt barristers who didn't pay any tax," his father continued. "They used the bankruptcy laws to extinguish their taxation debt and then they just carried on as normal without having to pay any tax at all."

"There is a lot of hypocrisy there," his son chimed in. "Barristers who hold other people to account under the law, but use the law to avoid their own civic duties."

"Yes," his father replied, "We had to bring about a change in the law to expose that practice and I must say, that is one thing I am proud of in my career."

"What were the easiest cases you investigated dad?" his son asked.

"Well, the easiest cases were when barristers simply broke the law and got convicted. The facts that led to the conviction itself were usually enough to get the barrister struck-off," his father replied.

"Ok," his son asked looking for something a little more interesting. "Tell me about the most difficult borderline cases you investigated."

"Well, there were of course the judge-shoppers. They fell roughly into two kinds. The first kind would commence several proceedings in the Courts that had a docket system, like for example the Federal Court. That meant that for each case they started, a docket would allocate which judge would be assigned to hear the case. Then when they got the judge that they liked, they either didn't serve or didn't proceed with the cases that were assigned to the other judges and simply amended the pleading before the judge that they wanted to include all of the other withdrawn or discontinued actions." Watkins rolled his eyes as he told that story. He truly believed in the integrity of the system and being the stickler for ethics that he was, anything that brought the system into disrepute was conduct that needed prosecuting.

"You said there was another kind of judge shopping, what was that?" his son asked.

"Oh, that was a harder kind to prove, but it happened all the time," his father began again. "Often a barrister would be waiting in a list-court waiting to be allocated one of a series of judges awaiting in neighbouring Courts. But instead of approaching the bar table and announcing their readiness to be allocated a judge, they instead held back and kept a close eye on the state of the list and an eye on which judge would be allocated the next case."

"Then," his father continued, "in a cunningly timed way, the barrister would announce his case to the list-judge with a cunningly manufactured estimate of time so that the list-judge felt that the judge the barrister secretly wanted, happened to now be the most time-appropriate judge to hear the case."

"Gosh", his son responded, "You exposed even that sort of stuff?"

"Of course," his father responded. "It wasn't exactly the worst kind of professional misconduct but it was unsatisfactory professional conduct that would bring the system of justice into disrepute and so that sort of conduct was always on our radar."

"Fancy that!" his son exclaimed. "What about even more difficult cases to prosecute?" his son enquired wondering just where it would end.

"Well, there were barristers running jury trials that believed that in the morning a jury's attention was at 100% but that after lunch, their attention became around 40%. And so, to take advantage of the system," his father continued puffing ever so more on his cigar, "certain barristers would drag-out or time their legal objections or points of law in such a way so that the opposing side's witnesses would ultimately be heard by the jury after lunch, and their own party's witnesses would be heard in the morning when the jury was fresh and paying attention."

"That's amazing," his son beamed, "They would really try every trick in the book, wouldn't they?" His son was genuinely amazed at his father's recollections and simply wanted to hear more. "What about the most difficult case that you ever did, can you tell me about that?"

"There was one case that I will never forget," his father said pausing and looking into the distance. He stopped smoking on his cigar as a rather forlorn countenance fell upon him.

"There was one barrister by the name of William Hunter," he said as he appeared somewhat uncomfortable and shuffled a little in his chair.

"We received reports that he never lost a case and his manner of running cases was, shall I say, somewhat unique."

"What happened?" his son asked.

"Well, I followed him around and watched a few of his cases. He hardly brought a piece of paper with him to Court. He hardly took any legal objections or ran any legal arguments at all. He would just sit in Court looking at the judge, the jury, and the witnesses all with a rather stone-cold expression on his face and he was just rather inscrutable. Then when he did eventually rise to cross-examine a witness, he just asked some very simple, seemingly innocuous questions in an almost polite, sorry-to-trouble-you way, and the witness would then give an answer that would always blow-away his opponent's case. They just couldn't win from there, and he never lost."

"How was that possible?" his son asked with immense curiosity.

"Actually, I never found out," his father said, "But at the time, I just thought there had to be something wrong. Perhaps there was some kind of coercion going on like bribery or blackmail or he was being fed some confidential secret information or something, but I just had a feeling that something was not quite right."

"So, what did you do?" his son asked wanting to hear more.

"Well, I investigated and I investigated. I widened the scope of the investigation to even look at his tax records but I couldn't find anything. He seemed squeaky-clean. Then eventually, I asked for an interview with him in his Chambers."

Watkins extinguished his cigar and wiped his forehead and his face with a handkerchief. His son wondered if he was wiping away a tear.

"I had nothing on him you see," his father continued after a pause. "But I just felt that I had to try something. And for the first and only time in my career, I thought I would attempt to bluff the barrister that I was investigating, and I actually told a little fib." His son did not ask what it was; he simply waited for his father to continue from the discomfort that his father was in.

"Mind you," his father said honestly, "If I ever exposed a barrister as telling a fib either to the Court or to us investigators or to the Bar Association, we would always come down on them like a ton of bricks. I had resolved never to do it myself. But in this particular case," his father said, "I did tell a fib and it has haunted me ever since."

His son's eyebrow went up as he waited to hear what it was.

"I said to him something like, 'Mr Hunter, evidence has come to light that you have engaged in improper conduct in respect of the cases that you have been involved in.' I didn't really give any detail or volunteer anything else. I just rambled a bit until I finally asked something like, 'Do you have anything to say?'"

His father looked ever more uncomfortable and troubled by the second and explained, "Of course no evidence had come to light against him at all. In desperation, I thought I would just shake-him-up or something, see what would happen."

His father shifted again in the chair and couldn't look his son directly in the eye.

"What happened?" his son asked quietly.

"The barrister stared at me with a gaze that seemed to penetrate my very soul," Watkins said as his focus again shifted to some undefined point in the room as he continued to recall the incident. "I couldn't tell you what he was thinking. I didn't know if he knew I was bluffing or if he thought I had exposed an entire conspiracy. But I actually felt dumbstruck and powerless and guilty and for a moment I thought I was actually immobilised. And his next two words have haunted me right up until this present day and I will never forget them."

After pausing for another moment, Watkins added a little commentary. "I had always thought I was a straight-shooter, a fair-minded person, honest and never a bully. But I can't say that my conduct with Mr Hunter lived up to that standard, and I really regret any harm that I may have caused the man."

"Why?" his son asked gently needing to hear the rest, "What did he say?"

"He said," Watkins replied with an even longer pause still focusing in the distance, "He said, 'I quit!'"

Chapter 2

The Shrewd Scientist

Dr Saanvi Patel was a shrewd, no-nonsense Indian woman. She had graduated first at her university in science and had always wanted a career at DrugTech. She had thought that coming first at her university would have been enough for her to be accepted at DrugTech after her graduation, but as it was, the one position advertised for the year that she applied for, was given to another scientist by the name of Benjamin Jones. Dr Patel suspected some kind of nepotism at the time.

Saanvi remained at the university as a post-graduate student where she continued her research under her Professor and Mentor, Philip Kurtis and she finally obtained her doctorate. Since her rejection at DrugTech, she had attempted to learn all that she could about the company, their hiring practices, how they worked, what they did and what they were looking for. She knew that Philip had once been employed at DrugTech but she had never managed to get her questions answered by him and the Professor always seemed reluctant to talk about it. Now, seven years on, Saanvi had had a major break-through in the lab.

Type I Diabetes is a pernicious disease where a person's immune system attacks the insulin producing cells in the pancreas. Accordingly, the treatment of diabetes requires the person to have insulin administered externally either by a series of injections or from an insulin pump. But that requires the patient to monitor their blood glucose levels constantly because as food increases their blood glucose level, insulin is required to reduce it. But if the blood-glucose is reduced too much from excess insulin then the brain (which feeds on glucose in the blood) will shut-down resulting in coma or death. But on the other hand, too much glucose in the blood over time will lead to nerve and organ damage resulting in rather horrible diabetic complications such as blindness, amputations, kidney disease, stroke, heart disease and the like.

Much of the technological breakthroughs that have come about for the treatment of Type I Diabetes over the past 100 years have been in better insulins, better glucose testing and monitoring, and better and more innovative insulin pumps. All of these devices and medications improve over time and all of these devices and medications cost money and therefore earn money for pharmaceutical companies such as DrugTech.

Dr Saanvi Patel had finally made the breakthrough that authors of scientific journals had only ever dreamt about. She had found the cure. Her breakthrough was in reversing and preventing the immune system from attacking the insulin-producing cells in the pancreas and thereby allow the patient to produce insulin normally once again. But Saanvi had been bitten once before by DrugTech when she was passed-over for the position that she had applied for and she was too shrewd to allow it to happen a second time. She knew that scientists had often been pawns of the economists and that there was no way on earth that a relatively young scientist like herself was going to waltz-on-in to DrugTech and announce a cure for a disease that brings in one of their most lucrative sources of income. On the other hand, she believed that she was too valuable not to be employed by them lest she offer the formula to a competitive company. She had shrewdly kept the breakthrough to herself and had not informed her university.

Her job interview was in 14 days' time and this time she wished to leave an impression. She once heard stories that the Bedouins who found the Dead Sea Scrolls were so shrewd, that they did not sell them in one lot to the scholars interested in the history obtained from them. That would not have been good for profit. Instead, the Bedouins tore-up the scrolls and sold them in pieces. Such an exercise, though contrary to the interests of the customer, was much more profitable. Saanvi believed that it was that kind of thinking, if anything, that would land her the job into a new and exciting career at DrugTech.

Ideally for Saanvi, the best result would be to 'dumb-down' the cure. In other words, to find a way to cure the illness but only for a week or a month at a time. That would require the patient to purchase a constant source of medication, and the company that would own that medication (that she as a scientist could provide the formula to) would monopolise and capitalise on the diabetes market putting all other competitors out of business. But there was no way for her to do all that in the next 14 days.

Dr Patel felt that she should discuss the topic with her Professor. The trouble was that her Professor was the most ethical man that she knew and he rarely if ever spoke about DrugTech. But she needed his help in two respects. Firstly, she needed his biochemical knowledge to help her 'dumb-down' the cure; and secondly, she needed his knowledge on how best to broach the subject in her interview at DrugTech. But if she asked for Professor Philip's help, it would mean firstly disclosing her major breakthrough that she had discovered whilst working at the university and thereby causing the university to claim half her royalties, and also asking the ethical Professor Philip for scientific advice on how to 'dumb-down' a cure which would surely run up against every ethical principle that he had. This was quite a dilemma.

For the next week Dr Patel agonized over her choices. And in the end, she felt that the only way to proceed was to tiptoe around the issue with her Professor and attempt to gain as much information as possible whilst saying very little, at least at first. It was now only a week to her interview and she thought that even a little information on how to proceed was better than nothing.

Dr Patel knew that more often than not; Philip would relax on a Friday night at the university bar for the usual Friday night drinks. And as luck would have it, next Friday was the night of the annual Science Ball and so many of the science students would be absent from the bar which meant that Saanvi might be able to have more time alone with Philip to ask for advice on how to proceed.

She waited at the bar and after spotting Philip come in and sit down, she purchased two beers and brought them to Philip's table where she sat down next to him and offered him one. She started an ordinary Friday night conversation with her colleague and mentor. She began by being a patient listener to Philip, seemingly eager to hear about his latest publications, his latest research on red-blood cells and the latest series of lectures that he had planned to give to the scientific community abroad when he would next travel. He was always travelling. At an appropriate pause in the conversation, she plucked up the courage to change the topic.

"Philip, in about a week's time, I am going for an interview at DrugTech," she began. "I am attempting to make an impression but I was wondering if you had any advice on how to do that. There is only one position open this year for a scientist of my level and I realise that the competition for that position is extremely fierce, so anything that you can say would be very helpful to me."

Philip looked surprised and appeared to contemplate his options on how to answer. The shrewd Saanvi observed his reaction and considered that she should probably say something more at this point before he answered in case his response was one of unhelpful circumspection. So, she continued.

"I realise that DrugTech is a company that exists for the purpose of profit and the directors are answerable to its shareholders," she rambled, "and so I suppose ideally, they would be looking for someone who can ultimately help them in that regard. I mean science is important of course, but so is their bottom line."

Philip leaned back in his chair and raised his eyes to heaven as he thought about the best way of responding. "Who is interviewing you?" he asked, "Do you know?"

"One of their chief scientists I am told," she answered.

"Well," Philip responded, "It's not so much what you say at the interview, but how useful you can be to them."

"Can you give me some examples about what you mean?" she asked hoping that he would open up a bit more.

"Well, your scientific field is in immunology and particularly, Type 1 Diabetes. So, for example, even if you were to announce, hypothetically, an actual cure for diabetes say," Philip continued, "their first thought would probably be to hire you for the purpose at least of signing you up to a confidential agreement to prevent you from giving it to their opposition. But then when they obtained the formula from you and had assigned to them all the rights to the patents of such a cure, you would become expendable to them. They could market the cure whenever they choose to and would only keep you on if they still found you useful."

"I suppose ideally then," Saanvi replied, "If hypothetically I did have a cure say, I should hold-back in giving it to them until I had signed them up to the deal that I wanted."

Philip leaned forward and beckoned Saanvi to also lean in giving the impression that what he had to say was for her ears only. Saanvi was only too willing to respond.

"Listen Saanvi," Philip began, "There is no point trying to bluff them. If as you say one of their chief scientists is conducting the interview, then he or she will be able to read your face like a book. I know this sounds incredible but he or she can take one look at you and know exactly what you are thinking. If you pretend you have a cure for diabetes and you don't, the interview will be over then and there."

Saanvi thought for a while and wondered whether she would question how they were capable of reading her face like a book or alternatively, whether she should continue to probe for more useful information while she had Philip talking.

"So hypothetically, if I wasn't bluffing and I told them I had a cure for diabetes, then..."

"Then...," Philip cut her off mid-sentence, "They will know immediately that you have held that breakthrough back from the university and they could threaten to expose you for telling them instead of your university, and they could trash your reputation or even force you to sign-up with them on terms that would be equally unpalatable to you." Philip said. "My advice would be to find another place to work."

Philip then leaned backwards, finished his beer and rose from the table.

The shrewd Dr Patel knew not to question the Professor any further. She understood the situation.

Seven days later, she was sitting behind the desk of the Chief Scientist in an interview room at DrugTech. The interviewer was tall and slender and his face appeared steely cold, almost blue in fact and he was perfectly unreadable.

"Tell me Dr Patel," the Chief Scientist asked quite politely, "What can you bring to DrugTech if we were to employ you?"

Dr Patel remembered what Philip had told her seven days earlier. Each word was as clear as a bell. They can read her face and know exactly that she had cured diabetes and that if she admitted it, they could effectively extort from her the fruits of her labour.

"Well," Dr Patel answered with beaming eyes and smiling her broadest smile, "I think I have found a way to grow naturally blue roses!"

Chapter 3

The Separation of Powers

In the European glory-days of old, the power of government was generally shared between the various Kings of the land, and the ubiquitous Church. As with most marriages, they had their fair share of problems. But in modern times, after the people had long wrestled power away from the Kings of old and divorced themselves from the power of the Church, a new style of government was fashioned allowing the people to choose from amongst themselves, their representatives for the making of laws. And to keep the checks and balances of that new system in place, the power of government was divided into three arms. These were the legislative, the executive and the judiciary.

In most Western democracies of today, it's the legislature that attracts the most attention. Generally, this arm of government represents the ordinary person in the street. In America, they are generally referred to as "We the People" after their great and sacred Constitution. In the UK, they are referred to as the "commoners". Some European countries use the term "hoi polloi". The Russians use the term "proles" or the "proletariat". But depending on one's perspective, a great deal of people simply referred to them as the riff-raff or the plebs.

The three arms of government each have different kinds of power. There is a saying that "the lawgiver is above the law" and so they argue that the legislature is the most powerful since the legislature creates new laws. Others have argued that there is not much point saying one thing if the judiciary says it means another; and that therefore the real power is with the Courts. These jurisprudential arguments may occupy philosophers for some time but over time, one thing has become clear. The actual abuses of power occur more often than not in the administrative arm of government.

When Public Servants do not carry out their lawful obligations, then they have their own agenda. They are not Public Servants. They are in fact Pirates. Some people say that such a thing does not exist today. Others swear that it does; and the name that some people give to this level of corruption of today is called, "The Deep State".

I of course know that it does exist. But let me take you back to a time when it not only existed, it was in fact not so deep. That is because at that time, there was no such thing as the separation of powers. The year was 1529 and a young child with an heredity rank of Viscount had just been born. The place was Florence and the Viscount Giovanni Terracini was born into the powerfully great and rich Medici family.

Historically the Medici family was a family of physicians, and so round balls representing pharmaceutical pills figure prominently in the famous Medici coat-of-arms. As with many medieval names of the time reflecting the house's chief occupation (as in Butcher, Baker, Chandler), the Medici name properly stems from the Latin form of medicine.

But the Medici family was not powerfully great and rich because of medicine. They were powerfully great and rich because of money. They were essentially the Bank-of-Europe at the time. And whilst they did not in name hold any high offices of Government, with the exception of course of Pope Leo X in1513 to his death in 1521 at a time when the Pope governed the Papal States, they nevertheless held 'influence'. And that influence effectively governed the Governments of Europe.

Viscount Giovanni Terracini grew up in many respects as a normal rich boy. From his adolescent years, he had moved to Venice and had become a mariner. He had purchased an apprenticeship as a naval cadet in the Venetian Navy. He had been trained in hand-to-hand combat. He had been trained in how to use a sword. He had been trained in the ways of gunpowder. And he also had a few Medici pills in his armoury to tackle any matters that might require the skills of a physician. And with all of these skills, he was more importantly trained on how to be a Venetian Spy. He was then charged with a secret mission of infiltrating enemy lines, which he carried out with distinction for the past decade.

Now the Republic of Venice at the time was governed by the Doge and several Councils that would convene in the Doge's Palace. But one Council stood apart from the rest. That Council was referred to, usually with fear and trepidation, as the Council of Ten. The Council of Ten had broad jurisdictional powers that included the security of the State. And at the point of time that concerns us, the security of the State meant securing the State from pirates.

It has often been said that "To the victor goes the spoils" and this was never more true than in naval battles. Ships, whether mercantile, naval or piratical, often carried the captain's treasure on board and capturing a ship was therefore a lucrative pastime. Of course, pirates and outliers who did not wish to bank their treasure in the Medici Banks, nor carry their treasure on board a ship, would find places to bury their treasure as a means of safe-keeping outside of governmental hands.

The Medici influenced Council of Ten was discussing the security of treasures carried by sea and the unofficial burying of treasure outside of the jurisdiction of the Government and the Medici Banks. The now Commodore Terracini of the Royal Doge's Navy had been called to testify before the Council and he was concluding his remarks:

"...and so, for the past ten years we successfully infiltrated the crew of the menacing pirate ship Douglas under the command of Captain Samuel. When the Captain had disclosed the whereabouts of the lost treasure of Count de Jager, he was summarily executed, and I assumed Command of the Douglas under the alias name of Captain Terrence. The lost treasure was retrieved and the crew was marooned on the Island of Mount Yearning. The Navy is now en route to arrest them."

And being the victor, he enjoyed the spoils. And he took the spoils and retired to Florence where he returned to his family's medicinal roots and started a small pharmaceutical enterprise to discover new and interesting drugs for the advancement of science and the betterment of economics.

Chapter 4

The Bank Heist

Lee Zhang Wei was finishing a long day at work at Miller and Davis Bio-Electrics. He worked in a cubical where he had spent most of his day coding and de-bugging computer software. As the day was drawing to a close, he decided to buy himself a burger on the way home when the telephone on his desk rang.

"Lee Zhang Wei speaking."

"Oh, hello Lee," his boss said, "Listen some FBI agents from America have spoken to me and they are investigating an incident that occurred six months ago when we sent you to install our bio-tech software at the Chase Bank in Alabama. Anyway, I have promised them our full cooperation, so tomorrow, can you head on down to the Surry Hills Police headquarters at 9am? I will email you the address."

"Yes Sir," Lee responded. His heart started racing.

"Good man," his boss replied. "When you come back to work, let my secretary know will you?"

"No problem, Sir," Lee replied as he hung-up the telephone.

Lee no longer felt hungry. He went straight home and started thinking about the events six months ago.

Lee had flown to Alabama from Sydney, Australia to upgrade the security system to the safety deposit boxes at the Chase Bank. Their old system had been a system of signatures and keys for any person gaining access to those boxes, but the new system would now involve a user number and a retina-scan.

The work had been routine and was completed in a day even though he had spent a week in Alabama. But unbeknownst to any other person, Lee had installed a very complicated backdoor into the software.

The backdoor operated this way. Between precisely midnight and 1am, if a person attempted to login to the Chase Bank's website with the username of "Don Trump" and the password "whitehouse" they would see the usual error message of "User name or password does not match. Please try again." But that particular attempt during that particular time period would cause a secret program to start running.

The secret program operated for the next business day only and at 6pm that night, it would erase itself from the system and would be effectively untraceable.

When a customer was at the bank and wished to gain access to the safety deposit boxes, he or she would key in a user number and the identification numbers of the safety deposit boxes that he or she was authorised for and wished to open on that occasion. The customer would then complete a retina scan to verify his or her authenticity. If the retina scan and the safety deposit boxes matched with the database, the customer was granted access to the authorised boxes. The whole thing would also be captured on CCTV footage.

But while the secret program that Lee had installed was running, any person who entered a user number of 6666 would pass any retina scan and any safety deposit boxes that that user nominated would be authorised and opened by the computer. Lastly, the computer system also had access to the CCTV security system and for the 20 minutes before and the 60 minutes after the time the user number of 6666 was entered, the CCTV footage would be replaced with the recorded footage for the same period for the previous day. Lastly, the electronic log of the incident would also be duplicated for the same time period the previous day thereby matching what was shown on the CCTV.

At roughly 30 minutes after midnight on the Friday before Lee was due to return to Australia, he had attempted to log online to the Chase Bank with the username of "Don Trump" and the password of "whitehouse". After receiving the usual error message, he erased his website history and turned his computer off.

At around noon that day, when most of the staff were out to lunch, Lee turned up at the particular Chase Bank in Alabama as an ordinary customer and keyed-in the user number 6666 and requested access to security deposit boxes 104, 105 and 106. They were just three random boxes that he had chosen. He did not wish to attract too much attention to himself.

The retina check was passed and Lee was told to go to the elevator and choose the basement level where the security deposit boxes were. When he exited the elevator, a rather short, fat and friendly black man in a bowtie met him.

"Good afternoon, Sir," the man said, "I hope you are having a wonderful day?"

"Fine," Lee replied wishing to keep any conversation to a minimum.

Lee thought the man must have Asperger's syndrome because his mannerisms were peculiar. Lee also remembered his nametag, which simply read, "Chuck". And Chuck couldn't stop smiling.

"Your deposit boxes have been opened for you Sir," Chuck continued. "You may take them out and place them on the table if you wish. When you are finished, just call out to me and I will take you up."

"Thank you," Lee said trying to keep a low profile.

All had been perfect. As he walked into the room, Lee noticed the red LED lights on each of the CCTV cameras indicating that they were recording. Only Lee knew better.

The first safety deposit box contained title deeds and other legal documents. "Useless," Lee thought to himself. "Hope they aren't all like that." He decided not to touch it in case he might leave some fingerprints behind.

The second box also contained a Will and a Bank Guarantee and other legal documents that he did not care to read. He decided not to touch them also.

The third box was the jackpot. There in the middle of the box was a black velvet bag. Inside the bag, Lee counted five diamonds. His first thought was to take the lot and leave as quickly as possible. But Lee thought that the best kind of heist was one that was not discovered. So, Lee pocketed three of the diamonds and left two inside the bag. That way he thought, there would be doubt by the owner as to whether they were stolen or lost or the result of an unknown mistake. He made sure to use the velvet bag to wipe any fingerprints off the remaining diamonds that he may have touched.

Lee closed the doors to the deposit boxes and called out to Chuck.

"Ready," he said.

"Right-you-are, Sir," Chuck said as he approached still smiling. "I am running late for my lunch myself, so I will come up with you in the elevator."

This made Lee a little uncomfortable. The elevator ride seemed to take forever and Chuck continued smiling at him refusing to take his eyes off Lee as if he was studying every aspect of Lee's face.

At precisely 6pm that evening when the secret computer program that Lee had installed deleted itself, Lee was in his hotel room getting ready to fly back to Australia the following morning.

Six months later, Lee still had the diamonds. He knew that the best way to completely cover his tracks was not to attempt to trade them too quickly. But for the life of him, he could not figure-out what had gone wrong. Why did the FBI wish to speak with him?

As Lee thought about it, it made him sick. He went over every aspect of the plan and couldn't think of anything that went wrong. There would be no security footage of him in the bank. There would be no log of the security boxes being opened by him. There were no fingerprints, and even if he did leave any, and he knew that he didn't, there was no fresh crime-scene to have preserved them. The heist was now six months ago and there had been nothing about it in the media.

Then how or why was the FBI led to him? Lee was more and more troubled. He opened up a book on a bookshelf where he had hidden the three diamonds for the past six months. They were beautiful pristine stones that caused a rainbow to dance all over his room. "What if the FBI and the Police came with a search warrant?" he quickly thought to himself. "Or worse," he continued thinking, "What if he was now under surveillance?" Much as he hated doing it, Lee flushed the diamonds down the toilet. Now there was absolutely no way of connecting him to the bank heist.

The following day, Lee was in an interview room at the Surry Hills police station that his boss had asked him to go to.

"Mr Zhang Wei," one of the agents began. "I am Special Agent Johns and this is Special Agent Downs. We wish to ask you some questions about the time you went to Alabama last year for your company. Special Agent Downs is recording this conversation on camera. We hope you don't mind. You should understand that this interview is entirely voluntary. Do you understand that?"

"Yes," Lee replied trying to appear as calm as possible.

"You left the US to return to Australia on a Saturday. We wish to ask you where you were on the Friday just before you left, particularly around noon that day. Can you remember what you did?"

"Let me see," Lee replied pretending to recall the precise time period he had already been thinking about. "The day before I flew back to Australia, I was in the park next to my hotel reading."

"Mr Zhang Wei," Special Agent Johns continued, "a person by the name of Chuck Smith has given your description to a sketch artist." As he said this, he unfolded a document from his pocket. Lee looked at it and saw a hand-drawn sketch of himself.

"So, we just want to confirm whether you were there on that day, particularly around noon."

Lee feigned confusion. "No, I was not there that day at all," he said. "He must have seen me when I was there a few days earlier installing software on the bank's computers."

"Thank you, Mr Zhang Wei," the Special Agent said. "That's what we thought too. Will you just wait a bit while we get this interview typed up and you can sign a transcript for us? That's all we need."

"Sure," Lee said wondering if that would be the end of it.

The two agents left and returned after about 15 minutes. Lee read the transcript and saw that it was accurate. He signed each page as the agents asked him to.

As he stood to leave, Lee asked, "What's this all about anyway?"

"Chuck's been charged with bludgeoning his landlord to death on that day. He swears he was at the bank at the time and that he spoke to you who could be his alibi. But the security cameras show that neither you nor him were there at that time." The Special Agent continued, "With his alibi witness neutralised, the DA is going to ask for the electric chair on this one."

Chapter 5

The Rat Race

Friday night dinner at the Grayson household was sacrosanct. The family would always start their meal precisely at 8pm and each member would be expected to relay to each other the interesting part of their day. Dr Grayson would usually go first. She was an Oncologist who worked in the hospital adjoining the university that her son attended as a biology student. Mr Grayson was a statistician who worked as a Public Servant in the Australian Bureau of Statistics.

"Work was as busy as usual," Dr Grayson began. "I treated about 30 patients today. But what I don't understand are the male doctors. They always seem to treat a lot more patients than us female doctors. Maybe you should run an audit on the payment of male and female doctors from Medicare, Mark," she said looking at her husband. "I guarantee you the male doctors' notes are a lot more-shoddy than us female doctors." It was a usual complaint and didn't need any elaboration. "How was your day?" she asked.

"Today I was given a new assignment," her husband answered. "I am to run a statistical analysis on corporate enterprise and the bureaucracy," he said. "It's a three-week project, and I am hoping to get promoted at the end of it."

"Is that likely?" Dr Grayson asked her husband taking an interest.

"I think so," he replied. "I'm in line for it and a vacancy has come up in the Auditor General's department."

"Which corporate enterprises in particular are you focusing on?" his wife asked.

"I have chosen McDonalds, BHP and DrugTech," Mr Grayson said chopping a fine piece of meat from his T-bone steak.

"DrugTech is a wonderful company," his wife chimed in. "Their drug reps at the hospital always prepare the doctors the best meals for their drug presentations and they always seem so well prepared with them."

"How was your day today, Tommy?" Mr Grayson asked his son.

"Today was the first of the Summer Rat Races," Tommy began. Both his parents looked confused. "The Summer Rat Races is a tradition amongst the biology students. On Friday nights after lab, the biology students each grab their lab rat and we race them in the student common room. We each give our rat a name in accordance with the theme of the race for that night and register our rat online with wagers. The winner each night takes home $50 plus their winnings if they also wagered in favour of their rat. Since my friends and I are experimenting with steroids on our rat in the lab, we have the best chance of winning each Friday."

"How many rats compete in the race and what do you mean by, 'the theme of the race'?" his mother enquired

"There are about 50 of us all up, and tonight the theme of the race was American States," he replied. "I registered my rat as Texas but unfortunately, Texas came in second to California tonight."

And so, the conversation continued.

The following Friday was similar to the last. The meal was prepared at 8pm and Dr Grayson began again.

"I had this one patient today that just couldn't get it," she said with rising frustration. "You know you are losing when a patient starts taking advice from their Naturopath," she said with obvious disdain. "I mean did their Naturopath spend six years at medical school and another four years in specialist training? I don't think so," she said answering her own rhetorical question with an emphasis on each word. "Naturopathy is just quack science," she said grabbing her glass of red wine and taking a rather large gulp. "How was your day, Mark?" she asked her husband.

"Well, it was the strangest thing," he said. "Corporate enterprises are often involved in litigation both as plaintiffs and defendants. Today I ran a statistical analysis on how long it took on average for a trial to be heard in the District, Supreme and Federal Courts from the moment the action was filed in the registry to the moment judgment was given by the judge."

"And what did you find?" his wife asked.

"Well for cases involving McDonalds and BHP, whether they were the plaintiff or the defendant, the case on average took about 3 years," he said as if he was stating a simple fact. "But this was not the case with DrugTech. When DrugTech was the one suing, their case only took two years on average. But when DrugTech was the one being sued; their case would always take around four years."

"Maybe that's because their issues are medico-legal and quite different to those of McDonalds and BHP," his wife volunteered.

"I thought so too at first," her husband responded. "But I looked a little deeper," he said. "I found that when cases against DrugTech were commenced with wrong-spelling, or with a typo; I mean when the last letter of DrugTech was spelt with a 'k' instead of an 'h', I noticed that those cases proceeded through the system at exactly the same rate as all the other cases. But almost from the moment the defendant's name got amended to the correct spelling with an 'h'," Mark continued looking a little perplexed, "the case would get bogged down in the system again and start to blow out."

"How do you explain that?" his wife asked.

"I don't know," he said, "But that's not the only thing. I also noticed that when a corporation lobbied government officials for a change of regulations affecting their industry, whether it be a Union Award or a reporting obligation or whatever," he said, "McDonalds and BHP would spend a lot of money and a result would be given in roughly six months' time. But whenever DrugTech sought a change to the legal status quo, they hardly spent any money at all, and it would usually be effected in two."

"That is strange," his wife replied wondering if there was a simple explanation.

"What about you Tommy? How did the Rat Race go?" his father enquired.

"I only came third tonight," Tommy answered. "The theme of the race was Pop Stars. Mine was registered as Katy Perry. But apparently Katy Perry came in behind Madonna who came in behind Taylor Swift."

The following Friday night was windy and rainy and Tommy was running late. His parents were forced to start dinner before Tommy came home.

"I'm not very hungry tonight," Dr Grayson said. "The drug reps from DrugTech gave us a magnificent feast for lunch and I am still a little full from that."

"What was the drug they were pushing this time?" Mark enquired.

"Nothing much for Oncology," she answered. "These days it all seems to be about Type I Diabetes. I hear big things are happening there," she said. "How was your day?"

"Well, it was another strange day," Mark began. "I took my findings in to the boss and I thought he would want me to explain more the discrepancy between DrugTech's treatment in the bureaucracy compared with other corporate enterprise. I was a little relieved when he didn't ask because I don't think I could have explained it. He just asked me to leave it with him and he went all quiet."

"What about the promotion? Do you think you are still in line?" his wife enquired.

"I'm not sure," he answered. "No one upstairs seems to be talking to me anymore about it. If I didn't know better, I'd say I was blacklisted. And as I was leaving today, I got a hint that they want to move me sideways to bookkeeping." This time Mark had a big gulp of red wine. "Sometimes I wish I never heard of corporate enterprise and DrugTech," he said looking a little despondent.

At that point they heard the front door open and Tommy came home. He took off his raincoat and made for the dinner table.

"Sorry I'm late," Tommy said, "I'm starving." Tommy started devouring his steak that was left for him on the dinner table.

"How was your day?" his mother enquired.

"Terrible," Tommy replied. Tonight, my rat actually won. But when I went to claim my money, the organisers refused to pay-up saying that I failed to register my rat online before the race in order to place my wager."

"So why didn't you register your rat?" his mother asked.

"I did," Tommy said in boiled-up frustration. "It's not my fault if their stupid computer glitches. As if I wouldn't register my rat before the race," Tommy said a little angrily. "They kept telling me that rules were rules and that it was my responsibility to ensure that the computer registered the name before I logged off."

"Now son," his father admonished. "It's a bad tradesman who quarrels with his tools. You should just learn from the mistake and move on. Next time you could take a screenshot of the registration or something. What name were you trying to register when the computer glitched on you anyway?" his father asked.

"We had to choose from the top 50 companies," he said. "I tried to register mine as DrugTech."

Chapter 6

The Flip Side

It was Friday night at the university campus where professors and students would meet at the end of the week. Charlie was watching Philip saying goodbye to two elegantly dressed suits, a woman and a man.

"Thank you for your time," the woman said, "If we need anything, we know where to find you."

"My pleasure Detective Summers," Philip responded, "I'm sure it was just a tragic event."

With that the two plain-clothes detectives left the bar.

"Who were they?" Charlie enquired of Philip making sure they had gone first.

"They were detectives from the Surry Hills police station," Philip answered. "They were investigating the suicide of an old friend of mine Marty Hanson."

"Well, they looked a little too elegantly dressed to be cops if you ask me," Charlie volunteered. "Martin worked with you at DrugTech didn't he?" Charlie enquired.

"Yes, for many years," Philip said. "Poor soul, he was quite delusional in the end. I hear he jumped from a 9th floor balcony after screaming that a horse with 12 legs with the head of a lion was chasing him. Go figure right?"

"Were you critical of DrugTech when you were speaking with those guys just now?" Charlie asked out of the blue.

"Critical of DrugTech?" Philip enquired. "Why would I be critical of DrugTech?"

"I mean, do you think it was a real suicide? Do you really think Martin was delusional?" Charlie asked looking a little agitated.

"Of course he was delusional," Philip responded. "The last time we spoke he said that I had a genetically engineered monkey brain."

Charlie leaned forward beckoning Philip to do the same, obviously wishing to continue the conversation in whispers.

"Have you ever heard of the suicide drug?" Charlie asked.

"No, what's that?"

"I first found out about it when I was working at DrugTech researching my cure for cancer. Since leaving DrugTech I have been looking at historical documents and doing a bit of research into it," Charlie whispered.

"Listen," Philip said, "Usually you make a little bit of sense Charlie, but I haven't got a clue what the devil you are talking about."

"The year was 1925," Charlie said, "A person in Centennial Park was having a picnic with his fiancée when he suddenly froze and told his betrothed that he just saw a 12-legged horse with the head of a lion. A rather majestic creature moving through the trees in the distance," Charlie said. "His fiancée didn't think much of it at the time, but a couple of days later, she went to an art gallery and she happened to see a painting of a horse with 12 legs with the head of a lion."

Philip seemed intrigued. "Go on," he said.

"She enquired after the artist but was told that the artist committed suicide by jumping into the lion's den at Taronga Zoo about six months earlier." Charlie made a quick scan of the room to see if anyone was watching them or listening to their conversation. Satisfying himself that they were not being observed, Charlie continued. "The following weekend she was due to meet her fiancé again at Centennial Park only this time he didn't show-up. She later found him hanging in his garage at home. He had committed suicide."

"What happened?" Philip asked wondering where this was leading.

"Two cases," Charlie continued, "of two seemingly unrelated suicides, yet both hallucinated a strange identical creature. An investigation was opened to see the connection between these two apparent suicides. It was later discovered there was a connection." Charlie surveyed the room one more time.

"Well?" Philip asked almost impatiently, "What was the connection?"

"Leo Mitch and Morley was the biggest pharmaceutical company in the early 1900s in Australia. They had all kinds of hospital products, medicines, even ladies' cosmetics. Turns out that both suicides were taking the same anti-depressant medication made by Leo Mitch and Morley. They concluded that it was a powerful psychotropic hallucinogen that induced patients to commit suicide."

"What about the 12-legged horse with the head of a lion," Philip asked sceptically. "That's a pretty specific hallucination for a simple drug don't you think?"

"It turned out," Charlie continued in whispers, "That the Leo Mitch and Morley Company logo was embossed on the pill. That logo consisted of the word Leo on top of two 'M's. Obviously 'Leo' was interpreted as a lion and sitting on top of two 'M's side-by-side looked like six legs on the one side of a horse. The patients became susceptible to their environment and they latched on to the image on the pill which formed the basis of their hallucination later."

"Then what happened?" Philip asked wondering how much was real and how much was conjecture.

"There was a big investigation and the medicine was recalled from the market. The shares of Leo Mitch and Morley plummeted and the company went into voluntary administration. And then a little-known pharmaceutical company by the name of DrugTech purchased the shares and took over the company."

"So, what are you saying?" Philip asked almost sarcastically, "That DrugTech poisoned Marty with a suicide pill to murder him?"

"Well, it seems awfully suspicious don't you think?" Charlie replied. "When Martin left DrugTech, he was always very critical of them."

"Well, it seems a little far-fetched to me," Philip replied. "There's no evidence to support any of this. It's just a campfire ghost story. Just another conspiracy theory."

"Look whatever man," Charlie said, "Just don't come running to me if you ever see a 12-legged horse with a lion's head chasing you."

"Don't worry," Philip said, "I won't."

"Well, I'm off to Israel on a sabbatical tomorrow. Take care," Charlie said as he rose and made another scan of the room before leaving.

"Strange guy," Philip thought to himself.

Philip never believed Charlie's suspicions were true. But the story troubled him somewhat. The following morning Philip decided to telephone the Surry Hills Police station to ask Detective Summers a few more questions regarding Martin's death.

"I'm sorry," the receptionist replied, "We have never had a Detective Summers working here. Sergeant Skipper Johns has always been in charge of the Martin Hanson case."

Chapter 7

The Craziest Kind of Crazy

Cafes are usually the best place to plan conspiracies. The movies would have you believe that conspiracies are usually conceived of in saunas. Perhaps that's because in a sauna, the co-conspirators are in a state of mutual undress and thereby incapable of concealing a listening device. But movies rarely reflect real life and saunas are simply too impractical. Similarly, conspiracies are rarely planned at the office because there are too many interested ears about and way too many distractions and interruptions. But cafes on the other hand are the places that people meet when they wish to discuss all kinds of troublesome issues.

Now at the café at the corner of Elizabeth Street and Park St in the Sydney CBD, one retired barrister was reminiscing to one retired company director about the crazy kind of troublesome issues that he had had to put up with in the course of his brilliant career and the solutions that he had employed to fix them.

"There are four kinds of crazies when it comes to judges," the retired barrister said. "The first kind is the judge who's good at mathematics."

"What's the problem with that?" the director asked.

"Well decision making in human affairs rarely comes down to a mathematical model," the barrister said. "Mathematicians just assume the unreal."

"How would you fix that?" the director wondered.

"Usually, you could appeal that kind of judge on the basis that they failed to take into account relevant matters and took into account irrelevant matters. It was very tiresome."

"So, what's the second kind of crazy?" the retired company director asked with much amusement.

"The second kind was the academic kind. You know, the one who thinks that in educating their students, there is no such thing as a dumb question. Courtrooms are not classrooms. The academic kind of judge usually assume an authority to decide an issue when no such jurisdiction to do so exists."

"Did that happen often?" the director asked.

"Oh, all the time," the barrister answered. "Judges have a lot of power but they are loath to think that there are limits on their power. We would also appeal those decisions on the grounds of lack of jurisdiction."

"That sounds pretty crazy to me. What could be crazier than that?" the director asked.

"Well crazier than that were the botanists," the barrister replied.

"The botanists?" the director enquired, "What do you mean by that?"

"Well take Chief Justice Rex Klein for example," the Barrister said. "Rex had this principle that roses only come with an admixture of thorns. And more than that, every legal principle had to be given a Latin name or he failed to recognise it."

"So how would you deal with that?"

"Well, those kinds are very difficult to deal with. They like to be the boss of everything, poor souls. And not many Appeal Court judges know that much Latin you see. I mean they'd get bogged down in whether certiorari should issue when a ejusdem generis interpretation of the Act demonstrated the judge acted ultra vires or not."

"That's all Greek to me," the director retorted. "Did things like that happen often?"

"From time to time," the barrister replied nodding his head.

"So, what would be the craziest kind of crazy?" the director asked with much amusement.

"Oh, the craziest kind of crazy were the clockmakers," the barrister answered. "I mean the actual clockmakers who would make clocks in their spare time and attend the Horological Societies or the Society of Clockmakers. Their homes are adorned with all kinds of clocks, most of them not working and none of them keeping accurate time and every hour or so a reminder is given of just how cuckoo they really are."

"But why?" the director enquired. "What's wrong with a judge having that kind of hobby?"

"Well, it's a twisted philosophy. Life isn't a clock and they think it is. In a clock, cogs follow upon cogs, gears are set and interwoven and things just tick as they are supposed to tick. That's clockwork. But when a judge tries to impose that kind of system on real life, they get into all sorts of bother. It's a clog on the equity of justice."

"So how do you fix that kind of crazy judge?" the director asked whose amusement was growing by the minute.

"Well, you just can't," the barrister answered. "It's not a matter of time, they are too far gone. At least you can't from within the four corners of the courtroom."

"What do you mean?" the director asked.

"Well, we had this one case once involving a woman named Dorothy Wilcox and her husband, a former submarine Captain," the barrister began.

"They were crying-out, in fact begging for some kind of justice against a private detective and a law firm over certain issues in their past, but the judge just refused to be reasonable. The judge just saw the pendulum swinging from left to right and left to right and there was no way to get him to see the problem from outside the box. Besides it's terribly difficult when you are suing a law firm who often briefed the judge's colleagues. And that happens more often than you'd care to think."

"So, what did you do?" the director asked.

"Well, it was just a hopeless situation," the barrister began. "I was looking for ways to break the news to my clients that the situation was hopeless. But then the darndest thing happened."

"What?" the director asked. "What happened?"

"Well, I was walking back to Chambers after another difficult day in Court and I ran into your former boss sitting just where you're sitting now," the barrister said. "I nodded at him and he offered me a seat."

"My former boss?" the director enquired.

"Yes," the barrister said, "Dr Jamieson, the CEO of DrugTech at the time."

"Oh yes," the director responded, "What happened then?"

"Well, I told him about the troublesome judge and all the difficulties that we were in and he seemed very understanding and wished he could help if he could," the barrister said. "I think he knew Captain Jackson or something and had some rudimentary understanding of the case."

"So, what happened?" the director asked.

"Well, we returned to Court the following Monday and the judge was just as bad as ever, and he reserved his decision."

"So, nothing happened?" the director questioned, "Is that what you're saying?"

"Well, I'm not really sure what happened to be honest," the barrister said. "But we were expecting a decision in about two months; but instead, we got the decision in two days and it was a resounding win," the barrister said. "But that wasn't the strangest thing."

"What was the strangest thing?" the director asked.

"The strangest thing was that that judge then stepped-down from the bench and never practiced law again."

"Really? What did he do?" the director asked.

"Well, I'm told he gave a few lectures in law at several universities," the barrister said, "But then about two years later, I noticed that he turned his career towards corporate enterprise. Then, the last I heard, he served as a director on the board of DrugTech until his retirement."

Chapter 8

Prejudice and First Impressions

Matt Pike was a famous Australian actor and a typical heartthrob to adolescent girls. At the peak of his acting career, he had starred in several Hollywood action movies. But four years ago, he stood trial in Australia on one count of insider trading brought by the Australian Securities and Investments Commission over a suspicious transaction involving Qantas shares. At the time he had retained the services of Barrister William Hunter and was ultimately acquitted by a jury of his peers. The trial was a media-packed event and was sure to have ended his acting career if he had lost.

His career never returned to the same heights that he had reached prior to his arrest but it was also fair to say that it was far from over. On this particular day, as a publicity event for his career, his manager had arranged for him to watch the female State finalists in the Wood Chopping competition at the Royal Easter Show as the guest of honour. He would then be asked to present the trophy to the winning team and to have lunch with the female competitors. The winning team would be seated at his table during the luncheon.

It was a packed open-air arena. Each team representing each State consisted of 3 women. The first woman from each team would need to complete the "Underhand Chop". This required the woman to stand with one foot on each side of a log that was fixed in a cradle in a horizontal position. It was a race. The first to cut the log into two with the axe would allow the second member of the team to proceed with the "Standing Block Chop".

In the Standing Block Chop, the log is secured vertically in a dummy and the scarf is cut from each side until the block is severed. When the woman succeeded in completing that task, the final woman was then allowed to start the "Tree-felling Chop".

The Tree-felling Chop was the most spectacular to watch. A log about 4.6m high represented the tree. The woman would cut notches into the log called "board holes" in order to insert a board or a plank. She was then required to stand on the plank in order to insert a higher plank until eventually she climbed all the way to the top of the log. Then whilst standing on the uppermost plank, she was required to lop the top of the tree off. But usually that meant chopping half-way through the log and then coming down to start again by inserting planks into the other side of the tree to recommence lopping the top of the tree from the other side in order to accomplish the job. The winning team was the first to lop the top off the tree.

The sport was a tradition in Australia from around 1870 but this was the first year that the sport was open to women.

Matt Pike observed the three-women teams from each of the six States. But from the moment the event started, the New South Wales team attracted his and the crowd's attention. The first woman was a rather attractive blonde woman with shoulder-length hair. She was a slim woman and her axe looked smaller and lighter than the others. But she wielded it with such vigour and excitement that she managed on average to get two chops in to everyone else's one. She was the first to turn around on the log that she was standing on and commence chopping from the other side. And each time a log was cut, the crowd went wild. Upon the blonde's final blow, Matt Pike couldn't help but wonder if the woman was married. His first impression was that she was an attractive, fit and very eligible woman to any man.

The second member of the New South Wales team was a brunette in glasses. She appeared to Matt Pike as a strong middle-aged woman. She would heave a mighty blow with the axe into the standing log. The blows were slow but powerful. At this point in time New South Wales was blow for blow with the Queensland team and it seemed to be a tie when the standing-block was split in two. Matt Pike wondered what the brunette's occupation was as he couldn't quite venture a guess. "Could be anything," he thought to himself.

Matt Pike then turned his attention to the third member of the team. She was a large stocky woman with a shaved head. As she swung the axe to create the board-holes, her muscles protruded through her stocky arms. "Definitely a lesbian," Matt Pike thought to himself as he looked at her shaved head. In Matt Pike's mind, there was no other explanation for a woman so strong having a shaved-head. "Definitely not undergoing cancer treatment with that strength," he mused to himself.

After a nail-biting finish, which sent the cheering-crowd to their feet; Matt Pike presented the trophy to the New South Wales team. Lunch was in an hour and all the women went off to shower and get changed before lunch.

"Ladies and Gentlemen, please welcome Superstar Matt Pike," was the announcement over the microphone to a cheering hall of women waiting at tables for their lunch. Matt Pike was ushered through the room. All the women appeared quite differently now with makeup on and cocktail dresses.

The women's wood-chopping event was sponsored by the Dominican Nuns and Matt Pike was led towards a table where three sisters in habits were standing to greet him. Upon seeing the nuns in their habits, his first impression was to watch his manners and not say anything too controversial.

"Welcome to the winner's table," the first nun said with her hand outstretched and indicating an empty chair for the actor to sit. "I'm Sister Mary-Joseph". To Matt Pike's surprise, he recognised the nun as the third woman in the team.

"My goodness," Matt Pike said, "After watching the way you felled that tree, I would never have picked you for a nun in a million years."

"Why not?" she enquired innocently. "Did I do something wrong?"

"No, it's just..." Matt felt a little lost for words. "I mean you are wearing a veil now, but with the shaved head I must admit, my first impression was that you were a cancer survivor."

"That's funny," Sister Mary Joseph responded. "Most people mistake my shaved head for being a lesbian."

"Oh!" Mike Pike exclaimed with laughter from an unexpected quip.

"Actually, I was married once with three children," Sister Mary Joseph continued, "but many years ago, they all went to God after a tragic car accident."

"Oh, I'm sorry to hear that," Matt Pike said.

"Besides," Sister Mary Joseph said, "She's the lesbian," indicating another nun who was standing and smiling with an outstretched hand.

"I'm Sister Mary Thomas," she said, "Yes, I'm a lesbian."

Matt Pike was even more surprised when he recognised her as the attractive slim blonde-woman who was the first to start the race.

"Oh?" the actor said with raised eyebrows. "I didn't think lesbians could join a nunnery?"

"Nonsense she said," still smiling and shaking his hand. "It's only practicing lesbians that they have a problem with. I've had same-sex attraction ever since puberty," she said with a notable lack of embarrassment. But I have always loved Jesus Christ and have chosen a life of chastity," she continued. "And I have never met more interesting women in my life than in the Order of St Domonic."

"It's funny," the actor said, "Maybe I'm just prejudiced, but I would never have thought that a nunnery would allow women to compete in wood chopping of all things."

"Well in their spare time, I allow them to do anything they want," the brunette with glasses, said. "I'm Mother Patricia, the Mother Superior."

After shaking her hand, they all sat down and Matt Pike said, "Well you three would have to be the most fit and active members in the nunnery I'd say."

"Oh, I don't know about that," the Mother Superior said. "Do you remember four years ago when you were on trial for insider trading and you had the barrister William Hunter represent you?"

"Yes," Matt Pike answered with even more embarrassment wondering how they knew the details.

"Well, that barrister had a work-experience student named Jennifer at the time who watched your trial," she said. She joined our Order a few years ago and I'd say that she's the strongest and fittest of all of us."

Matt Pike remembered the dainty law student in her mini-skirt at his trial and wondered how she could be fitter and stronger than the three 'axewomen' before him as the Mother Superior continued.

"She just came first in this year's open boxing competition."

Chapter 9

The Charlatan's Sister

In my earlier work, I introduced you to the Charlatan, Madam Mandy Kizana who dressed up as a Gypsy and preyed on the vulnerable with the use of her crystal ball. Now let me tell you about her sister, Beatrice.

Beatrice Kizana was a single middle-aged woman with three grown-up children. In her spare time, she fell into the now, not so uncommon habit of surfing the web, commenting on twitter, updating her Facebook page, and just a few years ago, she took to publishing a few stories of her own on Amazon Kindle detailing her recent life-experiences. None of the stories contained any literary merit but they were published none-the-less and they became the backbone of her contention that several taxation deductions that she had claimed in her last filed taxation returns were in fact legitimate.

On this particular day, Beatrice Kizana was selected for an audit by the Australian Taxation Office and Investigator Rawlins with his sidekick Anne Trundle had just entered her apartment for an official interview.

"May I call you Beatrice?" Investigator Rawlins had asked after the customary introductions.

"Of course," Beatrice said smiling and showing her visitors in to her small lounge room where they all proceeded to sit around a coffee table. "What seems to be the problem?"

"Beatrice," the Investigator began, "The Australian Taxation Office is concerned about a number of deductions that you have claimed. We are concerned that they are not legitimate expenses but rather, your own private living expenses."

"What do you mean not legitimate expenses?" Beatrice asked looking a little confused.

"Well, you are only allowed to claim an expense as a deduction," the Investigator answered, "if the expense was legitimately made for the purpose of helping you achieve your business income."

"Ah yes," Beatrice said answering calmly, "All of my expenses are legitimately made for that reason, I am a writer."

"Well, we would like to go through these with you Beatrice," the Investigator continued. "For example, you have claimed several restaurant meals for two in last years' taxation returns." Inspector Rawlins opened a folder he had been carrying under his arm and pointed to a few highlighted entries in a spreadsheet. "These meals were three-course dinners with wine and ice-cream for dessert between yourself and a male companion?"

"Of course," Beatrice answered looking almost shocked at the impertinence of the question. "I'm a writer. I write about my experiences including these dates and I publish it on Amazon."

"Yes, but you see, the meals add up to several hundred dollars, and your e-books are only priced at 99c and you have only sold about three or four of them to close friends and family. It's not exactly a thriving business, is it?" The inspector's sarcasm was palpable.

"Oh yes," Beatrice responded nonchalantly, "But I am just getting established. J K Rowling wasn't an established author overnight you know?"

"And here," Inspector Rawlins said flipping over a few pages, "Here you even claimed a trip to Venice and that trip looks like a simple holiday. But you have claimed several thousand dollars as a legitimate deduction. How can you justify that?"

"Yes," Beatrice replied with a similar level of frustration, "As I have tried to explain to you, I'm a writer, and here I was writing about the time I visited Venice. You can check it out for yourself if you buy my book on Amazon?"

"But really Beatrice," the Inspector said almost rolling his eyes, "You don't have to go on an expensive trip to Venice to just write about it in your published works."

"Well, how am I supposed to write about Venice otherwise?" Beatrice questioned.

"Well, you could read about Venice…" the Inspector said looking for an argument before he was interrupted.

"Inspector," Beatrice complained, "Really. I am writing about visiting Venice. I am not writing about 'reading about visiting Venice'. As an artist I need to get my inspiration."

"Look Beatrice," the Inspector said with a slightly agitated tone, "I am trying to help you. It's alright for you to just dismiss this investigation as something flippant, but really, these are not legitimate deductions and worse than that, if it appears to us and my Office to be willful cheating, then this matter could be handed over to the prosecutorial branch for criminal prosecution."

"My goodness," Beatrice said looking shocked, "Criminal prosecution? I think I will write a book on taxpayer harassment from the investigators of the Australian Taxation Office. Criminal prosecution? How absurd?" Beatrice started looking around for a notebook and a pen looking evidently flustered. She found such a notebook and pen from a telephone-table desk-drawer nearby. "How do I spell Inspector Rawlins and what was your name again?" she asked looking at the sidekick.

The sidekick was taken aback at being asked a direct question and she stopped taking notes of the conversation at that point. Inspector Rawlins came to her defence. "There's no need for that Beatrice," he said with his hand outstretched almost as a peace offering, "Everyone should just calm down. There's no need for threats. We don't need to bring a criminal prosecution against you and you don't need to write about any harassment from us, OK? But really, you have to be more circumspect with your taxation deductions. Can we at least agree on that?"

"Fine," Beatrice said, "I will discuss the matter with my accountant tomorrow.

"I think that would be a very good idea," the Inspector said feeling that they had reached an impasse and looking for a way out. "When you have done that, just ask your accountant to give me a call and we can sort out these issues once and for all, OK?"

"Fine," Beatrice said again as the Inspector and his sidekick rose to leave the apartment.

As she showed them out and shut the door, Beatrice adjusted a small microphone that was pinned to her bra under her blouse. "Have you got enough?" she yelled to the kitchen as she walked back to the lounge room.

Two Federal Agents with their badges pinned to their coats walked out of the kitchen. "I think so," the first Agent said, "We have Inspector Rawlins on tape agreeing not to prosecute you if you agreed not to write about them. That bribe should at least be enough for us to get us a search warrant for his home and office."

Chapter 10

The High-Tech Criminal Merchant

Detective Sergeant Derrick was deep undercover. Over the years he had infiltrated drug gangs, bank robbers and organised crime syndicates. He was currently a high-ranking member of an Australian money-laundering operation but rather than bring this organization down, he was too useful to the police as a secret informant of the criminal clients of such an organization. In this way, the police could covertly monitor and capture various major drug syndicates in need of money laundering services.

But recently reports had been received of a new kind of high-tech criminal organization. Such rumours were dismissed as mere gossip at first, but more and more reports were received of criminals evading capture by police with almost supernatural powers from the use of high-tech equipment that would at every stage out-fox standard law enforcement.

After much internal debate within the higher echelons of law enforcement, a decision was made to infiltrate this new organization even at the expense of exposing their most valued informant. Accordingly, the Detective had made several enquiries with his clients and other affluent criminally minded persons, and all reports seemed to direct him towards a person known only as Dr Lazer. Apparently, Dr Lazer and his cohort had come from Silicon Valley in the US to peddle their high-tech wares to the high-end criminal organizations around the world thereby giving those organizations the edge they were looking for over standard law-enforcement technology.

On this particular night, Detective Derrick was met by teenage boys dressed in hoodies and sneakers, who frisked him to make sure that he was unarmed and not in possession of any listening devices. They took him to a white van and the Detective allowed himself a smile when he saw that the van had P plates alongside the registration plates. He had agreed to ride in the back of the van with the windows-blacked out so that he was unable to see where the van was driving to. After approximately 60 minutes of driving, the Detective heard a roller-door open and the van drive inside what was obviously a warehouse. The roller-door was closed behind the van and the Detective was let out.

"Follow us," his two companions said. They walked into an elevator. After a short ride when the doors of the elevator opened, they exited into a corridor. At the end of the corridor, the Detective was led into a magnificently decorated showroom.

"Good evening," a handsome young man said in a white lab coat, which the Detective estimated to be in his twenties. "I'm Dr Lazer. Welcome to my showroom."

The Detective peered around him. He was standing on plush red carpet and various items, some in glass cases, were positioned neatly at various places in stands that resembled articles in a museum. The display immediately to his left contained a simple baseball hat on the head of a mannequin.

"Let's start here," Dr Lazer said pointing to the mannequin and picking up a sample baseball cap from the bottom of the display.

"This cap is fitted with high-tech cameras on each side and high-tech speakers all around, but they are hardly visible to the naked eye."

"What's it for?" the Detective asked.

"The cameras have a 360-degree view around the person wearing it. When they detect a charging police dog coming towards it, the micro-computer automatically activates the speakers to emit an ultra-high frequency tone, completely deafening to dogs, but wholly undetectable to humans." As he said these words, Dr Lazer pointed out the cameras and speakers that blended in well with the cap.

"The microcomputer is woven into the visor here," Dr Lazer said indicating a small-thickened part of the visor. "Have a look at the cap in action."

Dr Lazer pointed to the television mounted to the wall behind the stand. It displayed two police dogs charging towards a man in a standard k9 bite suit used to train police dogs how and where to bite their targets.

"Now watch again when the trainer wears the cap," Dr Lazer said pointing to the cap that the man in the bite suit was now wearing. As the dogs started running towards the man, they stopped short and whimpered away almost in pain. The dogs refused to go near the man.

"That's amazing," the Detective said. "How much are you selling a cap like that for?"

"We don't sell our equipment," Dr Lazer responded. "You may hire as many caps as you want at a price of 10k each per night. They must be returned when you are finished."

"Fair enough," the Detective said.

"If you are actually interested in hiring them, we can do a live demonstration with a real dog so that you can convince yourself that the dog is quite aware of the sound and won't approach the cap. You will be convinced."

"I believe you," the Detective said feeling quite impressed with the technology. He had seen nothing like it in his career as a detective but started to think that a new wave of high-tech and young band of criminals were about to make their mark.

"What else have you got?" the Detective asked walking to the next stand.

The next stand also had the head of a mannequin but instead of wearing a baseball cap, it was wearing a pair of glasses in a black frame.

Dr Lazer picked up the display model of glasses nearby. "These glasses are fitted with ultra-powerful LEDs at either end of the frame here and here," he said pointing to a cluster of clear LEDs blended into the frame at either side of the lenses. "When activated, the LEDs emit high power radiation both in the ultraviolet and infrared bands of the spectrum, completely invisible to the human eye. In other words, they emit invisible light," he said.

"What's it for?" the Detective asked with evident curiosity.

"The invisible light completely overwhelms the sensors inside cameras, so the person's face cannot be recorded on CCTV. Watch this."

Dr Lazer put on the pair of glasses and pointed to the television screen behind the display. "You can see that both of us are visible from that camera at the top of the screen. Now look what happens when I turn on the glasses."

Dr Lazer tapped the glasses between the lenses and looked again at the screen. As he did this, the image on the screen completely whited out similar to a camera being pointed at the sun.

"Notice what happens when I turn away," Dr Lazer said turning his back to the screen.

The white-out on the screen dissipated and the figures of the Detective and Dr Lazer's back reappeared first as silhouettes but then in colour as the camera adjusted itself back to the normal lighting of the room.

"You can try it out yourself," Dr Lazer said handing the glasses to the Detective. The Detective put them on and turned and ducked and weaved around the camera. They obviously worked and his face was incapable of being displayed on the screen.

"How much to hire these?" the Detective marvelled at the technology.

"These are 20k each per night," Dr Lazer said taking the glasses back from his customer and carefully putting them back in the display position.

"Over here is one of our most popular items," he said pointing at a small container that appeared to contain two lip balms standing upright in the middle of a display case. One had a reddish hue, the other a bluish hue.

"This looks like lip balm and can even be used as such," Dr Lazer said putting the red container lip balm on his lips in the usual way as an example. "No reaction occurs unless it is applied to the inside of the wrists. But look what happens when it is applied to the inside of the wrists."

At these words, Dr Lazer summoned one of the two persons that had driven the Detective to the showroom. The young boy came and pushed the sleeves of his hoodie up his arms exposing his wrists. Dr Lazer then applied the red lip balm to the inside of one wrist, and the blue lip balm to the inside of the other.

"Watch carefully," he said as the Detective moved closer for a better look.

The wrists of the boy started to fatten. It looked like a severe allergic reaction. The Detective had seen something similar on television when persons suffered allergic reactions to bee-stings or peanut butter, but this reaction was contained solely on the wrists and did not progress to any other part of the body.

"I think I know what this is for," the Detective said. "How long does the reaction last?"

"It lasts for about three hours," Dr Lazer said as he picked up a pair of handcuffs and put them on the boy. "Unless," Dr Lazer continued pointing at the boy's handcuffed wrists, "Unless the chemical on one wrist is rubbed into the chemical of the other wrist."

As he said that, the handcuffed boy rubbed his wrists together and for a moment it appeared that the chemicals on his wrists produced small bubbles and a slight gas was given off. Within seconds the circumference of his wrists returned to normal. The boy was then able to slide his hands out of the handcuffs without needing to unlock them first.

"Amazing," the Detective exclaimed. "I haven't seen anything like that in my life."

"A pair of these lip balms will set you back 30k per night. The containers must be returned even if the contents are all used up."

The Detective was dumbfounded. It was like a cornucopia of high-tech criminal wares. "Did you guys ever work for the British Secret Service?" the Detective quipped.

"No," Dr Lazer replied without missing a beat, "They couldn't afford us."

Each of them chuckled at the banter as they walked to the next display. This display looked like simple clothing all folded neatly as they would be seen in a clothing shop. Several folded-up hoodies similar to what the boys were wearing were among them as well as jeans, shorts, socks and T-shirts.

"Don't tell me these stop bullets?" the Detective asked incredulously.

"No, they don't stop bullets," said the Merchant, "But they do stop Tasers. Woven into the fabric is an electrical conducting foil designed to short out Tasers. We give these out free of charge to all of our customers."

There were many other displays that the Detective was eager to get to, but at this point, the watch on the Detective's wrist started to vibrate.

"I'm afraid you guys are not the only ones with high-tech equipment," the Detective said. "I didn't think it was worth blowing my cover on you guys but after seeing this, I think it was really worth it. You see this watch?" The Detective said holding up his wrist. "It has been transmitting my GPS coordinates to the Tactical Response Squad all of this time. I have just received a notification that this building is surrounded and there is no escape."

As he said these words, a group of about 12 police officers with semi-automatic assault rifles burst through the doors and surrounded Dr Lazer and his two young assistants.

"Get on your knees and put your hands on your heads," shouted one of the armed police officers through his balaclava.

To the Detective's astonishment, Dr Lazer and his two associates burst into laughter.

"What's so funny?" the Detective asked cautiously.

"All you have done is trigger the alarm," Dr Lazer said almost unable to contain himself with laughter. "Within two minutes from now, this building and everything in it will blow up. I suggest you get your men out of here fast!"

"What about you?" the Detective said. "You three are under arrest and you are all coming with us."

The Detective could not understand why they started to smirk and guffaw.

"If you look at each corner of this room," the Merchant said, "You will see three lasers each representing the primary colours red, green and blue focused on where my friends and I are standing."

Leaving their weapons still trained on the Merchant and his assistants, the Detective and each police officer turned their heads to the side to look at each corner of the room and saw the strange devices, each somewhat illuminated from within and obviously turned on.

"This whole ruse was just to expose the police informer in our midst. I'm afraid you are out of a job," Dr Lazer exclaimed; and as he said these words, the lasers powered-down and the three holograms vanished from sight.

"Everyone out of here fast!" the Detective screamed as he and the police officers bolted from the room.

Chapter 11

The Scientist Who Came In from the Cold

Scientist Bruce was found Not Guilty by reason of mental illness of the murder of his friend Thomas, and the attempted murder of Gary, a stranger who had wandered onto his premises. He had been incarcerated at the Mary Immaculate Psychiatric Hospital and he refused to speak with any of the psychiatrists.

"Go away," were the first words spoken by the scientist to his new visitor.

The new visitor looked over her shoulder to ensure that the staff of the hospital could not overhear her. She then moved her seat closer to the scientist and spoke in a soft voice.

"I am not a psychiatrist," she whispered. "My name is Dr Saanvi Patel; I am a scientist at DrugTech."

This introduction had its desired effect. Scientist Bruce sat up on his bed and looked at the visitor in his cell.

"Why should DrugTech care about me?" the scientist enquired, "I have been incarcerated here for six years now. DrugTech is only interested in profits."

"That might have been true when Dr Jamieson was in charge," the visitor continued whispering, "He was not very interested in scientific breakthroughs. But my boss, Benjamin Jones is of the scientific guild. His father, Benjamin Jones Snr, was one of the three scientists with you at DrugTech."

"Your boss is Benjamin Jones Jnr?" he asked.

"Yes," Dr Patel responded. "He wants you to come back to DrugTech."

"The Trans Warp Inducer doesn't work," he said. "It is of no use."

"You transported yourself through it?" Dr Patel asked rhetorically.

"Oh yes," Bruce replied, "Several times. And each time I suffered delusions. The first as a servant in the household of Barshimon about two-thousand years ago; the second as the cook Sebastian to the Pirate Captains Samuel and Terrence about a thousand years ago; the third as a janitor to the drug company Leo Mitch and Morley about a hundred years ago."

Scientist Bruce stood from the bed and started pacing around the cell. "Delusions mean that the neurons in the brain that hold the memory patterns have been disarranged. So, it doesn't work! Besides, if a person suffers delusions, then such a person can't be certain of reality. I am not capable of admitting that my science project worked at all, I could just be insane!"

"They are not delusions," Dr Patel responded glancing over her shoulder to ensure that they were still not overheard. "They were observations."

"What are you talking about?" the scientist asked pulling up a seat closer to his visitor. "How can you observe the past like I have?"

"We see the historical past every night," Dr Patel answered. "Haven't you ever looked at the brightest star in the night sky, Sirius? That is nine light-years away. When you look at it, you are seeing how Sirius was nine years ago, not how it exists today. Sirius could have gone supernova 8 years ago and you would never know it until one year from now. Every time you look up at the night sky you are seeing how the stars were many, many years ago. You are not seeing how the stars are now. The Andromeda galaxy is two and a half-million light-years away. When we see it, we are seeing two and a half-million years into the past. There is no limit to it. If a person in a distant galaxy were to look at earth through a telescope tonight, they would see dinosaurs roaming the earth."

"What does that have to do with my experiment?" the scientist asked.

"The Trans Warp Inducer," Dr Patel answered. "Remember folding a piece of paper in on itself so that point A meets point B? Don't you see what happens when the universe warps in on itself that way? Anyone taking that ride through the 'doctrine of relative stillness' will experience the waves-of-time that are released. It is the very fabric of space-time."

Scientist Bruce seemed to consider this for a moment. After a short pause he replied.

"Well, whatever," he said. "The observations are so strong, they overwhelm you. No person can function effectively when the ride is over."

"We can fix that Bruce," Saanvi said smiling. "Do you remember Project Gamma Alpha Kappa. At the right dose, it can remove those memories. You will just see a golden glittery effect at the point of transportation and you will be immune from the waves of time."

"Project Gamma Alpha Kappa," the scientist reminisced. "That was a memory wiper," the scientist said to himself as he recalled it, "At the right dose, maybe it could..."

The scientist collected his thoughts and gazed at his visitor. "Can you get me out of here?"

"That is not going to be easy," Dr Patel replied. "You are still held at the pleasure of Her Majesty by order of the Court remember?"

"I just have to convince them that I am no longer delusional right?" Scientist Bruce asked with restrained excitement.

"Take this," Dr Patel said removing a small chocolate bar from her handbag. "It has been laced with Project Gamma Alpha Kappa. Your delusions should go almost immediately. Then after a bit of time, we will try and convince the authorities that you should be released."

Dr Patel stood and left the chocolate bar on the side table before signalling the nurse that she had finished with her patient.

"Get well soon," she said to the patient, "We need you back and healthy."

About 20 minutes later, Dr Patel finished a cafe latté next to Benjamin Jones at the café adjoining the head office of DrugTech.

"Why is Scientist Bruce so important to DrugTech anyway?" she asked.

"We've tried and we can't get it to work without him," Benjamin Jones answered putting his hot-chocolate down. "The Trans Warp Inducer is by far the most important scientific breakthrough that DrugTech has ever engaged in. Its power can unlock the very fabric of the universe. It is capable of winning wars. It can make the Manhattan Project look like a schoolboy's science experiment. It could quite literally change almost every aspect of life as we know it."

Benjamin Jones removed his glasses and wiped the moisture that had gathered underneath with a napkin. Upon putting them back on, he rose from his chair and added under his breath, "Either that or it's the most expensive piece of science-junk that DrugTech has ever invested in."

Chapter 12

The Deep State Deepens

"Just tell me all about it," were the comforting words spoken by the Special Agent's wife. Special Agent Mick Lovejoy had just risen with a tremendous hangover from being drunk the night before.

"The worst night of my life," he said grabbing his wife's double-strength coffee. "We had received word that every scientific company in the world were eager to get their hands on some scientific experiment that a scientist by the name of Bruce had been conducting in some country town somewhere."

"What was so special about it?" his wife asked curiously.

"I don't know," he said, "I never found out. But there were all sorts of allegations of stolen intellectual property rights, theft of software, theft of hardware, theft of patents, of designs, you name it. It was a total shemozzle. There were conspiracy theories raised against law enforcement at all levels and now the shack out in the country was a crime-scene for a murder of a man known as Thomas something or other."

"Slow down, you're losing me," his wife said, "Just start at the beginning. What happened when you got there?"

"I was one of the first on the scene, but my boss stayed in the car still receiving instructions from his superiors over the radio. My orders at that stage were simply to observe what was going on."

"So, what happened?" his wife asked.

"The State Police were there hanging tape around the premises saying, 'Police Line Do Not Cross". That's when the first lawyer showed up."

"The first lawyer? What was that about?" his wife asked looking a little confused.

"So, this lawyer turns up and he says, 'I represent an Irish Pharmaceutical Company. I have an Anton Piller injunction from the Supreme Court. The contents of this laboratory and all things connected with the experiment known as the Trans Warp Inducer must be handed over to us by order of the Court."

"That must have shocked them," his wife said, "Did the Police comply?"

"No certainly not," the Special Agent continued. "It got handed up to the police officer in charge and he came in and said, 'This is an active Crime Scene young man, we are investigating a murder. All goods in this house have been seized under the *Law Enforcement (Powers and Responsibilities) Act*. Your injunction is just a civil matter, it will have to await our investigation."

"That must have stopped the lawyer," his wife volunteered.

"It stopped him alright, but it didn't stop the second lawyer," her husband replied.

"The second lawyer?" his wife asked almost shocked, "What happened there?"

"Well about five minutes later, a second lawyer comes bursting in and he says, 'I represent the Chinese Government. We have an Anton Piller injunction from the Supreme Court. Everything in this house should be handed over to us by order of the Supreme Court."

"He must have received the same response," his wife volunteered.

"He did," the man said drinking more from his coffee and becoming more alive with every sip, "Only that lawyer was ready for it."

"How?" the wife enquired, "What did he say?"

"He said, 'Not so fast Commander. This injunction names the Commissioner for Police as the Second Defendant to the lawsuit. This lawsuit alleges a criminal conspiracy between the accused Scientist known as Bruce and the Police. If you read the order carefully, you will see that the Supreme Court is literally ordering the Police to hand-over the contents of this laboratory to us. Anything short of that will be a contempt of Court by the Police! Are you prepared for that Commander?' the lawyer asked him."

"Gosh, that's telling him," his wife said fascinated at the development. "What did he do?"

"Well, it took the Police Commander aback I must admit," the sobering man replied drinking more of his coffee. "He was on the phone with his superiors and he was waiting for them to get legal advice, I think. Anyway, it looked like the Police were about to comply with the order when my boss came in from the car outside."

"Go on," the wife asked seeming even more fascinated at the development.

"Well, my boss said, 'I have an electronic search warrant here on behalf of the Federal Police. The contents of this laboratory are to be handed over to the Federal Police."

"What a quagmire," the wife responded almost laughingly. "Then what happened?"

"Well, they started arguing over whether a search warrant issued under a Federal Act overrode the State's Jurisdiction to issue an injunction from a State Court because of section 109 of The Constitution," the man said. "Section 109 of The Constitution says that to the extent of any inconsistency, the Federal law will prevail over any State law."

"So that was checkmate then," his wife volunteered. "The Federal Police got it."

"Well, that's when the third lawyer came busting in."

"You're kidding," the wife said. "What now?"

"This middle-aged woman with glasses carrying a folder of material says, 'I represent the Government of the United States and I have an Anton Piller injunction here issued out of the Federal Court of Australia. It joins the NSW Police and the Federal Police as co-defendants to the lawsuit and the Federal Court is hereby ordering both the Federal Police and the State Police to hand-over the contents of this laboratory to us!"

"My goodness," the wife says. "How did they deal with that?"

"Well, everyone was getting legal advice you see," the Special Agent said finishing his coffee. "All arguments about Federal jurisdiction trumping State jurisdiction and search warrants and crime scenes seemed to be all out-ranked by a Federal Court injunction issued against both levels of law-enforcement ordering the contents of the lab to be given to the lawyer representing the US Government."

"So that lawyer won?" the wife asked, "The US Government got the contents of the lab?"

"I thought so," the Special Agent said. "I mean it took an hour or so of argument and everything, but in the end, there was just no way around that kind of Federal injunction."

The Special Agent poured himself a second cup of coffee.

"We were getting ready to go," he said taking a big gulp. "But then we heard a whole lot of sirens coming towards us."

"Sirens?" the wife asked incredulously.

"Well about a dozen military police came in, and then this highly decorated soldier walks in and says, 'I'm Major General Frank Collins. Dr Jamieson from the Australian pharmaceutical company known as DrugTech has just spoken with the Defence Minister and an Infrastructure Declaration has just been made under the *Defence Act* in respect of this shack and everything in it. It is all now seized by the Australian Military. I must ask you all to step outside."

"Unbelievable!" his wife replied. "Then what happened?"

"Well, we all went outside and started asking, 'Who the hell is this Dr Jamieson guy?' and 'Where do we all go from here?'"

"Well?" his wife asked, "Where did you all go?"

"The only place left that seemed to have jurisdiction to deal with the matter," he said taking another gulp of coffee. "We all went to the pub."

Chapter 13

The Compassionate Murderer

Macey was having a very bad day. As a single woman with a three-month old baby, she had found it incredibly difficult to juggle work and child-minding services with her mother. She worked as a bookkeeper at Miller and Davis Bio-Electrics. On this particular Friday, she was forced to leave work at 4:30pm to pick-up her daughter from her mother who had a late afternoon appointment, but Macey was forced to return to work at 6:30pm that evening with her baby in tow in order to collect some items that she needed to work-on that evening.

It was now about 7pm, and leaving work with her baby under one arm and a satchel under the other, she entered the elevator on the 21st floor. As the doors closed, she dropped her satchel on the ground, and started rocking her baby with both arms who was starting to become a little irritable. The elevator stopped at the 19th floor and a black man with a leather jacket and dreadlocked hair with a cloth bag slung over his shoulder entered. He nodded hello at the occupant, but Macey's first thought was to pretend that she had not noticed and she decided not to make direct eye contact with the stranger.

Somewhere between the 16th and 17th floors, the gears of the elevator let out a tremendous groan and the elevator car seemed to buckle, with the back part of the car falling below the front part where it scraped along the lift shaft and skidded to a stop. The carriage remained off balance tilting slightly backwards.

"That didn't sound good at all," the man said as he tapped the open-door button several times. "I think we are stuck." The man started pressing the alarm button and several other buttons on the elevator panel, but there was no response.

At that moment, Macey felt very protective of her child and started to fear the stranger who was trapped in the lift with her.

"I'll call police-rescue," she said bending down to pick her satchel up off the floor.

"Oh, you can't call the police, lady," the man said looking a little defensive.

"Nonsense," she said finding her phone and dialling emergency. She tried several times. "No signal," she said.

"Inside the lift shaft, I don't think you can get a signal," the man said.

The man opened the panel door just under the elevator buttons and picked up the phone that was inside.

"This is a recorded message," the voice on the other end of the phone said. "The automatic distress beacon has been activated. Your elevator carriage and your location have been reported to elevator repair personnel who are now on their way to you. You shall be contacted shortly. Please stay calm." The message repeated itself.

It was not necessary for Macey to hold the phone to her ear; she had heard the message through the speaker. After shaking her head when the phone was offered to her, the man returned the phone to the cabinet and shut the door.

"Well, that's just perfect," Macey said in exasperation. "I've brought home work that was supposed to have been done yesterday. If I don't submit it tonight, I will probably get fired!"

At this point in time, the woman's baby started crying.

"Look, I have to feed her," the woman said in desperation.

"Go right ahead," the man said before realizing that the woman meant she needed to breastfeed her baby. "Oh," he said, "I'll just turn around."

The man turned to face the front of the lift. "I think we are going to be here for quite some time," the man said sitting on the floor.

Macey also sat on the floor and started breastfeeding her child.

"Look lady, I have an unopened bottle of water here," the man said fishing around in his cloth bag. Without looking backwards, he swung the bottle behind him and placed it on the floor between himself and the woman.

"No thank you," Macey said feeling quite nervous. There was obvious fear in her voice and she did not trust the stranger. And even though she was extremely parched, especially whilst breastfeeding, she decided to decline the invitation.

"What's the real reason you didn't want me to call police-rescue?" the woman asked quite boldly wishing to get her fear out into the open. "You didn't know I wouldn't get mobile phone reception in here when you said that. What did you do, kill a man?"

The question was blurted out almost sarcastically. Macey's character was to put her cards on the table when she was frightened. She was not really expecting a response.

"No lady, I think I killed three men," the man replied.

"Oh my God," the woman gasped.

An awkward pause followed. After a few minutes Macey put her daughter on her lap and started rocking her to sleep.

"So how come you killed three men?" Macey asked, her voice still quivering with fear.

"They were members of a gang, I knew them," the man said. "I was sitting in my van parked on the side of the road when they walked past and I heard them talking about the schoolgirl about 50 meters in front of them. The schoolgirl was about 12 years old. I wasn't prepared to let them hurt the girl. So, as they crossed the road to head towards the schoolgirl, I ran them over with my van."

Macey did not know what to believe. After a short pause she asked, "So if it was in defence of the schoolgirl, why don't you just explain it all to the police?" she asked.

"Because I have stage four terminal cancer," the man replied. "I'm going to be dead soon anyway. I just don't want to spend the last few days I have in a police cell or in jail awaiting trial."

As the man was sitting on the floor, he started to cradle his stomach and lean to one side. Macey noticed a small pool of blood towards his left side.

"You are bleeding," she said. Her initial thought was to stay as far away from the blood as possible, as it might contain any number of transmissible diseases.

"As I came into this building tonight," the man said now not trying to hide the growing agony in his voice, "I got mugged."

"You got mugged?" Macey repeated.

"Yeah, a group of boys took the cash I had in my wallet and one of them stabbed me," he said.

Macey took the bonnet off her daughter who was now fast asleep. "Do you want this?" she said offering the man the bonnet.

"Thanks," the man said taking the bonnet and pressing it to his wound. His shirt under the leather jacket was drenched in blood.

"Do you want to clean the wound with the water?" Macey asked looking again at the bottle of water.

"No, you have it," the man said. "I think the bleeding will stop soon anyway."

Macey couldn't hold out any longer. She took the bottle of water and started drinking it.

"How long have you been on the run from the police?" Macey asked.

"Three days now," he said.

"Don't you have any family or friends who can help you?" she asked.

"No," the man replied not wishing to elaborate.

Macey felt a little sorry for the stranger and tried to change the subject. "I'm a bookkeeper," she said. "I need this job to pay the mortgage on my apartment."

The man shuffled back and to the side so he could now sit with his back against the wall. But he stayed huddled over cradling the wound in his abdomen.

"What do you do?" Macey asked.

"I'm a courier," the man replied. "I just dropped off a package on the 19th floor."

"So let me get this straight," Macey said looking a little confused. "You're on the run from the police, you got stabbed by a group of boys, you're dying of cancer, but you still delivered a package to the 19th floor?"

"Yeah," the man said. "I had the package and I know people are relying on their couriers to deliver it, so I just wanted to finish what I started."

Macey couldn't believe what she was hearing. Either the man was some kind of selfless saint, or he just couldn't be taken at his word.

"I think we are going to be here for a while," the man said, "I think I will just have a little sleep now."

"Aren't you supposed to stay awake or something?" Macey asked.

"I think that's for head injuries," the man replied tilting his head back and closing his eyes.

Macey had not really looked into his eyes before, but catching a glimpse of them, they appeared to be bloodshot.

At this point, Macey picked her mobile phone up again. "I wonder if I can at least get a text out," Macey said trying madly to send a text. "At least let my boss know I am stuck in his lift," she said emphasizing the word 'his'.

"Would he really fire you if you don't get that thing submitted tonight?" the man asked.

"I think he would," Macey replied feeling a little depressed.

"I can give you something," the man said as he reached for his wallet in his back pocket.

"I thought the boys took your money," she said almost defiantly.

"They did," the man said. He opened up his wallet and there was no money in it. "But they didn't take this."

The man opened a small compartment in the wallet and pulled out a lottery ticket. "Take it," the man said. "It is a winning ticket. It is worth one million dollars. Take it, I can't use it. I am dying anyway and I have no friends or family. So just take it."

The man dropped the ticket on the floor between them. He then leaned his head backwards and letting out a slight sigh, he breathed his last.

Chapter 14

The Contessa Medici

Benjamin Jones did not like corporate governance much. He was a scientist. Being the Managing Director of DrugTech was to him a necessary evil to allow him to pursue his dream of scientific discovery. But having recently accepted the position of Managing Director, the young Dr Benjamin Jones was prepared to do all that was required of him both for the company's success and his own. His predecessor, Dr Jamieson was a calculating and ruthless businessman and cared little for scientific discovery. As a Nobel laureate in biochemistry, Dr Jamieson spoke more about economics and power than the Nobel laureate in economics.

Dr Jamieson had taken the company from financial success to financial success and the board members were only too pleased to allow him to do so. The well-connected Dr Jamieson had managed to ward off several hostile takeovers but none was more determined than a particular international company known as Medici Pharmaceuticals.

Medici Pharmaceuticals had its global headquarters in Ireland and its Managing Director was the famous Contessa Medici. She had an Italian heritage and an Italian rank but she was as Irish as the Cliffs of Moher. Her Irish family had Irish names, but the Contessa enjoyed her rank and its privileges and she used them to her advantage as she ruled her company with an iron fist. In the years that Dr Jamieson was head of DrugTech, there was only one reason that Medici Pharmaceuticals had not launched a successful hostile takeover of DrugTech. That reason was Dr Jamieson.

Dr Jones knew he had big shoes to fill. The board members were particularly keen to avoid a hostile takeover. A hostile takeover usually meant a new board of directors, which would of course leave them out of a job. The Contessa Medici had travelled to Australia and she had organised a meeting with Dr Jones. Obviously, she wanted to talk about a takeover. She did not need DrugTech's board approval, but she would prefer it. Usually, the shareholders would vote in favour of a takeover if the price was right but the shareholders always wished to avoid a managerial bloodbath. The board of directors on the other hand usually always resisted being taken over. Several of them were wary of Dr Jones' corporate ability in outwitting or outmanoeuvring the notorious Contessa Medici.

The boardroom meeting discussing the various issues of a hostile takeover within DrugTech had just concluded and Dr Jones returned to his office awaiting several reports from various corporate personnel. If there were several things that Dr Jones was weak at, doing his research and homework was certainly not one of them. The meeting with the Contessa was scheduled for morning tea at the café on the corner of Elizabeth St and Park St in the Sydney CBD. The meeting was too formal for an office meeting, too hostile for a dinner meeting and too important for a telephone meeting or videoconference. In such a situation, such corporate meetings took place in coffee shops. This meeting was to be between the Contessa Medici and Dr Jones alone.

"Who's first?" Dr Jones asked Dr Patel who would often fill the role of Dr Jones' personal assistant.

"The first report is on the Contessa's history of corporate takeovers all over the world and a group of economists and stockbrokers wish some time with you tonight to update you on her previous attempts to takeover DrugTech. Dr Jamieson had used several poison pills to avoid the takeovers by borrowing heavily and granting rights to shareholders and staff and allowing them to acquire more shares at substantially reduced prices and redistributing the voting rights."

"Why can't we just do that again?" Benjamin Jones asked.

"They say it won't work this time because Medici Pharmaceuticals has recently come into a lot of money and this time, they think they will just swallow whatever poison pill you throw at them."

"It's the Trans Warp Inducer you know," Benjamin said softly. "Medici Pharmaceuticals have always been interested in DrugTech but because of our possession of the Trans Warp Inducer and the potential power that that could unlock, they now want us at all costs. Maybe we should try some sort of angle with that?"

"Well, if you give them that I think they will agree to back off," Saanvi Patel said. "And since it doesn't work yet and may never ever work, the economists here would love you forever. But I think the scientific guild would go on strike. They would see that as a complete capitulation and it would tear the company apart. They'd say you threw the baby out with the bathwater."

"Who's after the economists and stockbrokers?" Dr Jones asked.

"The next report is from the chief scientists and their understanding of the state of Medici Pharmaceuticals' scientific breakthroughs," Saanvi said. "If DrugTech is seen by the shareholders as being far ahead of Medici on the scientific field, the shareholders might reject the price that Medici offers on any hostile takeover."

"Is that likely?" Benjamin asked.

"Probably not," Saanvi answered. "The scientists want to brief you on what breakthroughs Medici Pharmaceuticals have made. I hear it's fairly impressive. They will also update you on where we are at and what we are ready to announce to the market in response."

"And then what?" Benjamin enquired further.

"After that the lawyers want about an hour or an hour and a half with you," Saanvi said. "They want to brief you on your legal options as well as their research in how the Contessa Medici has dealt with political and legal interference in the past. I'm told she can be quite ruthless and only Dr Jamieson with his political connections had been able to resist her."

"Talk about a swamp," Benjamin said shaking his head and flicking the report that he had been studying off to his side. "I don't have the same connections that Jamieson had."

"After the lawyers, our contract private detectives have prepared a report on the Contessa and her family and their personal lives. There might be some angle there for you to manoeuvre also, or at the very least," Saanvi said, "You should familiarise yourself with that aspect of her life as well."

"Ask them to bring me all their written reports," Benjamin Jones said attempting to make a clearing on his desk. "I'll study them the best I can before the meetings and then I will study them more tonight. I intend to be fully prepared for the meeting tomorrow."

With that Saanvi left her boss as a line of corporate personnel from different departments started making their way into his office carrying several folders and leaving without them. Saanvi did not envy her boss' workload and was thankful to be occupied mostly in the scientific aspects of the company. She wondered if her boss would return home that evening.

The following day, a rather dishevelled and tired-looking Benjamin Jones shuffled in to the café on the corner of Elizabeth St and Park St.

"The Contessa Medici I presume," Dr Jones said as he approached a 63-year-old woman, elegantly dressed in a business suit and pearl necklace with Prada shoes. "I'm Dr Jones."

She rose from her chair as the two shook hands. Upon sitting down again, a young waitress attended to take their order.

"We will have two skim flat whites," the Contessa said.

"I'm impressed," Benjamin said, "You obviously have studied me as much as I have studied you."

"Of course," the Contessa said matter-of-factly. "Shall we get down to it? Tomorrow we wish to announce a takeover bid of DrugTech. I would like it to be with the approval of the board of directors but if it is not, we will do it anyway. I will not bore you with the price we are offering or attempt to negotiate that with you now; I will leave you with our full report and your people can talk to my people about that later."

"Many of the board of directors are concerned about their position?" Dr Jones said.

"If the takeover is amicable," the Contessa replied expecting the question, "Half of them can stay but the other half will be replaced by our people. Control of the company will be with us."

"You have obviously done your homework," Benjamin stammered. "What would my predecessor have said?"

This time the Contessa smiled at the question.

"That cunning devil," she said. "Well, if you must know, he would have leaned on the Finance Minister to block the takeover as not being in the best interests of Australia."

"Well?" Benjamin replied. "Is it?" he asked, "In the best interests of Australia I mean?"

"I have just come from a meeting with the Treasurer and the Finance Minister," she said. "And they agree that it is. There is no political problem whatsoever."

"I can stop you," Benjamin said looking the Contessa Medici directly in her eyes, "Or at least make life very difficult for you," he stammered before looking away.

"I know all about you," the Contessa replied. "Dr Benjamin Jones, previously a student of Sydney University. I know your parents were counsellors at DrugTech. And don't try anything either," she said squinting her eyes and lowering her voice. "I know all about your bag of tricks from the scientific guild of your company. Your Project X23, your Project Spectrum 77 and the like. They won't work on me."

Benjamin Jones was amazed but he pretended to take it in his stride. "I know all about you too Contessa," he replied without altering his voice. "I have studied your family, your private life, and their private lives."

"Is that supposed to be some sort of threat?" the Contessa asked hardly amused.

"Not at all," Benjamin said smiling sweetly. "I have a simple proposal for you."

"What's that?" the Contessa said bracing herself.

"You can have DrugTech," Benjamin said almost dismissively. "You can replace as many of the board of directors as you want. I won't fight you. But the company will keep its name 'DrugTech' and I will stay on as the Managing Director of the Australian Branch of the new multi-billion-dollar conglomerate. I am happy to confine most of my duties to scientific research anyway."

"And what's the price for such a generous offer?" the Contessa asked waiting to hear what Benjamin's research had led him to.

"The price," Benjamin said remembering his university days and thinking about his future. "The price is your daughter Kathleen's hand in marriage to me."

Chapter 15

A Day in the Life of a DrugTech Counsellor

The counsellors at DrugTech were a rare and precious breed. Rarely, if ever, was a counsellor brought in from outside. Usually, they were company personnel nearing their retirement age who had a good working understanding of the requirements of the job, the role of the company and the needs of the staff. Such personnel, if acceptable, and upon obtaining the necessary professional qualifications, would be permitted a transfer to the counsellor role.

One such counsellor was Dr Jeremy Pitts who was in the twilight years of his life having worked previously at DrugTech in the field of red blood cell research and the ever-expanding role of MRI machines in biotechnical sciences. From within the company, Dr Pitts was a devout and loyal servant. He had their back. He was one of them through and through and helped guide the scientists, employees and their departments through the evermore-complicated minefields of legal ethics, public opinion and social wellbeing.

Dr Pitts had a brass plaque outside his therapy room setting out his philosophy. It was read by all and encouraged free and open communication. The plaque read:

"What we say here,
What we hear here,
When we leave here,
Stays here".

And by such doctor-patient confidentiality could the patient and doctor sleep-well at night. Dr Pitts always slept well at night. He discharged his counsellor duties with typical aplomb. And on a typical dreary afternoon he had only a few more clients scheduled to see him at which point he would return home to a waiting dinner, a night-time scotch, and an evening paper.

"Next!" Dr Pitts would yell into his intercom to his young assistant outside his room who presided over the slightly bigger-waiting room. The intercom was not really necessary given the volume at which he would yell the word owing much to his advanced age but Dr Pitts ran things his way.

As the last patient left, another patient entered and was directed to a sofa adjacent the rather large desk that Dr Pitts would sit at.

"What can I do you for?" he enquired of his patient.

The patient was a young good-looking scientist, a man in his early thirties, fit and muscular and had a security clearance of level two.

"I think we are near a breakthrough in the lab," he began with muted enthusiasm. "We have manufactured a serum that could be used in social settings. In particular, when a guy is dating a girl. With the pheromones at play, it can help breakdown the girl's inhibitions and leave her much more confident to act on her animal instincts so to speak."

"We already have that son," Dr Pitts replied, "It's called alcohol."

"Oh no," the scientist retorted, "Oh no, this is much more effective and much better too. Alcohol leaves you dreary and tired and intoxicated, but this makes you happy and excited and fully in charge of your senses; it just makes you want to, well, you-know, jump on the guy!"

"So, it's like ecstasy then?" Dr Pitts enquired.

"No, no," the scientist said looking a little flustered. "It has no intoxicating effect on the blood at all. This works by opening up certain neurotransmitters in the brain to be much more effective and efficient."

"OK fine," Dr Pitts said sounding somewhat convinced. "I guess there could be a market for that kind of thing, but the authorities would never approve a drug that you could just hand out in that kind of social setting and I'm pretty certain the law would not allow you to administer such a drug without the female's consent."

"Yes doctor," the young scientist replied. "That's why I was told to see you."

"Well, your job," the doctor said scribbling-down a few notes and talking in-between pen strokes, "Is to make the drug potent in an aerosolised form. We can then market it as another 'irresistible perfume' for men or something. Keep me updated on your progress, will you? Next!" the doctor shouted into his intercom that his assistant heard quite clearly through the door.

As the young scientist left, a grey-haired woman in a lab coat entered and sat on the sofa. From the notes that were transmitted to his computer, Dr Pitts could see that she was an animal researcher with a level 3-security clearance.

"What can I do you for?" the doctor repeated his usual mantra.

"We have discovered ways of utilizing the nose of a dog into a computer," the scientist began getting right down to it. "A dog's nose is about a million times more powerful than our own and hundreds of thousands of times more powerful than any existing computer."

"So why would we need that when we can just use dogs to sniff out cadavers or drugs or escaped criminals?" Dr Pitts asked also coming straight to the point.

"Well through our inter-company dialog, we have learnt that Lockheed Martin is developing autonomous machines to send into the theatre of war," she said trying not to sound too excited.

"You mean terminator machines?"

"I guess so, yes," she replied. "They are working on telescopic and infra-red camera technology to hunt down their prey, but our dog-nose assisted computer technology would make those machines a million times more effective. It would be impossible for any human target to hide from them."

"So, what's the problem?" Dr Pitts asked agreeing that such an advancement would be profitable to the company.

"Well, the problem is that it means keeping the dog in a comatose state while we insert electrodes into its nose and brain. If it dies the nose stops working you see. And if the dog is conscious, it's no use to us either. But the dog would never be normal again, it would be the ultimate sacrifice and would have to be all boxed-up inside the robot or terminator."

"I see, I see," Dr Pitts said nodding as he appreciated the problem. "The anti-vivisectionists would go crazy. Yes, that could create quite a political storm that could kill the project."

"I agree," the scientist said, "That's why I thought I should see you doctor."

The doctor started scribbling some notes. "Leave it with me," he said. "I will send someone up to you with level six-security clearance. They have found a way to genetically engineer animal brains and keep them alive after removing them from the animal. If you had just the dog nose and the living brain, then you could insert your electrodes into them without the rest of the political baggage; it could be sold politically as stray or sick dogs donating their organs for the good of the armed forces."

"Oh, thank you," she said this time with more enthusiasm that she cared to show.

"Next!" the doctor screamed.

Dr Pitts' next patient was a 49-year-old scientist with a level four-security clearance.

"What can I do you for?" the doctor asked again.

"There is a Public Inquiry going on into corruption of several Government officials and politicians," he began. "They are looking at political or administrative favours granted to corporations. The Feds have camped outside our Western Australian lab waiting to serve subpoenas on anyone entering or leaving that building. We suspect that any moment now they will go on in with search warrants."

"So, what's the problem?" the doctor asked. "DrugTech has always managed to stay above board?"

"My problem is not with the Inquiry *per se*," the scientist replied. "I just have to relay a top-secret formula to my counterpart in Western Australia for a time-sensitive experiment. If I transmit it to him, it will be intercepted by the Feds. If I send someone to see him, I can't risk him being served with a subpoena and being forced to disclose the formula to the inquiry."

"I see," the Counsellor said leaning back into his chair and closing his eyes for the moment. "I heard of something similar to this in the sixties."

The counsellor stood and walked to his filing cabinet where he retrieved a file from the back of the top drawer.

"I'll send the company chaplain over to see you. Major Davis is a highly decorated and retired veteran and military chaplain during the Vietnam war," he said looking through the file. "You can tell him the formula and he'll relay it to your counterpart in Western Australia. If he's served with any legal process by the Feds, he can resist it on the grounds that no Inquiry can compel a priest to disclose anything said in a religious confession."

"OK great!" the scientist said as he rose looking much relieved.

It had been a long day, and the Counsellor looked at his watch before calling for the last patient of the day.

The next patient was a doctor with level five-security clearance. She was a physician who worked in the immunological sciences department.

"What can I do you for?" Dr Pitts enquired.

"I have a slight problem," she began with a few tears welling in her eyes. "My niece has just been born and is in the hospital adjoining DrugTech. The doctors don't know it yet, but I observed the way the baby was breastfeeding and a few other symptoms and I suspected that she had Type I diabetes. So, I tested some of her blood and I was correct but I carefully did not share that diagnoses with anyone."

"I see," Dr Pitts said looking concerned. "Go on."

"Well, confidentially, a Dr Patel in my department has found a cure for this doctor," she said. "I have done my research and have confirmed that legally, we don't need a TGA approval to release a medication for personal reasons if it is not being marketed to the public for profit. And anyway, I can administer the medication myself before work tomorrow morning without anyone ever finding out. No one would ever know that the baby ever had the condition. It can remain confidential."

"Sounds good to me," Dr Pitts said looking at his watch, "So what's the problem?"

"Well, nothing really," the patient replied somewhat surprised. "But before releasing the medication to me, I was told to run it by you first."

"Well, I see no problem," Dr Pitts replied. "These things are sanctioned by the Company when it is a last resort. Type I diabetes cannot be cured otherwise. See me an hour before work begins tomorrow and I will have it ready for you, but you must agree to keep it absolutely confidential."

"Of course, doctor, absolutely," she said as she rose and left his room.

It had been a long and successful day for Dr Pitts. He completed his notes and returned any open files to his filing cabinet. He left his room and closed the door behind him.

"Good night," he said to his assistant as he grabbed his hat and his scarf from the hat stand.

"Goodnight, Dr Pitts," his assistant said as she was completing her computer entries for the day.

As he was about to leave the room, Dr Pitts turned and said, "Listen, type an email for the Managing Director to let that last patient go, will you?" He asked as he wrapped the scarf around his neck, "She's too unstable for DrugTech."

"Sure thing, Dr Pitts," his assistant said without looking up.

Chapter 16

The Confession

Mrs O'Leary awoke in a police-holding cell. She had been arrested last night at a pub on suspicion of the murder of her husband. Being slightly intoxicated, the police did not conduct the standard electronically recorded interview at the police station that evening, but waited until this morning for her to reach an acceptable level of sobriety when she was brought into the interview room with two male plainclothes detectives.

"Mrs O'Leary, we want you to know that this interview is being recorded. You are not obliged to answer our questions, but if you do answer our questions, anything you say will be recorded and it may be used as evidence against you. Do you understand that?"

"Yes," she replied rather sheepishly. "I don't mind, I'm happy to answer your questions. I am a little tired though. Can we hurry this up?"

"We can suspend the interview now if you wish us to allow you to rest?" the Detective asked politely.

"No," she said, "I'd rather get it over and done with."

"And you mentioned to me last night that you do not wish to call a lawyer," the Detective said. "Is that still the case?"

"Yes," she said. "I don't want a lawyer."

"For the purposes of the recording, my name is Detective Sergeant Cambridge and I am present with Detective Constable Manning. The time is now 10:30am. Before us is Mrs Patricia O'Leary who has voluntarily agreed to conduct this record of interview."

At this point the Detective Sergeant nodded to the Detective Constable to proceed with the interview.

"Mrs O'Leary, last night we declared your residence a Crime Scene and among other things, we seized the computers that were in your house," the Constable began.

"Yes," Mrs O'Leary said looking rather dazed.

"We noticed that about 3 months ago, you took out a 20-million-dollar insurance policy on your husband," the Constable continued. "That is rather a lot of money to insure a simple butcher. Why would you take out an insurance policy like that on your husband?"

Mrs O'Leary started fiddling with the fingernails on her right hand and seemed rather uninterested in the question.

"I took out a large insurance policy on my husband because I intended to kill him and cash-in on the money," she said rather nonchalantly. "He did manage to pay the mortgage and keep the bills paid and I figured I would need some money after he was gone."

Both of the detectives were not expecting such an admission so quickly into the interview. They both looked at the camera to ensure that the light was on and that there was no hiccup with the recording.

"How were you planning to kill him?" the constable continued.

"Well, my husband kept an unregistered gun under the seat of his car," she said. "At first I took his gun and put it in my chest of drawers."

"We found that gun Mrs O'Leary," the Constable said, "and the Crime Lab confirmed your fingerprints on the weapon."

Mrs O'Leary nodded her head still playing with her fingernails.

"Next to the gun we found a vial of insulin and a needle and also in the drawer we found some noxious white powder. Do you know what that white power is?"

"Yes," she said. "It's arsenic."

"What were you planning on doing with arsenic or insulin?" the Constable asked, "No one in your family is a diabetic."

“Well, you have my computers,” she said. “If you analyse them, you will see that I was Googling ways on the best way to poison someone.”

“When did you get them?” the Detective asked.

“The insulin I got about a month ago when a friend of mine accidently left it behind in the living room. The arsenic I found last week in my husband’s garage,” she answered putting her hands by her side and slumping back in her chair. As she looked up to face the police officers and the camera, her eyes were rather bloodshot.

“Mrs O’Leary,” the Constable said, “Why don’t you just tell us in your own words what happened last night.”

“Well, my husband Sam recently installed a cold-room in our house. He figured he would buy his meat from the abattoirs in the afternoon when prices were cheap. He would keep them in the cold-room at home over night and then take them to his butchery the following morning.”

“Go on,” the Detective Constable said.

“Well last night, I was walking home from across the park, and I noticed the front door wide open and my husband’s van doors wide open. So, I walked inside and I heard my husband calling me from inside the cool-room.”

“What did he say?” the Constable asked.

“He said: ‘Patricia can you let me out. The wind blew the door shut and the inside latch is not working.’

I said: ‘How long have you been in there?’

He said:‘Not long, I just put the meat down and a gust of wind shut the door. It’s freezing in here, please open the door.’

I said: ‘You know what? I’m not going to. I hope you freeze to death.’”

Mrs O'Leary smiled to herself as she recalled the incident. "Then he started swearing at me the same way he always does and so I started taking some selfies of myself next to the cold-room door."

"Then what happened?" the Detective asked rather shocked.

"Then I just walked straight out the way I came," she said. "I didn't touch the freezer door. I didn't touch the front door, I left it open. And I didn't touch his van, I left those doors open too. I left the place as I found it and I just walked straight out. My handbag was still on my shoulder so I went to the pub to celebrate."

The Detective Constable looked at the Detective Sergeant and they nodded to each other.

"Mrs O'Leary, the Crime Lab says that your husband's fingerprints were on the outside of the cold-room door handle, which means that you didn't touch the handle after your husband entered," the Detective Constable said.

"Yes, I didn't touch the handle," Mrs O'Leary said.

"But how do we know that you didn't kick the door shut when he was inside?" the Detective asked.

"Well, you know what?" she said contemplating the idea. "I probably would have if I had that opportunity, but like he said, the wind must have blown it shut."

"The time is now 10:30am and I am suspending the interview," the Sergeant said as he turned the camera off. "Please wait right here Mrs O'Leary, we will be back shortly."

The two police officers walked to the Sergeant's office across the corridor from the interview room.

"We have a problem," the Sergeant said. "That dragon lady hasn't actually confessed to a crime. She is only relaying a tragic accident."

"Oh, come on Serge," the junior police officer remonstrated. "Even if what she says is true, she didn't open the door. She didn't call the cops. She just went and celebrated and that's even after taking selfies!"

"But that's just it, you see," the Sergeant said. "There is no duty to rescue. She was actually under no legal obligation to open the door or to call the cops."

"Well, what about that case we once prosecuted of a man who had two prostitutes in a hotel?" the Constable asked. "They all took cocaine and one of the prostitutes died. That was a tragic accident too, but we got him on manslaughter."

"That was slightly different," the Sergeant said, "In that case they were behind the locked door of the hotel and their failure to report the incident prevented any possible rescue from occurring behind that locked door. But in this case, the front door of her house was well and truly left open. She didn't shut it. She didn't interfere with any phone lines or anything?"

"OK then," the Constable said, "Why can't we allege that she kicked the door shut. No jury would acquit her after what she has just confessed to, she's like the wife from hell."

"I don't think we'd be able to get it before a jury," the Sergeant said. "Maybe she did kick the door shut. But maybe she didn't. Without any kind of proof, the judge will toss the case even before a jury gets to deliberate. The law gives her the benefit of the doubt."

"Well, we can at least get her on possession of the unregistered gun, and the insulin without a prescription and the arsenic?" the Constable enquired looking rather cheated.

"We will look into that," the Sergeant said, "But it was her husband's gun and her friend's insulin and her husband's arsenic. I am not sure we are there on possession."

"So, what then?" the Constable asked. "We just let her go?"

"I think so," the Sergeant said. "We can keep looking of course, but at the moment we have nothing."

"I can't believe it," the junior police officer said.

"That's not the worst thing," the Sergeant said.

"What do you mean?" the Constable inquired.

"The worst thing," the Sergeant said, "Is that she will probably get away with her $20 million insurance claim when she puts that in too!"

Chapter 11

The Scientist and the Priest

The scientist, Bruce, was taken under prison guard for an appointment with a specialist to the neurological wing of the hospital adjoining DrugTech. He was to be assessed for the purposes of the *Mental Health Act* to determine whether he would be released from his incarceration after his successful insanity defence at his relatively recent murder trial. DrugTech had petitioned the relevant authorities for his release in order to secure his help in the experiment regarding the Trans Warp Inducer which had come at considerable expense to the Company.

The waiting room of the specialist was always packed with patients and clients (not necessarily waiting patiently) to see the specialist who was often called upon for his expert reports to disentangle the legal webs associated with antisocial behaviour connected somehow with neurological conditions. And Scientist Bruce's discomfort was particularly heightened by the presence of a priest in a traditional priestly collar seated next to the only vacant seat that would soon be occupied by the scientist.

Removing his handcuffs and having escorted the scientist to his seat, the prison guards were more than content to wait outside. The scientist shook his embarrassment from the several glances of patients and their support personnel who all turned to view the odd spectacle, but the murmur of chatter did not desist and the scientist sought to deflect his predicament by turning himself and addressing his chief discomfort directly.

"What brings a priest to a neurological specialist?" the scientist began with obvious disdain.

"Oh, I'm not here for him," the priest answered with surprising mirth, "I am here for the patients."

"Oh?" the scientist queried, "And what about the patients? You going to pray for them?"

"Some more than others," the Priest quipped, "And you look like you could do with a great deal," the priest said smilingly.

"I don't believe in religion," the scientist retorted, "I believe in science."

"Oh really?" the Priest enquired. "And what is it about science that you worship?"

"Well since you ask priest," the scientist began, "I just so happen to be working on the most important discovery in the history of the world, ever! It's a breakthrough that will unleash the power of physics in a way that has never before even been imagined."

"Well at best I would half agree with you," the priest replied.

"What do you mean, half agree with me?" the scientist enquired.

"Well, there are breakthroughs to be made in physics for sure," the priest answered. "But the most important discovery in the history of the world, ever?" the priest questioned, "That belongs to the realm of metaphysics, not physics."

"You know it would take a religious zealot to say something like that," the scientist said smugly and slightly offended, "Only the scientific community can truly appreciate breakthroughs in physics."

"I beg to differ with you on that point," the priest retorted. "Physics is material by nature, it is rooted in the concrete. Anyone can appreciate breakthroughs in that. But metaphysics is beyond the physical order. Only the true intellect can appreciate that."

"Ahh now that's where you're wrong priest," the scientist replied. "Only a truly gifted person in physics can possibly appreciate the value of physics."

"You mean like Albert Einstein?" the priest asked.

"Yes Albert Einstein," the scientist answered. "But not just him. Niels Bohr, Werner Heisenberg, Erwin Schrodinger, Robert Hofstadter, all of them Nobel laureates in physics and all of them making some contribution to the science."

"There was a saying in the Middle Ages," the priest argued, "That an appeal to authority was the weakest argument of all. There are a great many famous metaphysicians in history too you know? Aristotle, Plato, St Paul, St Augustine, Thomas Aquinas."

"Yes, but none of them understand physics you see," the scientist retorted.

"But if they did understand science," the priest enquired tilting his head slightly, "You think they would agree with you that science is the most important thing ever?"

"Of course," the scientist replied. "How could they not? And it just so happens that the specialist will write a report about my breakthrough in physics and the world will see again that breakthroughs in physics are the most important thing ever."

"Ahh but" the priest retorted looking somewhat confused, "He is a specialist in neurology. And by your argument, you need someone who understands physics to ratify your work."

The scientist had the priest right where he wanted him and he smiled his broadest smile while exhaling loudly and deeply to achieve an expression of maximum satire.

"Well, as a matter of fact," the scientist finally answered, "He is introducing me to Sir Charles Maxwell the most recent Nobel laureate in physics who only last year advanced Einstein's theory on general relativity."

The scientist was interrupted by a man in a white coat clearing his throat from behind. He turned to see the specialist holding a clipboard and surveying his notes accompanied by a female nurse.

"Are you Bruce the Scientist?" the specialist enquired.

“Yes, indeed I am,” the scientist replied somewhat enjoying his title.

“Oh good,” the specialist replied. “I am glad you two have met,” the specialist said indicating the priest with a flick of his head. “This is Sir Charles Maxwell, the man I wanted you to meet.”

Chapter 18

The Airport Kaprekar

Professor Philip was lamenting the commencement of exam-paper-marking in his private office at Sydney University when the two so-called detectives that once introduced themselves as investigators in the Martin Hanson suicide re-appeared at his door. And that immediately caused Philip to remember the last conversation he had had with his friend Charlie. Charlie had left for a sabbatical in Israel and was due to return any day now.

"Excuse us Professor," the two elegantly dressed detectives began, "a moment of your time again if you please?"

"Ah, detectives," Philip responded somewhat sarcastically but also a little cautiously. "How goes the police investigation into Martin Hanson? Are you still at the Surry Hills Police station?"

The man and the woman exchanged glances as if expecting the question. The man replied, "We know that you telephoned the Surry Hills police station when we left."

"Let's just say we are consultants with the police," the woman interjected.

Philip did not know what to think. He doubted the police would need 'consultants' but he was also mindful of Charlie's cautious suspicion about the well-dressed detectives who were inquiring into Martin's affiliation with DrugTech. He decided to appear outwardly calm.

"How can I help you?" Philip asked nonchalantly moving a stack of exam papers off to the side.

"Charlie Horovitz has just been arrested," the woman answered. "He is currently being held at the Surry Hills Police Station."

Philip was stunned. "Arrested, what for?" he asked.

"He is in possession of a highly classified chemical," the man responded. "In the wrong hands, it could be fatal to a lot of people. All we want is to get it back."

"I'm not following," Philip replied. "What would Charlie want with anything like that?"

"Someone we were following connected with the Hanson case had stolen a stone from a lab at DrugTech. We believe it is radioactive and unless handled properly, it could pose a real danger to the community," the man replied. "Now either Charlie had something to do with it being stolen, or the thief simply sought Charlie out to analyse it, but either way, we know that Charlie knows where it is but he is not talking. Our main concern is just to retrieve it safely."

"Well, how can I help?" Philip asked somewhat surprised. "I don't know anything about this."

"Yes, we know that," the man said reassuringly, "We just want you to wear a wire and go talk with Charlie."

Philip remembered the first time he had met Charlie outside the bioscience labs on the sixth floor of the building above Philip's office many years ago. He was a hothead then and apparently prone to crazy ideas. "Nothing seems to have changed in that regard," Philip thought to himself. But Philip then remembered his last conversation with Charlie a few months ago when Charlie seemed dubious about the very 'detectives' asking about Martin Hanson and Charlie's conjecture regarding the 'suicide drug' from Leo Mitch and Morley that was taken-over by DrugTech. Something inside Philip distrusted the visitors in his office, however, he decided to play along for the moment.

"What makes you think he will talk to me?" Philip enquired.

"We know he trusts you," the woman answered. "In Charlie's mind, it's us against him. Seeing you might get him to open up to an ally, someone on his side."

"There are many lives at stake here, Professor," the man interrupted. "If we can't recover the stone in time, Charlie will be charged with terrorism related offences. He could go to jail for life. But if we can recover it fast and safely, it could be a simple goods in custody charge. With his good record and releasing him into your recognizances, we'd probably let him off with a warning. But it's very important we act now."

"Well, how would we do this?" Professor Philip asked.

"It's simple," the woman answered. "Just come with us now to Surry Hills Police Station. Let us hook you up to a wire, and just go and speak with him. Tell him you heard he was arrested at the airport and ask if you can help with bail or something."

20 minutes later, Philip was tucking his shirt into his pants having been fitted with the latest in wireless technology. The cells in the station were on the bottom floor, and the elevator doors opened. He was escorted to his cell but was not allowed inside.

Philip stood outside the caged cell looking back at the police guard leaving the room until he was left alone with Charlie.

"I heard you were arrested at the airport," Philip began when Charlie immediately stood up and approached him with his finger held up to his lips.

"This place is probably bugged," Charlie interjected. "Be careful what you say."

The irony was not lost on Philip and he admired Charlie's insight. "Is there anything I can do to help?" Philip asked.

"All I want to say," Charlie answered, "Is that the refractometer is in the Airport Kaprekar. You got that? The refractometer is in the Airport Kaprekar."

"Yeah," Philip answered, "Got it."

"That's all I'm gonna say," Charlie said. And just like that, Charlie turned around and walked to the back of his cell. He lay down on the metal bench and covered his eyes with his elbows as if to go to sleep.

Five minutes later, Professor Philip was removing the tape from his body where the transmitter was.

"What the hell does that mean?" the woman asked. "Where or what is the Airport Kaprekar? And what is a refractometer?"

Philip knew he had a decision to make. It was Charlie or the detectives. And looking into the eyes of the detectives, he quickly made his decision.

"It's a reference to a certain locker number 6174," Philip replied. "That is the Kaprekar constant."

"What do you mean?" the woman asked. "What is the Kaprekar constant?"

"Well, you take any four-digit number with at least two different digits. Then arrange the digits in descending order to get a bigger number and ascending order to get a smaller number. If you subtract the smaller number from the bigger number to get another four-digit number using leading zeros if necessary, and you keep doing it, eventually you will always end up with the Kaprekar constant 6174 and certainly within 7 iterations and every iteration thereafter. It is a mathematical certainty."

"My God, he's right," the man said looking at a webpage on his phone. "There were lockers at the airport where he was arrested. No time to waste, let's go."

"Thank you, Professor," the woman said hurrying after the man who had just left the room.

"Don't mention it," Philip replied calling out after them.

As he exited the Surry Hills police station alone, he hailed a taxi cab back to Sydney University as he fondly recalled again the first time he had met Charlie outside the labs in the biochemistry building.

"This place is like an airport locker-room," Charlie had quipped. "And I've been assigned the 'Airport Kaprekar'" he said tapping locker number 6174.

Chapter 19

The Novitiate and the Cure

The Novice had donned the robes of the Dominican Order and was thankful to cover his head and face with the extra-large hood on such a cold night. He had been driving now for several hours into the Country until he found the dirt track that his map had indicated. He proceeded along this road for approximately 20 minutes when he arrived at what appeared to be a shack in the middle of nowhere.

The door was left open for him and he entered the shack into what appeared to be a rundown living room. He saw three similarly robed priests. A bearded elder man at a table reading a book by candlelight. A middle-aged man adjusting a picture frame of Pope Pius the Fifth on a wall behind him until it was properly squared with the room. And a younger youthful-looking priest scrubbing a scuff-mark off the wooden floor at the base of an empty bookcase.

The Novice intuitively made his way towards the elder priest and sat himself down on the other side of the table.

“You will have to forgive us,” the elder priest said, “The electrical generator is not properly fixed yet and we have to get around by candlelight at the moment.”

Shivering a little, the Novice responded, “I would have thought you would be more concerned with the…” But he was interrupted with an immediate blaze from a fire triggered by the youthful priest in a fireplace to the right of the bookcase.

“How can we help you?” the elder priest asked looking at the man in front of him.

“I spoke to a priest who was the recent Nobel laureate in physics, eh, Sir Charles Maxwell,” the Novice began. “I was impressed with his attitude towards metaphysis and…”

"Oh, you want to speak with our leader, Father Dom," the elderly priest said. With obvious pain from his age, the elderly priest stood from his chair and taking his book, he walked out of the room. The middle-aged priest had finished with the picture frame and followed closely behind him.

The youthful-looking priest was scrubbing the dust from his knees from kneeling on the floor and starting the fire. He walked to the empty chair left by the elderly priest and sat in it. "I'm Father Dom," he began, "Only the most inquisitive scientific minds are sent to us."

The Novice, still with his hood enveloping his head and face, covered any emotion that he may have displayed from the unexpected turn of events. He continued in any event. "Sir Charles had said something which I found peculiar," he said. "When I used the expression, 'Three's a crowd...' Sir Charles said, 'No, three's a joke, two's a crowd and one's a tragedy." When I enquired into what he meant, he referred me to you.

"Yes," Father Dom said. "Three's a joke, two's a crowd and one's a tragedy."

The light from the fireplace and the candles only heightened the mysticism of those words, and the Novice who never displayed emotion, began to feel a little impatient.

"There is something mystical about the number three," the youthful-looking priest said. "It is spawned of mirth. All jokes have the number three in them. The first entity sets the course of action. The second entity confirms the course. But then the third entity, instead of reconfirming it, does something completely unexpected. That is the essence of a joke. Humour is found amongst the most logical of people; where logic usually dictates one course of action, but another is chosen."

"I thought highly logical people displayed little emotion and had difficulty with the concept of humour," the Novice replied.

"Nothing could be further from the truth," Father Dom replied smilingly. "You know when Gene Roddenberry invented Mr Spock and spawned a race of Vulcans, he thought he was creating a race of logical people that displayed no emotion. But in fact, he created a race of illogical people acting as logical robots who had no mirth. But the greater the intellect, the greater the mirth because the intellect is that which foresees one end, only to be pleasantly surprised when it gains insight into another."

"Well, what about the Trinity?" the Novice retorted. "Isn't the Trinity the creator of the universe and the author of science and logic? What are you saying that the three-person God is the greatest joke of all?"

"Of course," the youthful-priest replied much to the Novice's confusion. "That is why trees grow apples instead of candlesticks. Because the Trinity created it that way. Scientists can fuss about the cells of apples all they like, but why apples grow from trees instead of growing candlesticks is a question of a much higher-order. And only someone with a sense of humour can appreciate it. Much like a bio-scientist burying his head in the physical nature of red blood cells instead of the metaphysical nature of the human soul."

"OK, well why would you say that 'two's a crowd'? That rather implies that two don't get on, that they soon part company," the Novice enquired trying to keep an open mind.

"Of course," the youthful-looking priest answered. "A story of 'Two' is a story where each part company in the same way that two sticks make a cross. They are diametrically opposed to each other. The parable of 'The Prodigal Son' begins with the words, 'A man has two sons.' The moment you hear those words, you immediately know that there is division amongst them. If they ran parallel to each other, then the story need only say 'a man had one son'."

"And I suppose, if a man had three sons, it would be..."

"...yes," the priest interrupted as they both said at the same time, "...a joke."

That caused a smile from the otherwise emotionless Novice and for the first time in many years, he felt he could learn from his interlocutor more so than he had learned since the time he was a child.

"Ok," the Novice began again, "'The Prodigal Son,' is a rather famous example, can you give me another?"

"Well, it's easy," the priest replied, "Any story that begins with a group of two is a story of the Prodigal Son. Take Macbeth when he visits the witches. He is in the presence of the second person Banquo. Macbeth will be king but Banquo shall generate a line of kings. There is a crowd right there. Diametrically opposed to each other. Not a harmonious relationship. The very nature of two implies that one goes one way and the other goes another. That generates the cross, which has a paradox at its centre. The eastern religions have a circle as their symbol. The circle of life. A swastika is an ancient religious icon of a cross becoming a circle because the circle is at war with the cross. But the cross is at the centre of our religion."

"So, you are saying a cross is formed from 'two' and that 'two' is a crowd? Doesn't that imply that there is *not* room for everybody? Sounds a little anti-Christian, doesn't it?" the Novice enquired with interest.

"Oh, there is room for everybody alright," the priest replied still smilingly, "But the 'crowd' implies that many are called, but few are chosen. Stories with two sides imply a right side and a wrong side. They both can't be right because then nobody's right."

"Fine," the Novice said wishing to advance the conversation. "Explain to me then how one is a tragedy?"

"One is a tragedy because if it is not, then the one is the storyteller not the story. When Abraham only had one son, he was tragically asked to sacrifice him."

"I suppose you will say that when God sent his only son into the world, that was a tragedy?" the Novice enquired.

"Of course," the priest answered. "That is the same story as Abraham, only this time, God's only son was in fact sacrificed in the same way as the sacrificial lamb that Abraham killed in his son's stead."

The discussion evoked many emotions in the Novice, and many thoughts and ideas that he wanted to ridicule or at least debate with his interlocutor. But before he could continue, the priest interrupted his line of thought.

"Tell me," the Priest began again solemnly but still smilingly, "Are these really the questions you wanted to come all this way to ask me? What is your real story? What brings you to see me?"

"I don't know if there is room in your religion for me priest?" the Novice replied finally removing the hood from his head and revealing a pale white stone-cold face. "My name is William Hunter. In my former life I was a barrister. And in the life before that I was a scientist. But now, I'm just a vampire. I drink the blood of humans to survive. Is there room in your religion for someone like me priest?"

"Of course," the priest replied smiling even more. "Before Christ died, us vampires roamed the earth somewhat aimlessly. But now we feast on the blood of Christ. And whoever drinketh his blood shall have an eternal spring welling-up inside him and he will never thirst again."

With those words, the youthful-looking priest removed his own hood from his head allowing the firelight to shine on his even paler stone-white cheeks.

"There is not only room in our religion for you," the priest continued, "But there is no room anywhere else for you," he said still smiling. "We are the antidote. The cure." And with that, the priest extinguished the candle.

Chapter 20

The Bloody Bastard

The wedding between Benjamin Jones and Kathleen Medici was a secluded affair. The venue was Lord Howe Island and for this occasion, the Island had been fully booked. The Jones family occupied the Pinetrees Resort. The Medici family occupied the Arajilla Retreat. And the married couple occupied the Capella Lodge. The ceremony itself was celebrated at the Boat House alongside the Island Lagoon. The geographic location of the Island just 600km from the Australian mainland in the Pacific afforded it year-round perfect weather, and the weather on this occasion was typically perfect.

The Contessa Medici had successfully replaced the members of the Board of Directors of DrugTech loyal to Dr Jamieson with members loyal to herself. These members formed the economic guild of DrugTech and both sets of members (along with the right wing of politics) had several common philosophies between them, being:

(1) personal ownership of property;
(2) wealth; and of course,
(3) power.

And so, nothing much had changed at least as far as the scientific guild of DrugTech was concerned. The scientific guild on the other hand, (along with the left wing of politics) also had common philosophies between them being:

(1) individual personal rights;
(2) honours; and of course,
(3) power.

And whilst the power of the left and the power of the right would by its nature interfere with each other, it formed a well-recognised interference pattern that became the golden tapestry of the company as well as in many modern-day governances.

My story is not particularly interested in the political side of governance. Each wing waxes and wanes with the politically changing times. Rather, my story is more concerned with the good and with the evil which exists in both sides of politics. Or more to the point, the evil which exists in the good. Ontologically, all things are good. That is why things exist. But the evil is not an existence *per se*. Rather it is a privation or the absence of a due good. Take blindness for example. Blindness does not exist as a thing, but it is evil in a man because it is proper for a man to see. But we do not describe a tree as blind, merely sightless. It is not within the natural order for trees to see.

And so evil is rather like a tear in the fabric; the fabric which surrounds the company of DrugTech as a cloak. A tear cannot exist without the cloak, it subsists within it. But a tear in a cloak leaves a hole, and every tear diminishes the fabric and is a thing usually kept secret. And the cloak of DrugTech had become so torn and become so secret that it was effectively a cloak of invisibility. Many spend their time with the battle that exists between the right and the left. It is only natural that many on one side wish as many as possible on the other to abandon that side and to join forces with the other. That battle is fought in the horizontal plane. But the battle that exists between the forces of good and the forces of evil takes place in the vertical. And when that occurs, you either go up, or you go down. And those that choose to go down, wish to take as many with them as possible.

Often a battle may appear to be taking place on a horizontal plane. The naval battle of Lepanto between the Ottoman Turks and the Christian forces was a physical battle between the East and the West in the Gulf of Patras. The date was 7 October 1571 and the Turkish invading forces from the East had just sacked the city of Famagusta in Cyprus and flayed its beloved leader, Marco Antonio Bragadin. Approximately 300 Ottoman ships under the command of Ali Pasha were en route to invade the Christian forces of Europe where they were met with a similar number of ships from the West. Ali Pasha was completely loyal to his sovereign, the Sultan Selim II. And Sultan Selim II had vowed to speak the name of his Commander as the first words from his lips upon his victory over the Christian forces.

You may ask, what has this got to do with DrugTech? Well, I will tell you. In every wicked and evil institution, there becomes one person that, against all odds, resets the natural order. But it is not done within the natural order. It is essentially supernatural. DrugTech will be taken down by a similar superhero. Its evil ways had infected all forms of Government and it solidified the Deep State.

In the days of Lepanto, Sultan Selim II could not naturally lose. His navy was invincible. But his counterpart was Pope Pius V and Pope Pius V was not known for playing fairly. Whilst Selim II was playing fairly and squarely on the horizontal plane, Pius V was invoking the powers of the vertical. The powers of the vertical are more devastating than a nuclear bomb. No earthly power can beat omnipotence. That's what omnipotence means. But the vertical weapons of Pius V manifested themselves in two humble earthly things. The first was the humble Rosary. The supernatural beads of the Dominican Order that, like a telephone to God, communicates with the Omnipotent. The second was the illegitimate son of the Holy Roman Emperor Don John of Austria, the 24-year-old boy who was already renowned from fighting victorious bloody battles against the Alpujarra in the Kingdom of Granada. The illegitimate 24-year-old Don John of Austria, by the anointing of Pius V, became the Supreme Commander of the Christian forces. He was to take on the irresistible forces of the Turkish naval veteran, Ali Pasha.

And by all that is natural, when the battle had been lost and won, Selim II should have spoken the name of his Naval Commander. And so too would DrugTech have been naturally victorious. But by all that is Holy, Selim II instead spoke the three words which has now gone down in history as referencing any supernatural entity that disrupts the ordinary natural order. And those immortalised words have now been spoken in many a defeat since then. And the same thing will happen with DrugTech. I am sure of it.

I began this chapter by speaking of the wedding feast of Benjamin Jones and Kathleen Medici on Lord Howe Island. If you read my earlier book, "Spellbound – The Workings of DrugTech" you would have already been introduced to this island. Except you would know it as the Island of Mount Yearning, the island that Captain Terrence marooned his crew on when he recovered the lost treasure of Count de Jager. At the beginning of this book, "DrugTech – the Deep State Deepens" I told you how Captain Terrence had revealed his true identity as Commodore Terracini of the Royal Doge's Navy and then had his crew arrested for piracy. That was an example of how, at least to the crew of the Douglass, a seemingly supernatural entity disrupted the ordinary natural order. But as the forces of evil were destroyed at Lepanto, a new evil remained with the pharmaceutical company created by the former Commodore Terracini. And in the wake of the victory of Lepanto, the company solidified and began to expand.

Now if you ask me what were those three words spoken by Selim II upon hearing of Ali Pasha's defeat at Lepanto, I will tell you that also. They reference his Commander's counterpart; the illegitimate Don John of Austria and the words form the name of this chapter.

Chapter 21

To Play the King

The Court of King's Bench was a newly opened establishment within walking distance of the Criminal Courts and many a barristers' chambers. And every Friday night, more and more barristers would attend the establishment to drink, let off steam and generally discuss their upcoming trials with their professional colleagues of good repute in a less than professional setting.

Black, Stone and Colfax were three learned friends each with less than 15 years at the bar. It is difficult to say the least for women barristers to juggle home life and traditional prejudices in a very traditional profession, but these three ladies were exceptional barristers with exceptional intellects and not the kind of ladies who would succumb to bullying in any of its forms.

Stone returned with a second round of beers form the bar as Black and Colfax eagerly replaced them with their empty schooners. The tray with the empty schooners was moved to the side allowing the ladies to lounge more and more on the table in front of them and warm-up to each other and their ice-cold beverages.

"I have a case on Monday before Magistrate Burwood," Colfax said in a loud tone to carry her voice over the general chatter of her surroundings.

"He's a really nice man," Colfax continued. "I've done many cases in front of him. He smiles, he's courteous and polite and he really helps you along. I think he is a really understanding Magistrate."

"Smiling death if you ask me," Stone replied. "I bet you have never won a single case in front of him?"

"Let me think," Colfax said rolling her eyes towards heaven. "Come to think of it, I don't think I have."

"Of course you haven't. He's a hanging judge. Impossible to win in front of," Stone said. "Oh, he listens very politely alright, and he's the most courteous man on the bench. But if there is a contest between your witnesses and the prosecution witnesses, it doesn't matter how ridiculous you make the prosecution witnesses sound in cross-examination, he will simply always believe the prosecution witnesses and you lose."

"And if there's a point of law," Black said, "He will listen to both sides of the debate from the defence and the prosecution and even encourage the defence along often agreeing and sparring with the prosecution. But then he goes away and comes back on the bench and then gives a judgment that sounds like he reluctantly had to side with the prosecution; and again, you lose."

"It's like the Queen's gambit," Stone said. "You make an opening move that seems like you have an advantage over the prosecution, but then he corners you in the way you opened and uses it against you in his final judgment. It's a lose, lose situation, you can't win."

"I heard," Colfax said with her eyes beginning to squint and tilting her head to one side to glance at Black, "that Black actually won a case in front of Burwood the other day."

"Yes, I heard that too," Stone said adopting a similar pose and looking at Black. "Is that just rumour or did you actually win in front of the smiling assassin?"

Both barristers were now gazing at Black who soon realised that she became the centre of attention. She gulped another mouthful of beer before returning the glass slowly to the table to allow herself time to empty the contents of her mouth into her stomach before speaking.

"Well as a matter of fact, I did happen to win a case in front of Magistrate Burwood the other day. Burwood ultimately said that the prosecutor failed to satisfy the heavy burden to the very high criminal standard of proof beyond reasonable doubt," Black said in a mocking imitation of Magistrate Burwood's speech patterns.

"Tell us how?" both Colfax and Stone asked and both straightening-up in their seats and not wanting to let this one pass.

"Well, like you guys, I had my fair share of cases in front of Magistrate Burwood," Black began, "And I lost the lot. The losses never seemed to trouble me, he would always let you down gently and you got the feeling that you did a wonderful job, only you just happened to have the losing case and better luck next time."

"We've all been there with him," Stone said, "So what did you do?"

"Well, I got this case where an 18-year-old kid was charged with robbery-in-company," Black replied. "It was alleged that he and two other blokes held an innocent couple up in a park wearing ski masks and producing knives. The other two guys had already pleaded guilty."

"So, how could you possibly win?" Colfax asked.

"Yeah?" Stone added, "Especially in front of Burwood?"

"Well, the kid and his mother came to my chambers and they swore to me black and blue that he was tricked by the other two blokes," Black answered. "He said that his friends told him that they actually knew the innocent couple in the park and that the whole thing was just going to be one big schoolyard-type prank. So, he went along with it thinking the whole thing was a joke. In his mind, he was not really robbing the couple, he was just having fun with friends of friends. Except of course they didn't really know the couple and the whole thing went south very, very quickly."

"That's a likely story?" Colfax said. "You believed that defence?"

"Well, it doesn't really matter whether Black believed it," Stone answered for her, "There is no way on earth that Burwood would believe it. How could you possibly win that one?"

"I had the same misgivings as you guys about Burwood," Black replied finishing her beer. "Normally I would just go to Court, do my best, get complimented by the Magistrate on my stella performance, and then have to explain to the poor mum why her son was sent to jail."

"Welcome to life at the Criminal Bar," Colfax said.

"Only, something about the kid and his mum truly convinced me of the kid's innocence," Black continued, "And I couldn't sleep that night knowing that there was nothing that I could possibly do to save this innocent kid."

"So, what did you do?" Stone asked, "How did you pull it off?"

"Well at first I read up on all the most recent law on robbery-in-company," Black said. "Then I expanded my research into how to cross-examine the Crown witnesses and especially the other two guys that pleaded guilty, but then it occurred to me."

"What?" Stone interjected. "What occurred to you?"

"Well, that nothing I would do would have any effect on Burwood," Black answered. "It wouldn't matter what anyone said in Court, Burwood would simply say that he doesn't believe that my client was engaged in a prank and he would simply convict him."

"With you so far," Colfax interjected impatiently and wanting Black to get to the solution.

"Well about a week before the case," Black continued, "I was having a coffee by myself at the corner of Elizabeth Street and Park Street and I overheard a retired barrister telling an elderly gentleman about the 'craziest kind of crazy' judges that he had come across in his day at the Bar. So, I waited for him to finish with the man that he was talking to, and then I went an introduced myself to him, explained the problem that I had with Burwood and I asked him for advice."

"You're kidding?" Colfax said, "That's ballsy."

"Never mind ballsy," Stone said, "What did he say?"

"He said," Black replied beginning to smile, "He said a good lawyer knows the law. But a better lawyer knows the judge."

"What's that supposed to mean?" Stone enquired. "He's either your friend or you offer him a bribe or something?"

"No, that wasn't it at all," Black said. "He said sometimes you have to play the person, not the argument. Magistrate Burwood, like many other new Magistrates and Judges of today, are only worried about two things."

"What two things?" Colfax asked finishing her beer.

"Being ridiculed in the media," Black answered, "And being ridiculed on Appeal. Other than that, they really don't give a crap about your client or the case, only their own reputations. And since being a hanging-judge hardly ever gets you in trouble with the media, then many new magistrates and judges of today have become brutally cruel. But many of them adopt a pleasant and courteous demeanour to encourage you not to appeal them. Welcome to the criminal justice system of the 21st century."

"Well, that sounds like Burwood alright," Stone said looking at Colfax and looking back at Black, "But I still don't see what you did with that little gem of knowledge. How did you win?"

"When the case started, instead of dragging in my trolly of books and folders of research that I had done and planned for the case, I left it all back at my chambers. I took a single sheet of paper that I placed on the bar table in front of me but I never wrote anything on it. It just stayed there for the whole proceeding."

"Go on," Colfax said, "What happened?"

"The prosecutor opened the case and then Burwood asked me if I wished to make an opening statement," Black answered. "I simply said that I did not. I kept my eyes on the plaque behind the Magistrate and only turned to look at the Magistrate directly in the eyes when he asked me a direct question. Other than that, I sat there like a statue throughout the whole proceeding while the prosecutor called witness after witness. I never wrote anything down, I just kept a poker face and never let the Magistrate know what I was thinking."

"Gosh," Stone interjected, "That's a high-risk strategy if ever I heard of one."

"What happened then?" Colfax asked.

"Well after the prosecutor made a closing statement, the Magistrate then asked me to make my closing statement," Black answered. "Like before, I would turn my gaze from the plaque behind the Magistrate, look him directly in the eyes, and I simply replied, 'No thank you, your Honour.'"

"Gosh," Colfax gaped incredulously, "So what happened then?"

"Well, at this stage, the nerves of the Magistrate became completely shot," Black answered. "Burwood lost his cool and looked at me harshly and then he bellowed almost at the top of his voice, 'Ms. Black, you haven't made an opening statement; You haven't asked the police any questions; You haven't asked any of the lay witnesses any questions and you haven't made a closing statement. Let me ask you. Why are you even here?'" Black said cracking a smile at her two colleagues who were stunned into silence.

Seeing her friends could not ask, Black continued. "As before I turned my gaze from the plaque behind the Magistrate and this time I looked as coldly as I possibly could with as much sarcasm and disdain as I could possibly muster dripping from my very lips; and then I looked him straight into his eyes and I said very calmly, 'Your Honour, I'm here for the appeal.'"

Chapter 22

The King and the Queen

"Now that you have level six-security clearance," Benjamin Jones said to his personal assistant, "I would like you to come with me to a crossover meeting."

Saanvi Patel barely had time to grab a notepad before grabbing her white coat and following her boss down the corridor. They proceeded to basement level six which was off limits to most of the DrugTech personnel.

"What's a crossover meeting?" Saanvi Patel enquired of her boss on the way.

"The Counsellors here at DrugTech usually have some little insight into almost every project being researched," he said as they walked to the meeting room. "But as many of them are top secret, one project doesn't know what is going on with any other projects. Every now and then, the subject matter of one project seems to crossover into another project and when that happens, the Counsellors are instrumental in bringing it to our attention. But both of these projects are level six-security clearance and it is unusual for there to be a crossover on such highly classified projects so I have been asked to look into it," Benjamin said.

Benjamin Jones and Saanvi Patel made their way through various security doors and corridors of the basement six level. They came to a room with a boardroom table and a television screen on the wall. Dr Jeremy Pitts, a DrugTech Counsellor was waiting for them in the room with his briefcase open on the table and several handwritten notes spread-out in front of him.

"Let's just get down to it," Benjamin said upon entering the room and taking a seat. Dr Patel sat alongside her boss ready to take notes.

"As you know, we managed to get Scientist Bruce released from psychiatric custody so he could continue his work on the Trans Warp Inducer," Dr Pitts said flicking through his notes and turning pages. Dr Pitts was not one to mince words. "Now from what I understand, the Trans Warp Inducer is a Star Trek type transporter device," he said casually rustling through his notes as if he was reporting the invention of the typewriter. "Scientist Bruce was complaining that it transports inanimate objects and animals alright, but it always seemed to go wrong with humans."

"OK," Benjamin said waiting to hear more, "Please go on."

"Well in one of our meetings, I asked Scientist Bruce what was the problem with humans," Dr Pitts continued pulling another notepad of handwritten notes and turning to the relevant page. "Scientist Bruce said that matter was transformed and digitised at one end. The digitization would go through several iterations until it was reproduced and reformed at the other end. But with humans, the computers needed to complete more than eight iterations due to their complex nature. But after the sixth or seventh iteration, the digitization would get locked on the number 6174 and then enter an endless loop thereafter. It could not progress beyond 6174."

"Is it a computer problem?" Saanvi asked wanting to understand where this was headed.

"No," Dr Pitts said. "Scientist Bruce said something about a God-given universal constant in the nature of mathematics that prevented him from going beyond seven iterations on computations of four digits. He called it the..." at this point Dr Pitts paused to glance over a few other notes before coming back to the document he was reading from, "he called it the Kaprekar Constant."

"The Kaprekar Constant, what's that?" Benjamin Jones enquired.

"I'm not sure," Dr Pitts said. "That's where my involvement with the first case ended. Then sometime later, another case came across my desk when a video tape was handed in by Sergeant Johns from the Surry Hills Police Station."

"Video tape?" Benjamin Jones enquired, "What video tape?"

Dr Pitts reached inside his open briefcase and retrieved a remote-control. Pressing play, he turned around to the screen behind him and all three occupants watched the television that flickered to life.

The scene was obviously the footage from CCTV recorded from a security camera in the corner of a room showing a closed police cell. A man was standing talking to another man through the bars. The audio of the television was quite distinct and began:

"All I want to say is that the refractometer is in the Airport Kaprekar. You got that? The refractometer is in the Airport Kaprekar."

At this point Dr Pitts paused the tape.

"Is that it?" Benjamin asked looking a little puzzled.

"That's it," Dr Pitts said packing his papers into his briefcase and closing it leaving the remote-control behind on the table. Dr Pitts knew enough not to enquire further, nor did he want to. He had reported what was supposed to be reported at such a crossover meeting and he promptly left.

Upon shutting the door, Benjamin Jones stood up to pace around the room and eventually sat at another seat around the boardroom table facing his personal assistant.

"Do you recognise the man in the video?" Benjamin asked looking at the paused television image.

"Yes, I do," Saanvi said. "He was our former Professor at Sydney University, Professor Philip Kurtis. What has he got to do with the Trans Warp Inducer?"

"I don't know," Benjamin said. "Maybe nothing. But before my time, when Dr Jamieson was in charge, one of his last acts as Managing Director was to appoint two detectives to look into a former employee's suicide by the name of Martin Hanson. I didn't know that the detectives were still on the case. But Dr Jamieson once referred to a trio of former employees who worked for DrugTech as the Old Fart Martin, Charlie Sleazebag and Professor Monkey Brain."

"Well," Saanvi said also looking confused and puzzled, "If there is a connection between the Trans Warp Inducer and that trio of former employees, maybe we should find out what it is?"

"It's not that simple," Benjamin Jones said. "I don't know who the two detectives are and Dr Jamieson is not the most approachable of people. He certainly doesn't owe me any favours. He is like a King in his own right."

"Well," Saanvi said proceeding cautiously realizing the delicacy of the situation. "If he's a King in his own right," she said wondering how to choose her next words, "Then you may need to bring out the Queen to corner him."

"What do you mean?" Benjamin asked squinting his eyes.

"I mean," Saanvi said looking rather uncomfortable, "I mean your new mummy-in-law, the Contessa Medici."

Chapter 23

The Luckiest Guy on Earth

Tommy Grayson was best friends with Jake Peterson and had been from his early school days. They shared most things with each other. Jake was now studying Engineering and Tommy was studying Biology, each at the University of Sydney. This weekend Tommy was picking Jake up for a weekend of skiing at the 'Man From Snowy River' hotel at Perisher Smiggins.

"Say, that's a fine set of wheels," Jake commented as Tommy pulled-up in a brand-new utility truck, "How did you score that?"

"Thanks," Tommy said. "I won this in the McDonalds Monopoly promotion. I just registered online for the second chance draw when my burger tickets came up empty."

"Far out!" Jake exclaimed, "That's amazing, I never win anything. Next time you place a bet on the Summer Rat Races," Jake continued, "Remind me to spot you!"

"Will do," Tommy said smiling to himself.

"Come to think of it," Jake said settling into the passenger seat after unloading his luggage into the back of the Ute, "Didn't you win this weekend getaway as well?"

"Yes, I did," Tommy said somewhat smugly. "The student union had an online raffle and this was the lucky prize that I won."

"Wow," Jake exclaimed again. "You seem to be the luckiest guy on earth. Didn't you recently win a Court case about a mugging in a park with two other uni guys that pleaded guilty?"

"I did," Tommy said embarrassingly, "But I don't think I got very lucky there."

"What do you mean?" Jake said.

"Well, I was tricked into the affair. I tried to explain it to my barrister and everything, but she just didn't buy it. In fact, she was really quite hopeless in Court. I think I only won because the judge saw through the prosecution case, no thanks to her. At least I had a decent judge!"

"Still sounds lucky to me," Jake said.

After stopping for dinner along the way, and a couple of more hours of banter between them, they arrived quite exhaustedly at the Man From Snowy River hotel.

"Don't forget to register for the lucky door prize," the receptionist said with a lovely smile. "Just scan the QR code and register online. First prize is an all-expenses paid week long skiing holiday at our sister lodge in Switzerland!"

"Thanks," the boys replied scanning the code with their mobile phones.

"I swear to God, if you win this," Jake said, "I am going to throttle you!"

The skiing over the weekend was otherwise uneventful and when Tommy received an email on the last day advising that he had won the holiday to Switzerland, he discreetly kept it to himself.

On the way home, the boys pulled into a service station to refuel the truck. The service station was running a promotion with a sign above the fuel pump that read, "For your chance to win free fuel and a meal for two, scan the QR code and register your details online."

"Hungry?" Tommy enquired as he scanned the QR code.

"Starving," Jake replied. "Hope this place has some good steaks."

As Tommy lined up to pay for his fuel, he received a text message on his telephone that he promptly showed to the attendant.

"Congratulations," she said hitting a few buttons on the cash register and handing Tommy two tickets. "Here are your meal tickets, please leave us positive reviews!"

"Will do," Tommy said taking the tickets.

"Wait," Jake said seeing what had happened. "Don't tell me you won that promotion too? This is excellent! I don't know what it is man, but you are on a roll."

"Well, you know what they say," Tommy said smiling, "It never rains but it pours!"

The two boys filled their bellies with luscious steak, chips and salad and took their soda cans with them to the truck to continue the drive home.

The banter continued as before and when Jake was removing his luggage from the back of the truck after being dropped off at his home, he said, "You make sure to remember me before your lucky streak runs out, you hear?"

"Sure thing," Tommy said as he drove off waiving and smiling.

Tommy's lucky streak didn't stay with him much longer that night. Several minutes after leaving Jake's place, Tommy was distracted when his mobile telephone fell from his pocket onto the floor. Reaching down to pick it up, his truck collided rather abruptly with the back of a fully-marked highway-patrol car.

"OK, out of the truck," the Policeman said walking up to Tommy. "You're under arrest."

"Not again," Tommy thought to himself, "What would mum say?" He could hear the lectures being already, "Another round of expensive conferences with Barrister Black!"

Approximately two hours later, Tommy was sitting in an interview chair at the Surry Hills Police Station. He had remembered the advice that Barrister Black had given him, "If you ever get arrested again, say nothing to the police."

Following the good advice, Tommy remained silent throughout the interrogation process. The highway patrolman completed the 'Facts Sheet' which alleged Tommy was guilty of Dangerous Driving, or in the alternative, Negligent Driving, and nominated a Court date for him to attend. The officer completed Tommy's address and contact details, however, when the highway patrolman attempted to save and process the document, the computer whistled indicating that an error occurred and would not proceed further.

After hitting the same button a few more times and getting the same result, the highway patrolman printed what he had done and commanded that Tommy, "Stay right there." He proceeded to knock on his Sergeant's door to explain the problem. Sergeant Skip Johns listened very politely and gazed at the paperwork that his highway patrol officer handed him. He looked it over and noticed the telephone number in the contact details of the accused.

"Leave it with me," the Sergeant said. "I'll fix it up and talk to you shortly."

Dismissing his officer, the Sergeant took the paperwork and proceeded to the interview room where Tommy Grayson was waiting nervously and patiently.

"Hello, I'm Sergeant Skip Johns," the Sergeant said looking like a fatherly figure to Tommy. "I'd like to ask you some questions about your telephone number."

The words, "Say nothing," were ringing in his ears from his Barrister, and Tommy remained silent. "How did you come by that number?"

Tommy was amazed at his perception. Since the computer glitch that Tommy had noticed when the internet failed to register the name DrugTech for his rat with the Summer Rat Races, Tommy secretly investigated further. Tommy had changed his mobile telephone number to the same number of the Australian Company Number of DrugTech's registration with the Australian Securities and Investments Commission. And having done that, whenever that number was entered online, Tommy had become, let's just say, very, very lucky.

"You don't want to speak with me?" Sergeant Johns said smilingly. "You don't have to, you know, but if you do, things might go a bit more smoothly for you."

Tommy still did not answer. He had been secretly suspicious of DrugTech ever since his father had explained to him his futile attempts to run a statistical analysis on the company over many a conversation at the dining-room table.

Tommy's silence seemed to irritate the Sergeant and he was doing his best not to show it. The Sergeant stood and walked to the tea and coffee making facilities at the side of the room. With his back to the accused, he made a cup of coffee and slipped into the beverage a 'suicide pill' that had the embossed logo of Leo Mitch and Morley.

"Here's a cup of coffee for you," the Sergeant said putting it on the table in front of him, his hand showing a red scorpion on its back.

"Thank you," Tommy said looking quite relieved. "I haven't had a drink all day."

The Sergeant saw him grab the coffee and take a big gulp.

"Let me see if I can get this sorted out with my officer, and maybe we can let you off with a warning this time. You just keep your nose clean for the next 48 hours and we will see what happens then, OK?" the Sergeant said sweetly as he took the papers from the room. "Just wait here please."

Making sure that the Sergeant had completely left the room, Tommy emptied the contents of his mouth back into the cup, spitting to make sure that all of it was gone.

Chapter 24

A Cafeteria Chat

Scientist Bruce was exhausted. He had spent the last 48 hours attempting to debug and reprogram his computers without success. With dishevelled hair and two-day stubble, he wandered from the DrugTech laboratories into the neighbouring hospital cafeteria. After filling his tray and paying for his items, he looked for a place to sit when he saw a familiar face sitting and eating alone.

Now a fight between a priest and scientist is not an unknown thing *per se*. The intellectual fights have existed ever since the priesthood discovered science in the Middle Ages and the later breed of scientists then thought that they no longer had any need for priests. Galileo was one such scientist who attempted to ram his scientific discoveries down the throat of the Church but was unfortunately met with rather amateurish priests who felt unnecessarily challenged by the whole affair. But, in any event, an actual 'fist-fight' between a scientist and a priest is a truly remarkable thing, and if you care to read further, you will come across how a scientist and a priest came to fisticuffs from a simple cafeteria chat.

"Can I ask you a question priest?" Scientist Bruce said sitting in the chair opposite to Sir Charles Maxwell. He didn't wait for an answer. "When you won the Nobel Prize in physics, did you dedicate your two-million-dollar prize to the Church?"

"No," the priest responded. "I received the prize when I became a priest, but it was awarded for the work I did as a physicist whilst I was lecturing at the University of Sydney. So, I felt conscience-bound to donate the money back to the university in the furtherance of science."

"Render unto Caesar, eh?" the Scientist quipped.

"Perhaps," the priest replied.

At this point there was an awkward pause whilst the priest finished his lunch and began on his coffee and the Scientist rotating his muffin in his hand looked for a way to ask the physicist for assistance on his project.

"Does the number 6174 mean anything to you?" the Scientist began again.

Fr Maxwell had an eidetic memory. He closed his eyes to think for a second and then responded. "It is the Kaprekar constant. Has this got something to do with your big invention that is going to change the earth as we know it?"

"You know about my Trans Warp Inducer from my Neurologist," Scientist Bruce answered. "Now how do I get your Nobel laureate physics brain to help me with my problem?" the Scientist asked in frustration. "I can transport animals and objects alright, but humans need more than seven iterations of computer digitization, and I keep running into the Kaprekar constant and can't get past it."

"Your problem is not physical," Maxwell replied, "It's metaphysical."

"Here we go again," the Scientist said rolling his eyes around.

It didn't take long before the Scientist realised that the conversation would be as stifled as his experiment if he didn't allow the priest to proceed so he decided to indulge the priest a little and asked, "Ok, how is it metaphysical?"

"Consider an angel," the priest began again. "Aristotle referred to them as 'the intelligences'. Entities that are made up of form but not matter. In modern day parlance, they are wholly spiritual beings. Do you think your Trans Warp Inducer, in its current form, could transport an angel?"

Scientist Bruce was forced to confront his prejudices. He could either remonstrate with the priest about the non-existence of angels, or he could humour him to see where this Nobel laureate was going, to see if it could unlock the equation that stumped him. Either way, the question was surely unique and to Scientist Bruce it was a new way to approach the problem.

"Well," Bruce hesitated, "Assuming angels exist and one of them stepped into my Trans Warp Inducer," he paused again as he thought about the problem, "Then no, I don't think there would be anything physical there to digitise."

"That's your problem right there," the priest interjected.

"I don't follow."

"A human being is not a wholly physical being you know," the priest replied. "There's the spirit to worry about as well. When you transport the physical human and leave his soul behind, of course you will get a corpse at the other end."

"You know that's exactly the kind of rot I was expecting a priest to say," Scientist Bruce said in an exasperated tone. "Can't the physics Nobel laureate turn his mind to the problem at hand, or has your conversion to religion left you that twisted?"

"What makes you think that human beings don't have a spirit anyway?" the priest said deciding to challenge his interlocutor.

"Because you can't touch it or see it or otherwise measure it in the laboratory. If it is not comprised of particles, then it doesn't exist," the Scientist retorted.

"And that's your definition of existence, is it?" the priest replied. "I can well understand 'material' existence fitting that definition, but 'spiritual' existence by its very definition is something that cannot be measured in a laboratory or be attracted to gravity for that matter."

"Ok fine, I'm giving you that on the definition of 'spirit'," the Scientist said, "Maybe that's what a spirit is defined to mean. But you can't prove that a spirit actually exists. With you religious lot, it's just an article of faith. You can't prove it."

"Of course you can prove it," the priest replied somewhat indignantly. "The existence of a spirit has been proved many a time. That is what Aristotle did in his work on 'De Anima'."

Scientist Bruce looked perplexed and frustrated, "How do you prove a spirit exists?" This was actually the last thing that Scientist Bruce wanted to know. He felt manipulated by the priest to side-track the conversation into what he undoubtedly considered an attempt at his own conversion. But from a straight scientific point of view as to how the priest claimed this impacted his experiment, he was certainly intrigued. And perhaps a minute or two down this path wouldn't go completely astray.

"Well, it's all about knowledge," the priest replied. "We know things exist but we also know that we know things exist. When we 'know that we are knowers' then that is our very consciousness."

"We know things because our neurons form a pattern that causes an electrical impulse in the brain," the Scientist was quick to retort.

"I know the scientific definition of knowledge," the priest replied. "To a scientist, the brain is just a sausage machine. A combination of neuro-chemical reactions that are predestined to occur by the laws of biochemistry and humans therefore have no real free will or independent thought for that matter. If that was true by the way, and no doubt scientists really believe that it is, then Courts and tribunals would all be in vain because nothing would be done voluntarily; human thoughts and intentions would have been as assured of happening just as magnesium dissolves in acid."

Scientist Bruce's head started to hurt. "Well anyway, none of that is proof of anything, you're just telling me what intellect is not. What's the proof that a spirit actually exists?"

"Well consider an analogy. Suppose the human intellect to be a plastic bucket for example. If you put a banana in the bucket, then that is the same as the intellect knowing the banana because the banana is within it; and the knower and the known are one. But let me ask you a question," the priest challenged. "What is the one thing that you cannot put in the bucket?"

"What?" the Scientist asked wishing he would come to the point.

"The bucket!" the priest answered. "You can't put the bucket into the bucket," the priest explained. "If you tried to do that, it would eat itself and cease to be a bucket. So, from that simple thought experiment, a material intellect like a plastic bucket could never know that it knows. In order for an intellect to know that it knows, it needs to perfectly reflect upon itself without destroying itself. Matter cannot do that, including neurons. Only a spirit. Therefore, the human intellect is spiritual. That's the problem that your experiment is running up against. That's why you can't get past the Kaprekar constant."

"That's just a bunch of crap," the Scientist said without quite knowing where to begin. "For one thing..." at this point, the Scientist felt challenged enough to reveal confidential information to his interlocutor for the simple point of winning an argument. But before he would do so, he decided to question the priest further.

"Anyway...assuming you are right," Scientist Bruce began again trying a different tactic, "How would you get the Trans Warp Inducer to transport a spirit?"

"The answer is music," the priest replied.

"What do you mean 'the answer is music'?" the Scientist asked quite frustratedly. "You know it's answers like that which make me want to murder you. What the hell has music got to do with it?"

"Music," the priest replied, "Is something that is uniquely appreciated by the human spirit. Animals have no appreciation or even concept of it. Music sings to the soul. It gives praise to God. It is a material thing that can transform one spiritually."

"This makes no sense to me whatsoever," the Scientist said looking confused.

"That's your problem," the priest retorted. "It goes from one sense to a completely different sense. It is a kind of synaesthesia. Like people who see colours in numbers. You need a synaesthesia formula to materially transport the spiritual form from A to B. That will then get you past your Kaprekar Constant and allow more spiritual iterations."

At this point the Scientist had had enough. "You know, I thought that talking with you could possibly progress my experiment. I see now that it has been a complete waste of time when you prattle on about your metaphysical crap. I can't believe they even gave you a Nobel Prize; I reckon they ought to strip you of it given the nonsense that you go on about."

"And what makes you so sure that I am wrong?" the priest enquired. "If you analyse your objections, you will see that they are not scientific in nature, they are actually faith based. Your own twisted faith prevents you from broadening your horizons."

That was the last straw and Bruce decided to open-up in a way that he had not disclosed to anyone previously.

"Ok fine," he began, "You say that my experiment can't transport the human spirit and that's why my experiment fails? Well, that's where you're wrong priest. Nobody knows this, but after I attempted to transport my friend Thomas through the Trans Warp Inducer and killed him, a person by the name of Gary wandered on in to my shack. I successfully transported him!"

"I know about your shack which was your laboratory out in the Country," the priest replied somewhat nonchalantly. "The Dominican Order eventually took it over. And do you know what happened to Gary?" the priest retorted.

"I didn't know you knew him," the Scientist replied somewhat sceptically.

"He committed suicide," the priest replied. "He left a note saying that he felt like his soul had died inside."

The scientist stood-up rather exasperated. "For one thing, I don't believe you. But for another," he said pushing his tray to one side and preparing to leave, "I didn't just transport Gary, I also managed to transport myself. Now how is it that I have managed to live without my soul being transported?"

Scientist Bruce was not expecting an answer, but he got one anyway.

"That's because you're a psychopath," the priest replied. "You are spiritually dead inside and have been for a very long time. Yes, you transported your soul, or what was left of it anyway, but being the psychopath that you are, you found that you didn't have much need for any of the human virtues resident in the soul anyway."

There was not much talking between them after that.

Chapter 25

When Serpents Fight

Lee Zhang Wei was exhausted having spent the early evening hours at work. He had bought dinner for himself on his way home and was now looking forward to a night alone in his studio apartment when he arrived at the front door of his apartment. It was now around 8pm and as Lee opened the door, his heart skipped a beat as he witnessed a stranger sitting at his desk playing a computer game on his computer.

"Who in the hell are you?" was his immediate question as he reached for his mobile phone and kept the door open in case he needed to flee.

"Ah, Lee Zhang Wei," the person said without looking up from his game, "Come in, come in, come in."

For a moment Lee wondered if he knew the person, but quickly came to the conclusion that he did not. The stranger was a man in his young twenties.

"I'm calling the police," Lee said as he unlocked his phone.

"Damn," the stranger said as the computer made a noise indicating that his game had been lost. "No need for that Lee Zang Wei, I only want to talk to you about that computer worm you installed at the Chase Bank a few years ago."

Lee remembered the time he had stolen three diamonds from the Chase Bank in Alabama after installing a backdoor in the computer system. He had previously been interviewed by the police, but no allegation had since been made.

"I don't know what you are talking about," Lee said somewhat perplexed.

"Do you ever give that fellow, what's his name, Chuck Smith, a second thought?" the young man asked. "You know they executed him last week and he swore black and blue at his trial that you were his alibi on the day of the killing."

"Are you a detective?" Lee answered the question with a question. The truth was that Lee often thought about the peculiar man with Asperger's syndrome that he had met in the elevator when he carried out his bank heist. Lee's conscience had often haunted him about the fact that his failure to disclose his own crime, resulted in the electrocution of an innocent man. But, Lee Zhang Wei reasoned, or rather, rationalised, that it was simply not fair that another man accused of a crime should rely exclusively on Lee for his evidence at that moment in time. Lee had his own life to live and he did not see himself as responsible for saving another.

"No, my name is Dr Lazer," the young man replied. "You could say that I am a high-tech criminal merchant and I wish to contract you for some computer services for us. It has taken years for us to track you down."

Lee was taken aback and didn't know how to respond. He was curious as to what the man knew and what he could reveal to authorities about his crime, but at the same time, he was frightened to make any admissions that may be recorded and used as evidence against him.

"Are you wearing a wire?" Lee asked rather nervously.

"No, of course not," Dr Lazer responded lifting his shirt and rotating on the spot to reveal both sides of his bare trunk. "The only thing I have is my mobile phone, and I will now turn it off," he said showing the phone powering down.

Still, Lee thought to himself, he could have planted a bug in the apartment before he came home. Lee thought for a moment and then said aloud, "Hey Google set volume to maximum." After his Google Home complied, he then commanded, "Hey Google, play heavy metal music."

Google complied with a cacophony of sounds that would drown-out the recording of any listening device and Lee closed the front door of his apartment and proceeded to open his cupboard. He retrieved two gaming helmets and switched them both on. He placed one on his head and gave another to Dr Lazer indicating that he should do the same. Lee then whispered into the microphone attached to his helmet.

"These are gaming helmets that are connected to each other by Bluetooth. If you whisper into your microphone, I can hear you just as you can hear me, but nothing can be recorded over this noise," Lee said rather softly as his Google Home bashed out heavy-metal music. "You happy to play along?" Lee asked feeling safe to continue the conversation.

"Fine," Dr Lazer whispered back. "I like how you think," he said.

Dr Lazer sat back down at the computer desk and looked at Lee who backed off to the sofa on the other side of the room with the heavy metal music booming loudly between them.

"My people have integrated a computer worm into most parts of the internet," Dr Lazer began. "It is still infiltrating major networks but when it installs itself, it has the power to alter the database that that network accesses. This can provide us unlimited power," he continued. "For example, it can change the account balance of a bank account. It can alter a criminal record. It can even modify a birth certificate or create one for that matter. You get the picture."

"That sounds pretty sophisticated," Lee considered how such a worm could possibly work.

"Well, it's not sophisticated enough," Dr Lazer replied. "The problem is that if and whenever it is actually used, it can modify the database all right, but it still leaves a trail behind indicating that the database has been hacked into. Even if we make the trail untraceable back to us by routing it through countless VPN servers, the fact that such a trail exists is enough to make any modifications useless to us. We need to make it invisible."

"Go on," Lee said as he started to think about the problem.

"Then a few years ago," Dr Lazer said his eyes beaming and unable to contain his smile from within his helmet, "We were looking into the database of the Chase Bank, Alabama. And wham bam!" Dr Lazer said above a whisper, "The code rewrote itself and old code was deleted. That was a stroke of genius," he said in a whisper tone again responding to Lee's gesturing. "It was absolutely untraceable. The only way we were able to suspect you is from the interview you gave to the detectives at the Surry Hills police station six months later that our worm was able to access and the defence raised by the late Chuck Smith at his recent trial. When we married those events together with the fact that you were working at the Chase Bank at the time, we were able to deduce that you are the computer expert who is capable of writing code that could delete itself from a system without leaving a trace. So, we want you to write a computer function for us that can attach itself to our code so that it deletes itself without a trace. We need to be invisible on the net. We can certainly make it worth your while."

"If I was interested," Lee said wondering if he had hit the jackpot or whether it was all an elaborate hoax or a trap, "How would we communicate and negotiate the terms?"

"It's simple," Dr Lazer replied. "When I leave here tonight, I will give you the name of a computer game to download on your iPad. Create a character and give it the username Stealth25. You can then type a chat in the game itself to us. We have registered another character on the game with the username of Timer52. After a couple of chats, we will rotate through several computer games and chat servers and usernames. It is all untraceable. If necessary, you and I can meet again at a place that you nominate if we need to clear-up anything just before we commercialise our worm. Are you interested?"

"I think so," Lee replied feeling rather excited about his new job prospects. "But I will have to see what worm you guys are talking about and how you have infiltrated the net so far."

"Very good," Dr Lazer said as he stood up and took his helmet off. He reached into his back pocket and pulled out a business card that simply had the printed name of a computer game and the user names Stealth25 and Timer52. "See you in hyperspace," he said as he handed Lee the card and left the apartment.

About seven days later, Lee had had multiple communications on game chats that he downloaded but never played. A somewhat complex Chinese computer fire-wall system was put in place between Dr Lazer's infiltration code and Lee's stealth self-deleting code that he would append to each data packet, so neither of them could actually see fully what each other's computer code was, but they could clearly see the effects.

Dr Lazer's worm had infiltrated major databases and it was only growing. At first small and insignificant changes were made to databases that were accessible from the net. A fictitious phone number was added to the phone book. A spurious online recipe was changed from two eggs to three eggs. The official sunrise in Zimbabwe was changed from 6:03am to 6:02am. Eventually the alterations began to become bolder. The tax file numbers of company directors were probed, their bank balances were inspected and driver's licence information was also revealed. Then accumulated points for driving offences started to diminish in specific cases and criminal records started to be altered. Even a prison sentence for an otherwise relatively insignificant criminal was reduced by a number of months. Dr Lazer's plan was succeeding and as his worm would grow, so too did his power, and Lee was along for the ride.

It was now about six months from the time Lee had first met Dr Lazer in his apartment and Lee's nominated PayPal accounts had significantly grown in the meantime. The plan appeared to be quite successful and Lee had started to develop a certain amount of trust regarding his new partner in crime. But now Dr Lazer had indicated that he had run across a problem and that it was not practical to solve it via the usual game chatrooms. They had met twice before in person to iron-out difficulties along the way. A third meeting was now organised in the cafeteria in the hospital that adjoined the University of Sydney after work on a particular Thursday night.

Lee arrived at the hospital cafeteria around 7:30pm and saw Dr Lazer already seated and flipping through his mobile telephone. The cafeteria had the usual hustle and bustle of patrons associated with the hospital being both medical personnel and patients alike. As Lee sat opposite Dr Lazer, Dr Lazer began.

"Our work has grown quite significantly since we started," he said. "Strictly speaking it is no longer an internet worm. I'd say it has fully grown into a serpent."

"I agree," Lee said with muted excitement. "It won't be long before our serpent swallows up the entire business world."

"That's what I wanted to ask you," Dr Lazer said. "What happens if our serpent encounters another serpent in the net?"

"What do you mean," Lee asked wondering where he was coming from.

Dr Lazer put the phone down and adopted a rather circumspect composure as he looked towards the ceiling.

"Do you remember the Bible story when Moses was before Pharoah and Moses placed his staff before him and it turned into a serpent?"

"Vaguely," Lee responded wondering what Dr Lazer was getting at. "Refresh my memory," Lee said.

"Then Pharoah accused Moses of a cheap magician's trick and Pharoah's own sorcerers put their own staffs on the floor which also turned into serpents," Dr Lazer continued. "Apparently if you hold a serpent upside down by its tail for a long enough time, it goes stiff and can resemble a staff. But do you know what happened then?"

"Not really," Lee replied feeling a little confused.

"Well apparently, by the power of God," Dr Lazer said rolling his eyes about, "Moses' serpent swallowed up the Pharoah's serpents and then only Moses' serpent remained."

"Ok," Lee said still wondering where this was leading.

"So, I was wondering," Dr Lazer asked, "If that's what happens in a real serpent fight," Dr Lazer continued shifting a little in his seat, "Could something like that happen if our internet serpent encountered another bigger internet serpent?"

"I think you had better tell me precisely what has happened," Lee said.

"Well, we were using our serpent to categorise the databases of the top ten companies on the Wall Street Stock Exchange. But when we came across the major pharmaceutical company DrugTech, our serpent crashed and it failed to come back online," Dr Lazer said looking at Lee in a rather confused way. "I mean DrugTech is a top ten blue-chip company," Dr Lazer continued, "It is supposed to be very reputable. But do you think that they could have their own internet serpent?"

"It's possible," Lee replied thinking about the problem. "But here's the thing," Lee continued this time Lee shifting in his seat rather uncomfortably. "If they actually do have a serpent already there and watching the internet, then if our serpent attempted to penetrate the company firewall without seeing or suspecting their serpent first, then it is very possible that their serpent would have seen our code before it deleted itself. If that is the case, then they could easily trace us in the very way that we were afraid of being tracked in the beginning. In fact," Lee said feeling his usual suspicious self again and making a quick survey of the room, "In fact, we could even be under surveillance right now."

"Now you are just starting to sound paranoid," Dr Lazer said. "If you start believing in conspiracy theories, then you can start chasing shadows forever," he said dismissing the suggestion.

Lee was not completely convinced. "But what if..." he began again when the Tactical Response Group stormed the cafeteria with guns drawn.

"It has been a long time since I finally got you in my sights again," a Detective Sergeant Derrick said to Dr Lazer as he and Lee were led away in handcuffs past two rather elegantly dressed detectives.

Chapter 26

A Quest

The camp fire was now more of a small bonfire as the blaze flickered across the reddened faces of the three students that sat around it on logs. Each of them shared their time gazing at the open stars, their cans of drink, and the several other camp fires that were each surrounded by other students engaged in a similar exercise as them. They had just finished eating the fat sausages that they had been given in fresh buns with a can of Coke.

"I am the Mother Superior of the Dominican Order of Nuns," a woman dressed in a nun's habit said as she approached the campfire where the three students were seated. "Welcome to the second night of the retreat for the new students of the St John's College and the Santa Sabina College of the University of Sydney. This year as you know," the Mother Superior continued, "the retreat is being run by the Dominican order of nuns. We have selected several exercises for you to partake in. This exercise was given to you at lunch time today for you to prepare something tonight. It is an informal thing. Each of you is to first introduce yourself, and then to state the strangest experience in your life. This exercise is scheduled to last 45 minutes, so take the opportunity to get to know each other and hopefully make yourself some lifelong friends in the process. Are there any questions?"

The two boys and the young woman looked around at each other to see if anyone would interrogate the nun, but after a short pause with no volunteers the nun began again. "Very well, this will conclude in 45 minutes when you can each return to your dormitories. Good luck." And just like that, the nun turned and left as quickly as she came.

As the students gestured each other to see who would go first, one of the boys suggested, "Ladies first," and he motioned towards the young woman. Rather than argue, she was happy to comply.

"My name is Patricia O'Leary," she began. "I am a mature-aged student in my first year at Sydney University in a combined science-law degree. I was married at 19 for four years before my husband died in a tragic accident at home. Two years later at the age of 25 I started this degree."

Patricia paused at this stage as she was about to shift topics to address the exercise that she was confronted with. The boys maintained a respectful silence as they waited for her to continue.

"I think the strangest thing that I have ever experienced would literally be about 20 minutes ago when I had a conversation with a nun in the dormitory just over there," she said indicating the building about a hundred metres behind her. "I was being interviewed by a nun, a arm...," she paused attempting to recollect her name, "a Sister Jennifer," she said evidently recalling her name with certainty when it came to her.

"Sister Jennifer was a tall slim woman, youngish, rather attractive in her own way. I couldn't see much of her with her vale on but she had very pale cheeks that never smiled. In getting to know me and seeing how I would fit in at Santa Sabina College, I was asked by Sister Jennifer what the most troubling thing in my life was. I explained that I was the beneficiary of an insurance policy to the tune of $20 million dollars on my late husband's life, but that the insurance company was jerking me around and refusing to pay. I told her that I had to engage a lawyer to sue the insurance company and that it was understandably causing me considerable stress."

At this point the boys murmured to themselves and under their breaths at the amount of money involved and the obvious problem that had befallen the speaker. They were curious to see how it unfolded.

"But then," the speaker continued looking puzzled and a little stressed as she wondered how to choose her next words, "The strangest thing happened," she continued. "Sister Jennifer looked directly at me with a gaze that sent shivers up my spine. Her face looked stone-cold white and I couldn't read her at all. And then after a short time, she said in a very gentle but somewhat commanding voice, as if nothing else in the universe mattered, the words, 'That's not quite true is it.' So, I naturally asked her what she meant. And then she said, 'You are actually more troubled by your own conscience in failing to rescue your husband by opening the fridge-door that he was trapped in.' So, I said to her, 'How do you know that? Have you spoken to someone about me?' and I was wondering who on earth she could have spoken to about me because no-one knew about this incident except the police who interviewed me, so I was wondering if she was connected with the police somehow. And she answered as if she read my very thoughts, 'No, I haven't spoken to anyone about you including the police.' So, I asked, 'Then how?' and she raised her hand to stop me and she said, 'It is written on your very face.'"

Patricia looked a little troubled in relaying the story at this point and looked at the boys to gauge their reaction. The firelight was dancing over their faces but they appeared mesmerised by the story and motioned for her to continue. "So, I said to her, 'Well I have taken steps to address my troubled conscience,' and Sister Jennifer then looked deeper at me and I felt frozen again and she said to me, "I know that you have enrolled in a new drug study at DrugTech to try an experimental drug for people who suffer from PTSD. You are hoping that that might help you find relief. I know all about DrugTech,' she said in a curt and rather expressionless way without any hint of emotion. 'At best the drug they will give you might help you forget the incident in the short term. But in the years to come, the truth will come back to you in haunting flashbacks. And in the end, no drug can comfort a soul in pain like that. You need spiritual healing.' Well at this point I was almost knocked off my feet so I said to her, 'How on earth did you know that I enrolled in that study? Are you stalking me or something? You seem to know everything about me?' And she goes, 'Anyone with eyes to see can see that it is written all over your face. I suggest you take on board what I have said and search your soul, for your own sake,' and then she left me alone, and I have been going crazy ever since wondering how she knew all those things about me."

"Gosh," one of the boys responded, "That is almost like a ghost story."

"I have always been suspicious of nuns," the other boy said. "But then I have started to grow suspicious of DrugTech too," he continued. "Are you going through with that study?"

"I don't know," Patricia answered. "I'll think about it. Anyway, one of you guys go next," she said gesturing with her hand towards them.

The boys looked at each other and then one of them started.

"My name is Jake Peterson," he said clearing his throat and putting his can of Coke down beside him. "I am a second-year Engineering student. I have been friends with Tommy here since my school days," he said indicating the boy next to him. "We are both new to St John's College this year so here we are both on this retreat."

Patricia nodded her head in acknowledgment and smiled gently at her new friends.

"I'd say the strangest thing that has ever happened to me was when I was in year 8 at High School," Jake said as he looked off to one side in recollecting the incident.

"I remember walking home from School through the park at Milson's Corner when I noticed a golden glittery effect under one of the bushes. So, I went to investigate and I found this magnificent Wizard's book with the words 'Book of Spells' on the cover. It had golden edges that just shimmered and I could have sworn that the book hummed like it was electric or something. I looked around for the owner but there was no one about, so I put the book in my bag and thought I would study it on the bus."

Jake looked again at his audience and saw that they were listening intently. He had never previously relayed this story to anyone and he wasn't quite sure how it would be received but he thought that his story was no-crazier than the story he had just heard and the others were not laughing so he continued.

"When I got on the bus, I studied the book more closely and saw that each page contained a beautiful picture with a spell," he said remembering the incident quite well. "There were things like 'How to make yourself invisible', or 'How to breathe underwater', or 'How to always know the time'. A different spell on each page. I must admit, I was fascinated and wanted the book to be real. Then I came across one spell called, 'How to remove magic spells,' and I thought to myself, 'I may as well try that one right here and right now on the bus just to see if the book was real. So, I said the incantation and looked around but nothing seemed to happen. But then when I had another look at the book, the pages of the book were blank. I almost died right there."

Both Tommy and Patricia each reacted in their way to the story they were hearing, but before they could voice their concerns, Jake continued. "I know you don't believe me," he said as they settled down to hear the rest. "For years I tried to convince myself that it was just a dream. I put the book with blank pages under my bed but the following morning it was nowhere to be found. I said to myself, 'I must be delusional' and so I decided never to tell anyone about the episode in case they thought I was crazy. It was my own personal secret for many years. But then recently, I started having flashbacks about it. The other night I woke from my dream, at least I thought it was a dream. I remembered walking through the park at Milson's corner but this time I didn't pick up the wizard's book. Instead, I went into a shop and saw a silver casket on the counter and heard the people there saying something about it coming from DrugTech. And then the casket morphed into the wizard's book and I was in the park again. These flashbacks have continued and I must admit they are a little haunting and they are only getting stronger. The name 'DrugTech' has been ringing in my ears now. I know it sounds weird but that's the exercise, right?" Jake asked. "Well, this is the strangest experience of my life," he said finishing his story.

"Wow," Patricia exclaimed.

"Far out," Tommy said.

"Your turn," Jake said pointing at Tommy, happy for someone else to start talking.

"My name is Tommy Grayson, I'm a second year Medical Student," he began. "I had just finished my biology lab class the other day and as I was leaving, I saw Professor Philip studying an item in a locker with a Geiger counter. I didn't think much of it at the time, but a couple of days later I made a mistake and went to the lab at the wrong time, and when I opened the lab door expecting to see my class mates, I saw Professor Philip and his associate Charlie both in full-blown radiation suits studying a camera on their desk which they then picked up with tongs and carried to a microscope. I thought it was quite a bizarre sight to see guys in radiation suits and handling something as basic as a camera with tongs, but a couple of days later, something even stranger happened."

It was now Tommy's turn to look at the faces of Patricia and Jake and he saw that both of them were interested in his story and wanted him to go on.

"As part of our psychiatry class, we had an excursion to the Mary Immaculate Psychiatric Hospital. Each of us were assigned one patient that we were to interview. I interviewed a scientist by the name of Bruce. He had been acquitted of a murder charge on the grounds of insanity and so he was being held by law at the hospital. He had been released just recently but he breached his conditions of release by getting into a fight with a priest of all people so he was re-arrested."

"A fight with a priest?" Jake quipped.

"I know right?" Tommy answered, "Go figure. Anyway, he said he was employed by DrugTech as a scientist and he was ranting about his new invention that he had been working on which he called the 'Trans Warp Influencer' or something. Apparently, he was under the delusion that he could transport a human from one place to another with his experiment but he hadn't quite perfected it for some reason or another. When I asked him how such a thing could even be theoretically possible, he raved on about some kind of physical discovery he had made called the 'Doctrine of relative stillness' and he rattled off all sorts of equations and I must admit that I was a little bored with his delusion, but then he said something that made me sit up and pay attention."

"What was that?" Jake enquired wondering where this was going.

"He said the thing he needed to get his invention to work was a thing called the Medusa Stone. When I asked him what was that, he said that his former cell-mate had found a piece of radioactive meteorite which he had covered with molten lead and then he placed it inside a camera. He then scraped a bit of the lead away so that the radiation could proceed through the aperture of the camera which he had also coated with led. Then whenever he looked through the lens and clicked the aperture of the camera open, he could zap any living creature and they would fall down dead instantly. Well up until this point," Tommy said taking a quick gulp of his coke and continuing before he had fully swallowed it all, "I had thought it was all one big delusion. But then I remembered seeing Professor Philip and Charlie with a Geiger counter and radiation suits and handling a camera with tongs. So, I thought to myself, maybe they had found the Medusa Stone that this patient wanted so badly."

"So, what did you do?" Patricia asked.

"Well, I said to him, 'That's funny you should describe such an odd thing, because I have just seen some scientists with a Geiger counter and radiation suits checking out a camera.' Well, at this point, he just froze and his eyes became wild and he insisted that I tell him when and where and who and he wouldn't rest until I did."

"Did you tell him?" Jake asked.

"Well, I had no reason to keep it a secret," Tommy replied. "I told him I saw my lecturer, Professor Philip and his associate, Charlie, back at the university mucking around with it."

"What did he do then?" Jake asked.

"He went completely nuts. It's as if his mouth seized up and he was foaming and dropping saliva all over the place and I just got the hell out of there as soon as possible. But when I wrote up my report the next day, I tactfully left out the fact that I had mentioned Professor Philip or Charlie or anything to do with a radioactive camera. I just didn't want to get involved in anything that was going on between them. Well, that's it," Tommy said shrugging his shoulders, "That's my story."

"You know," Jake said pausing a little before continuing, "It's funny that each of our stories mentioned DrugTech in some way or another. Patricia mentioned a drug study that she was going to do at DrugTech, and I said that I recalled DrugTech being mentioned in the shop with the silver casket. And you said that the scientist that you interviewed worked for DrugTech."

"That is strange," Tommy said looking at Patricia who was in full agreement. "We should make it our personal quest to find out what exactly is going on with DrugTech I reckon."

"You know," Patricia said, "That Sister Jennifer said that she knew all about DrugTech. I wonder what would happen if we all approached her and asked her what she knew."

"I'm not sure I'd be game enough," Jake said. "But it is strange that Sister Jennifer did happen to know all about you and the DrugTech trial that you were interested in even before you mentioned it."

"It couldn't hurt to ask you know?" Tommy said taking Patricia up on her offer, "We could all approach her tonight when this exercise finishes."

"Fine," Jake said and Patricia agreed.

About 45 minutes later, Tommy, Jake and Patricia had walked about a hundred metres to the building that Patricia had been interviewed in by Sister Jennifer when they were greeted by the Mother Superior.

"Can I help you?" the Mother Superior enquired.

"We were wondering if we could speak with Sister Jennifer," Patricia asked.

"She is on her way with the other sisters to Mass right now," the Mother Superior replied before being tapped on the shoulder by Sister Jennifer.

"It's OK, Mother Superior, I will be no more than a minute and I will go straight to Mass afterwards."

"Don't be any longer my child," the Mother Superior said before leaving them alone.

Sister Jennifer turned to look at each of her visitors directly in the face. Before they could speak, she lifted her hand to silence them and each of them froze as they waited for Sister Jennifer to speak first.

"I haven't got time to have a full conversation with you," Sister Jennifer began, "But I know what you have come to ask me," she said to three fascinated faces before continuing. "Ultimately everyone wants to know the causes of things. Mankind cannot achieve contentment without it. You have come to ask me what I know about DrugTech. All I can tell you is this. Ask yourself what you really want to know. If you want to know the scientific causes of DrugTech's projects that have fascinated you all so much, then you must speak to a person you know as Professor Philip Kurtis. But if you want to know about the legalities of DrugTech and its all-pervasive influence in the media, the internet, the Courts and the politicians, then all I can do is refer you to an honest cop by the name of Detective Sergeant Derrick at the Surry Hills Police Station. But if you want to know ultimately how every person with an interest in DrugTech is related to each other through DrugTech and what each of them are after; then you will have to seek out a Father William Hunter of the Dominican Order," she said just as stone-faced as when she began. "So let me now ask each of you a question," Sister Jennifer said to three stunned students. "Which one will you seek out?" she asked as she looked each of them again in the face. None of them had time to voice their thoughts before Sister Jennifer said, "I see." And just like that, she turned on her heels and proceeded to Mass.

Chapter 27

A Directions Hearing

"Call the next matter," Magistrate Burwood said as the accused from the previous matter was ushered back to the cells by the Corrective Services Officers.

"DPP and Dr Leon Lazer," the Associate called.

Dr Lazer was now ushered to the dock by the Corrective Services Officers.

"Do you have legal representation?" the Magistrate enquired of the accused.

"No, Your Honour," Dr Lazer replied, "I will be representing myself today."

"Very well," the Magistrate said politely, "But you do understand don't you that the DPP are seeking to have you committed to stand trial in the Supreme Court on 215 charges of computer fraud. They are very serious charges and if you are convicted of them, you could expect to receive a substantial custodial sentence. I would strongly recommend that you seek legal advice before the next occasion."

"Your Honour," Dr Lazer replied. "I have an application to make."

"Yes," the Magistrate responded, "What is the application?"

"I respectfully ask that you recuse yourself in this matter," Dr Lazer began.

"On what grounds?" the Magistrate enquired politely as if the application was of little consequence.

"Your Honour," Dr Lazer answered, "The defence in this matter will be raising some very serious allegations against the company DrugTech. A quick ASIC search has revealed that you personally are the holder of shares in DrugTech. That means that legally you are a part-owner of the company and are technically financially interested in the outcome of this matter. It would not be proper for you to be seen to be involved in this matter because a reasonable person in the back of the courtroom might suspect that you might not bring an impartial mind to the matter."

"I am also a taxpayer too Dr Lazer," the Magistrate quipped. "Does that mean I should recuse myself of every tax fraud case as well?" he asked smiling wryly.

The prosecution along with the rest of the courtroom chuckled at the joke. But Dr Lazer did not find the question funny. As with most self-represented litigants, he struggled to keep up with the flow before he was interrupted by the Magistrate again.

"If I own DrugTech shares," the Magistrate continued, "And in fact I do not know whether I do or I don't, but if I do, then it is only because they comprise part of my Superannuation share portfolio which my family stockbroker has put together. I am not an active shareholder in any of those companies, and I don't see how any of that can be seen to make me any less impartial in this matter. What do you say Mr Crown?"

The prosecutor rose to his feet and responded. "This issue is well-settled Your Honour. On that basis, there is absolutely no problem with Your Honour continuing with this case."

"Yes, I think so too," the Magistrate replied still maintaining the utmost courteousness and politeness, "the defence application for me to recuse myself in this matter is dismissed. I shall publish my reasons at 2pm this afternoon." At this point the Magistrate looked at the accused.

"Dr Lazer," Magistrate Burwood began again in still a polite and softly-spoken voice. "I shall give you every opportunity for you to make whatever allegation you like against the company DrugTech or any other company for that matter. It will either provide you with a defence or it will not. But what concerns me is that you receive a fair trial and I am not satisfied that you are capable of representing yourself."

At this stage the Magistrate looked around the courtroom and spotted a barrister sitting at the back looking over her notes.

"Ms Colfax," the Magistrate enquired directing his attention to the back of the courtroom, "Are you up to receiving a dock brief?"

"Yes, Your Honour," the barrister replied clumsily putting her notes to one side and standing to address the Court.

"Dr Lazer," the Magistrate said turning to look at the accused, "The Court is assigning Ms Colfax to represent you further in these proceedings. I suggest you go downstairs and have a conference with her and give some serious consideration to continuing to retain her to represent you in this matter. Do you understand that?"

"Yes, Your Honour," Dr Lazer replied rather sheepishly.

"What's happening in this matter Mr Crown," the Magistrate enquired of the prosecutor.

"The prosecution seeks service of brief directions and a date for the committal hearing of the accused," the prosecutor answered.

"How long do you need to serve your evidence?" the Magistrate asked.

"28 days," the Crown responded.

"Very well," the Magistrate said. "I direct the prosecution to serve the accused with any evidence that the prosecutor intends to rely upon against the accused within 28 days. The matter can then return to Court in seven days after that to set a hearing date for committal. Is there anything else?" the Magistrate enquired of the parties.

"Yes, Your Honour," Dr Lazer answered. "I was charged with another person by the name of Lee Zhang Wei but we were separated when we were taken into custody. He will be instrumental in my defence and I wish my committal hearing to be heard at the same time as his. Also, I wish to make a bail application."

"One thing at a time Dr Lazer," the Magistrate said proceeding cautiously. "Mr Crown, if this accused was charged at the same time as another co-accused and the matters are related, shouldn't they be proceeding together?"

"Yes, Your Honour," the Prosecutor said rummaging through his papers and looking at his instructing solicitor for guidance on the matter. "I am not sure what the story is there."

"Alright," the Magistrate said. "I will stand this matter down for 20 minutes. In the meantime, the prosecutor can make enquiries as to what is happening with Lee Zhang Wei and the accused can go downstairs and talk to Ms Colfax about making a bail application. Call the next matter please."

Dr Lazer was then escorted back to the police holding cells beneath the Court. It wasn't long before he was taken to a small interview room where he was seated behind a desk fronting a pane of Plexiglass. On the other side of the Plexiglass was a similar facing desk and a door where barrister Colfax entered and shut the door behind her before spreading out her notes on the desk.

"I have received the charges and the facts sheet from the prosecutor," Colfax began. "The charges are quite voluminous and pretty serious. Why don't you just tell me what your side of the story is?"

"It's all a setup," Dr Lazer answered. "We were looking into simple security protocols on the world wide web and we came across an internet worm that DrugTech had installed behind it's firewall."

"Hang on, slow down," Colfax interjected attempting to make notes. "This is all way too technical to me. You need to explain it as if you are speaking to a school student who knows nothing about the intricate technical details of the web. Certainly, you can't expect the jury in this matter to have any idea about the technical workings of the internet."

"It's difficult to explain," Dr Lazer began again. "We were searching and scanning internet web sites and carrying out an audit to characterise how secure certain websites were. But when we came across DrugTech's website we saw that they had installed a computer worm that could access all sorts of websites and get around the security protocols. They are engaged in some serious computer fraud. They are the ones who should be charged with what we are charged with. Lee Zhang Wei can explain it better than me. You have to speak with him."

"Well, they are some pretty serious allegations that you are raising," Colfax replied. "I don't know how you are going to prove something as conspiratorial as that against a top ten company on the Australian Stock Exchange. I must admit that most juries are suspicious of conspiracy theories, especially when they are advanced by people who are themselves charged with serious crimes. Do you have any way to demonstrate this to the courtroom?"

"Oh absolutely," Dr Lazer replied quite enthusiastically. "Lee Zhang Wei can demonstrate it quite easily on his laptop. All he needs to show is that when he masks his identity behind a VPN server that mimics that of DrugTech, then all the web servers that normally keep out unauthorised users are suddenly open up to it. DrugTech can penetrate the security system of banks, the taxation office, the ASX, prison records, you name it. I expect the matter will attract great publicity. I doubt very much that this will actually go to trial in the end."

The barrister was not so easily moved by the story. "Most of my clients think that their case would attract great publicity," she said still making notes. "But most of the time, their cases are rather dry and boring and not up to the standards set by the salacious media. How are we going to get Lee Zhang Wei to demonstrate this, isn't he in custody too?"

"Yes," Dr Lazer answered. "But if you speak to him and bring a laptop with you, he will show you what sites to log in to, to demonstrate what I am talking about. He has all the computer expertise in this matter. He has computer robots installed and ready to go to demonstrate what I have said and how we are the effective scapegoats for DrugTech's own internet fraud. We are just charged because we are the ones who have found them out!"

"Well, it all sounds rather airy-fairy to me," Colfax replied still taking notes, "But I will speak to him like you insist."

At this point, Colfax's mobile telephone started vibrating.

"Hang on," she said reaching for her phone. "It's the prosecutor in this matter."

Colfax answered her phone and listened intently. "I see," she would say occasionally and she made more notes of the phone conversation. After about three minutes the call terminated and she directed her gaze back to her client.

"Lee Zhang Wei's committal hearing is listed in one month's time," she said. "The prosecutor will ask the Court to relist your matter on the same date as his so that any application for joint or separate trials can be made on that day."

"That's excellent," Dr Lazer responded, his eyes beaming. "Lee Zhang Wei will most certainly be able to demonstrate what I am saying to you on that day."

"I don't think so," Colfax replied putting the lid back on her pen and closing her notes. "The prosecutor just indicated that they expect Lee Zhang Wei to plead guilty on the next occasion. He has reached a deal with the prosecutor and will be the main prosecution witness against you."

Chapter 28

The Police Officers' Ball

The annual Police Officers' Ball was held this year on the last day in October and so it naturally took upon itself a Halloween theme. The black-ties and formal dresses gave way to vampires and witches but the usual dancing and fraternising remained the same. The venue this year was the Masonic Centre in Castlereagh Street, Sydney, a particularly plush establishment large enough to accommodate the officers and their guests from around the State, and in the heart of the CBD, it was central enough for a small ride or a medium walk from the Surry Hills Police Station.

It was pushing into the third hour of the event and the tables were thinned to allow the coffee drinkers and dessert eaters to speak to each other in relative peace whilst the others engaged in dancing on the dance floor. Towards the back of the venue was a table organised for the usual Red Scorpion Brigade. The Red Scorpion Brigade were highly trained officers in the fields of covert infiltration, homicide and tactical operations. It was an unofficial fraternity (not formally recognised by the establishment) so named after the red scorpion that each of them had tattooed to the back of their hands. Its new leader Sergeant Skip Johns had replaced the late Sergeant Adam Michaels, killed in a motorcycle accident several years ago.

The Kizana sisters had left the table with their partners for the dance floor. Sergeant Skip Johns and DrugTech Counsellor Dr Jeremy Pitts remained where they huddled together with their coffees and began to talk quietly to each other about their recent accomplishments.

"I'd like to thank you for helping me out with my grandson," Skip Johns said as he stirred his coffee and eyed the desserts. "He was a shy fellow, rather introverted, but he seems to be enjoying himself on the dancefloor."

"It was Project X23," Dr Pitts replied. "We use it for just such an occasion. But it can only be used once. It has some rather bad side effects if you try it again."

"I hear you managed to get Investigator Rawlins to resign," Dr Pitts began again changing the subject. "What was the story there?"

"Oh, he was a taxation investigator who was looking to commence an audit into DrugTech," Johns said, "But unlike you DrugTech counsellors, we don't often have the luxury of fancy scientific stuff at our disposal. We have to do it the old fashion way, with the carrot and the stick."

"So, what happened?" Dr Pitts asked sipping his coffee and looking rather bemused.

"Well, we arranged with our Federal buddies to get him to assist in an investigation into your very own Beatrice Kizana, as an author who was claiming some rather unorthodox taxation deductions," Skip Johns recalled with a wry smile. "Our Federal buddies managed to wrangle a search warrant out of a judge and they raided Rawlins' house causing much embarrassment to his division. Pressure was then put on him at work to throw in the towel and resign."

"That sounds like the stick alright," Dr Pitts volunteered, "But what about the carrot?"

"Well, his daughter Macey was a single mum who was struggling and relying on her dad for financial assistance every so often, which was really the motivation for her dad to stay at work anyway," Skip Johns replied. "We had one of our operatives organise an elevator accident where he got trapped in the elevator with her, and it was staged for him to slip her a winning lottery ticket before he carked it in front of her."

"Are you serious?" Dr Pitts asked showing his amusement. "I wish I could have been a fly on the wall in that one."

"Well, it worked," Skip Johns continued. "The last I heard; Macy with her daughter and Ex-Investigator Rawlins, her dad, all set up residence together at Lord Howe Island. Not a bad place for retirement I hear."

There was a small pause at this point while Sergeant Johns helped himself to the chocolate desserts which he consumed in-between coffee sips. "I hear you had some success too with getting that Asian guy, what's his name, Lee Zhang Wei to plead guilty. Could you imagine if he started raving on about the DrugTech worm he discovered in open Court?"

"Oh yeah," Dr Pitts smirked. "All you do is release a bit of Haldo 29 in the air while he spends the night with Mr Solitary. The guy can convince anyone to plead guilty. We did something similar with that bloke accused of killing a prison officer once. Apparently, he had become a nuisance to DrugTech too."

"Well, be careful because Detective Sergeant Derrick doesn't know anything about that," Skip Johns replied, "But he seems terribly happy about catching Lee's partner. I understand he has been chasing Dr Lazer for years."

There was another break in the conversation at this point as Sergeant Johns grabbed another dessert and Dr Pitts finished his coffee and stretched himself out in his chair as he wondered how much longer there was in the night before his wife would return from the dance floor with her sister.

"How's the Marty Hanson suicide case going?" Dr Pitts enquired after a brief yawn.

"We're about to wrap that up," Sergeant Johns answered. "By the way, I used the last of those suicide pills on a kid called Tommy Grayson who happened to have his phone number the same as the ACN of DrugTech. I don't think it worked on him, but then I got a report that his dad happened to be working at the Australian Bureau of Statistics and had attempted to run some kind of audit into DrugTech too. There's something about that kid that troubles me, I'd better keep him under surveillance."

"Sounds tiresome," Dr Pitts replied yawning again. "Let me know if you need me for anything there."

"Sure thing," the Sergeant said signalling the waiter for another cup of coffee. "So, how are you finding your new managing director, the young Benjamin Jones?" Sergeant Johns enquired before stuffing his mouth again with the dessert.

"Oh, he's not so bad," Dr Pitts answered. "He loves the science. It's probably about time the scientific guild grabbed the reigns again. Besides, that Jamieson was probably a bit too ambitious for the company's good. It's probably better that he has retired."

"Oh, he hasn't retired," Sergeant Johns replied. "The last I heard; he went back to the United States. Apparently, he's got two detectives wandering around the place keeping an eye on things for him here. I'm told they are looking into this new invention the company's working on called the Trans Warp Inducer."

"The Trans Warp Inducer?" Dr Pitts enquired. "I thought that was something Benjamin Jones was trying to get working. If Jamieson has left DrugTech, what's he interested in it for?"

"Oh, he hasn't left DrugTech," Sergeant Johns replied. "I mean, not completely. He's just left Australia."

"What do you mean?" the DrugTech Counsellor enquired.

"Well, I hear that not too long ago," Sergeant Johns answered, "Jamieson hooked up with the Contessa Medici and together they merged their companies to form some international pharmaceutical conglomeration with their headquarters in New York. That is now the New York parent company to DrugTech in Australia. And Dr Jamieson is now the Managing Director of that conglomeration in New York."

Chapter 29

The Ten-Year-Old Know-It-All Kid

Orientation day at the University of Sydney was always a spectacle. Tommy Grayson, Jake Peterson and Patricia O'Leary had signed-up to the Archery Club, the Society for Creative Anachronisms and the Rock-Climbing Club. The Fencing Club was a close almost. As they strolled across the university quadrangle, a group of students that had huddled around a central figure caught their attention.

"What do you think is going on over there?" Tommy enquired.

"Dunno," Jake said, "Let's go find out."

The three of them trotted about 50m to the corner of the quadrangle where a ten-year-old kid was surrounded by a group of students all asking him questions.

"Hey kid, when do you turn 11?" one of the students asked him.

The ten-year-old had blonde hair and was wearing glasses. He was miniscule in comparison to the crowd. He slumped on a bench with his newly acquired text books that seemed almost half his size in comparison.

"In a couple of months," he replied quite innocently.

"Is it true that you have a photographic memory?" another student asked amidst the growing fascination of the students.

"I guess so," he replied, "I mean, you could probably call it that. I don't forget things that I see and hear."

"What's Euler's theorem?" another student barked.

"It's just a number theory formula that if 'a' and 'n' are coprime integers then 'a' raised to the power of the totient of 'n' is congruent to one, modulo 'n'," he replied as if he was reciting a nursery rhyme.

"Unbelievable," the students replied.

"Wow," Patricia O'Leary joined in. "Where are you staying?"

"I am staying at St John's College," the child replied. "I have to find a Tommy Grayson. I was told he would be coming-by this way. He, has been assigned as my roommate."

"Well, I think I can help you there," Patricia beamed quite happily, "Here is Tommy Grayson before your very eyes," she said as she indicated with both hands the person standing behind her.

"Hello? Can I help you?" Tommy responded hearing his name and seeing the group open up to allow him access to the child. Before him was a kid who looked like he should have been entering year five, but instead was enrolling in first year university.

"I'm Simon Sage," the boy said. "I understand that you are my roommate at St John's College."

"Well, in that case," Tommy replied extending his hand, "I am very pleased to meet you. Have you finished enrolling in all your subjects?"

"Yes," Simon replied.

"Ok, then let's get you settled at St John's. Come with me," he said looking to help him with his bag and his books.

The crowd dispersed and Tommy, Jake and Patricia escorted their new young friend towards St John's College.

"I'm Jake," he said introducing himself. "Have you given some thought to what you want to major in Simon?"

"That's a good question," Simon replied. "I think it will either be applied mathematics, physics or biochemistry. My professors want me to come to a tentative view on that within six weeks so they can steer me into the appropriate extra courses that they have in mind."

"Gosh," Patricia exclaimed, "It must be hard being such a whiz kid. You're still a growing boy, I hope. What time do you get to bed each night?"

"I get in bed at 7:30pm and hope to fall asleep by 8pm," he answered.

"Well, I'll tell you what kid," Tommy said. "On Tuesdays Wednesdays and Thursdays, I usually catch up on my lab work or study in the library, and on Friday nights I usually go out late with these guys, but I'll make a deal with you. Every Monday night, I will catch an early night with you at 7:30pm and you can fill me in on what you have been up to and let me know if there is anything I can do to help you out at Uni, OK?"

"Sounds great," Simon replied.

The following Monday night, Tommy had an early dinner and wandered on in to his dorm. Simon was already in his pyjamas and was climbing in to bed.

"What can you tell me about Professor Philip?" Simon enquired.

"He's pleasant enough. Very jovial. Quite no-nonsense when it comes to bioscience, especially red-blood cells. He respects everyone's questions but his answers usually go right over everyone's heads. Way too technical if you ask me," Tommy answered quite candidly. "You'll probably love him actually," he added remembering the intellectual calibre of the person he was talking to.

"What about Professor Jordon," Simon enquired again.

"Excellent mathematician," Tommy answered. "A little bit arrogant. He loves poker. He says he got into the game to assess the odds of each hand, but a lot of us students reckon he actually got into mathematics to do that."

"Tell me," Tommy asked, "How are you finding university so far?"

"It's pretty cool," Simon answered. "Much better than school. A lot more freedom."

"How are you finding the workload?"

"Not so bad," Simon replied. "I find it is progressing rather slowly actually. I have already read the text books and the lessons are just reiterating them so far."

"Far out," Tommy exclaimed. "I wish I had your brain."

Within minutes the conversation died down and the ten-year-old fell fast asleep.

For Tommy, the week proceeded slowly. Much of the classes were introductions to new topics and new concepts. Many of the students were still settling in. When Monday night came around, Simon was already in bed before Tommy came in.

"Anything interesting happen this week kid?" Tommy asked climbing into bed.

"Not too much," Simon responded.

"Given any more thought to your possible majors?" Tommy asked.

"It's still a toss-up between physics, biochemistry or mathematics," Tommy replied.

"Well, I suppose it all depends on what you want to do in life kid," Tommy volunteered. "Do you want to cure cancer? Do you want to cure diabetes?"

"I think those things can already be cured in today's technology," Simon answered. "It's really just a financial or economical question about whether the pharmaceutical companies want to fund or progress such a cure."

"What are you talking about?" Tommy asked rather sarcastically.

"When you look at the state of the science," Simon replied, "There's nothing really too obscure or difficult about taking the next step and finding a cure for those diseases. It's really just a question of funding."

"Well," Tommy replied, "Whatever you say kid."

The weather had grown progressively worse during the night and in the morning, a storm-front had arrived. Much of the week was dark, wet and miserable.

The following Monday, Simon was late as the first years were returning from a weekend retreat.

"Meet any new friends on retreat?" Tommy asked.

"Quite a few," Simon answered.

"Boy, I remember our retreat," Tommy began again. "We met this one Sister, Sister Jennifer, who for all intents and purposes, could quite literally read our minds. I think she was telepathic."

"There is no evidence to support telepathy," Simon answered quite matter-of-factly. "She probably could just read your face."

"Actually, she said something similar. What do you mean read my face?" Tommy asked.

"Well, colour is the object of the eye and we can only see seven shades of them," Simon answered. "But there is a theory that there are a lot more colours than that and certain adapted eyes can see and process those extra or 'super' colours which in turn can give away what a person is thinking. She is probably well adept at reading peoples' faces that way."

"Well, it's certainly got to be something," Tommy replied feeling quite overwhelmed with the explanation.

"By the way," Simon said changing the subject, "I think you are being surveilled."

"What are you talking about now, kid?" Tommy asked almost dismissively.

"You could say that I have a photographic memory of the people that surround us in the food courts, the lecture theatres and the corridors and there is this one guy who on average keeps the same radial distance from you on every occasion," Simon said. "Then the other day when you walked past him in the Chem building, he made as if he was talking on his mobile phone, however, in the basement level of the Chem building, there is no mobile phone reception."

"You're serious?" Tommy asked starting to take an interest in what he was being told. "Well, who is he?"

"Judging by his haircut," Simon answered, "I would say he's a cop. And judging by the tattoo of a rather un-aesthetically-pleasing red scorpion on the back of his hand, I'd say he is a member of a fraternity or a squad."

"Well, what do I do? How do I shake him?" Tommy asked starting to feel a little anxious about the situation.

"Well, the best way," Simon answered, "Is to just be boring."

"What do you mean 'just be boring'?" Tommy asked further.

"You just go where you are expected to go and do what you are expected to do. If he's a cop and you are boring, then there's nothing to report and he's bound to lose interest. Surveillance costs time and money and they just don't have the resources to surveil you forever. So, unless you are involved in anything illegal, just be boring."

"Thanks, kid," Tommy replied making plans for himself for the forthcoming week. Tommy knew that the surveillance definitely had something to do with DrugTech and that cop he had met not too long ago at the Surry Hills Police Station. Tommy recalled seeing a tattoo of a red scorpion on the back of his hand. However, Tommy decided not to corrupt Simon with his theories on the evil DrugTech at this stage. That was a quest that he and his other friends had decided to get to the bottom of, but it was way too cynical for a freshman, let alone a ten-year-old. Perhaps when the kid was more worldly-wise, he could be brought up to scratch on the likes of DrugTech.

"Tell me something," Tommy asked after a short pause, "What would a kid like you want? I mean, if I could get something for you as a kind of a reward, what would you like? A laptop? A night out with some friends? A movie? What?"

"Are you serious?" Simon asked, "No one has ever really asked me that before."

"Sure," Tommy replied. "Just name it."

"Well, to be honest," Simon said, "I think what I would like most of all..."

"Yeah?" Tommy interjected impatiently, "What?"

"I think I'd like Pokémon cards," Simon answered.

"Pokémon cards?" Tommy asked quite surprised at the answer.

"Sure," Simon answered. "I'm still just a kid you know."

"Alright, kid," Tommy replied. "I'll tell you what. Next Monday, I'm going to treat you to a plethora of brand-new Pokémon cards. What do you say?"

"It's a nice thought," Simon answered somewhat bemused. "But actually, this is my last night here."

"What do you mean?" Tommy asked sitting up out of astonishment.

"I got a letter today," Simon said. "I have been given a scholarship from a pharmaceutical company in New York and have just been accepted to finish my degree at Harvard. Then I will have a job as a research scientist at DrugTech, New York. I have an appointment with a Dr Jamieson in two days' time so I am leaving tomorrow."

Chapter 30

The Finger of God

The St Regis was a particularly swanky hotel located at 2 East 55th Street, Manhattan, New York. The Contessa Medici alighted from her limousine and proceeded through one of the two golden rotating doors leading up to the Hotel's foyer. On this occasion, she had no need for luggage. She took the elevator to the seventh floor and knocked on the door of room 735.

"Well, if it isn't the Bloody Mary Medici herself," Dr Jamieson said wrapped in a bathrobe.

Dr Jamieson's wife would always look the other way. Her only condition was that her husband not bring his floozies to the matrimonial home. On the other hand, the Contessa Medici was hardly a floozy. She was as unsexed as Macbeth's wife and Jamieson knew it. But the situation was delicate and too secretive to be discussed in a café let alone a business office.

"It's done," the Contessa said kicking off her shoes and putting her hat on the console table as she entered the room ignoring the greeting she received. She grabbed a croissant from the basket on the breakfast table in the living room and sat herself down on the sofa kicking her feet up behind her. "The Trans Warp Inducer is simply missing the Medusa Stone to get it working. That is a small radioactive stone that is the missing piece of the symphony that Scientist Bruce has been raving on about from his psychiatric cell. Apparently, that will penetrate the Kaprekar constant that has been frustrating the experiment up to this point and allow any kind of transportation. You can have your two detective flunkies pick it up from Monkey Brain and Charlie Sleazebag whenever you want." She took another bite of her croissant and wiped the flakes from her mouth with the back of her hand. Her attempt to catch them with the same hand was not a genuine one.

"Is Scientist Bruce needed to complete the project?" Jamieson asked.

"I don't think so," the Contessa replied. "Best to leave him where he is."

"Finally," Jamieson said slumping into the chair alongside the breakfast table. It was one of those rare occasions when he smiled for his own sake and not to make an impression on his audience.

"It's not like you Jamieson," the Contessa began again before shoving the rest of the croissant into her mouth and licking her fingers. She allowed herself time to finish it before proceeding. "You are typically associated with the economic guild of the company. What makes you so particularly interested in the latest scientific breakthrough?"

"You really don't get it?" Jamieson said looking towards heaven and focusing his gaze on a point somewhere above the ceiling. "It is ultimate cosmic power."

"How so?" the Contessa asked before grabbing another pastry from the basket and settling back down on the sofa.

"The Trans Warp Inducer can literally rearrange matter. It can do it on a small scale or on a large scale. Imagine the potential in an otherwise unsuspecting world. It could literally remove and replace ballots from a ballot box. So, you have the power to rig an election right there. On a larger note, you could quite literally remove the nuclear warheads from an enemy's nuclear arsenal, or even worse, blow them up, and all without sending a single operative anywhere near the place. You could transport the stern of a battleship five metres to starboard. You getting the picture? Imagine that? And you think Pearl Harbour was bad. You could remove the fuel from a fighter jet mid-flight. You could remove the bullets from a gun, money from a wallet, money from a bank, you name it. You could even transport the neurons out of a person's brain and make him stupid, or the heart from his chest and make him dead. What we are talking about is the very finger of God. Ultimate cosmic power. You would be limited only by your imagination. You could even transport the centre of the earth to the surface of the earth and destroy the planet in one go. It is quite literally unlimited and previously inconceivable power, and did you know the entire device can run off a single double 'A' battery?"

"Now, hang on," the Contessa Medici said with undisguised scepticism. "Even if the device is capable of re-arranging matter like you say, I do happen to know something about science. The power to transport something as massive as the centre of the earth to the surface of the earth would require more energy that anything that mankind has ever produced; even if you were to add up all the power stations in the world together and have them all working in unison. What about the conservation of energy? A basic law of thermodynamics that has to be obeyed."

"And it is obeyed," Jamieson said smiling even more broadly. "Did you know that Nikola Tesla tried to find wireless electricity? He tried it in this very city of Manhattan. The closest he got to was the invention of the radio."

"What has that got to do with the price of fish?" the Contessa asked sarcastically.

"He only had a radio transceiver to work with. Electromagnetic or radio waves can induce a small voltage in an antenna that can be used to reconstruct a signal. He couldn't transfer electrons themselves," Jamieson replied. "He tried and tried with larger and larger voltages of electricity in the air but only managed a plasma corona."

"So what?" the Contessa asked wondering if there was a real breakthrough at hand or whether it was just wishful thinking.

"But with the Trans Warp Inducer," Jamieson continued, "A simple battery is all you need to start it up. Then the first thing it transports to itself is a simple electron. Then another and another and some more and more after that. It can steal them from any electron source that it wants. This rapidly builds up a chain reaction so that it can steal more and more electrons for as much energy as it needs until it is even big enough to move the earth itself. But scientifically, energy is still conserved. The law of thermodynamics is preserved. The device just steals the energy it needs wirelessly and rearranges matter. Nikola Tesla would probably be turning in his grave right now."

"Ok," the Contessa said finally starting to realise the invention's potential. "How do we get it here?" she asked rising from the sofa and sitting in the chair opposite Jamieson.

"That's the point," Jamieson said still smiling, his eyes beaming. "It's all wireless. We don't need it anywhere near us. We can send it instructions remotely and it can rearrange matter remotely. What we really want is to place it somewhere far from us, somewhere where no-one will suspect it, where no-one will find it if they were even looking for it."

"Well, if it can run on a single battery," the Contessa volunteered, "Why not put it on a ship out at sea, or even a submarine? No one would ever find it there."

"Not safe enough," Jamieson countered. "For one thing, ships can sink and for another, they need to be manned with a crew."

"Well then what about on a satellite in orbit around the earth?" she volunteered again.

"Still too dangerous," Jamieson answered. "It may need to be serviced. We should still be able to access it if ever and whenever we want."

"Well," the Contessa responded, "If that's the case, if you need to be able to access it occasionally, but at the same time, you want to keep it generally out of sight, then you need to hide it in plain sight in a secluded spot, perhaps somewhere out in the sticks where it would never be suspected by the people around it."

"My thoughts exactly," Jamieson said. "The whole thing was cooked up in a laboratory which was nothing more than a rundown shack in the middle of the Australian outback by Scientist Bruce in the first place. It was put on a truck and taken to the DrugTech laboratories after he got arrested, but now that a fully working model is at hand, we need to put it back onto a truck and take it back to that shack in the middle of nowhere under cover of darkness and where no-one would ever suspect or know what the hell was going on. Does DrugTech still own that shack?"

The Contessa was already flipping through her mobile phone that linked with her office computer.

"I'll check," she said as she flipped through various screens on her phone looking into the company's land-titles database.

"We could ship it there and set it up in the basement. Then we need to find a reputable unsuspecting business that can operate on top of it which is otherwise beyond reproach."

The Contessa found the screen that she was looking for and then replied. "We certainly do," she said looking up from her phone to face Jamieson. "And if I'm not mistaken, it is currently being leased to the Dominican Order of Priests," she said looking up. "So, I guess they are a reputable, 'beyond reproach' business that is unsuspecting and harmless enough."

"Perfect," Jamieson said.

Chapter 31

A Parliament of Owls

The Old Wise Owl Café was the last commercial establishment on the outskirts of town before one enters the sticks. Tommy Grayson and Jake Peterson were already seated when Patricia O'Leary entered through the saloon doors, and after carefully scanning the dining room, she made her way over to her waiting companions.

"Detective Sergeant Derrick should be here shortly," she said.

"Great," Tommy said. "What about Sister Jennifer?"

"She said that she would meet us directly at the shack where Father William Hunter will be waiting for us."

"The Detective is here now," Jake said as he turned to look at the saloon doors where a tall, casually dressed man entered carrying his large leather jacket and taking off his sunglasses. It was nearing dusk anyway. He spotted Patricia and her two companions and he made his way over to them.

"This is Tommy Grayson and Jake Peterson," Patricia said standing and pointing at each of them in turn as the Detective nodded and took his seat at the table, "And guys," she said turning to her friends, "This is Detective Sergeant Derrick."

"Last chance for a meal before we meet them," Tommy said, "I don't think they will be giving us dinner."

"Just a long-black for me," the Detective said to the waitress who approached them.

"Skinny-latte," Patricia said who had not yet ordered.

The boys had ordered and were finishing their beverages.

"Did you have any luck with Professor Philip?" Patricia asked the boys.

"He's not interested," Jake said. "He said that two detectives took possession of a radioactive substance that he and Charlie had been studying a few months ago, but that he had finished with it and was now finalising a paper on it to the scientific community. Honestly," Jake said almost exasperated and taking the last sip of his coffee, "All that guy does is publish scientific papers."

"It's in his genes," Tommy said sarcastically. "What about you Detective?" Tommy said looking at their new guest. "What sparked your interest in this meeting?"

"I couldn't help but overhear some talk, almost rampant excitement actually, among the red scorpion squad back at the station. They were raving on about DrugTech acquiring a new weapon of sorts, a Trans Warp Inducer, that makes them all powerful. Ordinarily, I wouldn't have cared less, but a few months back, a fellow I arrested by the name of Dr Lazer was talking about DrugTech in the same kind of way at his trial. That guy was already a tech genius and for someone like him to be raving on about the power of DrugTech, then something really big must be going down. But I couldn't get a straight answer from anyone I spoke to, including the cops at the station that only seemed to speak in the shadows, so when Patricia here said that she had some information about DrugTech, my curiosity was piqued."

"Sister Jennifer said that you were an honest cop," Jake volunteered.

"Well, I don't know any Sister Jennifer," the Detective replied. "So, I don't know how she is able to say anything about me. Most of the time, I am out of uniform anyway, so I find it quite strange that she happened to single me out."

"She could probably read your face," Tommy said. "Apparently, she has this ability to read what someone is thinking by looking at a person's face."

"Listen," the Detective said rather abruptly, but he was interrupted by the waitress returning with the table's outstanding beverages.

"Long-black for you," the waitress said as she placed it carefully in front of him, "Skinny-latte for you."

It all took too long for the Detective as he waited for the waitress to leave and then turned promptly to his companions where he began again in a whisper.

"Listen," he said, "I've looked up Sister Jennifer and the Dominican Order that she belongs to for that matter. And I must say," he continued with a certain level of disdain, "If these wise old owls are going to start prattling on in metaphysical terms that that Order is renowned for, then I am out of here." The detective motioned with his thumb to some point over his shoulder as if that is the track that he would take when he decided to leave the premises, and then nodding at his guests, he believed that he had made his point and decided to drink to it with the long-black that was placed before him.

"Well, whatever man," Tommy said in response. "All I know is that something really weird happened the last time we saw Sister Jennifer. Then not long after, I had this ten-year-old genius kid as a roommate who was already proceeding through the sciences in his first year at uni you know? It was like it was nothing to him. Well anyway, he started to work out all kinds of things and just as I was about to get him to turn his genius brain towards DrugTech, he then gets a letter from the Chief Executive Officer of their New York head office."

"Are you referring to Dr Jamieson?" the Detective enquired and Tommy nodded. "I have looked into him too," the Detective continued, "And strangely, I have heard his name mentioned a few times in whispers by several of the other cops at my station. I heard them talk about a Trans Warp Inducer. Have you guys heard anything about that?"

Tommy responded. "When us students had a day at the Mary Immaculate Psychiatric Hospital, I was assigned an in-patient to interview who was referred to as Scientist Bruce. He used to work for DrugTech and mentioned something about that thing being the most important scientific breakthrough in the world that could give you ultimate cosmic power. I guess they have managed to perfect it eh?"

"Well, we'll see," the Detective said gulping the last of his lukewarm coffee. "Shall we meet up at the shack?"

After securing nods from the other three, the Detective left the same way that he came; through the saloon doors and into his four-wheel-drive truck.

Tommy and Jake had also arrived in a truck. As previously arranged with Patricia, they placed the ramp that they had brought with them into position to allow Patricia to ride her motor Vesper onto the back of the truck. Then after securing the bike in place with the appropriate straps and retracting the ramp, Tommy entered the driver's seat followed by Patricia and Jake.

It wasn't too long before they had caught up to the Detective's truck on the roadway which soon become a dirt track. After several hours of following the Detective, the two vehicles parked at the front of the shack and the occupants alighted.

They were met at the door by Sister Jennifer in her nun's habit and she had the same chilling effect on the group that she had the night of the university Colleges' retreat. They were led to a room with a stone table where the four of them were ushered by the nun to four empty chairs situated on one side of the table. Sister Jennifer herself sat at the head of the table, and on the other side of the table were three empty chairs which the newly arrived guests sat facing as they waited for their hosts to arrive.

The twilight hour had passed and the night was dark. The room was poorly lit and the fire in the corner of the room produced most of the light. The room smelled of smoke from the fireplace and the burning logs produced the usual crackling and popping noises of a fire that otherwise filled the silent room.

After a few minutes, the impatient Detective was about to enquire about the absent hosts when Sister Jennifer rose from her chair as the door to the right of the guests behind the table opened and three priests dressed in Dominican robes entered. The first was a man who appeared to be in his young thirties. He walked to the chair closest to the door from which he came and stood behind it. "I'm Father William Hunter," he said still standing.

The priest directly behind him, a man who appeared to be in his sixties walked past Father William as well as the empty centre chair to stand behind the left-most chair to the facing guests. “I’m Father Charles Maxwell,” he said.

The last priest was a youthful looking man in his twenties who walked past Father William to stand behind the centre chair. “I’m Father Dom,” he said as the three priests then pulled their respective chairs out from the table in unison and they all sat down together. When they were seated, Sister Jennifer sat back down.

The Detective smirked as he had seen the ceremony repeated dozens of times in the Court of Criminal Appeal when three judges dressed in what he referred to as, “Santa Claus Suits” would enter the Court and do the same thing, only when judges did it, the most senior judge occupying the centre seat would walk first instead of last.

“In fairness, Detective,” Father Dom said looking directly at him, “The Court of Criminal Appeal copied the ceremony from us priests in the Middle Ages from when we priests ran the Courts. Our Order was doing it long before them.”

As surprised as the Detective was that the priest appeared to have read his thoughts, he did not wish to waste time on that. The Detective began immediately.

“Father Dom,” the Detective said, “I wish to open an investigation into DrugTech. I was wondering if you have heard of, or know anything about something known as the Trans Warp Inducer?”

“Yes,” Father Dom said rather calmly. “It’s here. It’s in the basement.”

The Detective was not expecting such a direct answer and he shifted in his seat. “Well do you know what it does and what they are using it for?”

“It is a matter re-arranger,” Father Charles said. “It is capable of transporting materials from one place to another without passing in-between the two points. It’s as if the universe warps in on itself like folding a piece of paper so that point A touches point B.”

Father William took over the conversation at this point. "Dr Jamieson used it to rig the last election in the United States," he said answering the second part of the Detective's question.

"How did he do that?" the Detective enquired.

"He transported out several genuine Republican ballots from the ballot boxes of several States that would ultimately hold the balance of votes in the Electoral College," Father William continued, "And then he transported in several fraudulent Democratic votes instead. When the votes were ultimately counted, the Democrats appeared to have won the Electoral College and their man was declared President."

"That's a pretty far-out allegation," the Detective said curbing his astonishment with a healthy degree of scepticism. "How do you know this?"

"I read it in the Wall Street Journal," Father William said turning around and taking a copy of the recent Wall Street Journal from the bookcase behind him. He opened it to an article entitled, "The Rise and Rise of Dr Jamieson," and placed it on the table in front of the Detective.

"I have read that article too when I was researching Dr Jamieson," the Detective said flipping through the pages in front of him. "It only speaks about how Jamieson used to be the head of NASA during the failed Atlantis mission when they lost four astronauts; and then how he became the Managing Director of DrugTech, Australia and ultimately became the Chief Executive Officer of DrugTech, New York when Medici Pharmaceuticals merged the companies. It doesn't say anything about the Trans Warp Inducer in here."

"No, not in the text," Father William replied as calmly as Father Dom. "I was referring to this," he said pointing at one of the pictures located on the bottom right of the page.

"That's just a picture of Dr Jamieson and the Contessa Medici celebrating one year of Dr Jamieson's position as CEO after the recent US election," the Detective said trying to understand what the priest was referring to.

"No," Father William said, "You are reading the caption underneath the photo. I was talking about what Dr Jamieson and the Contessa Medici were each thinking when this photograph was taken as shown on their very faces."

"Well, how the hell can you tell that?" the Detective asked starting to lose his cool.

"When I was a scientist at DrugTech many years ago, I was injected with Project Spectrum 77 which allowed me to see many more colours than the seven colours that you can only see. Together, those colours can illustrate what a person is thinking."

"Even if that's true," the Detective said trying to choose his words carefully, "And I don't actually believe a word of it, there is no way that such a thing would be admissible evidence in a Court of law."

"Detective," Sister Jennifer said from her side of the table. "Father William has been a barrister for the past 25 years. He knows the rules of evidence."

"Hang on," the Detective said trying to do some quick mathematics. "You look like a man in his young thirties. Yet you have been a barrister for 25 years and you say you were a scientist at DrugTech before that. Just how old are you?"

"I am approximately 250 years old," he said as calmly as if he was reciting the time of day to a stranger.

"Ok," the Detective said rising from his seat. "You're cracked. I don't suppose you would demonstrate the Trans Warp Inducer to me if it is here?"

"It is locked in the basement," Father Dom said. "You're more than welcome to it, but I would suggest that you should probably get a warrant. DrugTech is a pretty powerful company and it might be difficult to explain yourself to the appropriate authorities if you just start personally mucking about with it."

The Detective knew that it would be difficult to get a warrant with the little information that he had, especially against DrugTech, which appeared to him to be a particularly favoured company in the legal system. He thought he would shift tack a little and try something else.

"I thought you guys were the defenders against evil. How come you guys are not like the Dominican Pope, Pope Pius the Fifth, who famously said he would 'take up arms against the Turk' and formed the Holy League against the impending forces of evil in the battle of Lepanto. Have you all gone soft in your old age?"

"That was a battle against the forces of evil that threatened the whole of Christendom," Father Dom said. "That is not the case here."

"What do you mean?" the Detective said still standing. "I thought that this was the most powerful discovery in the history of man."

"It's not the most powerful discovery," Father Charles said. "The Trans Warp Inducer is not evil in itself. One of these days, it may form the basis of the very engines used in mankind's star ships hurtling it through space from point A to point B faster than the speed of light. It simply takes advantage of the physical natural laws according to the laws of physics that were previously unknown. It is no more evil than any other scientific invention whether it be a cure for cancer or the atom bomb. What is evil is what people decide or not decide to do with it."

"So, what is the most important discovery in the history of man?" the Detective said recomposing himself and sitting back down more out of curiosity than anything else.

"Knowledge is power, and the ability to read face provides one with more knowledge than anything previously known to the senses," Father Dom said.

"Well, I thought that that came from Project Spectrum 77 which he got from DrugTech," the Detective responded. "And how do you explain your super human age for that matter?" he asked looking again at Father William.

"I was also injected with Project Vat 00," Father William replied. "I didn't know it until I came here, but both drugs are extracted from the one blood-borne virus that came into existence in the Dark Ages. The virus can allow you to read face, and it also slows your aging facility down considerably. But it also has some pretty nasty side effects too if you are not prepared for them."

"Are you buying this?" the Detective said looking around him at the stunned faces of his colleagues on his side of the table as well as Sister Jennifer. "And what do you mean you didn't know it until you came here? Are you also infected with this blood-borne virus?" the Detective asked looking at Father Dom.

"Yes, he is," Father Charles said answering for him. "Father Dom here founded the Dominican Order. He was born in the year 1170 and is over 850 years old."

"Ok, I've heard enough of this crap," the Detective said rising again from his chair. "I don't know about you guys, but I am out of here."

The three university students did not seem to share the Detective's desire to vacate the premises, so the Detective nodded to everyone present and said, "See you later," as he headed towards the door and closed the door on his way out.

"Many are called," Father Dom said.

"But few are chosen," Father Maxwell replied.

The three priests and the nun now turned their attention towards the three university students still seated on their side of the table. Tommy was in the middle with Patricia to his right and Jake to his left.

"There are three kinds of police officer," Father Dom said, "And for that matter judges and barristers too in our cherished legal system. The first kind are the ones that seek answers to the truth. The Detective is actually one of them, but he was a little overwhelmed with the truth that he was receiving all at once. Sort of like a night owl suddenly exposed to the sun. He will eventually come around."

"And the second?" Tommy asked.

"The second are those that seek power for the sake of power," he said. "Many of the police officers form squads or brigades with that intention in mind. But there are also corrupt judges and barristers who do the same thing."

"What about the third kind?" Jake asked injecting himself into the conversation.

"The hoy polloi," Sister Jennifer answered.

"The riff-raff," Father William added.

"The proletariat," Father Charles also added.

"In other words," Father Dom said, "The working class. They are in it for the money. It's just a job to them. They don't actually see it as a calling."

"I suppose you can say that about any profession," Tommy said. "Even the scientists at DrugTech," Tommy said looking at Father William and remembering why he had come.

"You can," Father William answered. "Ultimately mankind seeks to know the causes of things. The first kind of scientist seeks to know the causes of effects in the natural order. They are the scientists *par excellence*. They observe natural effects and search for natural material causes. An example is the person you know as Professor Philip. He has made a life study exposing the natural causes of the red blood cell. But these scientists have their extreme side too."

"What do you mean?" Tommy asked.

Father Charles answered. "They get into trouble when they are presented with a supernatural effect outside of the material order. An example is the death and resurrection of Christ. Their belief in their science prevents them from seeing anything supernatural, so when they are presented with the fact of Christ being stabbed in the heart on the Cross by a Roman soldier's spear, their science tells them that a stabbing in the heart would totally ensure his death. But coming back to life again is an anathema to their science and so in order to explain that, they have what you may call a 'Trans Warp Confuser' in their brain which rearranges the facts a little. And so instead of being stabbed in the heart from which blood emanated as well as water being the build-up of serous fluid in the pericardium, they prefer to say he was stabbed in the gallbladder, with the mere loss of bile."

"It's monkey-brain thinking," Father William added. "Excellent physicians, but hopeless metaphysicians."

"What about the second kind of scientist?" Patricia asked.

"Insofar as the material causes are not readily known to mankind, they immediately appear to be supernatural," Father Charles answered. "The Trans Warp Inducer is just such an example. Scientist Bruce thought that he was making a supernatural breakthrough outside of the material order when he was working on his Trans Warp Inducer. Many of the DrugTech scientists are the same."

"They keep a collection of scientific breakthroughs to themselves, usually in a revered silver casket, and they use them as a means of extraordinary power," Father William added.

"But strictly speaking, there is another kind of scientist that also seeks power, but it is a benevolent power," Father Dom said. "They are distinguished from those that seek to find supernatural causes for things but not the ultimate cause of all things, which is God himself. You could say that *we* are the scientists of Sacred Scripture," Father Dom continued. "Our scientific search for the causes of things extends to the ultimate first uncaused-cause of things, and that is God himself. You could say that it goes beyond the supernatural to the *supranatural*."

"Well now I'm starting to feel a little overwhelmed," Tommy said smiling and looking at his friends as he rose from his seat. "You have given us much to think about."

"I agree," Jake said also standing.

"Me too," Patricia said as she stood up.

At this the priests stood and Sister Jennifer walked with the three university students to the door. "Please feel free to come back any time you like," she said as they left.

Sister Jennifer shut the door behind them and sat back down at the table where the other three priests were already seated again.

"Well, what do you think?" Father Maxwell asked of the others who himself did not possess the remarkable gift of reading face.

"I could read it in the face of Jake Peterson," Father William said.

"Me too," Sister Jennifer said.

"What's that?" Father Charles enquired.

"Jake Peterson will be the one to ultimately bring down DrugTech," Father William said.

"It's funny too," Father Dom added. "He had the exact same look in his eye as the young Don John of Austria which Pope Pious the Fifth commissioned to lead the Christian forces that formed the Holy League against the forces of evil. I met Don John of Austria you know, back in 1571 on the feast day of Thomas Aquinas when the Holy League was formed."

"No, I didn't know that, Father Dom," Father Charles said feeling curious. "What was he like?"

"He was the illegitimate son of Emperor Charles the Fifth," Father Dom continued. "And funnily enough, I see from Jake Peterson's face that he is also an illegitimate adopted child."

"Hang on," Sister Jennifer said, "You couldn't possibly have read that in his face, Father Dom," she said quite surprised at the suggestion. "For one thing, even if Jake is adopted, he doesn't know that, so you couldn't have possibly have seen that in his face, could you?" she asked.

"Yes," Father William added. "I too looked into Jake's face, and I saw no suggestion of the fact that he has any knowledge of being adopted or being illegitimate. How were you able to see that Father Dom?"

"It's simple," Father Dom answered. "Jake does not know he's adopted. But what he was thinking about which you two should have seen was a mental image of both his mother and his father. Did you see that? Can you remember those images?"

"Yes," both Sister Jennifer and Father William answered nodding their heads at the same time and each recalling the images of Jake's parents which they had extracted from reading Jake's face.

"Well, you would have seen that neither of them has a dominant cleft chin like Jake has," Father Dom said. "Therefore, Jake is adopted."

Sister Jennifer smiled at Father Dom's perceptiveness as she shook her head.

Father William also smiled and shook his head as he contemplated Jake bringing down DrugTech like the Don John of Austria of old and he muttered under his breath, "The bloody bastard."

Book 3

DRUGTECH

THE FINAL DOSE

Book 3:

To my father-in-law,
Emeritus Professor Philip Kuchel,
who I suspect, is starting to suspect,
that a certain character in the book is
not entirely fictional, and indeed, from
the last chapter of this book, is the very
person appearing on the front cover
of this book; but I must say in answer
to such preposterousness, that my
father-in-law does *not* drink coffee in
the mornings on his way to university
from Redfern Train Station.

Chapter 1

The Rather Odd Witness

There were three occasions that brought Detective Sergeant Derrick around, but it happened slowly and with much scepticism. The first was the case of the rather odd witness. He had been waiting for his case to be called in the Taylor Square Supreme Court Complex, but the trial of the semi-famous gambler charged with fraud, being heard before the same judge that he was assigned to, had unexpectedly blown-out. The detective had taken a back seat in the public gallery where he observed the female prosecutor, a long-time close friend of the detective, open her case to the jury. There had been several days of legal argument, and after the defence received an unfavourable ruling from the judge who refused to adjourn the case until November, the accused's legal team had withdrawn leaving the gambler to defend himself. Being on bail, the judge allowed the accused to leave the dock and sit at the Bar Table so that he had a better opportunity to defend himself and not be so prejudiced in front of the jury as he was now representing himself.

"Three million, one hundred and forty thousand dollars," the prosecutor continued her address as she eyed each jury member with her back to the accused. "That is the amount, ladies and gentlemen of the jury, that this self-proclaimed gambler is charged with defrauding vulnerable members of the public."

She took a sip of water from her glass so as to keep the volume of her vocal cords set to high as she continued. "Now the walls of this courtroom have seen many a charlatan attempts to predict the future. Predicting the future itself is not of itself wrong; many people try to do that. Scientists, stockbrokers, lawyers, accountants, meteorologists, they all attempt to predict the future in one way or another. But the difference between them and a fraudster is that they have a reasonable basis for such a prediction. Their prediction is grounded in logical cause and effect. So, for example, if I am standing on the earth, and I let go of the apple in my hand, then I can predict that it will fall downwards. That is a logical prediction based on observable cause and effect. It is based in reason. But ladies and gentlemen of the jury, crystal balls, tea leaves, horoscopes, palm prints, whatever the gizmo, whatever the gadget; these things are notoriously deceptive devices used by tricksters and fraudsters to enable all kinds of snake-oil-salesmen to cheat and deprive vulnerable members of the public from their money while the fraudster ruthlessly robs them blind."

"You will hear evidence, ladies and gentlemen of the jury, of the many witnesses whom the accused sold account passwords to enabling them access to a website. The sale-price of these accounts ranged from 150k at the lower end, to 1.5 million dollars at the higher end. The accused represented to each of these customers that the webpage would employ a computer algorithm to predict, logically and accurately, the outcome of any horserace in the world that they would care to bet on. Each customer was given a certain set number of races that they could purchase a prediction for, whether it be one race or two or three or four. He claimed that the computer would take into account everything known about the horses in the race, from its diet to its training sessions, its trainer, its rider; then it would combine all that data with even more data such as the weather, racetrack conditions, time of day, you name it, 'fairies on Pluto' for all the prosecution would care to suggest, and he claimed that the computer would then put all that together in a logical scientific-based algorithm and provide the first, second and third horses to finish the race. He even claimed it was a sure thing."

Detective Sergeant Derrick glanced at his watch as he realised that there was no way his case would be mentioned today. It was already 11:20am. The usual course was to receive word from the judge's associate of when his matter would be mentioned, probably at the conclusion of the case several days or even weeks from now. He was free to leave, but he waited this long, so he planned to have a word with his friend, the prosecutor, over the morning-tea adjournment. Besides, the outside weather was abysmal with dark rumbling clouds and a horribly uncomfortable drizzle in the air. The day was darker than the case he was watching, and as he sat intrigued with the prosecutor's opening address, he was also curious to see how the self-represented self-proclaimed gambler would defend himself against the charges.

"Luckily, ladies and gentlemen of the jury," the prosecutor thundered on, "AUSTRAC is the Australian Government agency responsible for disrupting criminal abuse of the financial system to protect the community from serious and organised crime. They tracked unusually large amounts of money being betted on even more unusual horses in the upcoming Melbourne Cup horse race, and they intervened. Thankfully the bets were cancelled and the accused was arrested. The prosecution says that the actual outcome of the Melbourne Cup in a few months' time is irrelevant. Win or lose, there was no reasonable basis for the 'sure thing' label that the gambler sold access to his webpage for, and so he stands charged with the matters now before the Court."

"Would that be an appropriate time Ms Crown?" the judge intervened addressing the prosecutor using the usual title.

"Yes, Your Honour."

"Very well," the judge said turning to look at the jury. "Members of the jury, please have your morning tea now, and when we return, the Crown will call its first witness."

The accused stood out of respect, as he was required to do under the law, as the jury shuffled their way out of the courtroom. Then the rest of the courtroom stood as the judge left; and finally, the crowd broke its silence as the courtroom's formality descended from that of a disciplined classroom to that of a busy train station.

There were a few coffee shops in Taylors Square within a stone's throw of the Court Complex. Usually, the defence counsel would go to whichever one the Crown didn't. But they were all as dreary as the 135-year-old Court Complex and were only kept in business because of it. Detective Derrick bought his coffee and moved to sit next to the prosecutor who was already drinking hers.

"Hi Deb," he began. "Great opening. I wonder how he will defend himself?"

"Hi Derek," she said with a smile that only an institutionalised prosecutor would give. "Well judging by what he told the police in his record of interview," she said blowing an opening in the froth of her cappuccino, "He bought the website from an unknown third party. So, he claims he doesn't know anything about the so-called computer algorithm or how the program actually works. He said he's just an innocent middleman who is passing on knowledge of what he truly and innocently believed to be so."

"Did they recover the $3.14 million from him?" the Detective asked.

"Unfortunately not," Debra said taking a sip. "But the judge won't let me tell the jury that. It's 'too prejudicial'," she said re-iterating the judge as she rolled her eyes towards heaven. "What brings you down this neck of the woods anyway?"

"Remember the case of Dr Lazer?" the Detective replied. "You prosecuted him for computer fraud."

"Oh yeah," she said paying more attention to her coffee than the conversation. "He got about three years or something, didn't he?"

"Yeah," the Detective answered. "But it looks like we will shortly be charging him with murder," the Detective continued. "Apparently, he murdered another inmate by the name of Peter McKinnon, otherwise known as Mr Solitary. Ever heard of him?"

"Nope," the prosecutor said putting her coffee down and looking at her friend. "Dr Lazer," she said slowly trying to recall the case, "He didn't strike me as the violent type. Thought he was just a computer fraudster, wasn't he?"

"I thought it was strange too," the Detective replied. "I was wondering if I could speak with you informally about the case, say at drinks on Friday night perhaps?"

"Sounds great," Debra said looking at her watch. She had another five minutes.

"You reckon this gambler guy has any chance?" the Detective said changing the subject.

"Knock your socks off," she said as she pushed a folder of papers across the table towards him.

He habitually flipped through the brief not expecting to find anything in particular. "That's odd," he muttered to himself.

"What?" the prosecutor enquired.

"Nothing really," the Detective said looking a little confused as he gazed more through the papers. "The website address has the name 'Kizana' in it," he said pausing as he now turned his gaze towards heaven. "I thought I heard of that name somewhere. Probably nothing. Say when do you think you will finish the Crown case in your trial?" he asked as he returned the brief and stood up.

"Probably Friday," she said wanting to finish her coffee before she too would rise and head back to Court.

"Good, I might catch some of the defence case then when I see you for drinks after Court," the Detective said smiling as he headed towards the door.

The prosecutor also smiled as she took her last few gulps of coffee and wiped the remaining traces of froth from her lips with her hand.

"Say, one last thing," the Detective said having abruptly turned around and taking a few steps closer to Debra. "Did you ever in your career meet a criminal barrister by the name of William Hunter?"

"No," she said, "But I've heard of him. He was way before my time. He had quite a big reputation."

"I don't suppose you would happen to know anyone who actually met him?" the Detective tried again.

"Well, there was this Legal Services Investigator by the name of Watkins," she said remembering the name from her Legal Ethics classes back in Law School. "Apparently he was investigating William Hunter when Hunter quit the profession. Dunno if that helps or not. Why?"

"Oh nothing," he said as he turned around again to head for the exit. The prosecutor now rose herself to head back to Court.

"See you Friday," the Detective said over his shoulder as he exited the Coffee shop. The Detective went one way and the prosecutor went another.

For those of my readers who wish to read stories in a linear chronological progression of events, then these DrugTech stories are probably not for them. A few chapters later in this book I provide some insight into where, chronologically speaking, the Detective Sergeant went after his coffee with the prosecutor. But for now, I wish to take you to the following Friday of this week where the Crown prosecutor had just closed her case to the jury, and the judge was calling upon the accused as to whether he wished to make an opening statement to the jury before calling his first witness.

Detective Derrick turned up to Court again and sat in the public gallery. He remembered the Crown's opening address and was curious as to the defence case.

It was early afternoon and the sun was now shining through the skylight roof windows. The stuffy courtroom never had air-conditioning, and at times like these, judges and barristers in their British woollen gowns and horse-haired wigs would often suffer and become irritable.

"Yes, thank you, Your Honour," the accused mumbled as he stood from his seat and turned nervously towards the jury. He opened the top button of his shirt to allow some kind of air circulation around his neck with his left hand while he held onto his handwritten notes in his right.

"Ladies and gentlemen of the jury," he said in a softly spoken voice that irritated the judge and caused him to lean forward in his chair. The judge was about to interrupt the accused to get him to speak louder when the accused continued.

"Um," he said nervously shuffling through his notes held out in front of him, "The prosecutor, ah, Ms Crown, um, she said that I said to my customers that the prediction my computer webpage would give them would be a, um, a sure thing. Well, that is true, but it is also not true," he said looking a little confused.

The Crown prosecutor smiled to herself and at this point the judge chose to intervene.

"What do you mean true but not true?" the judge enquired of the accused. "It is either true or it is not true. They can't both be true, the proposition is mutually exclusive. You may tell the jury which one it is."

"Um, thank you Your Honour," the accused said being obviously taken aback. "I mean it is true that I said it would be a 'sure thing', but," the accused paused at this point as he was searching for the words, "But it is not true that I said that their predictions would be a sure thing until, um, about one hour before betting closed before the race would start. All these people that gave evidence," the accused said looking both at the jury and the judge, "They received predictions, but the predictions were not yet 'sure things' because the AUSTRAC people shut it down before the race was due to start in a few months' time from now."

"Anyway, it is impossible for me to demonstrate that the predictions would be sure things," the accused continued, "until Melbourne Cup Day which is in early November. That is six months from now, and the judge will not let me adjourn the case until then."

"Mr Higgins," the judge said interrupting the accused again, "Your opening address to the jury is to outline the evidence that you anticipate calling in your defence, not to appraise them of the applications that you have made to the Court which do not concern the jury."

"Um," the accused began again with obvious difficulty in public speaking, "That is why I wish to make an, um," the accused said finding it ever more difficult to get the words out, "A um, an application," Your Honour.

"I have already ruled on the application refusing to adjourn this case until November," his Honour said anticipating the application.

"Yes, I know," Your Honour, "I'm not seeking that," he said as the judge waited patiently for him to get the words out. The accused began again. "But tonight, the Kentucky Derby is on in Louisville, Kentucky, in the USA. I wish to give my evidence at the same time as those horse races so I can demonstrate how my computer program is 100% accurate and will predict the winners of each of the races that are on within one hour before the betting closes in each."

"I am not quite sure I understand you," the judge said. "What exactly is your application?"

"My application is," the accused replied, "to adjourn this case until midnight tonight. That way, I can get into the witness box at the same time as the Kentucky Derby races are being run, and I can, um, have the opportunity to um, demonstrate my computer program in real-time by making real-time 'sure thing' predictions about the outcome of the races in the, um, Kentucky Derby. Since it will be live, there will be no room for error, or trickery or um, fraud as the prosecutor says. But that way I can properly, um, defend myself."

"Are you serious?" the judge asked sarcastically. "You want me to reconvene the Court after Court business hours, namely midnight tonight, so that we can have the Kentucky Derby streamed live to the courtroom to facilitate your evidence in this matter?"

"I'm just trying to defend myself Your Honour," the accused said almost inaudibly. There were chuckles from the jury box as well as the public gallery.

"I think I will ask the jury to step outside while I discuss this with the Court staff and the prosecutor," his Honour said nodding to the Sherriff's officer to usher the jury out. "In the meantime, could I ask each jury member to advise the Sheriff's Officer whether any of you have any practical difficulties with coming back tonight at midnight for this case to proceed at that time of night. We are all members of society each with our own family obligations. If things are not practical then they are simply not practical, so we can at least find that out before we proceed any further."

When the jury had left, the judge looked at the prosecutor.

"What do you say Ms Crown?"

"Your Honour, I object," she answered. "This is just a circus stunt where the accused is attempting to dazzle us with a magician's trick. This case does not depend on whether he manages to predict a couple of races correct; it is whether he had any reasonable basis for making such a prediction."

"That sounds right doesn't it, Mr Higgins?" the judge enquired of the accused. "What do you say about that?"

"Your Honour," the accused replied. "I am not going to demonstrate that I can accurately predict a couple of races. I will demonstrate that I can actually predict each and every single race in the Kentucky Derby 100%. This will conclusively show that my computer algorithm works. I can understand why the Crown prosecutor objects, because her case will then fall apart."

"That's not true," the Crown interjected. "A criminal trial is not a magical act."

"Ms Crown," the judge said silently intrigued by the accused's suggestion, "I am not sure of many magicians who subject themselves to cross-examination by a crown prosecutor. If it is all one big magician's act, then I am sure you can amply expose it with the accused in the witness box."

At this point the Sherriff's Officer came back in and handed a note to the Judge's Associate who promptly handed it to the judge.

"It seems the jury are happy to come back at midnight, provided they can go home now to clear up a few things. So, let me make enquiries with the Court staff," the judge said looking around him at the Court officers.

The Sheriff's Officer responded at this point, "Yes, Your Honour, we can organise for the Court to be opened and for adequate security to attend."

The judge looked at the Court Reporter and his Associate. They both nodded their heads in agreement.

"Bring the jury back in please."

The detective couldn't help but smile at the prospect of the courtroom sitting at midnight to follow the Kentucky Derby whilst the accused was giving evidence and being cross-examined in the witness box. That would surely make for a rather odd witness indeed.

"Members of the jury," the judge began when they had taken their usual seats. "I am proposing to adjourn the case now to allow you all to have the afternoon off to make the appropriate arrangements, and we shall reconvene here at 11:45pm tonight. Thank you."

And with that, the jury were ushered back out of the courtroom and the judge left the bench.

The frenzy started to grow, and the one or two odd journalists in the courtroom were already on their mobile phones. The story would be picked up in the evening news, and by midnight, the city streets would be packed with media vans and trucks each with extended satellite dishes and the courtroom gallery would be packed with journalists while the country would await news from the Court.

Chapter 2

Midnight Before the Battle

It was midnight, and the undefeated Pirate Uluç Ali, Naval Commander of an Ottoman armada of 222 war galleys, 56 galliots and other smaller vessels; put in anchor at Lepanto in the Gulf of Patras. It was for a pre-arranged war council with the Müezzinzade Ali Pasha, the Supreme Commander and Grand Admiral of the Sultan's Naval forces, in preparation of the forthcoming naval engagement with the Christian's so-called Holy League.

"You're late," the Müezzinzade said finishing his cup of black tea as the Pirate entered the tent. The tea leaves formed a pattern up the side of the cup which the Müezzinzade studied carefully as he placed the cup down slowly on the table before him.

Next to the cup was a silver bowl containing oil for fuel for the fire that was burning on top of it and providing most of the light for the tent. The map of Cyprus was pushed aside to make room for newly drawn-up battle plans for the anticipated naval engagement.

"A splendid victory in Cyprus," the Pirate replied ignoring the rebuke and complimenting his superior. "I hear the flaying of Bragadin has thoroughly demoralised the Christians."

"How so?" the Müezzinzade enquired not merely out of curiosity.

"The Christian Holy League is a ragtag group of inexperienced farmers. They have never seen battle before. They are no match for our trained janissaries. I hear they are commanded by a 24-year-old boy, the bastard, Don John of Austria. The Pope put him there because the Commanders of each fleet in the alliance won't take orders from each other. The Pope is just clinging on to power. He has ex-communicated the Queen of England for heresy; and she in turn has not contributed any ships to the fleet. The French have made a deal with our side since they are dependent upon our trade and they also have not contributed any ships. All they have left is Spain and Venice and a couple of Papal States. And they are fighting amongst themselves, with anger and surprise, as they deal with Calvinism infecting and undermining their religious beliefs. And now with their beloved Bragadin flayed, they feel a newer face of impending doom. Our spies have reported that the infidels are so scared, they even have a priest on board each galley to pray for them!"

"Good, good," the Müezzinzade said. "With the Christian fleet defeated, all of Europe will be ours. The time is right. Rome is a juicy apple and is ripe for the picking. You know what our Kahin is saying?" the Müezzinzade continued, "That she has consulted the Jinn and the weather favours our fleet leaving the port of Lepanto in the morning and intercepting the Christian fleet in the Gulf. The wind will carry us to victory. What is your opinion?"

"I disagree, my Lord," the Pirate answered.

"Why?"

"Because here in the port of Lepanto, our land cannons can decimate the Christian fleet. Let them come to us and we will send them straight to the devil."

"And if they don't come?" the Müezzinzade asked rhetorically. "The wind may change and we will lose our advantage. Suddenly our fleet will be the ones travelling up-stream. There is a time to strike, and now's the time. Behold the seal of Solomon," the Müezzinzade said as he directed attention to his hand and he slid a ring off his thumb onto the table next to the bowl of fire.

It was a golden ring that was lopsided, the thick part of the ring forming the shape of a crescent on one side.

"How did you get it?" the Pirate asked, his eyes widening at the treasure.

"Never mind," the Müezzinzade said. "We have set the seal of Solomon, on all things under sun, of knowledge and of sorrow and endurance of things done [*]," and he dropped the ring into the bowl of fire.

The chant had been said only a few times before. Then the fire in the bowl started to flicker. The smoke thickened in the middle and became sapphire in colour. Then it spun and spun until it turned itself into a mini-tornado that extended towards the top of the tent.

"Black Azrael and Ariel and Ammon on the wing [*]," the Müezzinzade continued the chant, "Giants and the Genii, multiplex of wing and eye, whose strong obedience broke the sky...[*]"

"When Solomon was king, [*]" the Pirate completed the chant.

Then the twisted sapphire smoke dissipated and the bowl took on the image of a great pearl that resembled a crystal ball. And within the pearl was seen a crescent of mighty ships in the Gulf of Patras. They flung great shadows forwards towards the Christian foe. The Venetian galleys of St Mark, filled with infidels, with their crosses and plumèd lions, became totally veiled by shadow as the victory of the Ottoman fleet was now predicted and shown with certainty. The vision was seen as a sure thing.

"It is they that saith, not 'Kismet'," the Müezzinzade spoke. "They do not believe in fate. It is time to put our feet down upon them, that Islam be on the earth [*]."

The weather outside was cold and uninviting. There was no moon and the darkness surrounding the tent and the Ottoman fleet was immense.

Meanwhile, in a tent many several kilometres away, under the same moonless night, a young 24-year-old bastard sat opposite a makeshift table where the elderly admirals of the Venetian, Spanish and Genoese armada sat on the other side.

"Bragadin was skinned alive," the Venetian Commander had said as the other Commanders appeared horrified.

"Now is not the time for emotionalism," Don John interrupted, his voice higher in pitch. "It is time for cool hard logic. When daylight breaks Admiral, I want you to remove the battering rams from all of our galleys."

"Remove the battering rams?" the Admirals asked stunned and almost in unison.

"Yes," Don John continued. "Their usefulness is outdated. But more importantly, they are preventing our front cannons from targeting the hull of the enemy galleys. There is no point firing our cannon balls through their sails, which is all we are capable of doing at the moment. We need to target their ships directly."

The Admirals saw the logic, but they remained silent to allow the young Supreme Commander, commissioned by the holy Pope himself, to continue.

"Next, I want all six galleasses to be placed in the absolute front of the armada, spread out equidistant from each other like the arms of a cross. The Turks will be in their usual crescent formation. That formation is designed to prevent us from outflanking them. But we will not be attempting to do that. Our formation will be a cross. We will head directly for the centre and directly for the heart. Domino Gloria, our God will give us the victory."

"But Your Excellency," the Venetian Commander questioned. "The Galleasses are our secret weapon. They are slow huge ships that the enemy will no-doubt think are commercial ships thrown into the fray out of desperation. They won't even know they are equipped with more cannons than a porcupine has spikes until the hatches are thrown open. If we move them up front, we will lose the element of surprise."

"Negative," the young Commander responded. "They will still think they are commercial ships that have been thrown into the fray, but they will think we are even more desperate and they will laugh at us. The Galleasses have never been encountered in battle before," Don John continued. "But their firepower will win us the war. Each one can sink ten or even 20 enemy galleys before their janissaries are even in range. They must produce for us an impenetrable barrier that will burst the battleline of the Turks."

"But Excellency," the Spanish Commander chimed in. "If the wind is against us, it will be almost impossible to row the ships into place and be anywhere useful in battle up front of our ships. It's the simple scientific law of inertia. The ships are too massive."

"Have faith," Don John answered. "At first it may appear as if the wind is against us," Don John said as his eyes focused into the distance as if he was recalling a spiritual vision. "The arrogant Turks will be singing and dancing on their ships, blowing their trumpets and banging their drums. Their sails will be raised high, for the wind will favour them. And they will laugh at our ragtag coalition, that have thrown commercial liners into the front of the battleline as we desperately row ourselves into position with all sails down."

The Commanders listened in silence. They had not liked what they heard so far. But Don John was not a fool and the Commanders knew it. His battle tactics and reasoning were sound. And as far as any so-called spiritual vision was concerned, they had faith in their Pope who was certain that he would bring them the victory. So, they listened in silence as the young Supreme Commander continued.

"But just before the ships come within range," Don John said now wide-eyed and regaining his focus on his Commanders, "The wind will change! It will change dramatically and everyone present will see it. Our crew may have been silent up until this point and they may appear demoralised now as we mourn the death of our beloved Marco Antonio Bragadin, who was flayed alive in Cyprus by the Müezzinzade devil against us; but when the wind will change, and it will change Commanders, have no doubt about that; our sails will be thrown up; and the Turkish sails will be lowered in despair. Our forces will let out a relentless cheer as they will then know that God will deliver to us the victory of the Ottoman Fleet, and the Ottoman Fleet will feel abandoned by their God in that moment, as the battle is just about to start!"

The doubtful Spaniard tried to remain optimistic. "I hope you are right," he said. "Because at the moment, our crew find their God forgotten, and many of them no longer believe in signs and miracles."

"Vivat Hispania!" Don John replied smilingly. This is written in heaven. Have faith Commander," Don John said smiling and almost winking, "It is a sure thing!"

---

[*] Adapted from G K Chesterton, "Lepanto".

Chapter 3

The Society of Creative Talent

It was the first Friday of the month and as pre-arranged, the Society of Creative Talent would meet tonight approximately 6km from the University of Sydney, in the Manhattan Superbowl in Mascot. The venue was a retro themed Tenpin Bowling Alley, mostly in darkness, with tacky neon lights flashing around the walls and UV lights illuminating the bowling alleys. Props and themes of Route 66 were outside the alleys and Tommy Grayson and Patricia O'Leary had already settled into a dinner booth adjacent bowling alley number eight, while they both waited for the others to join them.

Music was playing quite loudly in the background, and with the general chatter of patrons in other booths, it was necessary to raise one's voice just to barely be heard.

"We'll have six hot dogs, six fries and six diet cokes," Patricia O'Leary said to the waitress who wrote the order down on a pad and roller-skated away. "May as well order now for the rest of them," she said to Tommy.

"I agree," he said, "I'm starving."

The Society of Creative Talent was a sort of secret 'brains trust' or 'think tank' which Jake Peterson put together. Its objectives were to sort-out and solve life's mysteries, with a particular interest in bringing about the ultimate public exposure and downfall of the evil DrugTech.

"It looks like we are going to reach a settlement in my case against the Insurance Company over my late husband's death," Patricia O'Leary said to Tommy while they waited. "And with the potential of coming into possession of a few million dollars, do you know what Sister Jennifer said when I offered a substantial contribution to her religious order?"

"What?" Tommy asked somewhat bemused.

"She said she wanted nothing," Patricia said in exaggerated shock, "Can you believe that? Not a brass razoo. A charity of poor nuns turning down money? She said the Dominican Order is founded and in fact grounded in poverty and it would not befit the Order to take the money."

Tommy laughed. "Sister Jennifer never ceases to amaze you," he said.

"You can say that again," Patricia replied eyeing Detective Sergeant Derrick in a rather cool leather jacket enter the restaurant section of the Manhattan Superbowl. He was carrying a briefcase which seemed a little out-of-place in the setting they were in.

"Looks like we're early," the Detective said taking a seat in the booth. He looked around him and made a quick survey of the premises.

In bowling lane eight directly in front of them, was a beautiful blond woman around the age of 20, who, Detective Derrick thought to himself, was bowling with her blonde-haired brother aged at around 15. The bowling alley next to that was unoccupied and the one next to that was occupied by a group of schoolchildren celebrating somebody's birthday.

The booths located in the restaurant section could hold around six patrons each. In the centre of the restaurant section was a long table and several empty chairs set up on each side soon to be occupied by schoolchildren currently bowling in lane six.

"I did a little background investigating of our friend, Father William Hunter," the Detective began. "Turns out before he left the criminal bar to become a priest, he was under investigation by a Mr Watkins from the Office of the Legal Services Commissioner."

"So?" Tommy asked wondering where the Detective was going with this.

So," the Detective answered, "I went and spoke to him."

"You Did?" Tommy asked. "What did he say?"

The Detective leaned forward towards his listeners so that they could hear him more clearly over the music. "I showed him a recent photograph of Father William Hunter as he appeared on the day that he was ordained."

"Well?" Patricia asked.

"Well, he identified him clear as crystal," the Detective said somewhat surprised, "That was William Hunter, Barrister-at-Law, and he hadn't aged a day. Yet the old man I was talking to was remembering an event that occurred around 50 years ago when that priest was a barrister and had already carried on an illustrious life as a rather successful criminal barrister for many years prior to that."

"It's like he said Detective," Tommy said, "He and Father Dom and Sister Jennifer don't age like we do. They are incredibly old. Father Dom founded the Dominican Order, and he was even present at the Battle of Lepanto in 1571."

"And I've done a little calculation too regarding Sister Jennifer," the Detective continued. "Did you know she did work experience with Barrister William Hunter also around 53 years ago when he defended that actor who was charged with insider trading? Well assuming she was around 20-years of age then; that would make her around 73 years of age now. Yet when..." He was interrupted by the waitress bringing a rather large order of hot dogs, fries and cokes to the table.

The Detective stuffed a few fries into his mouth before he was about to continue, however, Jake Peterson arrived and the Detective moved around the booth to allow him to sit down.

"The Detective was telling us that he was doing a little checking into the ages of Father William and Sister Jennifer," Tommy said rather smilingly at Jake.

"Well," Jake said also stuffing some fries into his mouth, "You can check up all you like, but I choose to believe them. They are rather special people with rather special gifts and I think they can help us a lot in anything we need to do here in the Society of Creative Talent."

"I thought Sister Jennifer was coming tonight," the Detective said. "And weren't you bringing some kind of Sherlock Holmes bloke with you?" the Detective asked looking at Tommy.

"Yes," Tommy answered. "The genius Dr Sage. They're both here."

"Where?" the Detective asked looking around him.

"There," Tommy said pointing to the 20-year-old blonde and the 15-year-old boy in lane eight. They had completed their bowling and were now heading towards them.

"Sister Jennifer," the Detective said, "I didn't recognise you without your veil on."

The two shook hands. "It gets in the way when I bowl," she said as she moved one of the hot dogs towards herself.

"And you are?" the Detective said with his hand outstretched to the 15-year-old boy.

"I'm Dr Sage," he said shaking the Detective's hand, "But you can call me Simon."

"You're kidding," the Detective said not being able to contain his surprise.

"Nope," Tommy answered. "He's a kid who never kids. This is Dr Simon Sage, whiz-kid extraordinaire. Photographic memory. Degrees in physics, mathematics and biochemistry. Doctorate from and lecturer at Harvard University, currently on sabbatical at the University of Sydney, and generally one of the coolest kids I know." The two gave each other a high-five.

"Well, I'll be..." the Detective said rather amazed.

"How did you find the Flinders Rangers in South Australia," Simon asked quite innocently looking at the Detective.

"Gosh," the Detective asked taken rather aback. "How did you know I was there?" the Detective asked. "That information hasn't been made public."

Simon leaned forward and pulled a small twig caught in a hole in the Detective's leather jacket. "This is the very rare *Acacia araneosa*," Simon said twirling it in his fingers, "Otherwise known as spidery wattle. In this corner of the globe, it is only present in a small area in the Flinders Rangers. And given that your rank is one of Detective Sergeant and you are not directly connected with the South Australian police force, I can only guess that you were invited to help, possibly to help search for or recover a body in the vast region."

"Astonishing," the Detective said with beaming eyes. "You do botany too?" he asked.

"No," the boy replied. "But I read a book once in my spare time a few years ago which was a 'Field Guide to the Flinders Rangers'. There were lots of diagrams and I just remember that that was one of the species discussed."

"I told you," Tommy interjected. "Regular genius, extraordinary conclusions."

At this point, they distributed the food amongst themselves and with the chomping and slurping that followed, there was not much talking. When each had had their fill, Jake Peterson piped up, "So Detective, what mystery have you brought for us to solve tonight?"

"Well, you guys must have heard in the media about the case of the self-proclaimed gambler who managed to predict 100% accurately every single first second and third places of every single race of the Kentucky Derby? I would like to know how he managed to do it."

At this point, he opened his brief case and pulled out two photographs. "Cameras are not allowed to be used in courtrooms," the Detective said. "However, I managed to get these two stills from the CCTV footage in the courtroom."

"This is a picture of the accused Mr Higgins in the witness box being cross-examined. Sister Jennifer, can you look at it and read his face and tell me how he did it?"

The nun took the photograph and illuminated it with her mobile phone light.

"He genuinely believes in the computer program that he was selling access to, Detective," Sister Jennifer answered. "He doesn't know how the computer program actually works. Only that he believes the person who told him that it works and he has seen for himself and has demonstrated to the Court that it does in fact work."

"Are you able to tell me anything about the person that told him that?" he asked accepting what Sister Jennifer said, that she could read the thoughts in the witness's head by looking at his face in the photograph, at face-value.

"I'm afraid he isn't thinking any more precisely on that when this photograph was taken," Sister Jennifer answered quite innocently. "So, it is not recorded here. Maybe in other photographs during his evidence if you can show me those?"

"Say, whatever happened to that fellow anyway?" Patricia asked, "Did the jury return a verdict?"

"That's my next question," the Detective said taking back the photograph from Sister Jennifer and giving her the other one. "It was a hung jury. They couldn't decide whether he was guilty or not guilty. Here is a photograph of the jury at the moment the judge asked them if they had agreed upon their verdict or not. Can you tell me why the jury was hung?"

Sister Jennifer illuminated that photograph too with her mobile phone light and examined it closely. "About half the jury believe in the computer program and think that he has properly demonstrated to the Court that it works. They want to acquit him. But the other half, including the foreperson, think that they were subjected to nothing more than a magical trick, and they are not buying it. They want to convict him."

At this point there was relative silence as they all considered what they would have thought if they were sitting in the jury box themselves.

"Well," the Detective said breaking the silence. "Here is the million-dollar question. How did he do it?"

This time the silence was more pronounced. Smiles were replaced with squints, eyebrows were raised, and heads were cocked to the side.

After a few seconds, the Detective broke the silence again and said to Dr Sage, "What about you Sherlock Holmes? Do you know how he did it?"

"Yes," he replied rather matter-of-factly.

The others gasped and Sister Jennifer turned to look directly at the boy, then smiled to herself as she knew precisely what he had in mind.

"Science could not have predicted the first, second and third place holders 100% accurately of every single race," Dr Sage answered. "On the contrary, science tells us that the system is too chaotic and that such predictions with 100% degree of accuracy are actually impossible. The whole idea of knowing those kinds of things about the horses, their diet, their trainer and the racetrack, the turf, all those things, and then making such specific predictions as 'sure things', the hypothesis is logically flawed, it is not scientific."

"Well, I'm with you so far," the Detective said. "So how did he do it?"

"It is also not practical to suggest that there was such a big conspiracy going on involving all of the other riders of the horses in all of the races at the Kentucky Derby, not to mention those in authority surrounding the races."

"Go on," the Detective said still perplexed and waiting for the answer to the mystery.

"You know, when horses race, each race they do grades them and so to even the race up between them, and to make the outcome more unpredictable; but more to the point, to close the odds for betting purposes; they add a certain amount of lead in the saddle-bags of each of the horses," Dr Sage said. "Then at the end of the race, they weigh the jockey and the saddle again to ensure that the jockey has not disposed of the lead."

"So, what are you saying?" the Detective asked waiting patiently for the conclusion.

"The accused was not giving predictions of a fair race. Rather, the finely balanced lead in the saddle bags had been changed so that the winner, and second and third place holders became sure things and the other horses didn't stand a chance. The races were fixed."

"But how is that possible?" the Detective asked. "You just said that the jockeys and their saddles get weighed at the end of the race to ensure that the lead hasn't been mucked around with."

"That's true," Dr Sage said. "That leaves only one possibility."

"Well?" the Detective asked beginning to get a little impatient. "What is it?"

"Only one thing could alter the amount of lead in the saddle bags during the race, and then alter it back again after the race, without the jockeys or anyone else even knowing it," Dr Sage said.

"Well, what is that?" the Detective asked in immense anticipation, his patience had run out.

The other university students in the booth chose this point to break their silence too and also asked, "Yeah, yeah Simon, how is that possible? What is that one possibility that could do that?"

"I would have thought it was obvious," Dr Sage said looking rather innocently at his questioners. "It's the Trans Warp Inducer."

Chapter 4

A Race Against Time

"Only one thing could alter the amount of lead in the saddle bags during the race, and then alter it back again after the race, without the jockeys or anyone else even knowing it," Dr Sage said.

"Well, what is that?" the Detective asked in immense anticipation, his patience had run out.

The other university students in the booth chose this point to break their silence too and also asked, "Yeah, yeah Simon, how is that possible? What is that one possibility that could do that?"

"I would have thought it was obvious," Dr Sage said looking rather innocently at his questioners. "It's the Trans Warp Inducer."

"Oh my God!" the Detective exclaimed after he fully contemplated what had just been said. "I think the situation is even more desperate than you guys may think."

"How so," Jake asked.

"At the beginning of the case with the gambler, I had a coffee with the prosecutor because I wanted to talk with her about the police wanting to charge Dr Lazer with murder," the Detective began again. "She agreed with my instincts that as deceitful as Dr Lazer was, he was not the violent type."

"I read about Dr Lazer on the internet," Tommy volunteered to the bewildered faces of his friends (except of course Sister Jennifer who was typically poker faced). "He was charged with computer hacking, and his defence was that DrugTech had set him up."

"I think something is at play here," the Detective said shifting in his seat and looking rather concerned. "I am frightened that he has made an enemy of DrugTech and is now going to pay the penalty without him even knowing it."

"Can you explain that?" Patricia asked looking rather concerned.

"After I had coffee with the prosecutor," the Detective said, "I went to see Dr Lazer in prison. At first, he didn't want to talk with me and I was about to leave. But then I told him that I didn't think he was the violent type and neither did the prosecutor who prosecuted him in his computer-hacking trial."

"What happened then?" Tommy asked wanting to hear more.

"Apparently, he was put in a cell with a guy called Mr Solitary. It was Mr Solitary that persuaded the main witness against Dr Lazer, a fellow by the name of Lee Zhang Wei, to plead guilty and testify against Dr Lazer. Lee Zhang Wei did plead guilty and he became the main witness for the Crown against Dr Lazer in return for a reduced sentence for himself. I am now starting to think that placing Mr Solitary in his cell may have been a setup after all," the Detective said. The Detective was not prone to conspiracy theories, but after recent events, he was now not so sure.

"Why? What happened?" Tommy asked.

"Well Dr Lazer claims that he was simply chatting rather pleasantly with Mr Solitary, when all of a sudden, his head just exploded!" the Detective said.

"Horrible," Patricia said rather shocked.

"Naturally, no one believes him," the Detective said. "The medical experts will have no choice but to put it down to death by physical trauma, meaning that Dr Lazer will soon be charged with bludgeoning Mr Solitary to death with his bare hands. Up until tonight, I just saw it as Dr Lazer wildly denying the bleeding obvious, even though violence had previously been out of his character; but now I'm starting to think that the Trans Warp Inducer may have been involved in the death of Mr Solitary in order to frame Dr Lazer! In other words, things have taken a rather sudden and horribly dark turn!"

"That's terrible," Jake said looking exceedingly troubled.

"That's not the worst of it," the Detective said. "If DrugTech is involved and they are in fact using the Trans Warp Inducer, then either an innocent man will be wrongly convicted of murder, which means he will quite likely spend the rest of his life behind bars, or worse still, Dr Lazer may kick up such a stink trying to defend himself, that DrugTech will simply use the Trans Warp Inducer to eliminate him once and for all."

"It sounds like we now have a race against time to accomplish our main objective," Jake said. "Can't you as a Detective, get official wheels turning to open-up some sort of government enquiry into the workings of DrugTech?"

"Um, that won't work," Tommy answered the question. "I know from my own experiences, as well as the experiences of my father who worked as a government statistician, that anything in official circles, whether it be political or judicial or administrative or whatever; if it involves DrugTech, it will automatically cause computer alarm bells to go off somewhere and DrugTech will be one step ahead of it all the way. Take it from me, the tentacles of DrugTech run way too deep within the State for official channels to be its undoing."

"There must be something we can do?" Jake questioned.

"Can't we just go down to that shack in the country again, where they are keeping the Trans Warp Inducer, and break the machine?" Patricia asked. Suddenly all eyes were on Sister Jennifer.

"I don't even know if it still there," she answered. "Father Dom and Father William have been called to Rome, and the rest of the Order have left the shack. The Dominican Order no longer has any interest there at all, and we shouldn't even assume that the Trans Warp Inducer is still there."

The Detective and the rest of the company appeared stumped. They all sat back in the booth, but it was not out of comfort, but more so attempting to take a break from the intensity of the conversation. After a few seconds of silence, the Detective's eyes narrowed and he focused his gaze on Dr Sage.

"Ok, Einstein," the Detective said in desperation to the 15-year-old kid, "Any bright ideas on how to solve this conundrum?"

"DrugTech cannot be dismantled from the outside," Dr Sage replied. "It must be done from within. As Aristotle says, a being guards its unity as it guards its being. Without unity, it crumbles. A kingdom divided against itself cannot stand."

"Hey, aren't you already inside DrugTech?" Tommy piped up. "Your scholarship to Harvard University was from Dr Jamieson himself. You were offered a job there!"

"My connection is with the Manhattan branch of DrugTech run by Dr Jamieson," Dr Sage replied. "And from what I gather, confronting him with the issue is not going to create division, but rather, the opposite. It will multiply the problem."

Dr Sage was not finished with his analysis. He pondered the problem a little further and then continued. "Benjamin Jones is the weakest link," he said. "From what I can determine from having read the public reports about DrugTech, and from reading between the lines, whenever Dr Jamieson is mentioned alongside Dr Jones, there is somewhat of a distrust between them. In other words, the current Managing Director of the Australian Branch of DrugTech, Dr Benjamin Jones, and the former head and current Chief Executive Officer of the New York Branch, Dr Jamieson, don't like each other. Their relationship is not one of mutual trust. Dr Jamieson is concerned with the economics of DrugTech, whereas Dr Jones is concerned with the scientific aspects."

"He's right," Sister Jennifer continued. "Dr Jamieson cannot be approached under any circumstances. Moreover, he has used the Trans Warp Inducer himself to rig the last US election. Remember that conversation we had with Father Dom and Father William? We could all read that very clearly on his face in the photograph of the Wall Street Journal."

"So how would we get inside the Australian branch of DrugTech?" Patricia asked. "Why would someone like Benjamin Jones even want to speak with us anyway?"

"Professor Philip could get us in," Tommy replied in a low voice. "He used to work there when Dr Jamieson was running the place. And from what I can tell, he never really liked the man, and he goes all quiet whenever DrugTech is mentioned. Dr Sage is on sabbatical with Professor Philip now at Sydney University. The two of them have a rapport. We could approach him through that channel."

Dr Sage nodded in agreement.

"It's not that simple," Sister Jennifer volunteered. "Father Dom and Father William and myself are not the only ones who can read face," she said. "There are people at DrugTech who can do precisely what we can do, and they will no doubt have those kinds of 'sentry guards' (if I can coin that expression) already in place throughout the company. The moment any of you approach DrugTech with these kinds of intentions, it will be written all over your faces and they will know immediately what you are up to," she said. "That will sound the alarm bells well before anything is accomplished."

"You know I've actually been giving that a lot of thought," the Detective said. "I mean about how to thwart someone who has the gift of reading face."

All eyes shifted to the Detective as a plan started to unfold.

"When I was investigating Dr Lazer as an undercover detective, I was once shown around a warehouse where Dr Lazer, or to be more precise, a hologram of Dr Lazer, demonstrated some high-tech criminal wares for sale," the Detective said recalling the rather bizarre incident as if it were yesterday.

"Go on," Jake said intrigued at where he was heading.

"Well one of the things on display," the Detective said, "Was a pair of high-tech glasses in a black frame. The frame was equipped with ultra-powerful LEDs at either end which could emit invisible light; that is radiation at both ends of the invisible electromagnetic wave spectrum for the sole purpose of overwhelming sensors inside cameras so that the person's face could not be recorded on CCTV or even photographed. By my reckoning, if they can't be photographed, then they could also not have their face read, right?" he asked looking at Sister Jennifer.

"I agree," Sister Jennifer answered. "It is what you people call the invisible spectrum of light that we see as the ultimate language of how to interpret peoples' thoughts written all over their face. If our eyes are overwhelmed by artificial light in that part of the spectrum, then we would not be able to read their face."

"So," Tommy spoke up, "How do we get our hands on a couple of pairs of those glasses?"

"I don't know," the Detective said. "But Dr Lazer would know."

"Dr Lazer needs to be brought on board with the plan," Sister Jennifer said.

"That's not going to be easy," the Detective said. "He is terribly suspicious of the police, and the legal system. Can you blame him?"

Patricia O'Leary looked at Sister Jennifer. "We could go and see him," she said. "At least we wouldn't be police officers or people within the system. Besides, with you being able to read face and all, you have an advantage on how to persuade people about things, you know?"

"Agreed," Sister Jennifer said.

"Fine," the Detective said. "Meanwhile, Tommy, Jake and Simon should get to work on Professor Philip. And I'll have another word with my friend the original Crown Prosecutor of Dr Lazer's trial to see if she can come on board, or at the very least, let me know which prosecutor would be assigned to his murder case. This is a race against time people," the Detective said, "Let's all meet up again the moment we have something."

"Agreed," the rest replied.

And with that said, the Society of Creative Talent formally closed its meeting.

Chapter 5

Before Day or Battle Broke

"This is not just a battle on the physical plane of existence," Father Dom said continuing his sermon to the Christian fighting-forces of the Holy League. It was the morning of the 7th of October, 1571 where a massive armada of approximately 210 ships lay in anchor alongside the Gulf of Patras. In addition to the 40,000 sailors and oarsmen, there were approximately 20,000 soldiers. They had amassed for the pre-dawn service of what would either be their last Mass on Earth, or in the rather unlikely event of victory, their first day free of Ottoman aggression. The soldiers were kneeling in prayer and fear. It was not yet dawn, and the darkness was immense, broken only by the crimson torchlight on the altar. The altar was at the top of the hill, and the kneeling Christian forces around the hill, looking up at the altar, made the feeding of the 5000 appear somewhat as a Sunday picnic.

"Have no doubt that the spiritual forces of Mahound are at play here. For over that first hill to the East," the priest continued, "The great and terrible Müezzinzade has begun the Ottoman fleet's morning prayers. 'They gather and they wonder to give worship to Mahound.' [*]"

"And the Müezzinzade's voice is not just a battle-cry to his janissaries. It is a cry to 'Black Azrael and Ariel and Ammon on the wing, Giants and the Genii whose strong obedience is to break the sky [*]' and prevent the winds that blow from changing."

The simple folk of the Holy League had never encountered battle before. Many believed that they would die that day. This was their last Mass. They had said farewell to their families. They were making peace with their God. But heaven was at war with itself, and that war was spilling-over onto the Earth. And when the two armadas would meet, the end of the world would begin.

"They'll rush in red and purple from the red clouds of the morn, [*]" Father Dom continued with his sermon which was more of a battle chant itself, "And from temples where the yellow gods shut up their eyes in scorn; they'll rise in green robes roaring from the green hells of the sea, where fallen skies and evil hues and eyeless creatures be. [*]"

With their swords placed on the ground beside them, the soldiers clung instead to their rosary beads that had been distributed to each of them. The beads were providing them with the strength that they needed which their swords could not. 'They touched it, and it tingled and they trembled very soon. And their faces were as pale as lepers, white and grey. Like plants in the high houses that were shuttered from the day' [*].

And Father Dom continued. "On them the sea valves cluster, and the grey sea-forests curl, splashed with a splendid sickness, the sickness of the pearl. [*]"

"But have no fear," the priest continued turning his back to the congregation and looking up to heaven. "We pray to the humble Virgin. 'The last and lingering troubadour to whom the bird has sung, that once went singing southward when all the world was young. In that enormous silence, tiny and unafraid' [*], the wind will change and whence will begin, the noise of our Crusade."

"And over that second hill to the West," the priest continued turning to look at the other horizon. "'The Pope is in his chapel before day or battle breaks' [*], summoning the forces of St Michael and the Lady of Victory. The Lady as fair as the moon, resplendent as the sun, and terrible as an army with banners."

The sermon was having its effect. Rousing the soldiers into action and removing their paralysis to face what would otherwise be their impending doom.

"We do not fear death," the priest continued. "For on the third hill, the hill of Calvary, there were three thieves. The Good Thief to the West. The Bad Thief to the East. And in the centre, nailed to the cross, the Thief in the Night. We find ourselves ready, ready as the five bridesmaids with oil to await the bridegroom." And with that the signal was given to the other priests present to commence the Third Rite of Reconciliation, a general absolution *en masse* of the Christian forces of all of their earthly sins in preparation for the battle.

And as the service ended and the first tangent of the sun peeked its head above the horizon, the priests were replaced with Admirals and Commanders, and the 24-year-old Don John of Austria, Supreme Commander of the Christian Holy League, in his battle suit of armour. He was now giving the final commands directly to his fleet.

"Remember the 'one good shot' rule," he said from behind the altar which was now converted to a war table.

"As our ships approach their ships, you will feel an overriding urge to fire our cannons at them. This must be resisted," the young Supreme Commander said as the soldiers felt spiritually re-invigorated after the Mass. "As the battle begins, apart from the Galleasses which are too big to be boarded, we will not have time to fire and reload our guns and get in an effective second shot against the same ship. We must make the first shot count! So, aim the cannons at the centre of the hull of the enemy galley, or as best as your angle will permit. Fire only at point blank range. We cannot afford to miss. One good shot may even sink the entire galley, and if so, the process can then be repeated on the next ship."

"If it does not, then prepare the grappling hooks. Only those in body armour should be on the edges of the ships and throwing the grappling hooks. Any exposed area of the body will be susceptible to the arrows from their janissaries. Those without armour should take up positions behind them. Have your arquebus or musket ready to give them cover. But remember the same principle. There is only one good shot in each. Fire them only at point blank range. Aim for the centre of the biggest part of the enemy's body. You don't need to kill him. You only need to bring him down so that you won't be killed. Remember that their trained janissaries can get 30 arrow shots off by the time it takes for a soldier to reload an arquebus. So, make your one-shot count!"

The soldiers had heard it many times before, but they welcomed hearing it again from their Supreme Commander. In the heat of the battle, there was no room for mistakes, and well-rehearsed routine was your friend. The heat of battle did not favour experimentation.

"Those in body armour, remember your balance," Don John continued. "You cannot afford to slip or be pushed or thrown overboard. If you hit the water with the armour that you are wearing, it is all over. There will be no return. Swimming is not an option. Do not attempt to board the enemy ship until it is properly grappled or the gap between them may open-up and swallow you without warning."

"When you've fired your shot, then grab your sword," Don John continued. "You will remove the advantage of their janissaries if you can board their ship and rush them. Close the distance between you and them to neutralise the effectiveness of their bows and arrows. Remember your training. We recommend the cut-and-slash technique. A good slash is better and more efficient than a thrust. The janissaries have curved swords for just such a technique. If you are at absolute close range and you are forced to thrust, then remember to turn your sword sideways when it is in the enemy's body, or the suction will prevent you from pulling it out."

The soldiers did not wince. They either had too much adrenalin in anticipation of the event, or they were too worried about being sliced in two themselves by the curved swords of the janissaries.

"Lastly," Don John continued, "Listen out for orders from your Commanders on the poop deck. They will have a superior view of the unfolding battel around you and can coordinate troop movements in a way that you may not be able to see for yourself in the thick of battle. Their orders are designed to save your life, so listen carefully and be ready to follow their voice unquestionably."

Then the throbbing of the dim drums began again as the troops gathered in formation to the beat. They marched their way to their vessels in port, with sword in one hand and rosary beads in the other, as they prepared to stare into the very face of the devil himself.

---

[*] Adapted from G K Chesterton, "Lepanto".

Chapter 6

Down a Dark Alley

The meeting between Patricia O'Leary, Sister Jennifer and Dr Lazer at the Long Bay Prison Complex had gone quite smoothly. And Patricia began to appreciate the real talent of Sister Jennifer. As expected, Dr Lazer was frightened, suspicious and reserved. But Sister Jennifer patiently and gently revealed to him the things that he needed to hear to satisfy his inner scepticism and she did so without revealing her own hidden talent of being able to read face. But what Patricia began to realise that she admired more and more about Sister Jennifer, was not so much her wonderful talent of being able to read face, but rather it was Sister Jennifer's philosophical outlook on life. Sister Jennifer was not one to be concerned with the usual earthly side-tracks. Money was not her motivation, nor honours, nor power, nor fame, nor any hedonistic pleasures. Rather, Patricia came to realise that Sister Jennifer's motivation was none other than a genuine concern for the welfare of humankind and a practical, common-sense approach to life with more of a reliance on the use of reason than Patricia had thought normal for a religious person. But whenever Patricia would speak with Sister Jennifer about her religion, Sister Jennifer rarely if ever appealed to the faith of her creed (she had said that the creed of her religion was put together for believers by believers) but rather, she would meet any reasonable objection against her religion with a totally reasonable retort. Reason and logic were the backbone of her faith, and her faith was only a tool to behold the finer and more blessed truths over and beyond where reason could reach.

Having just finished at the Long Bay Prison Complex, the university student and the nun bussed it back to Kingsford. The sun had now set, and Patricia was more than a little hungry, but Dr Lazer had told them where his private garage was in Kings Cross of his high-tech criminal wares, and the two of them wished to retrieve the special LED glasses before dinner. As the twilight darkened, the two ladies alighted from the bus at Kingsford, and waited on the Light Rail Stop opposite the Souths Juniors Leagues Club. It wasn't long before they were seated on the tram for their several kilometre journey into the heart of the city. They would go as far as Wynyard Station, and then catch a train from there to Kings Cross.

Kings Cross was the State's Red-Light District, and two ladies travelling alone in the darkness was not the safest of plans. Having reached Kings Cross, Patricia O'Leary's focus was directed to her mobile telephone where she used Google Maps to guide them to the street they were looking for. But as they reached the street, Sister Jennifer put her hand out to stop Patricia.

The pair had spotted a garage at the end of the street that fitted Dr Lazer's description. But in-between the garage and the opening to the street where they had stopped were a group of four 'scary-looking' men standing and smoking. Patricia doubted whether the smoke was tobacco.

"Maybe we should come back in the daylight," Patricia said.

"Let me have a better look," Sister Jennifer said as she opened her handbag and retrieved what at first glance looked like an elegant cigarette case. But she pressed a button in the middle of the thin side of the case, and the case popped open revealing an elegant pair of opera binoculars. Sister Jennifer raised the binoculars to her eyes and studied the faces of the men approximately 50m ahead of her.

"One of them, their leader, is armed with a revolver in his jacket pocket," Sister Jennifer said. "But I believe it is most unlikely that he will fire it. It's more his style to pull it out and flash it around to impress his friends. It looks as if his motivation is to be seen as the tough guy."

"I really think we should come back in the day time," Patricia said again, especially having heard Sister Jennifer's analysis of the leader's face.

"I think it will be safe if you let me do all the talking," Sister Jennifer said.

It was one thing for Patricia to admire Sister Jennifer's talent. It was quite another to trust it with her life. But Patricia decided to do just that as the two of them began walking slowly down the street with Patricia closely behind the nun.

As the ladies approached the group of men, the men turned their attention towards them and started wolf-whistling and laughing. Two of the men moved immediately to out-flank them on either side and stood behind them so that the ladies were now completely surrounded.

"Animals," Patricia thought to herself. "Fancy whistling at a woman in a nun's habit and a girl in jeans and a jacket close behind her."

As usual, Sister Jennifer looked cool, calm, pale and poker-faced.

"Hello Steve," Sister Jennifer said looking directly at their leader who had his hand in his jacket pocket.

The greeting obviously took the man by surprise and the others started laughing.

"You know this *nun*?" they enquired emphasising the word "nun" as if any association with her tarnished the reputation of their leader.

While the leader was wondering how the nun knew his name and whether he actually knew her or not, Sister Jennifer answered the question.

"Of course he knows me," she said. "I am a close personal friend of his Aunty Maureen."

Sister Jennifer paused as the statement, as intended, evoked more thoughts within Steve and Sister Jennifer seized the opportunity to scrutinise them.

"Maureen has invited your family to another barbeque this Sunday at her place," Sister Jennifer said as if she was speaking from personal experience, "And if you actually turn up this time, you might see me there."

"Yeah, well I'm not really in to barbeques with Aunty Maureen," Steve said sarcastically causing the others to laugh even more.

The feigned familiarity had the desired effect of calming the situation. "I'll be sure to tell her that you asked about her," the nun said as she started walking on her way again.

An opening parted in the group allowing the ladies to pass through. "It's like Moses parting the Red Sea," Patricia thought to herself fascinated and staying close behind the nun.

As the ladies progressed down the street, the men no longer felt comfortable in their surroundings. They turned and started heading out of the street the same way that the ladies had come.

After about another 50m, the ladies reached the garage that they were heading for.

Patricia O'Leary jumped ahead of Sister Jennifer and bent down to lift it. But as she did so, she spotted a rather large steel padlock.

"Great!" Patricia exclaimed in frustration rotating the base of the padlock from the floor and flinging it back down again. She stood and turned throwing her hands up in the air. "Dr Lazer never mentioned anything about a padlock or a security system. He gave me the impression that he was just hiding his stuff in plain sight."

"Me too," Sister Jennifer said bending down to study the lock.

"Ha!" Sister Jennifer exclaimed. "If you looked closer, you would have seen it's unlocked!"

The sense of relief on Patricia's face was palpable. She turned around again to see Sister Jennifer partially lifting the garage door.

"Let me help," Patricia said as she bent down to grab a portion of the door. It was heavy, and it squeaked. A dank musty smell came from within.

Inside the garage were a series of toolboxes.

"Let's find the one with the glasses and get the hell out of here," Patricia said using her phone as a torch. "This place gives me the creeps."

It didn't take them long. Sister Jennifer retrieved a folded-up plastic shopping bag from her handbag and the two of them filled them with the glasses in the toolbox. If Patricia didn't know better, she would have thought that the typically unflappable Sister Jennifer was uncomfortable in her surroundings. Patricia certainly was. Without wasting any further time, the garage door was closed and approximately 20 minutes later, the two of them were once again walking into Wynyard Station.

"Well, do they work?" Patricia asked, "Let's have a look!"

Patricia took a pair of glasses from the bag and placed it on her face. Remembering Dr Lazer's instructions, she squeezed the button on the frame to turn them on. Patricia smiled as she felt like a clichéd classics' professor with big clear glasses and bulky black frames.

Sister Jennifer looked at Patricia and then looked at others on the platform. She repeated the gesture a few more times.

"They work," Sister Jennifer somewhat astonished that she was now unable to read Patricia's face.

"Well, it looks like we finally found your kryptonite," Patricia said in jest and removing the glasses from her face.

"You take the bag and get them to the others. I have to go now back to the convent before vespers begin."

"Just tell me one other thing," Patricia said quickly before Sister Jennifer had gone. "What would you have done if Steve had had a change of heart and produced his gun? Or if one of the other goons decided to take matters into their own hands and get violent?"

"Knowledge always gives you a certain sense of power to foresee certain situations to a certain degree," Sister Jennifer answered. "It's only natural among reasonable people that violence be used only as a last resort. Thankfully violence was not employed on this occasion."

"You can say that again," Patricia said exhaling in relief. "Because I didn't quite like our chances if your analysis of the situation wasn't quite right."

“Well, it was,” Sister Jennifer replied raising her hand to wave goodbye. She turned and started heading towards a different platform leaving Patricia behind.

As Sister Jennifer approached a rubbish bin at the top of the stairs, she looked over her shoulder to ensure that she was now out of visual range from Patricia. When Sister Jennifer was sure of that, she put her hand in her pocket and retrieved the several broken pieces of the large steel padlock that had secured the garage door shut and dropped them all in the bin.

Chapter 7

The Ugly Unspoken Truth

The Honourable Justice Croydon of the NSW Supreme Court Criminal Division was a fat, over-bearing, over-opinionated, self-righteous, pompous, complacent, moralizing, sanctimonious, holier-than-thou, interjecting, self-satisfied, smug prig. The other judges of the NSW Supreme Court Criminal Division were not so fat. Many in the legal profession referred to him as the Butcher of Burwood. Whereas Magistrate Burwood was known as the Smiling Assassin, the Butcher of Burwood omitted the smiles.

“Call the next case,” His Honour said slumped over the bench in his judge’s crimson red ‘Santa Claus’ robes. He was anything but Santa Claus, and the slumping was because he was sick of supporting all the extraneous weight.

“Number six on the list,” his Associate said from the table beneath him. “DPP and Leon Lazer.”

The little door from behind the dock cracked opened whereupon a Corrective Services Officer emerged with one hand on the doorknob and jangling keys in the other attached by a long chain to his belt. He was followed by Dr Lazer in ‘prison-greens’ who took his place in the centre of the dock.

“Before the Court, Your Honour,” the Corrective Services Officer said.

“May it please Your Honour, I appear for the accused,” Barrister Black said rising from the Bar table in her black robes and horsehair wig.

Mr King for the DPP,” the prosecutor said from the other end of the Bar table. “I present an indictment.”

The Sheriff's Officer retrieved the standard blue-coloured document from the prosecutor and handed it to the Associate. The Associate stood, turned around and handed it to the judge behind her. The judge briefly perused the document before sliding it back to the Associate who remained standing and turned to face the accused with the indictment in her hands.

"Yes, very well," the judge said probably thinking about how long it would be until his next lunch. "Arraign the accused."

The Associate beckoned the accused to stand, and when he had risen and faced her, the Associate began.

"Dr Leon Lazer, you stand charged that you, on 30 November last year, at Long Bay in the State of New South Wales, did murder one Peter McKinnon. How say you, are you guilty or not guilty?"

"Not guilty," the accused replied.

"Yes, very well," the judge said. "Set trial date for 7 October."

"Your Honour," Barrister Black complained. "We've only just been served with the full prosecution brief of evidence this week. We have not had a chance to reply. We were only committed to stand trial last week and this is the first mention before this Court. We respectfully seek a six-week adjournment for the purpose of confirming instructions and determining number and availability of defence witnesses."

"No can do," the judge said rather expecting the complaint. "A directive from above. This case has been selected as a trial for the new Case Management Practice Note that is soon to be introduced to all murder cases in this Court. A hearing date will be set at the first arraignment hearing, and a directions hearing will be set 28 days after the arraignment date to assess the readiness for trial and to make any consequential directions and orders. Vacating of hearing dates will only be allowed in exceptional circumstances. The Court has two weeks available from 7 October this year and if the case takes longer than that, then it will just have to continue until conclusion and push-out the other cases due to start after that. Court Registry will advise the parties of the date for the readiness hearing. Call the next case please."

Defeated, Ms Black sat back down and Dr Lazer was taken from the Court.

Approximately 20 minutes later, Dr Lazer was brought up from the cells beneath the Court to the conference room where Barrister Black sat behind a Perspex screen with her papers spread out over the narrow desk.

"I'm sorry I couldn't get the case listed at a later time," she began.

"Don't worry about it," Dr Lazer said with a slight raising and lowering of his head as if to say, "I know what is really going on here."

"The case against you is pretty solid," Barrister Black began again. "Basically, a couple of prison guards will testify that they let a healthy, happy Peter McKinnon into your cell late one evening, and by the following morning, a beaten-up corpse was taken out. And a couple of doctors will testify that the cause of death was severe blunt trauma to the head consistent with having it smashed against the wall or the floor. The Prosecutor will say to the jury that the severity of the trauma could only indicate a ferociousness consistent with an intention to kill. Also given the lack of injuries on you, the Crown will say that self-defence was simply not open on the facts. The Crown case is expected to finish in a simple day. Can you give me *some* indication of a defence?"

"You know the last time I was sitting in this very room with Barrister Colfax in my previous trial; I was raving on about how Lee Zhang Wei would be my defence witness and that we were both set up by the big pharmaceutical company DrugTech because I happened to stumble across something ugly and dark on the internet which the rich and powerful DrugTech wanted to remain secret."

"Yes," Barrister Black replied, "And she said that she didn't easily buy into these kinds of conspiracy theories and that neither would a jury. She was ultimately shown to be right."

"The last time I mentioned in Court that I was going after DrugTech and that Magistrate Burwood should disqualify himself, the next thing I knew, the only witness that could get me acquitted turned into the main prosecution witness against me."

"Lee Zhang Wei is not the first witness in these Courts to sell out his mates and put himself first," Barrister Black replied. "What did you expect?"

"Didn't you think it was odd that my case, of all the cases to be heard, was the very one selected by 'directions from above' to try out this new case management thingy; which means my hearing date is already fixed and all too soon for comfort?" Dr Lazer asked somewhat sarcastically.

"It may seem like that to you," Ms Black replied, "But any case whatever selected for trial of any new practice note is by definition the odd case. The axe has to fall somewhere."

"Well, it has a tendency to keep falling on my neck," Dr Lazer replied.

"Oh really?" Ms Black said beginning to get exasperated. "And where exactly do you think the axe fell on Peter McKinnon's neck? Do you think the State is out to get you because they happen to want to prosecute murder cases swiftly?"

"No, of course not," Dr Lazer said starting to look a little more circumspect, "It's just..." and at this point, his voice trailed off into silence.

"What?" Barrister Black prompted. "It's just what?"

"It's just that this legal system of yours; it reminds me somewhat of family politics. There is always an answer for everything, but the answers that members of a family give each other is just a bunch of nonsense. Nobody buys it. But they have the answers nonetheless. The nonsense answers just take the place of ugly unspoken truths."

"And what do you suggest?" Barrister Black prompted again. "You have the answer to all of this do you?"

"As a matter of fact, I do, Ms Black," Dr Lazer replied and this time it was he asserting himself over Ms Black's argument. "You know you as a defence counsel may put forward any defence given to you by the people you represent and just let the jury decide if they buy it or not. But every now and then, just, every now and then, you may actually come across an innocent person who is standing behind an unspoken ugly truth; and that unspoken ugly truth is all that stands between him and the guillotine."

"I've represented more than my fair share of guilty *and* innocent people Dr Lazer," Ms Black retorted. "And what is this 'unspoken ugly truth' that you are so afraid of? Do you think that I won't buy it? I have believed all sorts of ugly truths in my time. It goes with the job. I usually find that it is the truth that sets people free."

"I *know* that you won't believe it Ms Black," Dr Lazer answered, "You have already demonstrated that to me."

"How?" Ms Black asked somewhat surprised. "All I said was that I have believed a whole lot of ugly truths in my time."

"I'm sure about that," Dr Lazer said rising to end the conversation. "For barristers in an ugly profession, that part is easy for you to believe. That's not the part of the defence that I was referring to though."

"Well, what then?" Ms Black asked looking a little confused.

"The most important part of my defence case thus far Ms Black," Dr Lazer answered as he knocked on the door for the prison guard to escort him back to the holding cell. "In fact, not just my defence, but my very survival depends on it."

Ms Black was more bewildered than ever. She had not even begun to take notes of the defence case to assist her in preparation of the forthcoming murder case.

"So, what part have I demonstrated that I won't buy?" Ms Black asked again really wondering what her client was referring to.

The door opened and as he was led away, he said over his shoulder to a bewildered barrister with her papers still open on the desk, “The fact that it is ‘unspoken’.”

Chapter 8

The Emperor's New Clothes

It was the 10th of August and the Perseids Meteor Shower was always a spectacle for the astronomically minded in Australia. On a particularly moonless and cloudless night, Tommy Grayson and Patricia O'Leary were already camped out in some secluded space on the University campus where they had each extended their sleeping bags, put pillows under their heads, and watched the sky with interest as they observed the 'Tears of Saint Lawrence' dart across the sky from the constellation Perseus.

"What's keeping Jake?" Patricia asked, her hands behind her head.

"I'm not sure," Tommy said, "He said he'd be here."

Tommy sat up to face the pile of junk-food that had been dumped between them and he grabbed a small packet of chips.

"Simon said he introduced Jake to Professor Philip's associate, Charlie Horovitz," Tommy continued in-between his munching on chips and licking his fingers, "And that he has a plan to get Benjamin Jones to talk with Detective Derrick."

"Well, I can't wait to hear it," Patricia said. "Do you know any more about this big plan?"

"I only know that it is due to take place in five days' time when Professor Philip is having his Festschrift," Tommy said, "Has Jake told you anything about it?"

"Jake asked me to volunteer to be the one handing out tickets to the Festschrift," Patricia said. "I am not sure why though. A number of Professor Philip's academic colleagues and a number of ex-students will attend; and a select few will read-out and present Professor Philip with essays each in honour of his accomplishments over the years. Jake said that the most important thing was that Benjamin Jones and his assistant Saanvi Patel are ex-students of Professor Philip and they have already said they are attending. Other than that, I don't know what his plan is."

"I don't know why we don't just get Sister Jennifer to attend and let her work her magic on Benjamin Jones there," Tommy questioned.

"Because firstly," Patricia responded, "In five days' time, her convent is celebrating the Feast of the Assumption and so she's busy on that day. And secondly," Patricia continued, "It's one thing for a nun to visit a man in prison like Dr Lazer who may be in need of spiritual guidance," Patricia continued, "But it's quite another thing for Sister Jennifer to attend a Festschrift of a retiring Professor to speak with none other than the Managing Director of DrugTech about a plan designed to bring DrugTech to its knees. She would never be able to clear it with the Mother Superior. I'm afraid we are on our own with this one." It was Patricia's turn to sit up and she grabbed a chocolate bar from the pile.

"Awesome!" Tommy gawked as a meteor streaked across the sky. "Did you see that?"

"Absolutely!" Patricia exclaimed with a similar level of excitement.

"Hey wasn't Simon going to smooth it over with Professor Philip or something?" Patricia asked, "I thought he had a rapport with him and was going to broach the topic of introducing us to Benjamin Jones or something."

"Jake said that all the indications were that Professor Philip would not help us out if he knew what we were up to," Tommy answered. "In the end, Simon managed to introduce Jake to Professor Philip's associate, Charlie Horovitz. And when Jake found out that Charlie was hosting Professor Philip's Festschrift and that Benjamin Jones was attending, Jake volunteered to take the lion's share of the planning from Charlie, and Charlie was only more than happy to let him have it."

"Hi guys," Jake said as he trudged towards them. He had his hands in his pockets and his sleeping bag and pillow in a backpack slung over his shoulder. "Did I miss much?"

"Oh wow!" Tommy and Patricia said as another meteor streaked across the sky.

Jake added to the pile of junk food between them with sugar snakes, chocolate frogs and corn chips, then set out his sleeping bag on the grass next to Tommy and Patricia. The three of them had their pillows surround the junk food and extended their feet out in a star position in different directions equidistant from each other.

"So, what's the big plan?" Tommy asked.

"Yeah?" Patricia questioned also curious to know what he had come up with.

"The operation is called, 'The Emperor's New Clothes,'" Jake replied. "Simon and I reckon that Professor Philip will not willingly help us, so we have decided to get him to help us, *unwillingly*."

"Oh yeah?" Tommy questioned. "And just how are you going to do that?"

"Well," Jake continued, "Patricia will be handing out tickets to the lecture theatre where the Festschrift is taking place. We are going to arrange it so that Benjamin Jones and his assistant Saanvi Patel will be given ticket numbers K15 and K16 which will place them almost dead-centre of the theatre."

"Go on," Patricia said.

"Well towards the end of the Festschrift," Jake continued, "After the academics have given their speeches, I have arranged with Charlie that I will then get to show off my latest and greatest scientific invention from my psychology class. It will be half serious, half in jest, but I think Benjamin Jones will be in for one hell of a ride."

"How so?" Tommy asked wanting to hear more of the plan.

"We are going to sit Professor Philip on a stool in the front of the stage facing the audience. We will then place a Virtual Reality Helmet on him where he will simply see images of past students in labs, lectures, and university life," Jake continued. "But I will announce to the audience that this machine embodies the beginnings of a breakthrough in technology in that it has a rudimentary ability to 'Read Face'," Jake said almost chuckling. "We will then ask each member of the audience to look under their seat and retrieve a pair of 3D glasses taped to the bottom of their seat and ask them to switch them on."

Jake grabbed some Smarties from the pile and started munching on them about four or five at a time as he continued telling his friends the plan.

"Our particular glasses will be the ones we got from Dr Lazer," Jake said. "We will already have them on before we announce what the experiment is," Jake continued finishing the packet of Smarties a little too quickly and dumping the empty box back into the pile. "That way, if any DrugTech goons are there with the ability to 'read face' themselves, they will not know what we are up to."

"Ok," Patricia said, "And what *are* we up to?" she asked wanting to hear more.

"At this stage," Jake answered, "Patricia you will approach Dr Saanvi Patel seated next to Benjamin Jones and ask her to come back stage with you to assist in presenting Professor Philip with a plaque on behalf of the old students. That will leave Benjamin Jones sitting in K15 or K16 on his own for the experiment."

"Then what?" Tommy questioned wanting to hear more.

"Then begins our 'Mission Impossible' scenario," Jake said. "Unbeknownst to Benjamin Jones and the rest of the academics and the odd students who will all be invited to go to the next-door auditorium and help set up the refreshments, the remaining members of the audience will be my very own flash-mob of psychology students. They have already agreed to partake in my little psychology experiment on 'The Power of Social Conformity' where Benjamin Jones is the one that we are experimenting on. Professor Philip at this stage will be essentially blinded by our VR Helmet so he won't recognise any of the students in the audience anyway."

Jake began eyeing the pile of junk food for another snack.

"The way it works is like this," Jake continued as he grabbed a packet of corn chips.

"I will announce that the helmet that Professor Philip is wearing is 'Reading-his-Face' and displaying images on the screen ranging from his immediate thoughts and probing right down to the depths of his subconscious. He will be asked to think about each of his past students and university life. Then, I will say that the 3D glasses that everyone has, is blue-toothed to the helmet and that each lens is actually an LCD screen that will switch from being opaque to black for each eye in perfect synchronisation with the images that Professor Philip is causing to be displayed on the screen because of his thoughts. Accordingly, I will say that each student will see a unique image on the screen as the glasses are synched with the ticket number of each person for when Professor Philip is thinking about them."

"The only thing is," Jake continued, "Every one of my flash mob students are wearing fake glasses and all they will see are garbled images on the screen. But they have been told that with each 'slide' that comes up, they are to pretend to see something funny and starting with a chuckle in an ever growing crescendo as each 'slide' is shown, they will laugh in unison until the final 'slide' is shown which will then 'bring the house down,' in absolute laughter," Jake said. "They are being told that Benjamin Jones has not been let-in on the plan and will simply be seeing nonsense like the rest of the students, but that he is being videotaped for his reaction to everyone's laughter which will be studied later in my psychology class, and that this constitutes my practical psyche project where I perform an experiment on an unsuspecting individual."

"Ok," Tommy said, "But what's the catch? How is this going to help us?"

"The catch is," Jake said, "That the glasses Benjamin Jones will have on are PS4 glasses that are in fact actually radio synched to the images on the screen and the laptop that I have. And so, Benjamin Jones will not see garbled images with each 'slide' that is put up. Rather, he will see very incriminating and very embarrassing slides about DrugTech and Dr Jamieson that Detective Derrick and I have been working on, from going through his intelligence reports that Detective Derrick has managed to compile on DrugTech."

Jake continued outlaying his plan to the other two students who were excited but cautiously sceptical that the plan may fail at any point. It wasn't long before each passing meteor became less and less exciting as the plan became more and more so.

Five days later, the Festschrift of Professor Philip was drawing to a close and the Professor was asked to sit on a stool wearing a VR Helmet facing the audience as Jake took to the podium where he asked each student to retrieve the 3D glasses from under their seats and turn them on.

Saanvi Patel was now in the neighbouring auditorium with Patricia and the other academics where she was asked to prepare a small speech on behalf of the ex-students as she presented a plaque to Professor Philip. The rest were setting up refreshments and a cake to commemorate the occasion.

Jake's 'flash mob' of psychology students sat smirking to each other as Jake invited the Professor to think hard on each and every student that he had taught over the years and allow the VR Helmet to probe the depths of his memories. Jake's head was buried in his laptop on the podium before he announced, "Yes, an image is coming through, unique to each student. Ladies and Gentleman, here is slide one!"

Jake then tapped a key on the laptop. Each student continued to see white noise on the screen. But Benjamin Jones' 3D glasses filtered out the white noise and permitted him to read the words:

"Dr Jamieson had Professor Philip's friend Martin Hanson murdered by giving him a suicide pill developed by Leo, Mitch and Morley."

The flash mob of students giggled at the slide as if something light and entertaining was seen by them, but Benjamin Jones shifted back and forth in his seat and began to look rather uncomfortable.

"Well done, Professor," Jake continued, "Now please think of the first time that you met each of your students in the lab. What did you want to say to them but couldn't?"

Jake tapped another key on his laptop, and Benjamin Jones read, "Dr Jamieson had two private-detectives from the United States surveil Charlie Horovitz, Scientist Bruce, Professor Philip and Benjamin Jones in order to secure for himself the Trans Warp Inducer."

Immediately the audience burst into laughter as if they had seen something quite amusing concerning themselves.

Benjamin Jones continued to shift in his seat. He removed his glasses to look at the screen directly, and then placed them back on. He looked around to see if anyone else could see what he was seeing.

"Now Professor," Jake continued from the podium, "Think hard about what the future holds for each of us and where you think we will go from here?"

Jake tapped another key, and this time Benjamin Jones read:

"Dr Jamieson and the Contessa Medici are setting Benjamin Jones up to take the fall for the murder of Marty Hanson and Peter McKinnon, aka, Mr Solitary."

At this point, the audience members were splitting their sides with laughter and it was almost impossible for Jake to get a word in over the commotion.

"Tell us," Jake yelled into the microphone over the laughter, "Tell us the remedy Professor. What should we do to improve the future that we just saw?"

Benjamin Jones then read:

"Detective Derrick from the Surry Hills Police Station is an honest cop. Ask him about Dr Lazer and the Trans Warp Inducer or it will be too late for Benjamin Jones!"

At this point the audience members were falling off their seats and stomping their feet. Several of them were wiping tears from their eyes from too much laughter. The lights came back up and a red-faced Benjamin Jones stood from his seat, looked at his watch, texted Saanvi Patel that he was not feeling too well, and promptly left the University campus.

Chapter 9

The Face of the Devil

Müezzinzade Ali Pasha boarded the flagship *Sultana* and gave orders that the fleet proceed in battle formation. For the next several hours, his fleet of 300 ships stretched out into the dreaded and feared crescent formation of the Ottoman Empire. The *Sultana* was at the centre of the vanguard. The crescent of ships was thousands of metres long and stretched northwards from the mountains of the Albanian Shore to southwards off the coast of Morea. Accordingly, the fleet blocked the whole of the entrance to the Gulf. The battle formation of the crescent was the embodiment of a simple unfailing tactic. Advance, outflank and surround. Nothing had as yet survived it. The bulk of the Ottoman fleet were rowed by Christian slaves; all below deck, naked, sweating, and shackled at the feet on their bench at the oar. The Müezzinzade had treated his slaves better than most. Should they be victorious today, they were promised their freedom. But if the ship was to sink, the shackled slaves would go down with the ship.

The wind was strong and steady from the rear, meaning that the slaves were not required to row. They were ordered to keep their heads down lest they would be killed. The grand sails of the Ottoman fleet were raised to capture the wind to the fullest extent, and the Turkish armada proceeded like a hungry stalking beast assured of its prey. And amidst the dazzling display of coloured, triumphant and effulgent pennants and streamers of the Ottoman war galleys, fluttering high and proud in the breeze, from the centre mast of the *Sultana,* was the green Islamic pennant bearing the name of Allah in gold calligraphy no less than 28,900 times. It was rumoured to have been touched by the great Prophet himself and was one of the treasures of Mecca. It was not that it had never seen defeat. Rather, its presence assured the victory.

And so, the full and deep sound of wind in sails and loud fluttering pennants and streamers were only the undertones of the battle choir of the Ottoman fleet. For there, on the deck of each war galley proceeding in formation, a cacophony of drums, flutes, trumpets, cymbals and gongs filled the air. Soldiers were belly-dancing on deck, laughing, cheering, whistling and hollering, bathed in over-enjoyment of the anticipation of the war.

Janissaries took their positions kneeling in formation from the sterns to the bows of the ships. Arrows were put in positions, cannon balls, torches, arquebuses and matchlocks. And strapped to their waists, swords ranging from heavy rapiers, and broadswords to curve-bladed sabres, dusacks and cutlasses. And just as it seemed the noise could not get any louder, the frenzied and deafening sounds of horns burst out across each ship as the enemy had just been spotted.

"What kind of battle formation is that?" the Müezzinzade asked himself as he saw six huge galleasses sprawled out in front of a slowly advancing horizontal line of ships behind them. The Christian league was slow and panting, with sails lowered and their oars raising and dipping. Unlike the Ottoman fleet, the silence from the Christian fleet was ominous.

"It's like the rowing dead," the Müezzinzade thought to himself, as their skeletal ships with lowered sails and naked masts laboured against the wind. One of his janissaries hollered in humour, "They've put their commercial liners in front of their fleet!" and the rest of the crew belly-laughed at the amusing sight.

Then a slight howling hum arose from the Venetian line of the Christian ships. Still grieving the loss of their beloved Governor Marc Antonio Bragadin, flayed alive when the Cypriote City of Famagusta fell to the Müezzinzade, the Venetian ships were quietly chanting the words "Famagusta, Famagusta, Famagusta," all in unison, like the deathly howl of the unrested spirits of the fallen Christian soldiers.

There was no dancing on the Christian ships. Priests in dark robes moved like ghosts upon the decks. Armed with a crucifix in one hand and rosary beads in the other, they had their backs to the Ottomans as they continually blessed the Christians and continually forgave their sins. It was the day of judgment, and their sins were laid bare before their maker.

"Shore up the rear guard," the Müezzinzade commanded as he spotted, through a gap of the galleasses, the flagship of the Christians. "I think he's heading straight for us!"

There was a long-known naval convention in war, that the flagships of the opposing fleets did not themselves engage in battle. But nothing about the Christian League was conventional. "Signal our intention to engage the flagship," the Müezzinzade commanded proudly as he spotted a young 24-year-old with sword in hand clumsily attempt to command his ship and that of his fleet.

A cannon ball was fired from the *Sultana* towards the *Real*. Though it landed midpoint in the water between them, it clearly signalled her intention to engage. Encouraging blasts and shots then rang out from the rest of the Ottoman fleet as they backed-up and encouraged their leader engaging directly in the fight.

Don John immediately returned fire with a single cannon ball towards the *Sultana* also signalling *Real's* intention to engage. But apart from the single shot, and the humming of "Famagusta" from the Venetian ships, the relative silence of the Christian fleet hung around them like the silence of dark heavy rain clouds before an impending storm.

The Müezzinzade watched closely. The priests had finished their blessings and were heading to the poop deck. They kneeled in prayer on every ship and began singing an harmonious Gregorian chant in honour of their Lady, the Queen of Heaven. They were difficult to hear as the wind was blowing from the direction of the Ottoman fleet, but it could still be heard. It was an unusually sweet sound, like the gentle smell of frankincense, and certainly nothing like the sound of an impending battle. Several laughing soldiers on board the Ottoman vessels stopped in admiration and curiosity to hear it. Then the sound of the priests grew ever so slightly in crescendo and even the fluttering of the Ottoman pennants and streamers stopped to listen. The breeze had stopped in its tracks, and a deathly calm ensued. The pennants and streamers of the Ottoman fleet drooped and their sails were stymied. The advancing Ottoman fleet had stalled. The chant of the priests grew and surrounded the Ottoman fleet like the tentacles of a Kraken from beneath the waterline.

Then the wind began again, twisting and turning, like a waking hungry baby screaming for its food and looking in the direction of the Ottomans. Then a howling wind grew in force directly behind the Christian fleet. "Lower the sails!" the Commanders of the Ottoman vessels barked as the wind against them grew and grew. The whipping of the slaves commenced as the oarsmen were now required to row into the wind. Then a thunderous cheer broke out amongst the Christian fleet to the great surprise of the Ottomans as the Christian oars were put away and their sails were lifted high on the masts. The Christian fleet with sails and pennants blowing in the wind towards the Ottoman fleet appeared resplendent and unstoppable and a renewed sense of purpose rang through the Christian soldiers as they screamed and cheered, "God is with us today!"

As the oarsmen of the Ottoman fleet began rowing hard, an awkward silence fell upon them as the stunned janissaries wondered what on Earth had just happened. And from the deck of the *Real* the young shrill voice of the 24-year-old Supreme Commander rang out with a passage from scripture, "Do not resist the one who is evil. But if anyone slaps you on the right cheek, turn to him the other also!"

And with that Command, all six galleasses stopped and turned clockwise in unison, like a well-rehearsed dance, and they exposed their port side toward the Ottoman fleet. The janissaries froze in stunned silence as they wondered what this could mean, when suddenly it was laid bare before them. The cannon doors of the galleasses swung open as rows and rows of cannons rolled out taking direct aim at them. And in that moment, the Müezzinzade went ghostly pale as he began to contemplate for the first time that day, the Christian forces as a truly formidable enemy.

Chapter 10

A Question of Loyalty

The audio-visual screen came to life and Dr Lazer appeared seated at a table.

“The accused is before the Court,” the Sheriff’s officer announced.

“This is a readiness hearing into the case of DPP and Leon Lazer,” his Honour Justice Croydon announced. The rain was lashing the windows towards the ceiling and the room was dark. “This trial is listed to commence on the 7th of October, next month. Has the prosecution case been filed and served?”

“It has Your Honour,” Mr King replied.

“Defence reply filed and served?” the judge enquired.

“Yes, Your Honour,” Ms Black answered.

“How long is this case expected to take?” the judge proceeded down his checklist.

“Approximately two weeks,” Ms Black answered.

“Any pre-trial evidentiary rulings required?” the judge asked.

“Yes, Your Honour,” Ms Black answered. “Dr Lazer is charged with murdering his cell mate at Long Bay Jail. The allegation is that he bludgeoned him to death with his bare fists. It has nothing whatsoever to do with the reason that he was incarcerated in the first place, which is that he was found guilty of a series of computer fraud charges. The Defence objects to any evidence regarding the reason that Dr Lazer was incarcerated, it is irrelevant and merely liable to prejudice the jury.”

“That sounds reasonable, doesn’t it Mr King?” the judge asked.

"No, Your Honour," Mr King replied very softly. "The Crown will allege that the victim in this matter was instrumental in persuading the main witness to testify against Dr Lazer in the computer fraud charges for which he was sentenced, and that that constitutes the motive for the murder. Accordingly, its probative value outweighs its prejudicial value and it should be admitted."

"What do you say about that Ms Black?" the judge enquired.

"That's pure speculation on the Crown's behalf, Your Honour," Ms Black protested. "There is absolutely no evidence that the victim persuaded such a witness and furthermore, absolutely no evidence that it acted as a motive for my client. Speculation is not sufficient to admit such prejudicial evidence against the accused."

"Well," the judge interjected. "That is a matter for the jury Ms. Black. I will admit it, but I will direct the jury that the mere fact that he was incarcerated for computer fraud does not of itself prove the murder in this case and that should undo any prejudice. Anything else?"

"No thank you, Your Honour," Ms Black answered defeated.

"Very well," Justice Croydon continued. "Confirm the hearing date of 7 October, and call the next case."

The audio-visual screen was then turned off.

Ms Black packed up her file, grabbed her umbrella and headed back to Chambers. At four o'clock, the Court was running late. Upon exiting the Court, she crossed the road and hurried past a coffee shop where Detective Derrick was having afternoon tea with another prosecutor who happened to have finished early that day.

"Do you know whether they are going to try your self-proclaimed gambler again, Deb, after the hung jury?" Detective Derrick asked.

"We are still waiting on the DPP to make a decision on that," Deb answered. "How's your murder case going with your long-time nemesis, Dr Lazer?"

"It's proceeding," Detective Derrick said looking a little perplexed. "The hearing date is next month. Hey, we both agreed that he wasn't the violent type, right?" Detective Derrick questioned.

"Well, there's always a first time for everything," Deb answered.

"I don't know," the Detective responded. "I am starting to have some misgivings about the case. Is there anything you can tell me about the prosecutor in the matter, Mr King?"

"He's not a regular Crown Prosecutor," Deb answered. The DPP is briefing a member of the private bar on this one, so I don't really know anything about him."

"That's odd, isn't it?" Detective Derrick asked.

"It does happen from time to time," Deb said reassuringly, "It all depends on the caseload."

As the Detective questioned where his loyalties lay, a rather perturbed Benjamin Jones was pacing back and forth in his office at the DrugTech headquarters adjoining the University of Sydney, as he waited for his intercom to buzz.

"Dr Jamieson is on line one," his secretary announced.

Benjamin Jones pressed the flashing light on line one, and picked up the cordless phone from his desk. "Dr Jamieson," Benjamin Jones said rather confrontationally, "It's about time we had a talk about the Trans Warp Inducer and a couple of other things."

Benjamin Jones expected that such an opening to a conversation would cause some level of shock, but he wasn't expecting his mother-in-law, the Contessa Medici to respond.

"Where are you?" the Contessa asked through the phone.

"I am in my Sydney Office," Benjamin Jones answered. "Why?"

"Are you alone in the office?" the Contessa Medici asked ignoring the question.

"Yes, I am," Benjamin answered.

"Please stand in the middle of the room and wait," the Contessa said rather matter-of-factly.

Benjamin Jones was still pacing the office, so it was a little matter for him to come to a stop in the centre of his office. "What is all this about?" he asked.

As he stood talking into the cordless phone, the colours of his office walls began to shimmer in a golden glittery way as if his eyes were closed and someone was rubbing his optic nerve. The colours began to fade and for a split second, Benjamin Jones felt he was standing in pitch blackness. But then what appeared as a perfectly blue sky started to appear in lieu of the walls and his office, as if someone was turning up the colour on a television set. He felt a warm breeze on his face and then the sun on his head. When the shimmering effect finished, he looked around to see himself standing on green grass on a magnificent hill with a picnic blanket set out in front of him. And there on the picnic blanket was the Contessa Medici and Dr Jamieson each eating toast and drinking tea.

"Where am I?" Benjamin Jones asked looking around him at the magnificent scenery. Hills of green grass and trees surrounded him.

"You are in the Swiss Alps," his mother-in-law answered. "Welcome to our little breakfast picnic. It sure beats conventional travel don't you think?"

"The Trans Warp Inducer?" Benjamin Jones questioned.

"Indeed," Dr Jamieson answered spreading some more jam on his toast. "Please have a seat."

"I would have thought as the Managing Director of the Australian Branch of DrugTech, that I had a right to know that the Trans Warp Inducer was finally operational," Benjamin Jones complained.

"Maybe," his mother-in-law answered almost dismissively. "But did you have a need to know? The Trans Warp Inducer is top secret and currently is only disclosed on a need-to-know basis."

It was a rather odd sight, seeing Dr Jamieson and the Contessa Medici each in business attire, on a picnic rug on the top of a hill in the midst of the Swiss Alps. He only imagined that as he was instantly transported there from Sydney himself, then obviously, they would instantly be transported back to wherever a business meeting was that they apparently had scheduled. And since they seemed to have all the power in the world to have breakfast in any place in the world at a moment's notice, he supposed that the open-air of the Swiss Alps was as good a place as any. Benjamin Jones decided to sit himself down on the picnic rug as he chose his next words carefully.

"Please tell me about Martin Hanson's suicide," Benjamin Jones asked looking at Dr Jamieson. "He was dismissed on your watch, and his investigation has sparked a certain level of curiosity."

"What about it?" Dr Jamieson asked unperturbed and pouring himself a fresh cup of tea.

"Some people are speculating that he was murdered by giving him a suicide pill from the former company of Leo Mitch and Morley."

"He was given a sedative," Dr Jamieson answered as he sipped his tea. "The guy was a crank and a lune. He had made it his mission in life to bring down DrugTech because he was a disgruntled employee. Obviously, his passions got the better of him. It was either him or DrugTech and as it turned out, DrugTech survives. So, case closed."

Benjamin Jones was not convinced with the answer, but he decided to move on. "What about Mr Solitary and Dr Lazer?" Benjamin Jones asked next. "Wasn't he murdered with the Trans Warp Inducer and Dr Lazer setup to take the heat?"

"Where have you been hearing these rumours?" the Contessa Medici asked.

"Let's just say it was read on someone's face who happens to be extremely curious about the situation," Benjamin Jones answered.

"Mr Solitary had stage four terminal lung cancer," Dr Jamieson replied. "At *his* request, he was spared the indignity and the pain of a most unpleasant death. It was an act of mercy."

"What about Dr Lazer?" Benjamin Jones enquired again. "Is it justice that he should be thrown to the wolves?"

"Of course it's justice," Dr Jamieson answered putting his teacup down with only a slight hint of irritation. "Dr Lazer has made it his mission in life to expose the workings of DrugTech and has drawn a line in the sand. It is either him or us. If he wants to take us on, fine, he can roll the dice and take his chances. We will not allow him to be acquitted."

"Or what?" Benjamin Jones asked, "Or his head will explode too?"

"I don't understand your hostility," Dr Jamieson said, "You are the Managing Director of the Australian Branch of DrugTech. It is really a question of loyalty. Don't you see it as your fiduciary duty to be true to the company? Your parents trusted you with a silver casket which you yourself use as a last resort when you want to accomplish things. Do you really see this as any different?"

Benjamin Jones thought for a second before responding.

He grabbed himself a plate with a piece of toast and poured himself a cup of tea from the pot. He then took the time to make a thorough inspection of his surroundings. Switzerland in September was always a perfect time of the year. And the weather there was perfect compared with the Australian dismal rain. "I want full access to the Trans Warp Inducer," he said taking a bite out of the toast.

Dr Jamieson looked at the Contessa.

"Fine," she said. "Give me your cell phone."

Chapter 11

A Career Change

It was the first day that Professor Philip attended work as an Emeritus Professor. Other than the title, and the non-teaching of students, nothing else had changed. And since he was more interested in his research and less interested in titles, he found himself rather free for the first time in his professional career to pursue his research with less interruption. Most people would have changed the time that they came into work, but Emeritus Professor Philip strode on in at the usual time of 7:30 in the morning with a half-emptied takeaway cup of coffee that he had purchased at Redfern Station. He rarely drunk the second half. It's not that it was too cold for his taste, though the second-half always was. But rather, only about half the coffee had been drunk from the time that he had alighted the train at Redfern Station to the time that he arrived at his office at Sydney University, and by that stage, he was too distracted with his work to think about drinking any more coffee.

And so, it was the same this morning, except for the fact that Patricia O'Leary was waiting in his office seated on the other side of his desk.

"Good morning, Patricia," the Emeritus Professor said. She was an unwelcomed distraction, but his polite attitude and years of habit prevented any of that from showing. "It is a little early for students, isn't it?"

"Actually, I submitted my last assignment on Friday," Patricia said. "I have pretty much finished at University now. The others still have exams to do, but my courses are over."

"You must be happy," Philip said, "Have you given any thought to your career?"

"Actually, I have," Patricia said. "You know I was a mature-aged student when I came here, and at that time, I was pretty lost, I had just lost my husband, I drank a lot, and I didn't quite know what I wanted to do in life."

"You seem like you have pretty much found yourself here then," the Professor said, "I have noticed you have been quite happy here these past few years and have grown close to your new friends."

"It has been great here," Patricia said. "Do you remember some time back when you and a few other professors put in a grant request with the Australian Government for 20 million dollars for new nuclear magnetic resonance machines at this university and others?"

"Yes, I do," the Professor answered. "It would have made the Australian universities the most advanced in the world. It was a shame the grant fell through though. For a moment it looked as if we were going to be approved."

"How come the grant failed?" Patricia asked.

"Some snake from Singapore put in a bid for research between some Australian Labs and some Singaporean Labs and he promised a whole lot of nonsense that didn't make any scientific sense; but," the Professor lamented leaning back in his chair, "He had told the politicians everything that they were looking for in a grant and he didn't let the truth get in the way, and so the grant went to them." The Professor hated politics. But grant proposals were a necessary evil in his line of work, and sometimes it was a cutthroat business.

"In my former life," Patricia began again, "I was married to a butcher. He was a bit of a bully and I refused to be a battered woman, and not having the best of motives in mind, I took out a life insurance policy on his life for 20 million dollars. Whilst I didn't have the purest of motives at the time, he actually died in a tragic accident, and eventually, after threatening legal action and all, the insurance company has just cut me a cheque for 20 million dollars for his death several years ago."

"That sounds rather incredible," Professor Philip commented, wondering why she had brought this up. "I don't suppose you are willing to donate any of that to science?" he asked in jest.

"It's funny you know," Patricia said somewhat sombrely. "I met this nun, Sister Jennifer, from the Dominican Order of Nuns, and from the moment I met her, she seemed to know all that I had done in my past life and said that I needed to come to terms with my conscience. We actually became friends and when I eventually tried to donate the money to her Order of Nuns, she said that she was more concerned about my soul and not my money."

The Professor chose this moment to remain silent. Obviously, Patricia O'Leary was here for a purpose and she had something to say, so he decided to sit back and let her finish.

"I considered using the money for myself, as well as all sorts of things," Patricia continued. "When I asked Sister Jennifer what she recommended I do with it, she said 'render unto Caesar what belongs to Caesar, and give unto God what belongs to God.'"

"Goodness," Professor Philip said not being able to remain silent. "That sounds like you want to be a nun!"

"I do," Patricia said.

"What?" Philip asked incredulously.

"I have decided to become a nun," Patricia answered rather forthrightly, "Like Sister Jennifer."

"I can't believe it," Philip replied. "Are you sure about this? I never saw any indication from you that you were religious?"

"Well, I have always kept that aspect of things buried deep within," Patricia answered. "But it has always been there," she answered. "It has taken me a long time to realise it, but after much soul searching, I found that happiness doesn't come from money but from answers to the truth. Some people search for truth in a lab, others in a monastery. I have always respected science, good science, but in the end, I think I would rather dedicate my life to the author of science rather than science itself."

"Well," Philip said lost for words, "Let me be the first to congratulate you, I suppose," he said still trying to come to terms with the news. "I don't suppose you want to donate the full 20 million dollars to science though?" he asked jovially in an attempt to lighten the mood.

"I do," she said opening her handbag. "Here is a cheque for 20 million dollars. I was hoping that you could apply it towards those nuclear magnetic resonance machines that you so wanted. Make the Australian universities the best in the world in that area."

"I can't believe it," the Professor said looking at the cheque placed on the table in front of him. "You know, usually when someone makes a donation to that extent to the university, they get a building or a wing named after them so that they are immortalised on campus. The NMR machines would go into the East Wing of this building. We could call it the Patricia O'Leary Wing."

"Oh gosh no," Patricia said blushing and thinking to herself with a bemused smile on herself. "But if you must call it something," she added, "Call it the Sister Jennifer Wing, only..."

"Only, what?" the Professor asked waiting to hear the rest.

"Only don't tell her that I requested that," she said smilingly.

Meanwhile, in an interview cell at the Long Bay Prison Complex, Barrister Black spread her materials out on the table as she waited for Dr Lazer to be brought in.

He was wearing the traditional prison jumpsuit without pockets that prisoners are put in designed to prevent them from smuggling anything into prison that prisoners may be given during a meeting. The back of the jumpsuit was done up with a cable-tie that protruded from the back of the neck.

"Dr Lazer," Barrister Black began. "Your murder case is due to start in the Supreme Court tomorrow. I still can't see anything resembling any hope of a defence. From where I sit, you may as well be pleading guilty. We can put the Crown to strict proof and force them to prove their case beyond a reasonable doubt, but in the end, I don't see how they won't be able to do that without too much difficulty."

"When will the Crown case finish?" Dr Lazer asked.

"About one week from tomorrow," Barrister Black answered. "That's how long it will take to empanel the jury, allow the judge to give them a prep-talk, have the Crown Prosecutor open his case and call all his witnesses."

"And then the Defence case starts right?" Dr Lazer asked.

"What Defence case?" Barrister Black answered the question with a question. "I don't know what case to present because you haven't given me anything here."

"That's OK, Ms Black," Dr Lazer replied. "From what you are telling me, the Defence case won't be ready to start in Court until after the next weekend, right?"

"Yes," Ms Black answered.

"Then tomorrow," Dr Lazer said. "I want you to issue one subpoena and serve it on the Defence witness that I am proposing to call. I believe that he will get me acquitted."

"I need to have some idea as to what you are proposing Dr Lazer," Ms Black said in protestation. "Barristers are not mouthpieces for their clients. If this has no forensic benefit for your case, then I am afraid I cannot comply with your request, and if you insist on it, then you will have to brief another barrister."

"I understand," Dr Lazer said. "We have a whole week to fill you in on the defence case."

"Who is 'we' and what am I to be 'filled-in' on?" Barrister Black asked again a little exasperated.

"I have some people on the outside who have been helping me with my case and I trust them, Ms Black," Dr Lazer answered. "They are preparing a brief of materials for you to peruse and study and you will have more than enough time to satisfy yourself of the defence case before it starts."

"And when do I get this brief of materials?" Barrister Black asked.

"Tomorrow," Dr Lazer answered. "It should be delivered to your Chambers after the first day in Court."

"I don't know what all the mystery is about," Ms Black replied. "It just sounds like more of your conspiracy-theory-fear-mongering."

"You can make up your own mind when you see the evidence Ms Black," Dr Lazer said smiling.

'He may be a fool,' Ms Black thought to herself, 'But he certainly is sure of himself.'

"And who is this witness that you want us to issue a subpoena for tomorrow?" Barrister Black asked.

"The Managing Director of DrugTech," Dr Lazer answered. "Dr Benjamin Jones."

Chapter 12

Bursting the Battleline

The Ottoman Turkish fleet began firing all canons towards the Christian fleet. The thunderous claps and black plumes of smoke created an unearthly fog around the Ottoman ships. But the Christian fleet were under orders not to fire, under pain of death, until they were within point-blank range. And with the wind now blowing strongly from behind the Christian fleet, the six galleasses, with their port sides and cannons exposed towards the rowing Ottoman fleet, were now blown sideways towards them. And with the cannon fog of war created by the Ottomans, the Christian vanguard was barely seen before it was heard. Massive volleys of cannonades were loosed upon the Ottomans and cracking wood, sinking ships, broken masts and screaming men became the sound of war.

Then the flagship *Sultana* with its battering ram at its prow, crashed into the flagship *Real* as volleys of arrows from the trained janissaries swept across the deck of the Christian ship. Those in suits of armour aboard the edge of the ship were protected as the arrows bounced off them. Immediately grappling hooks were thrown from both ships over each of them tying them together but the attempted boarding parties of the Müezzinzade's ship were met by another unexpected sight. Aboard Don John's flagship were a crack Sardinian Regiment that had trained for just such an encounter. And as the Müezzinzade's boarding party approached the side of the *Real*, a stunning anti-boarding net was immediately raised trapping the enemy behind it as they fell over each other in their haste to charge the Christians. Row after row of janissaries crashed into one another as the bulk of them had not yet realised what was preventing them from boarding the *Real.* And in that moment of confusion, the crack squadron of Sardinians fired volley after volley of arquebuses, muskets and matchlocks through the nets and into the Ottoman Turks.

When the firepower was exhausted, and before the smoke had cleared, what was left of the shredded boarding nets of the *Real* were dropped and hundreds upon hundreds of Christian soldiers charged the deck of the *Sultana* with swords swinging and teeth grinding. Within seconds, approximately eight hundred fighting men were battling each other aboard the deck of the *Sultana*.

Three times the Sardinian squad pushed the janissaries back to the other side of the *Sultana*, and three times the janissaries fought their way back again. It was a bloody battle with heavy casualties. The wounded fell where they were struck, bleeding profusely, and the advancing soldiers from either side either proceeded over the bodies of the bleeding fallen men or simply kicked them overboard.

Then as Don John was dancing a jig on the poop deck of the *Real* as he was yelling orders in uncontained excitement to his men, an arrow struck him in the foot. He immediately fell. It was not unnoticed and several janissaries screamed, "Allāhu 'akbar." The body armour of Don John had protected all the vital organs from arrow hits, and the strike to the foot appeared merely to be a graze. Before any psychological advantage was secured, he had jumped back up, and with sword in hand, he yelled in defiance, "Domino Gloria!" and the Christian forces once again drove the janissaries back. But this time, the Müezzinzade himself was struck in the forehead with an arquebus bullet. And as he fell where he was hit, the swinging swords of the advancing Christian soldiers did not stop to pay their respects. They hacked the head off the Turkish Admiral and thrust a half-pike into it, hoisting it high above the men. The ghastly vision of their Commander being killed had the effect of demoralizing the Turks, and the *Sultana* was very quickly overrun.

The green flag that had the golden embroidery of Allah 28,900 times was cut down and, in its stead, a banner of the Papal league was raised from the mast of the *Sultana.* The demoralizing of the Turks continued throughout the fleet and by 4 o'clock that afternoon of 7 October 1571, the battle of Lepanto was over. The sea itself was now red with blood as that day, an empire was sacrificed to the war god.

And about a thousand kilometres away in Vatican City, as people outside the Vatican had been saying the rosary each day after day from dawn until dusk, terrified that they were soon to be overrun, the Pope was sitting around a board room table with his treasurer and trusted Cardinals. He was about to speak when he froze suddenly and received a monstrous vision of the gory battle. After a few minutes of stunned silence, the Pope suddenly rose from his seat and gazed out the window, saying, "This is not a moment for business; make haste to thank God, because our fleet this moment has won a victory over the Turks."

Chapter 13

Smoke and Mirrors

Dr Lazer sat uncomfortably in the dock. The Crown case against him had proceeded as predicted. Mr King opened to the jury on a rather 'garden-variety prison-house beating' with only one possible motive, one possible cause, and only one possible murderer. And all of that pointed to the accused, Dr Lazer. There was therefore only one possible verdict. At least as far as the Crown case was concerned. It was now the third day of his murder trial, and with the Crown case finally closed, the accused was now given the opportunity to call his first witness.

"The Defence calls, Dr Benjamin Jones," Barrister Black said rising at the bar table.

Naturally all eyes looked towards the back of the Court. When no one responded to the call, the judge looked at the Court officer and said, "Call Dr Benjamin Jones."

The Court officer walked to the back of the Court. He then turned back around to look at the judge before bowing, and then turned around again to open the courtroom door. From outside the doors, the Court officer could be heard to yell, "Dr Benjamin Jones, Dr Benjamin Jones, Dr Benjamin Jones."

The doors opened again with the Court officer entering and saying, "Before the Court, your Honour."

A middle-aged man in a suit entered the Court, but he was followed by a woman in barrister's attire who proceeded to the bar table and announced her appearance.

"May it please Your Honour, my name is Colfax, I appear for the witness Dr Jones, there is a matter that I need to raise with your Honour in the absence of the jury."

"Yes, very well," the judge replied. "Ask the jury to step outside for a minute please," the judge said to the Court officer.

The jury rose from their seats and the six men and six women shuffled out of the courtroom. When the last of the jury had left and the Court officer had shut the jury door behind them, the judge looked at the new barrister at the bar table standing between the prosecutor and the defence Counsel.

"Yes, Ms Colfax?" his Honour questioned.

"Your Honour, an urgent order was issued last night from the Chief Justice of the High Court under the *Defence Act*," she said opening a folder that she was carrying and producing some papers bearing the stamp of the Court. "It is anticipated that Dr Jones may be asked some questions regarding confidential materials of which an Infrastructure Declaration under the *Defence Act* is in effect. On that basis, the Court has directed that any questioning of Dr Jones be conducted in a closed Court and with a non-publication order being made."

Barrister Colfax then handed the order to the Court officer who handed it to the Associate. The Associate stood and handed it to the judge seated on the bench elevated behind her.

The fat Justice Croydon hated being told what to do, but he had little choice in the matter. That did not mean, however, that he wasn't allowed to complain about it.

"This is a murder case, Ms Colfax," his Honour stated with obvious disdain. "Isn't it in the public interest that murder trials be conducted openly?"

"Yes, your Honour," Ms Colfax replied. "That matter was weighed up by the High Court along with the public interest of keeping certain defence matters confidential."

"What do you say about this Ms Black?" the judge asked looking for some support.

"Well with respect, we agree with your Honour," Ms Black replied addressing the ego of the judge directly. "Justice must not only be done, but it must be *seen* to be done. The order only requires your Honour not to receive any evidence from Dr Jones in an open Court and with a non-publication order. But if justice cannot be attained in a murder trial that way, then your Honour still has the power to stay the proceedings indefinitely on the basis that justice for the accused can no longer be obtained."

It was a long shot, but it was a typical example of the kind of submissions made to a judge when a judge stubbornly holds-out for too long.

"Well, it is regrettable Ms Black, and I will certainly advise the jury that no adverse inference should be drawn against the accused by the unusual order that is made, but when all things are weighed up, I think it is in the public interest that we just proceed under the law in the best way that we can," the judge did not wish to hear any further argument. "I will have this order marked for identification," he said giving it back to the Associate who promptly stapled a pink slip of paper to it with a number and filed it away.

"Members of the public gallery," the judge continued addressing the people seated at the back of the Court, "I now have to ask you all to leave the Court, the Court will be closed for the duration of this witness's evidence. I will make a non-publication order concerning the evidence given by Dr Jones including the reason why the Court was closed. Yes, bring back the jury please," the judge said to the Court officer.

As the jury was brought in, the members of the public gallery walked out. A sign was hung on the outside of the courtroom doors indicating that the Court was closed.

As the judge directed the jury that for 'legal reasons' the Court needed to be closed and that no adverse inference was to be drawn against the accused regarding the closing of the Court, the jury began to wonder why Dr Jones was being treated so differently under the law. Nothing was mentioned about the *Defence Act* or the order of the High Court to the jury, and as Dr Jones was called by the defence, the jury couldn't help but feel apprehensive that the defence was up to something that was unusual and therefore not really in the interests of justice. And the judge's warning to them not to think that way against the accused was simply perceived by them as part of such a legal trick that the defence must have managed to gain to their advantage.

Ms Colfax excused herself from the Court and Dr Jones was sworn in as a witness.

The examination-in-chief of Dr Jones by Barrister Black then proceeded as follows:

Q. Will you please tell the Court your full name?
A. My name is Dr Benjamin Jones.

Q. What is your current occupation?
A. I am the Managing Director of the Australian Branch of DrugTech.

Q. You are not a voluntary witness here today, is that right? You appear here under subpoena?
A. Yes.

Q. Do you know my client, Dr Leon Lazer?
A. No, not personally.

Q. Dr Lazer is charged with murdering a person by the name of Peter McKinnon. Did you know a Peter McKinnon?
A. No, not personally.

Q. Had you heard of him?
A. Yes, I had heard his name mentioned.

Q. How had you heard of him?

Mr King: I object, your Honour. This is hearsay.
Bench: Ms Black?
Black: Not pressed, your Honour.
Bench: Question is disallowed.

Black: The allegation against Dr Lazer is that he bludgeoned Mr McKinnon to death with his bare fists. Were you aware of that?
A. I have been made aware of that.

Q. Dr Lazer contends, that he never laid a finger on Mc McKinnon, that in fact, his head appeared to explode from a force or from forces unknown. Are you aware that he has alleged that as part of his defence?
A. I have been made aware of that.

Q. You understand that you have taken an oath to tell the truth and of your legal obligation in this Court to do so?
A. Yes, I am.

Q. Dr Jones, from your position as Managing Director of the Australian Branch of DrugTech, are you aware of anything that could possibly explain such a thing?
A. Yes, I am.

Q. What could possibly cause a person's head to explode without anyone laying a finger on him?
A. The Trans Warp Inducer.

Q. What is a Trans Warp Inducer?
A. It is a matter re-arranger. It is a breakthrough in physics that allows any matter in the universe to be trans-warped to another place in the universe. It's as if the universe folds in on itself between the two points.

At this point, there were giggles from the jury.

Q. Have you ever seen the Trans Warp Inducer?
A. You mean the actual device itself?

Q. Yes?
A. No, I have never seen it. I don't know where it is.

Q. Have you ever witnessed the effects of the Trans Warp Inducer?
A. Yes, I have. At one point I was standing in my Sydney office talking on the phone. And in the next moment, I was standing on the Swiss Alps, in Switzerland.

At this point, the jury burst into laughter as each of them questioned the mental state of Dr Jones. The judge was forced to interject.

Bench: I beg your pardon? What do you mean one moment you were standing in your Sydney office, and the next moment you were standing on the Swiss Alps?
Jones: I mean I was physically transported by the Trans Warp Inducer from Sydney to Switzerland in a matter of seconds.

The jury continued to laugh and the judge couldn't help himself, so he asked, much to the amusement of the jury:

Bench: Dr Jones, have you seen anyone about this?

The judge was not expecting an answer, but he received one nonetheless from the witness who remained quietly spoken and polite at all times.

Jones: Yes, I spoke to Major General Frank Collins from the Australian Defence Force about it.

This had the effect of quietening the jury as they eagerly wished to hear more.

"Please continue Ms Black," the judge said.

Black: Are you able to issue a command to the Trans Warp Inducer?
A. Yes.

Q. How are you able to do that?

A. I have an app installed on my mobile phone which gives me full access.

Q. Do you have that phone on you now?
A. Yes.

Q. Can you please take it out?

The witness complied.

Q. Dr Jones, in front of me is an empty drinking-glass. Let me fill it with water.

Barrister Black took the metallic jug full of water usually kept on the bar table for barristers to keep their throats wet, and filled the empty glass with water.

Q. Can you command the Trans Warp Inducer to trans-warp that glass of water from the bar table in front of me, to the bench in front of you in the witness box?

At this question, the courtroom became deathly silent as all ears were awaiting the answer and all eyes a possible demonstration.

A. Yes, I can.
Q. Then please do so.

Dr Jones tapped an icon on his phone as if he was taking a photo of the filled glass of water on the bar table. He then pinch-zoomed into the photo a few times isolating the glass of water before clicking on it once again. He then pointed the phone at the bench in front of him in the witness box and tapped a few more icons.

The colours of the glass of water began to fade-out until it was no longer visible on the bar table. Then in reverse, the colours of the glass began to fade-in on the bench in front of the witness. There were gasps of horror and excitement from the jury.

"May I please have that glass of water?" Barrister Black asked the Court officer who retrieved the glass of water from the witness box. Barrister Black made an obvious display of sipping some of the water and placing the glass back in the original position on the bar table.

Ms Black then turned around and asked a man who was seated behind her to stand.

Q. Dr Jones, do you see my instructing solicitor standing up behind me?
A. Yes.

Q. Are you able to trans-warp him from his position behind me to the area in front of the bar table?
A. Yes, I can.

The jury gasped at the answer.

"Then please do so," Barrister Black said as several of the jury members in the back row shifted their positions to get a better view of the demonstration.

Dr Jones repeated the tapping on his mobile phone. The colours of the solicitor faded-out of view and the man disappeared. He then began to fade back into view in front of the bar table. The jury could not contain their excitement and several of them gasped and commented to each other as if they had just seen a ghost. Even the fat Justice Croydon was taken aback and gaped at the spectacle.

"You feeling, OK?" Barrister Black asked of her instructing solicitor in a voice that everyone could hear.

"Fine," the solicitor said. The solicitor then walked back to his original position and took a seat again behind Barrister Black.

Ms Black waited for the commotion in the Court to come to order before continuing.

Q. Dr Jones, what about someone who is outside the courtroom? You said that the Trans Warp Inducer can transport matter from any part of the universe to another part. Are you able to give a demonstration of transporting someone into this courtroom from outside?
A. Yes, I can. But for safety reasons, I should telephone them first. Is that, OK?

Q. Yes, but please keep your phone on loud-speaker and turn the volume up to high so that everyone can hear what is being said. The Court reporter will need to transcribe the conversation. OK?
A. No problem.

Dr Jones then dialled a number and the ringing on the other end of the phone was put on loud speaker. A female person answered with the words, "Hello DrugTech? Can I help you?"

Benjamin Jones answered, "Hello, this is Dr Benjamin Jones, can you please put me through to my assistant, Dr Saanvi Patel?"

"One minute please," the voice on the phone said.

"Hello Saanvi Patel speaking," a female voice answered after a few seconds.

"Hello Saanvi, Benjamin Jones here, you are on loud-speaker. I am ringing from the courtroom and I need you for a demonstration," Benjamin Jones said.

"OK?" she said, as if asking a question, a little nervously.

"Please stand in the centre of your office, I am going to transport you to the courtroom," Benjamin Jones said.

Dr Jones then tapped a few icons on his phone, and a shimmering image began to appear in the front of the bar table. A middle-aged Indian woman in a white lab coat appeared blinking and looking around her.

The jury gasped again in astonishment.

"Please take a seat here, Dr Patel," Barrister Black said to the woman indicating the empty seat next to her instructing solicitor. Barrister Black then turned to the witness and continued.

Q. Dr Jones, a moment ago, you said that for safety reasons, you should ring the person up first. What did you mean by that?
A. The person you are transporting should be made aware of the transportation so they can be ready and basically hold still and not be in shock.

Q. Is the Trans Warp Inducer capable of transporting a body part, for example a person's head, leaving a headless corpse behind?
A. Yes.

Q. What about exploding a person's head, can that be done?
A. Yes.

Q. Can it be done from a different location? For example, a prison, while the command is issued from some other place on Earth?
A. Yes.

Q. And you are aware of other people at DrugTech who have had access to the Trans Warp Inducer, is that right?
A. Yes.

Barrister Black sat down. The jury was astonished and their murmuring to each other took time to quieten down.

"Cross-examination?" the judge asked.

"Thank you, your Honour," Mr King said standing to look at the witness.

The jury became deathly silent again as they awaited to see what kind of cross-examination would take place.

Mr King rose from his seat. He was slender and tall and his cheeks were pale. He began in a very soft voice.

King: Dr Jones, you say you have never seen the Trans Warp Inducer, and you don't know where it is currently located, is that right?
A. Yes.

Q. So, as far as you are aware, you are issuing commands to it from a mobile phone, but for all you know, something or someone unseen is causing these things to happen?
A. Yes.

Q. What I mean is, since you are not seeing the Trans Warp Inducer in actual operation, you are presuming that it actually is the Trans Warp Inducer that is causing these things to happen as opposed to some other unseen thing that you may not even be aware of.
A. Yes, I have to concede that.

Q. For example, instead of the Trans Warp Inducer, there may be some other magic going on which I might call, 'Smoke and Mirrors'. You simply can't say with certainty one way or the other, is that right?
A. Yes.

"Thank you, Dr Jones," Mr King said and sat back down.

"Any re-examination?" the judge asked.

"No thank you, your Honour," Barrister Black said.

"Very well, you are excused," the judge said to the witness who then left the witness box.

"Any further witnesses, Ms Black?" the judge enquired.

"No thank you, your Honour," Barrister Black said again.

"Any case in reply?" the judge asked of Mr King.

"Yes, your Honour," Mr King said. "However, our witness is not in the courtroom and we can make him available tomorrow morning."

"Very well," the judge said. "The Court will adjourn until 10 o'clock tomorrow morning. I remind you that there is a non-publication order in place with respect to Dr Jones's evidence so you must not speak about it to anyone. Court will adjourn."

"Silence, all rise," the Court officer said as the judge left the bench.

Chapter 14

The Rebuttal Witness

The following day, Barrister Black enjoyed a slightly longer breakfast than normal. She had completed the defence case in the murder trial of Dr Lazer, and the testimony of Dr Jones she thought went better than expected. But she was more than curious as to what Mr King had in mind for his case in reply. The announcement of a rebuttal witness was unexpected.

It was now about half an hour before the case was due to recommence and Barrister Black headed on down to the police cells under the Court and requested that her client, Dr Lazer, be brought into the conference room for a legal conference.

"Excellent witness, Ms Black," Dr Lazer commented as he entered from the other side of the Perspex screen and sat down.

"I think it made an impression on the jury," Ms Black said. "Even I was surprised to see the Trans Warp Inducer in action like that. It's a good thing that Dr Jones co-operated the way that he did."

"We knew that he would," Dr Lazer said. "He had spoken with Detective Derrick before the case started. Detective Derrick has turned out to be the only honest cop on my side, and an ally in my quest against the evil DrugTech. He was the first to believe me that Mr Solitary was murdered by the Trans Warp Inducer."

"Don't you think that if DrugTech is so powerful now with their all-so-powerful Trans Warp Inducer, then they could easily silence you in the same way that they disposed of Mr Solitary?" Barrister Black questioned.

"That is unfortunately the ugly unspoken truth that I was forced to keep hidden from you Ms Black," Dr Lazer replied. "Of course, I am worried about that. I even contemplated pleading guilty to this offence just to protect myself in that regard. But in the end, Dr Jones and Detective Derrick decided to get that order from the High Court requesting that Dr Jones' evidence be given in a closed court with a non-publication order. We figured that the less anyone hears about DrugTech being exposed, the better."

"But what if you are acquitted?" Barrister Black continued. "The people against you at DrugTech will certainly hear about it and they might take action then?"

"We'll just have to cross that bridge when we come to it," Dr Lazer said. "What's happening in Court this morning?"

"Mr King has said that he wishes to call a rebuttal witness in reply to the evidence of Dr Jones yesterday," Ms Black answered. "Do you have any idea who that could be?"

"I haven't got a clue," Dr Lazer said. "Isn't the Crown supposed to disclose all their evidence to you?"

"Well, they do," Barrister Black answered, "But when it is in rebuttal of the defence case, they pretty much have a reasonable excuse for not doing so. Usually, the Crown is scrambling to throw together something and they either don't have time to disclose it, or perhaps even they are not really sure what will happen when their new evidence is presented in Court. We are going to just have to play this one by ear I'm afraid."

Barrister Black looked at her watch and gathered up her things. "I'll see you in Court."

The 'Closed Court' sign had been taken down and the members of the gallery were allowed back into Court. The jury was brought in and the judge explained to them that they were now at that part of the trial where the Crown and Defence had both closed their respective cases, and the Crown had elected to call evidence in reply to the Defence case.

"Yes, Mr Crown," the judge said addressing the prosecutor using his official title.

Mr King stood slowly at the bar table with a single sheet of paper in his hand. All eyes turned to him as the Court eagerly awaited the Crown's next witness.

"The Crown calls, Detective Sergeant Derrick," Mr King said.

Barrister Black turned to look at her client who appeared equally surprised at the call. The doors opened and Detective Sergeant Derrick entered from the back of the courtroom.

It's at moments like these that the defence counsel in a murder trial races to make a speedy decision. Barrister Black had the option to attempt to object to this witness in his entirety, but her time for doing so was fast evaporating. If she was to do so, she would have to do so before the questioning began, lest she be taken to have waived her objection. On the other hand, if she was overruled, she would undoubtedly leave the jury with the distinct impression that she feared what this witness might say. She looked once more at her client who shrugged and continued to look surprised and so she decided to jump to her feet and make the objection.

"Your Honour," Barrister Black said freezing Detective Derrick in his tracks who had not yet made it to the witness box.

"The Defence objects to this witness at this time," Ms Black complained. "We have been given no prior notice of his testimony. At the very least, a statement should have been provided to us as to what evidence the Crown is anticipating from this witness. We shouldn't be ambushed."

The fat judge did not attempt to question Mr King. Rather, he said sarcastically, "It's in reply to the defence case, Ms Black."

"Yes, your Honour," Ms Black said still standing and holding her ground.

"I will permit this witness to give evidence in reply to the Defence case that was called yesterday Ms Black," the judge said, "But if this witness starts to introduce evidence that is not in reply to the Defence case, then that will not be permitted. Fair enough Mr King?"

"Yes, your Honour," Mr King said in response.

"May it please the Court," Ms Black said sitting back down again. She had wished she had never objected.

Mr King remained standing. The witness was sworn in and the questioning proceeded as follows.

King: Would you please tell the Court your full name, rank and station?
A. Detective Sergeant Michael Derrick, attached to the Surry Hills Police Station.

Q. Can you please tell the Court when was the first time you met the accused, Dr Lazer?
A. It was approximately two and a half years ago.

Q. In what capacity did you meet him?
A. I was a detective engaged in an undercover operation impersonating someone interested in purchasing some high-tech criminal wares.

Q. What do you mean by high-tech criminal wares? What kind of operation was that?
A. Reports had been received of a new kind of high-tech organisation where criminals were evading capture by police with almost super-natural powers from the use of high-tech equipment.

Q. You were investigating that?
A. Yes.

Q. So how did you come to meet Dr Lazer?
A. A meeting was arranged for me to inspect and possibly purchase the equipment. I was met by some teenage boys who drove me to a warehouse where I then met Dr Lazer.

Q. What happened then?

A. Dr Lazer proceeded to show me around where he introduced me to all sorts of things, such as a cap designed to paralyse a police dog, a pair of glasses that prevented your image from being captured on CCTV, and some chemicals that could be applied to the wrists designed to frustrate the operation of handcuffs.

Q. Did you attempt to make an arrest?

A. Yes, I attempted to.

Q. How did you attempt that?

A. My watch was relaying my GPS coordinates to the Police Tactical Unit who stormed the building in an attempt to arrest Dr Lazer and his gang.

Q. And what happened then?

A. We surrounded Dr Lazer and his cohort, but they started laughing and told us to leave the building immediately because it was about to explode.

Q. And what happened to Dr Lazer and his cohort?

A. They vanished from sight.

Q. What do you mean they vanished from sight?

A. They just disappeared before our very eyes. So, we then ran out of the building before it exploded.

Q. You filed a police report of the incident?

A. Yes, I did.

Q. In that report, you didn't mention anything about a Trans Warp Inducer?

A. No, I did not.

Q. Why not?

A. I had not heard of a Trans Warp Inducer at that stage.

Q. What did you write in your police report to explain Dr Lazer and his cohort just vanishing from before your very eyes?

A. I wrote that I suspected that they were laser holograms.

Q. You say, 'suspected'. Does that mean you don't actually know?
A. No, I can't say for sure what it was.

Q. You must have thought you were subjected to some kind of magic show with the use of smoke and mirrors?
A. I didn't know what to think.

At this point Mr King sat down as the jury was buzzing with talk amongst themselves.

"Ms Black?" the judge asked inviting her to cross-examine the witness.

Ms Black arose slowly. She was not aware of the incident that the Detective had relayed to the Court. The instructions whispered to her from her instructing solicitor, who was in constant communication with Dr Lazer in the dock during the testimony of Detective Derrick, was that the evidence was true and fairly given. This did not leave her with much to work with.

Black: Detective Derrick, you are aware that Dr Lazer claims that Mr McKinnon was killed by the use of the Trans Warp Inducer?
A. Yes, I am aware of that.

Black: What is your opinion as to the truth of that assertion?

King: I object, your Honour. This witnesses' personal opinion is irrelevant to these proceedings.

Bench: That question is disallowed.

Black: Detective Derrick, you communicated with Dr Benjamin Jones before he gave his evidence to this courtroom yesterday didn't you about the Trans Warp Inducer?

King: I object your Honour. That is hearsay and inadmissible.

Bench: Yes, I disallow that question.

Black: You have carried out investigations yourself, haven't you, on the location of the Trans Warp Inducer used by DrugTech.
A. Yes, I have.

Q. Did your investigations lead you to where the Trans Warp Inducer was located at the time?
A. I believe so.

Q. Where was that?
A. A shack that was located several hours outside the outskirts of town down a dirt track.

"Nothing further," Barrister Black said sitting down.

"Any re-examination?" the judge asked the prosecutor.

King: Yes please, your Honour. Did you visit that shack where you believed the Trans Warp Inducer was located?
A. Yes, I did.

Q. And did you lay eyes on it? What did it look like?
A. I never saw it.

Q. Why not? What stopped you?
A. The occupants of the shack said that I should get a warrant, and I didn't have a warrant.

Q. So why didn't you get a warrant?
A. I didn't have enough evidence to get a warrant.

Q. And who were these occupants of the shack that didn't invite you to inspect this Trans Warp Inducer and instead asked you to come back with a warrant?
A. They were Priests from the Dominican Order.

At this the jury started to chuckle.

Q. They just wanted to get on with their praying and wanted to be left alone?

Black: I object to the witness giving evidence about what someone was thinking?

Bench: The question is disallowed.

King: No more questions.

Bench: The witness is excused. Any other witnesses?

King: No, thank you, your Honour.

Bench: Very well. Members of the jury that concludes the evidence in this case. We will now have an early morning tea, and when we return, the barristers will begin their closing address. Court will adjourn.

Court officer: All rise.

Chapter 15

Two Blackhawks

Monday morning and Emeritus Professor Philip had an extra-large spring in his step. Over the weekend, three brand-new, state-of-the-art, Nuclear Magnetic Resonance machines had been installed in three Australian universities, and the greatest of them was installed in the Professor's own lab at Sydney University. They were linked to each other through the internet, and a whole lot of experiments had banked up over the years in the Professor's "to-do" list, awaiting just the right machinery to conduct them on. And now was the day!

Having alighted from his train at Redfern Station, he was too excited to buy himself his usual morning coffee. Instead, he bounded up the stairs from the platform and eagerly joined the university brigade of students, lecturers and tutors making their usual morning stroll from Redfern Station to Sydney University. Apart from his sense of internal excitement, all was as usual, when all of a sudden, the sky above started to vibrate the area below as the thunderous drumming of a Blackhawk helicopter proceeded at rather low height in a slow and straight-line above the university students towards the university campus.

"By golly," the Professor thought to himself, "That's something you don't see every day." He had hoped it was a good omen. "Perhaps they are just practising anti-terrorism exercises," he guessed.

As he approached the university campus, the Blackhawk helicopter had stopped its forward motion and hovered over the Professor's Biology building. Then 4 ropes were dropped, and four crack SAS soldiers with machine-guns abseiled down the ropes. "Wow," the Professor thought to himself, "They're really going all out."

When the four soldiers had reached the ground, another four followed, and then another four, and then another four. 16 armed military personnel with camo gear, helmets and machine guns proceeded to surround the lab as half of them entered and the other half secured the perimeter.

"Darn it," the Professor thought to himself, "I wonder how long this exercise is going to take. I want to start my experiments." The Professor joined the ever-growing crowd of spectators as they waited underneath a thrumming Blackhawk all wishing to catch a glimpse of military personnel storming the building.

Now, in order to understand precisely what was going on here, it is necessary for me to take you back about 60 minutes, which was about the time that the Emeritus Professor had first caught the train from his home station to Redfern. About that same time, Dr Lazer was being put into the prison van on his way to the Courthouse. The jury had finally retired to deliberate on a verdict on the Friday afternoon and they were continuing their deliberations on Monday morning. Accordingly, Dr Lazer was required to be brought to the Court for each day that the jury deliberated. But as Dr Lazer was being put into the prison van, he was surprised to see Detective Sergeant Derick enter the van behind him.

"A fat lot of good you did me," Dr Lazer said opening the conversation with his unexpected guest. "My case was in the bag until you had to come and bombard the jury with all your hocus-pocus stuff about my high-tech criminal wares. I thought you were on my side."

"I am on your side," the Detective said, "I was saving your life."

"Yeah right," Dr Lazer retorted, "More like getting yourself a promotion."

"Listen, you idiot," the Detective replied, "There are things going on here that you are not aware of. Did you ever give any consideration to what would happen to you if you were actually acquitted of the murder of Mr Solitary? Don't you think DrugTech wouldn't forgive that? Did you want your head to be the next to explode?"

"So, what's the plan then?" Dr Lazer said looking confused.

"Since we don't even know where the Trans Warp Inducer is located, the plan is to get you a hung jury," the Detective replied. "You won't be convicted, but you won't be acquitted either. Then if things go according to plan, you won't be re-tried either."

"You want to let me in on this big plan of yours?" Dr Lazer asked, "It sounds like there are a lot of hypotheticals involved.

"At this very moment," Detective Derrick began again, "Major General Frank Collins is in his office at the Australian Security Intelligence Organisation liaising with Dr Benjamin Jones. And he has two Blackhawks on standby."

"Are you ready?" Major General Frank Collins said looking at a blank video screen on the wall of his office at ASIO headquarters.

"Ready," Dr Benjamin Jones said from his own office at DrugTech adjoining Sydney University.

"Then proceed," the General said.

Benjamin Jones then took the glasses that he was wearing off of his face and replaced them with an identical looking pair. As he did this, he squeezed a button on the frame and looked into a mirror.

The blank video screen in the General's office came to life and it showed a mirror on a wall with the image of Benjamin Jones in the mirror adjusting his glasses.

"Can you see me?" Dr Jones asked looking squarely into the mirror.

"Affirmative," the General said from his office. "The glasses are working perfectly."

"OK," Dr Jones said, "Ringing Dr Jamieson now."

The image on the screen then appeared as if the cameraman was walking away from the mirror towards an office desk and a cordless phone came into focus. A hand picked up the cordless phone and a number was dialled before it was raised to the right side of the viewscreen and held out of view."

"Jamieson here," a voice was heard through the phone with a slight echo in the background.

"Benjamin here," Dr Jones replied. "It is urgent that I speak with you now, where are you?"

"I am at Chifley Tower in Sydney," Dr Jamieson replied. "I am about to address a meeting of stockbrokers and media about the company prospects of DrugTech. Can this wait until after that?"

"I'm afraid not," Benjamin replied. "But it should only take a few minutes. I just shouldn't say it over the phone. Can I come to you now?"

"Fine," Dr Jamieson replied, "Hold still."

Major General Collins continued to watch his video screen in silence. The image of Benjamin Jones' office faded darker and darker until for a split second the video screen was blank again. Then the colours of a magnificent public bathroom with brown and red speckled granite floor and wall tiles faded into view with Dr Jamieson wiping his hands with a white flannel towel in front of a line of bathroom sinks.

"Where am I?" Benjamin asked.

"You are on the 42nd floor of Chifley Tower," Dr Jamieson answered, "Men's room. What's so urgent?" Jamieson said disposing of the flannel through a slit under the sink.

Dr Jamieson's image moved to the centre of Major-General Collin's viewscreen as Benjamin Jones moved to stand directly in front of him with his video glasses transmitting a clear video image.

"Some of my people are at the Courthouse of the trial of Dr Lazer," Benjamin Jones began. "They overheard some officials talking about getting a search warrant to search the shack in the country that was occupied by the Dominican Order of Priests in order to seize the Trans Warp Inducer from us. I just want to make sure that it is still secure. Is it still in that shack?"

"No," Dr Jamieson said slightly relieved. "It has been moved to a safe location."

"Where has it been moved to?" Benjamin Jones asked, "I just want to make sure that it's not going to be seized by any authorities."

"Never mind," Dr Jamieson said. "I can assure you that it is in a safe location. But disclosing its location is on a need-to-know basis only. And at the moment, you don't need to know."

"Very well," Benjamin replied, "As long as you know where it is, and you can assure me that it is safe. Is it safe?"

"Yes," Dr Jamieson replied.

"Very good," Benjamin Jones said. "I'm out of here. Enjoy your meeting."

At that point Major General Collings raised a remote control to his viewscreen and pressed a button turning it off.

He turned slowly to a person who was sitting quietly in the corner of his office also watching the viewscreen.

"You got that?" he asked.

"Yes," a female voice said. It was Sister Jennifer watching the face of Dr Jamieson closely throughout the encounter, on the General's viewscreen. "The Trans Warp Inducer has been relocated to the Nuclear Magnetic Resonance Machine that has been installed in the laboratory of Emeritus Professor Philip at Sydney University."

The General then picked up a telephone.

"Send the first Blackhawk to the Biology Lab at Sydney University and seize the NMR machine that is there."

"And the second?" the voice on the other end of the phone asked.

"Send the second Blackhawk to Chifley Tower in the Sydney CBD and pick up Dr Jamieson now."

"Roger," the voice on the other end of the phone said.

Meanwhile, the prison van of Dr Lazer was arriving at the Courthouse.

"But how can you assure me that the jury will return a hung verdict?" he asked. "If they convict, it is all over, and if they acquit, apparently it is all over too!"

"Don't worry," Detective Derrick said. "Things were put in motion well before your case started. You know the prosecutor, Mr King?"

"Yeah," Dr Lazer said looking rather surprised.

"Let's just say that that barrister happens also to be a Dominican Priest by the name of William Hunter. If there is anyone to have faith in, then have faith that he is capable of knowing exactly what a jury is thinking. Half of them want to convict you and the other half want to acquit you. The jury will be hung."

Chapter 16

The Aftermath

The Pirate Uluç Ali never agreed with his Commander to move the fleet from the Port of Lepanto to meet the Christian fleet in the Gulf of Patras. Uluç Ali commanded the left flank of the Müezzinzade's fleet, and when the wind had changed and the Ottoman fleet had started rowing towards the enemy, Uluç Ali broke ranks and commanded his squadron to row around the left-most galleass towards the open sea. In this way, he outmanoeuvred his direct opponent whilst he and his fleet were chased by the flagship of the Maltese Knights.

But the Pirate Uluç Ali was as cunning as he was tactful. And when the Müezzinzade's head had been hoisted high upon the half-pike on board the Ottoman flagship *Sultana* and the Christians had suddenly become overwhelmed with a sense of victory which had hereto before been unthinkable, Uluç Ali suddenly stopped and turned 180 degrees around firing full cannons towards the chasing Maltese ship. His pirate-crew were well-trained in the manoeuvre and they completely took the Maltese ship by surprise whose attention had been mainly directed behind them.

With the Maltese ship practically smashed to pieces, the Pirate's ship easily grappled the remains and then proceeded to kill all survivors on board. Then taking whatever loot was on board, he cut down and took with him the Maltese flag from the main mast. The Pirate Uluç Ali then sounded the retreat to all remaining Ottoman ships that were within range of his squadron and raced with them to the open sea thereby avoiding any further conflict with the otherwise overpowering Christian armada.

He returned to Constantinople with 87 ships, the only survivors to have escaped from the Battle of Lepanto, and he presented the great flag of the Knights of Malta to his Sultan, Selim II. Being politically astute, he spun the defeat as somewhat of a victory to his home crowd and their Sultan, and the Sultan gave him the honorary title of *Kılıç* meaning "Sword". He thereafter became known as *Kılıç Ali Pasha.* His first task was to rebuild the Ottoman fleet which he did giving orders to build bigger heavier ships modelled off his observations of the Christian galleasses that he had seen for the first time at Lepanto. On 29 October,

1571, the Sultan promoted him to the position occupied by the former Müezzinzade, making him Kapudan Pasha, or Grand Admiral, of the Ottoman Fleet.

And by around this time, three weeks after the victory and three weeks after the Pope had had his mystical vision of the outcome of the battle, the first of the Christian ships were returning to Christian Europe. They were initially perceived with dread as victorious Ottoman ships from the shore because the Christian soldiers on board were wearing the turbans of fallen janissaries. But upon closer examination of the ships and the banners being flown, the fear was replaced with a state of euphoria and members of the public who were still praying the rosary from dawn until dusk in fear of being overrun by the Turks, immediately broke into song and dance. It was the end of a war and streamers were released. The usual home-life, ordinary business and prayer were replaced with uncontained celebration. And the Pope echoed the words of Scripture, "Now you can dismiss your servant O Lord In peace, because my eyes have seen your salvation."

Chapter 17

The Disentanglement

It was always a treat for Tommy Grayson and Jake Peterson when Simon Sage would come to Australia to visit. The December holidays afforded just such an opportunity, and the university friends decided to have another meeting of the Society of Creative Talent. This time it was held at the Crystal Car Wash, Kingsford, opposite the Souths Juniors Leagues Club. Unfortunately, Patricia O'Leary and Sister Jennifer were otherwise occupied on religious matters, but on this particular Friday afternoon in mid-December, Tommy Grayson, Jake Peterson and Simon Sage were joined by Detective Derrick.

"Well, it's been two months since the Defence forces seized the Trans Warp Inducer from DrugTech, and Dr Jamieson was on that plane that went down over East Timor last week," Tommy said. "It has been all over the news, there were no survivors."

"And the DPP have decided not to re-prosecute Dr Lazer and he was released last month from prison," Jake said, "So it looks as if we have had some success in rectifying the evils of DrugTech."

"I am not so sure," the Detective said somewhat sceptically. He put his coffee cup down and pulled a notepad out of his inside jacket. "Let me run a few things past you guys and see what you think."

"What kind of things?" Jake questioned.

"Just a couple of odd facts that I have noted these past few months," the Detective answered, "I think something doesn't quite add up."

"Let's hear it," Tommy said grabbing a handful of chips and nibbling them one by one.

The Detective unfolded his notebook and turned to a particular page.

"Fact one," the Detective said looking at the notebook. "Two months ago, Dr Jamieson was arrested from the Chifley Tower Building in Sydney by Major-General Frank Collins from Australian Intelligence and Defence."

"Fact two. When that was done, I had one of my men stake-out DrugTech because I just thought it was prudent to keep an eye on Benjamin Jones and see what would happen, if anything, at around the same time that Dr Jamieson was arrested. Benjamin Jones was not observed to leave the building but his secretary, Saanvi Patel, did leave the building around 9:50am. She was seen entering the Hospital adjoining DrugTech where she stayed for around 40 minutes and then she was observed to leave the hospital and go back to the DrugTech building."

Detective Derrick then retrieved a surveillance photograph from the back of his notebook and placed it on the table for the others to see. "As you can see, she is carrying a barely eaten muffin in one hand and a takeaway coffee in the other."

"Fact three. When Dr Jamieson was brought to the Surry Hills Police station for processing, he was met by Federal Agents who informed him that he was being charged with murder," the Detective continued reading from his notes.

"Fact four. When Dr Jamieson asked who it was that he allegedly murdered, the Federal Agents replied, 'Astronaut Dr Helouise Dawson and her crew of the spaceship Atlantis.' Accordingly, he was to be extradited to the United States to face those charges over there."

Jake Peterson, Tommy Grayson and Simon Sage continued to listen intently as the Detective continued.

"Fact Five," the Detective said continuing to read from his notebook. "As cool as a cucumber, Dr Jamieson then asked to be allowed to make his one phone call. And do you know who he called?" the Detective asked rhetorically looking at his friends. "Not a lawyer. But a woman by the name of Mandy Kizana."

Tommy Grayson grabbed his phone to conduct an internet search.

The Detective saw what he was doing and interjected, "Yes, I checked her out too," he said somewhat surprised at what his investigations revealed. "It turns out that she was recently employed at the Australian Museum in College Street, Sydney where she works in the 'minerals and crystals' department. Sometimes she dresses up as a gypsy and entertains the patrons with a crystal-ball-reading of their future in the foyer of the Museum outside the minerals and crystals section in keeping with the theme of the department that she works in."

The boys continued to listen intently and the Detective continued.

"Fact Six," the Detective said, "From the moment Dr Jamieson was arrested, he was challenging his extradition to the United States on every legal ground imaginable. This continued for approximately two months when all of a sudden, he withdrew all his legal objections and consented to the immediate extradition to the United States. No reasons were given for him as to why he gave up on his legal challenges."

"Fact Seven," the Detective said continuing to read from his notes. "A week ago, Dr Jamieson was being extradited to the United States. He was placed on a commercial aeroplane where two Federal Agents and he occupied the last two rows of the jet, but when the plane left Australian skies and got about as far as East Timor, it suffered unexplained catastrophic mechanical failure and crashed killing everyone aboard."

The Detective then paused as he closed his notebook and put it back in the inside of his jacket pocket. "So, there you have it," he said. "What am I missing?"

Tommy Grayson and Jake Peterson looked at each other somewhat dumbfounded, but Simon Sage had his eyes closed deep in thought.

"What was the murder charge in the United States all about?" Jake questioned.

"Apparently," the Detective answered, "When Dr Jamieson was head of NASA, the spaceship Atlantis and everyone on board blew-up shortly after take-off. It was on a mission to Mars commanded by Astronaut Dr Helouise Dawson. One of the persons that worked with Dr Jamieson in what was known as the 'Upper Room' in Mission Control made a very damning statement about him holding him directly responsible. So, the US wanted to put him on trial for that. But Dr Jamieson was claiming that it was all a political witch-hunt for no other reason than the fact that one political party won the White House instead of the other in the last US election."

At this point Simon Sage opened his eyes and picked up the photograph of Saanvi Patel in the middle of the table so that he could examine it more closely. Seeing what he had done, the others quietened down to allow Simon Sage some time to study it and waited for him to speak.

After a short moment, Simon slowly returned the photograph to the table and looked at his friends.

"Well?" Tommy said a little impatiently. "Did you find something?"

"Yes," Simon said still processing the information.

"Tell us," Jake said probing further.

Simon processed the information for a few more seconds and then turned to look at the Detective and said, "Dr Jamieson is alive."

"OK kid," Tommy said, "Let's hear what you've got?"

Then all three of Jake Peterson, Tommy Grayson and Detective Derrick leaned in on the table to effectively huddle-up together and hear what theory Simon Sage had come up with.

"It was not 'minerals and crystals' that Mandy Kizana was interested in at the Australian Museum," Simon Sage said, "It was meteors."

"Meteors?" Detective Derrick questioned.

"Yes," Simon answered. "At the heart of the Trans Warp Inducer is a radioactive stone known as the 'Medusa Stone'. It is the driving force that allows the Trans Warp Inducer to function properly."

"But the defence personnel seized the Trans Warp Inducer at the same time that Jamieson was arrested," Jake interjected before he realised where the conversation was leading.

The Detective answered instead of Simon, "But he was building himself another one."

"Yes," Simon Sage said picking up the photograph. "That leads us to Saanvi Patel. She spent 40 minutes in the hospital on the day that Jamieson was arrested, but she was not eating in the cafeteria there. No one leaves work to eat at 9:50 in the morning and in any case, her muffin is barely touched and she is carrying her coffee as if it was full, meaning that she just bought it on her way back to work."

"So, where did she go?" Tommy asked.

"Remember your psychiatry class excursion to the Mary Immaculate psychiatric hospital that is part of the hospital adjoining DrugTech?" Simon said looking at Tommy.

Tommy thought back to the time he interviewed a patient who had just had a fight with a priest. He had forgotten that he had told the story to Simon.

"Scientist Bruce is the patient that built the Trans Warp Inducer," Simon continued. "That is who Saanvi Patel went to visit. She was finding out how to build another one."

"Then two months later when they finally built it," the Detective muttered to himself horrified, "Jamieson drops the extradition fight and consents to being put on a flight that was doomed to crash apparently killing everyone on board."

"Precisely," Simon said.

"My God," Jake Peterson said. "He was Trans Warped off the flight before it crashed."

"I don't understand something," the Detective said. "How were they able to build another Trans Warp Inducer while Scientist Bruce was incarcerated in the psychiatric hospital?"

"He only needed to tell Saanvi Patel and any other scientist who visited him throughout the last two months how to put the new Medusa Stone that Mandy Kizana apparently found inside a meteorite into his equipment," Simon answered rather blandly.

"OK," the Detective said leaning backwards. "This is a nice neat conjecture that fits the facts that I have read out to you. But we have no objective proof to verify this, don't we?" the Detective asked looking puzzled.

"I bet we do," Tommy Grayson said rather smugly. They all turned to look at him.

"Scientist Bruce," Tommy said, "He wouldn't do anything for nothing. He has made a deal with Jamieson. He helps Jamieson, then Jamieson helps him. What can you find out about that psychiatric hospital and Scientist Bruce, Detective?"

The Detective reached for his phone and made a call. "Hello, Detective Sergeant Derrick here," he said talking into the phone, "Can you please go into the database of prisoners being held at the Mary Immaculate psychiatric hospital and see if you can locate an inmate who goes by the name of 'Scientist Bruce'?"

The Detective put the phone down for a second and whispered, "Anyone know his last name?"

He was met by shrugs from all three.

"What's that?" the Detective said putting the phone back to his ear. He listened for a few more seconds to the answer and then replied, "OK, thanks."

"You're right," the Detective said returning his phone to his pocket. "Patient Bruce McClintock escaped from the Mary Immaculate psychiatric hospital the day Jamieson's flight went down. He was in his cell one minute, and apparently, he was gone the next."

Chapter 18

Directed Entropy

Three visiting friars to the Sacred Heart Monastery in Kensington were of the Dominican Order. And through some happy co-incidence, the three of them happened to be interested in astronomy. So, on a particular cloudless and balmy evening on the 15th of December, the three priests, Father Dom, Father William and Father Charles moved three deckchairs into the middle of the adjoining meadow to have a clear view of the Geminids meteor shower.

The youthful looking Father Dom, founded the Dominican Order in the 13th century. There are many interesting articles written about the man from his former life around that time, such as his supernatural vision of the Regina Caeli wherein he received the miraculous Rosary, a divine gift capable of winning wars such as the Battle of Lepanto. But in this story, we are more concerned with a rather less-known fact of his life, being the rather interesting effects of a naturally contracted blood-borne virus, not the least of which causes Father Dom to age very, very slowly. Accordingly, he was present at the Battle of Lepanto in 1571 and has since written some private memoirs of the occasion that Father William Hunter had recently read.

Father William Hunter contracted a similar blood-borne virus through artificial means from his former work as a scientist at DrugTech. But, unlike Father Dom, he was only around a quarter of a millennium years old and carried on life after DrugTech as a rather successful Barrister in private practice, again, not the least of which, was achieved from some of the aforementioned interesting effects of the said virus. Upon his retirement from law, he joined the Dominican Order of priests where he has since found fulfilment for his soul. But from a bureaucratic request that was rumoured to have begun from the office of Senior Intelligence Officer Major-General Frank Collins, Father William accepted a private brief, post his retirement, to appear on behalf of the Crown and prosecute the murder case of Dr Leon Lazer, which he did under the name that appeared on his practicing certificate, of William King.

Father Charles Maxwell on the other hand was relatively unremarkable. That may sound a little harsh because in this story he is being compared with relatively immortal, super-strong mind-reading 'vampires' (for lack of a better term). He was, after-all, a whiz kid in his own right who had obtained his first university degree at age ten. He was a descendent of the late great Scotsman, James Clerk Maxwell who discovered a set of useful equations that has sometimes been referred to as the second great unification principal in physics. And Father Charles was himself a Nobel laureate in physics and was knighted by Her Majesty, Queen Elizabeth II. He since joined the Mendicant Order of Itinerant Preachers where he too, like Father William Hunter, found fulfilment for his soul.

And on occasions such as these, when the three wise men would get together, they would often look at the stars and philosophise, theorise and generally discuss what was right with the world. But as their patron saint, Thomas Aquinas would say, you cannot know a thing without knowing its opposite, and so they would also often discuss what was wrong with the world. And with Father Dom in the middle, and Father William on his right and Father Charles on his left, the conversation proceeded like this.

"I said Mass today for the loss of the souls on that dreadful flight that crashed in East Timor," Father William said, "It reminded me a lot of your memoirs of the Battle of Lepanto."

"Oh, yes?" Father Dom piped up.

"Yes," Father William continued, "And, speaking of Lepanto, I couldn't help but find an awful lot of similarities between your expressions in your personal memoirs, and those of Gilbert Keith Chesterton's in his great poetic ballad of Lepanto which he wrote in 1911."

"Alas yes," Father Dom replied, "Chesterton wrote that poem after we had a long chat about the battle and in particular Don John 'bursting the battle-line'."

"Ha!" Father Charles laughed, "So basically what you are saying is that Chesterton has plagiarised you, is that right?"

"The guy was a literary genius," Father Dom said ignoring the question, "He wrote the poem in a hurry finishing the last stanza whilst the telegram boy was waiting to snatch it from him and send it to his editor. Did you know the soldiers in the Great War would often say the poem to each other in the trenches to find their inspiration as they fought against the Turks?"

A blazing meteor streaked across the sky from the zenith to the northern horizon, as a gentle breeze began blowing across their faces from the West.

"I hear you had some success in getting a hung jury in your murder trial," Father Dom said changing the subject.

"Juries are terribly suspicious that if you show them magic tricks," Father William said, "Then they think that you are just throwing dust in their eyes. I am curious about one thing though," Father William said scratching his head.

"What's that?" Father Dom questioned.

"When Dr Jones was asked whether he was aware of other people at DrugTech having access to the Trans Warp Inducer, he answered 'yes'," Father William continued, "But at that moment Dr Jones was thinking about a scientist in a lab coat which he happens to know by the name of Scientist Bruce. But the expression on Scientist Bruce's face was one who had lived as a servant to a Jew by the name of Barshimon and witnessed the crucifixion of Christ, as well as a person who lived as a servant to a pirate ship called Douglass under the commands of Captains Samuel and Terrence. I don't understand how he was able to have such honest memories?"

"He may have perceived them as personal experiences," Father Charles answered, "But they were in fact observations of past realities."

"But how is that possible?" Father William asked.

"As St Thomas Aquinas said," Father Dom answered, "Time is just the measure of the movement of matter."

"Exactly," Father Charles said, "The Trans Warp Inducer is a means of warping the universe in on itself like folding a piece of paper so that point A touches point B. When the piece of paper opens, it's like waves of time are released which can be witnessed by any person being trans-warped by the device. So effectively, any moving thing can be treated as an horological device, or a ticking clock."

"It's like looking into the night sky," Father Dom said, "You see that bright star in the sky?" Father Dom said pointing out the brightest star in the sky above them. "That is Sirius, which is approximately nine light years away. That means that you are seeing that star as it existed nine years ago. You are actually seeing directly into the past, and in this case, nine years into the past."

"That's amazing," Father William said, "Is the Trans Warp Inducer capable of altering the past?"

"No, that's impossible," Father Dom answered, "As Aquinas says, altering the past is something that even God cannot do. It is a contradiction, like trying to draw a squared- circle. It offends against the basic axiom of metaphysics. Nothing can be both true and not true at the same time and in the same respect."

"So, what you are saying is," Father William questioned, "You can see into the past, but you can't alter it?"

"Precisely," Father Charles answered, "You can see the past and you can also move forward into the future at a faster rate than others. You just can't alter the past. Any science which claims to alter the past is absolutely absurd, and can be rejected out of hand."

"So, what you are saying," Father William said almost as if he was cross-examining a witness, "Is that the Trans Warp Inducer could be altered in such a way that instead of moving through the universe, you could actually use it to see into the past in any place at any time?"

"Indeed," Father Charles answered, "There is no scientific barrier to directing the entropy of the device that way. It could conceivably be altered so that all the secrets of the past can be observed in the now."

"So, let me get this straight," Father William said. "Anything that has been done in private in the past, could actually be witnessed now in the present? So, murders could be solved; and sins could be exposed?"

"Afraid so," Father Charles said.

"So, for one thing," Father William said, "If Dr Jamieson happened to make another Trans Warp Inducer and if he trans-warped himself off that flight before it crashed, then a Trans Warp Inducer could be used to actually see where he went?"

"Precisely," Father Charles said.

"That Dr Jamieson reminds me of the Pirate Uluç Ali," Father Dom said, "Who managed to escape the Battle of Lepanto."

"Just out of curiosity," Father William questioned, "Does anyone know at what stage Major- General Frank Collins is at with the Trans Warp Inducer that he seized from Professor Philip's lab?"

"I hear he hasn't managed to get it working," Father Charles said, "I'm not sure if anyone in his department has the necessary scientific knowledge to set it up in working order."

"Speaking of Lepanto," Father William continued, "What's the latest with Jake Peterson, the guy who reminded us of Don John of Austria?"

"I anticipate that he will shortly attempt to acquire a Trans Warp Inducer for himself," Father Dom answered.

"How do you know that?" both Father William and Father Charles asked.
"Let's just say," Father Dom answered, "I know the type."

Chapter 19

Falling Dominos

"Thank you, Mr Banks," Jake said as he shook the hand of Quentin Banks Solicitor and left his office. He smiled to himself as he saw his plan unfold. It was complicated, but it was, finally, the plan that would bring DrugTech to its knees.

Jake Peterson dialled his friend Simon Sage on his mobile phone. "I just spoke with the lawyer now, he'll do it," Jake said, "I'll meet you all at the Pizza Parlour tonight."

That night Patricia O'Leary and Simon Sage had just finished go-karting at the Fox Studios at Moore Park. They grabbed their gear and headed on over to the Pizza Parlour where Detective Derrick, Tommy Grayson and Sister Jennifer were already waiting for them.

"Where's Jake?" Patricia said as she and Simon Sage sat around the table joining the others.

"He said he'd join us after dinner," Tommy said just as three different kinds of pizzas arrived at the table with Coke enough for all. "Here's to Patricia's soon-to-be new life as a nun," he said holding up a glass of coke.

"Hear, hear," the others said all in a festive mood.

For the next 20 minutes, the five of them consumed three large pizzas and drank their Coke. It wasn't much longer before Jake Peterson strolled on in wearing a thick pair of black-framed glasses and carrying a briefcase.

"So, what's the big plan?" Tommy said as people shifted around the table to allow Jake room to join them.

"Let me guess," Patricia O'Leary jumped in before Jake could answer, "Are you going to make a Trans Warp Inducer yourself and tweak it to find out where Dr Jamieson is hiding-out?" she asked having recently been informed of the three priests' Geminids' meteor discussion through her newly acquired connections at the monastery.

"Nope," Jake answered smiling. "I know exactly where Dr Jamieson is hiding out."

"Where?" they all asked.

The glasses he was wearing prevented Sister Jennifer from reading his face.

"Dr Jamieson, Scientist Bruce and Mandy Kizana are all hiding out in that shack that we visited when we met the Dominican Order of Priests for the first time out past the outskirts of town, deep in the sticks. That is where Scientist Bruce first invented the Trans Warp Inducer several years ago before he was arrested for murdering a fellow called Gary. I have already cased out the joint and confirmed it."

At this point Jake opened a brief case and pulled out a notebook and a photograph. Jake continued outlaying his plan.

"Just parked outside is a ute with four barrels on the back," Jake said dropping the key to the ute onto the table. "Tomorrow morning at dawn, Tommy and Simon will take that truck and pick up Dr Lazer at this address," he said giving a card to Tommy with Dr Lazer's address on it. "He'll be waiting for you. The three of you will then drive out to the shack."

Jake produced an aerial photograph from Google Earth and oriented it so that it faced Tommy and Simon. "Here is an aerial photograph of the shack," he said pointing to the centre of the photograph. "And these Xs at the four corners around the shack represent the distance of roughly 50 metres from the centre of the shack," Jake said pointing to the four Xs in black texter inked onto the photograph.

"It's your job to place these barrels at around each of these Xs," Jake continued, "But it is extremely important to do it in such a way that you are either not seen by anyone in the shack, or if you are, that you don't arouse too much suspicion. I shall leave the details for you to work out, how to go about, it up to you. But when you have done that, you must drive the truck to at least 100m away from any of those barrels and ring me up. When you have done that, then wait for me to arrive for the next part of the plan."

"So, what's in the barrels?" Tommy asked out of curiosity. "They aren't explosives or anything are they?"

"No, nothing like that," Jake said, "They are just a little something that I have worked out with the help of Dr Lazer. You could call them 'high-tech criminal wares'," Jake said broadening his smile. "But be careful because they each contain a lead acid battery, so try to keep them as level as you can."

"Now," Jake continued, "When I get your call, I will then meet with Major-General Frank Collins," Jake said, "Sister Jennifer has already spoken to him and he will be expecting me," Jake continued. "Then, I will telephone Detective Derrick, Sister Jennifer and Patricia" he said turning to look at them.

Jake continued relaying the plan to his friends throughout the night. Many questions were asked and Jake patiently ensured that each of them knew their part of the plan by heart before they left.

The following morning, Dr Lazer, Tommy Grayson and Simon Sage drove out to the shack beyond the outskirts of town, down a dirt track, deep into the sticks. Their plan was a simple one. Upon arriving within 50m of the shack, they popped the hood of the truck and loosened a wire away from the battery. If anyone was to look or ask, they would pretend that the truck had simply broken-down and that they were waiting for help to arrive. But when they thought the coast was clear, and doing their best to keep the barrels upright, they wobbled and rolled each of them on each of their bottom rim so as to place each of them around the four corners of the shack as best they could in accordance with the marked-up aerial photograph provided to them by Jake. When they were happy with the positions of the barrels, they drove the truck at least 100m from the barrels and parked the truck. They then telephoned Jake and sat inside the truck awaiting further instructions.

Upon receiving their call, Jake then proceeded to the Victoria Barracks in Paddington and announced his appearance to the guard at the entrance. "Jake Peterson here to see Major-General Frank Collins," he said producing his driver's licence, "He is expecting me."

Jake was given directions to the General's office which he promptly followed. After a few minutes he arrived at the office, and having been announced by the secretary outside, he entered the office with the words, "Thank you for seeing me, General." The General beckoned him towards an empty chair on the other side of his rather large desk. He walked towards it, but instead of sitting down, Jake came straight to the point.

"That was not Dr Jamieson on the plane that crashed in East Timor," Jake said keeping the existence of the second Trans Warp Inducer secret, "It was a doppelganger."

"How do you know that?" the General said rising from his chair behind the desk.

"Sister Jennifer confirms it," Jake said producing a piece of paper and putting it on the General's desk. "Here are the coordinates of a shack where Dr Jamieson, Mandy Kizana and Scientist Bruce are all hiding out. You visited that shack once before General when Dr Jamieson had spoken with the Defence Minister and issued an Infrastructure Declaration under the *Defence Act* about 3 years ago."

"I remember," the General said as he picked up a telephone on his desk and hit a button that caused a light under it to illuminate.

Without wasting time, the General spoke to his attaché on the phone, "Do you remember the shack we visited three years ago when we served an Infrastructure Declaration under the *Defence Act*?" the General said, "Dr Jamieson is hiding-out there. I want you to send in Bravo Company ASAP to arrest Dr Jamieson and the occupants of that shack."

The General then dialled another number. "Have my helicopter ready, I'm coming now," the General said grabbing the piece of paper with the coordinates of the shack on it. "Coming?" he asked looking at Jake as he headed towards the exit.

"Yup," Jake said running after him.

The helicopter flight to the shack was only about 20 minutes. Bravo company had already landed about a kilometre away from the shack. A crack squad of six soldiers had trained not to fly directly to their destination when making an arrest. That would only cause the occupants to flee. Instead, Bravo Company landed about a kilometre away from the shack, and proceeded by foot and by stealth towards the shack whereupon they broke down the door and stormed the shack ordering all the occupants to lie on the floor with their hands behind their heads.

Mandy Kizana did just that. But surprisingly, the two males kept tapping icons on their mobile phones again and again as they each became increasingly surprised that either they or the soldiers did not promptly disappear. The barrels outside of the shack were jamming the signals of mobile telephones, and so the commands to the Trans Warp Inducer located within the shack were simply not received by it. Within seconds, the crack squad of troops threw the two males to the floor and secured their hands with cable-ties.

The General and Jake were not far behind, and Jake seeing his plan unfold through the doorway as he entered the shack, kept his eye on and grabbed the mobile phones that were dropped by Dr Jamieson and Scientist Bruce as they were arrested.

Within minutes, Dr Jamieson, Scientist Bruce and Mandy Kizana were marched outside of the shack as the helicopter of Bravo Company arrived from where it had landed 1km away to take them back to Sydney.

Jake then headed towards a truck parked about 100m away with three excited individuals inside.

"Here are the phones of Dr Jamieson and Scientist Bruce," Jake said giving one to Simon and the other to Dr Lazer. "Quickly get inside the shack and work out how the Trans Warp Inducer inside works, these phones have an app that are linked to it. I need you to use the Trans Warp Inducer to transport these two files to these two coordinates now," he said as he gave two files to Tommy Grayson and a piece of paper with coordinates scribbled down. "I need to make a phone call. Let me know as soon as you have done it."

Jake stayed behind out of mobile telephone jamming range, and the other three of them ran towards the now empty shack and Jake dialled Detective Derrick.

"Now," Jake said as Detective Derrick acknowledged the signal. Jake then proceeded to de-activate the mobile jamming devices located in the four barrels before returning to the shack.

Detective Derrick, Sister Jennifer and Patricia O'Leary were each wearing thick black glasses when they entered the DrugTech building. Detective Derrick produced his badge to the receptionist and before long, the three of them had made their way to the office of Benjamin Jones. Benjamin Jones was seated at his desk with his assistant Saanvi Patel seated on the other side.

"Ms Saanvi Patel?" Detective Derrick asked.

"Yes?" she replied.

"You are under arrest for conspiracy in aiding Dr Jamieson's escape from lawful custody," Detective Derrick said producing handcuffs. "You are not obliged to say anything, but anything you do say may be used against you in a Court of law."

Detective Derrick then marched a crying Saanvi Patel out of Benjamin Jones' office towards his parked police car outside and drove her to the Surry Hills Police Station for processing.

Sister Jennifer and Patricia O'Leary remained behind with Benjamin Jones.

"Thank you," Benjamin Jones said sitting back down after he rose to his feet during the arrest. "I only trusted Saanvi Patel to a point," he said looking at his two new visitors, "But I suspected that she was ruthless enough to assist Dr Jamieson with his escape and betray me."

"At this moment," Sister Jennifer said, "A solicitor by the name of Quentin Banks is liaising with the Australian Securities and Investments Commission as well as the Securities and Exchange Commission of the USA. A public statement is being released about Dr Jamieson escaping lawful custody and using DrugTech assets and infrastructure to do it," she said. "It is expected that DrugTech's financial institutions will then be ordered to freeze the assets of DrugTech USA and DrugTech Australia. But DrugTech Australia's assets will be released if you issue a press statement now saying that you are dissolving the merger with DrugTech USA."

Benjamin Jones looked relieved and Sister Jennifer knew it.

"I'm more than happy to do that!" Benjamin Jones said, "I never wanted DrugTech to be involved in such a large corporate enterprise in the first place. I was only ever interested in the scientific aspects of DrugTech."

Benjamin Jones looked a little sheepish and looked around his desk before asking, "Um, do you know what I should say?"

Patricia O'Leary produced a piece of paper that Jake had already worked out with Quentin Banks and gave it to Benjamin Jones. "Just email this message to the main television stations and newspapers at these email addresses," she said pointing out the message and the addresses.

"Great," Benjamin Jones said.

"There's just one thing more," Sister Jennifer said broaching the topic with a little delicacy, "I was hoping you could do us a little favour?" she asked as Benjamin Jones raised his eyebrows.

Chapter 20

Secret Deals, Estrangements and Recriminations

Detective Sergeant Derrick was not the only police officer to hear of the impending arrest of Dr Jamieson. Sergeant Skip Johns from the Surry Hills Police Station was the leader of the red scorpion brigade, and as such, he had connections with the Kizana sisters, Dr Jamieson and their greatest sponsor, DrugTech, or at least, the economic guild of DrugTech. And when Detective Derrick set out with Sister Jennifer and Patricia O'Leary to DrugTech to arrest Saanvi Patel for conspiring in the escape of Dr Jamieson, Sergeant Skip Johns covertly followed them whereupon he parked his police car along a side-alley of the DrugTech building and waited at a vantage point to see what would happen. When he observed Saanvi Patel under arrest and escorted to Detective Derrick's police car, he attempted to get instructions from one of the Kizana sisters, but having failed in that attempt, his mind went into overdrive as he observed Sister Jennifer and Patricia O'Leary leave the DrugTech building alone.

Sergeant Johns did not have time to give his plan much thought. The plan comprised of one word. And that word was, "hostages." And so, as Sister Jennifer and Patricia O'Leary exited the main entrance of the DrugTech building, Sergeant Johns drew his gun from his holster, and covered it with a cardigan that he grabbed from the front seat of his car.

As Sister Jennifer and Patricia O'Leary approached the laneway between the DrugTech building and the hospital, Sergeant Skip Johns appeared and said, "This way ladies," as he beckoned with the covered gun aimed directly at Sister Jennifer.

"Stay behind me," Sister Jennifer said to Patricia as she moved to stand in front of Patricia facing Sergeant Johns directly.

"Come with me and nobody gets hurt," Sergeant Johns said. It was a strange sight having a fully-uniformed police officer, with a gun drawn covered by a cardigan, and walking backwards as he waved it at a nun and another woman who followed as hostages into the side alley towards Sergeant Johns' police car.

But as they entered the alley, Sister Jennifer stopped and looked directly at the man.

"Don't try anything," he warned.

"Donald Duck had Mickey Mouse for breakfast this morning," Sister Jennifer said smilingly.

"What?" the police officer said not really wanting to hear an explanation.

Then as quick as a snap, Sister Jennifer's right hand swung in front of her body grabbing the man's hand that was holding the gun, and she raised it high above her head looking like the Statue of Liberty.

The man was taller than Sister Jennifer and so the man's arm was still bent at the elbow as his hand, was still on the gun, but it was clamped under Sister Jennifer's hand, and try as he did, he was unable to free himself. Then the grip of Sister Jennifer's hand became like an iron vice and it started to tighten and tighten. And as the bones in the man's hand started to crumple, his knees gave way under the pain. But the deadweight of the man as he buckled under his feet did not alter the Statue of Liberty-like-stance of Sister Jennifer who suspended the man off the ground by his hand who was now forced to continue to clutch the gun, as his fallen and dangling body caused his elbow to straighten, and as he writhed in agony and he screamed in pain.

Sister Jennifer then looked into the man's eyes and it appeared as if her own eyes were glowing red. She then said, "The Coyote only caught the Roadrunner once," and then her hand tightened so much that even the steel gun began bending under the grip. The bones in the man's hand were now pulverized and with his nerves obliterated, the pain was reduced to numbness up to his elbow, and he looked as if he was about to pass-out.

Sister Jennifer then dropped the man and the broken and bent gun as he curled himself into a foetal position and immediately nursed his crushed hand into his abdomen and covered it with his other hand. She slowly looked left and right as she surveyed the street. To the left of her was the DrugTech building which was approximately ten stories high. To the right was the side of the hospital which was two stories high.

Sister Jennifer then grabbed Patricia's elbow and walked her across the laneway to the side of the hospital building. Then slowly bending her knees into the crouched position she forced Patricia to bend also. And with her head looking up towards the roof of the hospital building, she then leapt high into the air bringing Patricia up with her. From Sergeant Skip John's point of view, he heard a Doppler effect of Patricia's scream as she was whisked with Sister Jennifer, higher than two stories into the air before landing gently on the hospital roof and out of sight.

"What the hell just happened?" Patricia gasped.

"The man had quite nefarious thoughts," Sister Jennifer said.

"I didn't know you could leap tall buildings in a single bound?" Patricia said quite astonished.

"It was necessary to create an unbelievable set of facts so that he would not be believed if he chose to relay exactly what had just happened to anyone else."

"I can't believe it myself," Patricia exclaimed. "And what was all that talk about Donald Duck and the Roadrunner?" Patricia asked still stunned at where she was.

"Like I said," Sister Jennifer replied. "Just ridiculous nonsense that makes the man's story appear delusional if he attempted to relay the story to any other person."

Sister Jennifer then grabbed Patricia's elbow again and the two of them walked towards the fire exit on the top of the roof where they proceeded to leave the hospital without any further incident.

Meanwhile, in a shack outside the outskirts of town, down a dirt road and deep in the sticks, Dr Lazer, Tommy Grayson and Simon Sage were busy tinkering with the Trans Warp Inducer when a ute pulled up outside and three Dominican Priests walked in.

"Dr Lazer and Simon Sage, this is Father Dom, Father William and Father Charles," Jake said introducing them to his colleagues. "I believe you already know Tommy Grayson," he continued as they all waved a greeting to each other.

"I hear that Benjamin Jones has done us a personal favour at the behest of Sister Jennifer and just granted the Dominican Order a 99-year lease over this shack," Father Dom said smiling at Jake.

"Yes," Jake said, "I understand that Sister Jennifer can be quite persuasive."

Jake then pointed to the computer equipment behind him in the shack as he addressed the youthful-looking Father Dom directly. "This is a new, fully-functional, Trans Warp Inducer, that is secret and unknown to the authorities," Jake said. "My colleagues here have just altered the computer programming so that instead of trans-warping matter from one part of the universe to another, you are also now able to witness actual events in history. So, for example, you may choose to witness the Crucifixion of Christ, or the three wise men visiting Christ at his birth. You may choose to see the Battle of Lepanto, the tempting of Adam and Eve, the killing of Goliath, the assassination of JFK, anything you like. The thing is," Jake said scratching his head and wondering how to phrase his next words, "The world just isn't ready yet for such a powerful piece of machinery. And with such great power, it needs to be used ethically and responsibly. I can only trust you people to take custody of it and to use it as you see fit for the benefit of humankind."

Father Dom looked at the other two priests and then looked at Jake. "I think we can accept such a generous offer," he said as he extended his right hand and shook Jake's. Jake let out a sigh of relief as he contemplated a job well-done.

Meanwhile, at around 1:30am local time, a 200-foot superyacht, which happened to be named the *Sultana,* had just sailed around the Peloponnese and had now entered the Gulf of Patras where it dropped its anchors for the night. It had all the trappings of the rich, including a ballroom, a golf course, a casino, a nightclub, a helipad and several other luxuries that gave the 100 private guests on board an artificial and inflated sense of entitlement and expectation with their relationship to the world in general. As the ship was owned by Medici Pharmaceuticals, it also had a biolab on board for taxation reasons, but the lab, of course, was never actually used. And being only 1:30 in the morning, the night was still young and amidst the dancing and drinking, three of the partying teenage guests on board were each just tapped on the shoulder and asked to go up to the office of the hostess of the ship.

The Contessa Medici was seated on a red leather chair behind a magnificent glass desk. The office had plush apricot carpet with red velvet sofas. There was a video display on one wall, and an aquarium in the other.

As the teenage boy entered in his suit, and the two teenage girls entered in their semi-formal nightclub dresses, they took their positions on the sofas while the Contessa was finishing a telephone conversation at her desk. She replaced the handset to its usual position on the telephone on her desk and said in a rather irritated tone, "Your idiot father has just activated clause 25 of the merger agreement between DrugTech Australia and DrugTech USA, and has effectively demerged the companies."

The children of Benjamin Jones had lived more with their grandmother than with their parents. They liked her lifestyle and did not care much for an education. Benjamin Jones was too busy with the company to be able to protest too much at their attitude to life, and his wife Kathleen was a chemist at DrugTech who also could not find the time to properly parent her children. But the Contessa Medici was only all too-willing to spoil them and wouldn't hear of nursery-maids or day-care.

"What does that mean?" Greg asked, "To demerge the Companies." He was 19 and the eldest of the children, and had only just started to take an interest in the business affairs of his grandmother.

"We are heavily invested," the Contessa groaned. "If that demerger goes through, then Medici Pharmaceuticals will lose billions of dollars, including this ship and the lifestyle that you three have grown accustomed to."

"You said if it goes through," Gwynneth, the 18-year-old girl said, "Does that mean there is a chance that it won't go through?"

"We are investigating that possibility now," the Contessa answered. "But Dr Jamieson has been arrested, and if he is tried and convicted, there will be no way to salvage it."

"I thought he was killed in that aeroplane crash, wasn't he?" Rhiannon, the 16-year-old girl asked.

"Oh, you poor dear," the Contessa said, assuming that that was a sufficient answer to her inquiry.

"So, will Dr Jamieson be tried and convicted?" Greg asked.

"It's tricky," the Contessa said thinking aloud "But we have done many a secret favour for the President, and he certainly owes us a favour or two. The arrest and prosecution of Dr Jamieson can be sold to the media as nothing more than a political witch-hunt. I will ask the President for a Presidential pardon."

"Lady Catherine?" Greg asked calling the Contessa by the term of endearment that he had grown-up with, "Who is doing all this? How come this is happening? Is it Dr Lazer?" he asked remembering the name that was spoken of in spite in earlier conversations.

"I have given that a lot of thought," the Contessa said raising her eyes to the magnificent chandelier in her office. "I don't think it was Dr Lazer," the Contessa said, "But you are right, I think there is someone who is causing all these things to happen, someone who is totally against DrugTech."

"Who do you think it is?" Greg asked pressing the Contessa for an answer.

“The Trans Warp Inducer was seized and taken by the authorities when it was put inside an NMR machine at the University of Sydney. The lab that it was installed in is run by a man who never got on with Dr Jamieson.” The Contessa then looked at her grandson directly. “I think it is obvious,” she said already thinking of an adequate recrimination, “The man responsible for all of this turmoil is Professor Philip Monkey-Brain!”

Chapter 21

The Final Dose

The Pirate Uluç Ali rebuilt the ships that were lost in the Battle of Lepanto in record time. And the newer ships were bigger, better and faster. But the defeat at Lepanto did more than just lose a couple of ships of the Ottoman Empire. It smashed its morale. And morale could not be rebuilt in a shipyard. The Empire was not just previously undefeated. Its invincibility had been attributed to God Almighty, and such attribution was not merely a philosophy, it was fundamental to their theology. Accordingly, the defeat was irreconcilable with their beliefs and it served as a kind of Reformation of the Islamic religion. Financially, the Ottoman Empire was funded by the spoils of war that it gained from expansion. But the defeat at Lepanto was a watershed moment that instead brought stagnation. Bankruptcy was soon to follow. The Empire was then referred to as the Sick Man of Europe, which culminated ultimately in the Great War, which was in essence, the 'de-Ottomization' of the world.

But not every Ottoman Naval Commander felt the same way after the defeat at Lepanto. The Pirate Hamet Bey was a particularly savage Captain of a newly built Ottoman war galley and being the nephew of the great Barbarossa, who was the Supreme Commander of the Ottoman Naval Fleet before the great Müezzinzade at Lepanto, Hamet Bey had a reputation that he believed was worth protecting. And when the newly acquired war galley met one of Europe's finest, the *Santa Cruz*, Hamet Bey sounded the attack.

His crew however did not feel much like fighting. Of course, the slaves being manacled and shackled to the oars, did not have much of a say in the command decisions of the ship, but they could to some extent vote with their feet. And when the command to attack was given, the chief Oarsman did just that and tripped the Turkish Captain so that he fell headfirst onto the benches of the oarsmen. And with their teeth being their only weapon, and the slaves being starved for food, they each took a savage bite out of their detestable Captain, passing him from bench to bench, until after approximately a hundred or so bites, the Captain bled to death. The second in command threw the body of his captain overboard and surrendered to the advancing *Santa Cruz*. The boarding party of the *Santa Cruz* relieved the ship of its war chest and freed the slaves.

At that point the scene being observed by Father Dom went dark and Father Dom removed the virtual reality helmet from his head. "What happened?" he exclaimed, "It was just getting good."

Father Charles entered from the adjoining room. "The meteorite at the heart of the Trans Warp Inducer has decayed too much for it to be useable. Unless a replacement can be found, the Trans Warp Inducer is dead. What were you watching anyway?"

"Oh, just the wash-up of the Battle of Lepanto," Father Dom answered. "I couldn't help but see the analogies in the fall of the Ottoman Empire with that of Dr Jamieson and the DrugTech Empire."

"Do you think people will try to revive it to its former days of glory?" Father Charles questioned.

"There will be some," Father Dom said thinking of the Pirate Hamet Bey, "But I don't think people have the stomach for it. The demerger will go through and until then, the financial institutions will freeze their assets and cripple the enterprise. It will become known as the sick company of the exchange until it does."

Meanwhile, Sergeant Skip Johns was recovering from an amputation of his right hand. He could not only not operate his gun, but he could no longer ride his motorcycle. And that meant he could no longer be Captain of the Red Scorpion Brigade. And with its chief sponsor in dire straits, the brigade lacked purpose and soon disbanded. Sergeant Johns left the force a confused and broken man, literally torn between delusions of power on the one hand, and being overcome by a nun on the other. He made no attempt to relay the embarrassing and confusing story of the loss of his hand to others, and it led ultimately to the complete mental breakdown of the man. With the help of Detective Derrick, he was persuaded to check himself in to the Mary Immaculate Psychiatric Hospital where he remained for the rest of his life.

Dr Jamieson was found guilty in an American Court of the gross and wicked negligent manslaughter of Astronaut Dr Helouise Dawson and her crew of the spaceship Atlantis. His failure to abort the take-off when it was found that he ought to have been aware of the defective landing-gear on board the ship, meant that he bore the brunt of the failed endeavour. The Contessa Medici was not successful in persuading the President for a full Presidential pardon, but she did manage to have the sentence commuted on the grounds that he was becoming severely demented. He spent the rest of his life being looked after by relatives in a humble abode in Texas where he soon forgot who he was nor had any idea what DrugTech was or did.

The Contessa Medici had lost billions in the demerger of DrugTech. She was still a wealthy woman with influence and power, but the pinnacle of her success was over. She retired to Australia where she accepted the largely ceremonial role of Chancellor of the University of Sydney. After her first official role as Chancellor, she asked that Emeritus Professor Philip join her for a cup of tea in her office overlooking the jacaranda tree in the main quadrangle.

Up until this point, the Contessa had blamed the Professor for the ultimate downfall of Dr Jamieson and the DrugTech empire, but upon Professor Philip entering the room with such a jovial happy-go-lucky smile, she had immediate doubts as to whether she had misjudged the man. "Only scientific idiots smile like that," she thought to herself, "Idiots who would much rather indulge in scientific breakthroughs than make money for their family which could benefit the rest of humankind! Definitely not my type."

"Good morning, Chancellor," the Emeritus Professor said as he was directed to a small round table with tea and scones prepared, "And congratulations on your recent appointment."

"Thank you, Professor," the Chancellor said.

"Please call me Philip," the Professor responded with his eyes growing wider with delight at the butter and jam scones on the table before him. The Contessa could not help but like the man.

"How goes the biolab since the NMR machines were seized by the military?" the Chancellor asked.

"Oh, that was a sad occasion," Philip said genuinely remorsefully, "We were so looking forward to conducting such wonderful experiments, when it all came crashing down around us."

"I see," the Chancellor said as she raised her cup of tea to her lips and took a sip.

The Professor's gaze was drawn to her wrist whereupon he noticed a "bag of worms"-like-movement in the muscles of her forearm.

"May I see that please?" the Professor asked in his medical doctor's tone. He extended his hand for a closer examination of the Contessa's wrist, and with the annoying twitching of her muscles in her forearm that she was eager to have looked at by an expert, she willingly complied.

"This looks like neuromyotonia," the Professor said, "Otherwise known as Isaac's syndrome."

"What's that?" the Chancellor asked with a little trepidation.

"Is it new?" the Professor asked.

"Only just started noticing it," the Chancellor answered.

"Well, then, it's a paraneoplastic syndrome of the nervous system," the Professor explained, "It may be the first symptom of a serious cancer."

"My God," the Chancellor said to herself as she looked more closely at her forearm and saw her muscles wriggling. "Can anything be done?"

"You know, Chancellor," the Professor said shifting in his chair and wondering how best to broach the subject, "When I worked at DrugTech many years ago, I came up with a pill that could cure any kind of cancer, even the terminal ones. The cure would leave the patient deaf, but that was nothing that a cochlear implant couldn't solve."

"Why did you leave DrugTech?" the Chancellor asked.

"When I took my cure in to the managing director at the time, he wasn't too fond of a cure for cancer," the Professor answered. "Also, he didn't really like referring such patients off to another company for a cochlear implant operation since DrugTech didn't own the patent for that operation and DrugTech was making far too much money from treating cancers instead of curing them."

"Is that what Dr Jamieson said?" the Contessa asked.

"No, I never met Dr Jamieson," the Professor answered, "This was before his time. But I heard later that the incoming Managing Director, Dr Jamieson did not much care for my line of work either."

"If I can get you back inside DrugTech," the Contessa asked, "Do you think you can use your cure on me if I have cancer?"

"Yes, I can," the Professor said smiling comfortingly at the frightened lady, "You will feel stronger and younger than you have felt for a very long time, and with the latest cochlear implants on the market today, you will be hearing better than you have also in a long time too!"

The Contessa was sold on the idea. Using her connections with her son-in-law, Benjamin Jones, the operation at DrugTech under the watchful eye of Professor Philip, went off without any complications. And with Benjamin Jones not really happy in his position as Managing Director, and with the Contessa Medici still being the major shareholder and persuading Emeritus Professor Philip to accept the position on condition that he would have access to the latest and greatest NMR machines on the planet, DrugTech Australia soon found itself with a new Managing Director.

Professor Philip was definitely of the scientific guild *par excellence* but with the Contessa Catherine Medici feeling that she owed him her life, the economic factions within the board of directors at DrugTech would not dare make a move against him. One of the first things he did as managing director, at Benjamin Jones' request, was to appoint Benjamin Jones a DrugTech counsellor where Dr Jones assisted with the mental well-being of his staff and scientists. Kathleen Jones, a respected chemist in her own right, and wife of Benjamin Jones, became the trusted assistant of Professor Philip. The second thing he did was declassify the cures of cancer and diabetes and a flood of patients and their loved ones from around the world were forever grateful.

But the patients and their loved ones were not the only ones grateful. The scientific community was abuzz with the breakthroughs made by DrugTech and in particular, the cure that Professor Philip had come up with for cancer, that Stockholm was soon to welcome him as a new Nobel laureate in medicine. And that meant that the Professor had to make a speech. Of course, he would never shy away from making a speech, but it didn't come naturally to him, as it did to people like Dr Jamieson. That meant that he needed to put in the proper research.

Kathleen had suggested that he speak with Sir Charles Maxwell, a former Nobel laureate in Physics, who had since become a Dominican Priest, and as it so happened, the Dominican Priests, where Father Charles was located, was in a shack at the outskirts of town, down a dirt road, that was under a 99-year lease with DrugTech. Professor Philip made an appointment to see him. But as he was nearing the shack, the old ute that he was driving hit a rock that caused a gasket to come lose, and the truck started to lose fuel. It broke down in the middle of the dirt track about a thousand metres from the shack.

"It's a good thing I brought some boots with me," he thought to himself as he put on his knee-high galoshes and started trekking by himself towards the shack. It was now dusk, and the mist and fog had descended making it difficult for him to see where he was walking. After a few hundred metres, with the truck well behind him and the shack well ahead of him, and the mist and fog all around him, he soon noticed an eerie green glow emanating from a rock in a small cavern ahead of him just to the left of the dusty track.

THE END

About the Author

As I grew up, I distinctly recall three distinct lessons which had a profound effect on the way I viewed life thereafter.

The first was my first science class in year eight where I was introduced to chemistry. I was absolutely astounded to learn that all matter, whether it be a horse, a human, a house or honey were all comprised of basic building blocks called elements – which were effectively the Lego of the universe; and that these were limited and listed in the periodic table (even if there were a few only mildly undefined ones towards the end). I had never before perceived matter that way. It is very seductive and taken to extremes can actually blind you to the reality of the horse in favour of its chemical composition. I remember going to Open Day at Sydney University and seeing this wonderful Professor reduce the human-being to just a composition of elements that he had on display. It took me a couple of decades later to realise that that professor was actually quite mad and that he turned out to be my father-in-law but that is a completely different story.

The second time I was similarly astounded was when I sat in a courtroom for the first time as a school kid, probably around year 10. I saw the judge and the barristers using words that I never understood like, "constructive trust" in a jargon which made me realise that these people were certainly speaking another language that I had not learned. But what I thought most strange was that whilst I thought I had a basic appreciation of what things were, I realised that these people had learned a whole new language to attach legal rights to the things that they were arguing about. Who would have thought that the "rules of the game" could not be gleaned by a simple knowledge of the reality of the subject of the things argued about, mixed with a bit of basic common-sense? In other words, a whole new legal language had to be learned and debated in order to secure such rights? As a debater, and someone whose curiosity was piqued, I wanted to learn that language. So, I bought a law book on contracts, read it and understood it, then went to law school and have now many times "talked the talk" in Court as I "walked the walk" with clients through such a minefield. That had its own fascinations and certainly changed the way I viewed the material universe thereafter. All of a sudden, I saw things with man-made laws imposed over them which governed relationships of man and matter called "property" laws which were "personal" (tangible), "intellectual" (intangible) and "real" (land).

Then of course there were two things that I either took for granted or had gleaned for myself whilst growing up. The first was an appreciation of mathematics and physics. Mathematics seemed to be universally inherent common-sensical rules of logic that could be applied to the real world and became a tool for the physicist. Whereas chemistry was the study of the composition of matter (which was not so self-evident), I had gleaned for myself that physics was the study of the movement of matter. Combined with mathematics, one could fascinatingly predict how future movement would occur from similar analogical experimentation. I found that the most fascinating thing of all.

There was another thing that as a child I took for granted without much thought about it. That was my being born into the Christian faith. Beginning with the "ten commandments", a natural law system was "God-given" that governed the relationship of humans with each other. Now as a child, I was happy to accept that this was "God-given" but was nevertheless a fundamental set of ethical principles that underpinned the modern-day western culture of law. This was the influence of Judeo-Christian society, and modern-day human laws in Western culture came from the priests of the Middle Ages who were the ones who became judges and lawyers because they could read and write. This was similar to mathematics underpinning physics. They worked hand in hand and were worthy of simple acceptance.

But what I also took for granted, is that whilst I took Moses to be a "God-given" receptacle of the laws of God, atheists simply saw Moses as a kind of Confucius, who went about "making-up" or "discovering for himself" the common-sense principles of ethics that work to govern the relationship of humans and so he, "appropriated for himself," the divine authority from whence his laws came. At first, that didn't matter to me. I was happy to accept on faith that God gave the laws, but I was content for the atheists to simply follow the laws as a matter of atheistic ethics. It mattered little for the governance of man that some people believed in the faith and others did not, so long as they lived harmoniously together following the same rules of ethics. And I ultimately believed that God did not much care either. What would it matter if someone believed that God exists or chose to love God if they nevertheless believed in or loved what God believed in and loved? In other words, live a natural good life according to ethics, and you happen to be living what others called a "holy" life and that was sufficient for salvation.

So that was my basic child-hood understanding of the universe and the laws of nature and the laws of man. It was a good working system and I am sure that many a professor still believes in such a thing as the underpinning of a good working ethical system of the workings of science and human relationships. But then, by a chance accident, I hit upon another thing that had a profound impact on me and certainly changed the way that I viewed the world.

When I was a young child, we used to play with the children of the neighbouring Jewish family. They were not exactly orthodox Jews, but they certainly did not believe in the Christian religion. That was never an element of friction amongst us, it was probably only mentioned in passing conversation and was only an academic thing in any event. But then the girl of that family, Rebecca, became a "born-again Christian" whatever that meant. I think I just viewed that as another version of Protestantism. Again, it meant very little to me, it was a free world and "each to their own". But then something strange happened. She started arguing with my brother that, "Mary had other children besides Christ," and she claimed that a line of scripture supported her statement. Now, when I heard that, my basic reaction was, "does it matter? Surely, that is simply a question of historical fact? The scriptures either answer it or it does not, and what does it matter if it was ambiguous?" That was my childhood thinking on the topic. The profound thing happened when my brother relayed that assertion to my father. My father's reaction was immediately, "That is anathema" and then he reached for a couple of books which I later learned was the "Summa Theologica" and he said, "Let's see what St Thomas Aquinas says about it."

So, my immediate reaction was, "Who the hell is St Thomas Aquinas and why would his opinion matter more than the born-again Christian's? Surely it was just a question of historical fact, wasn't it? Wouldn't a simple logical interpretation of scripture suffice?"

So, long after the matter was settled between my father and my brother, I kept gawking through the Summa Theologica. Here again I came across a jargon that I did not understand. He was speaking the language of another “science” which I later learned to be metaphysics, but I previously had no concept of it. But that was not what I found fascinating. What I found incredibly fascinating was this. The conclusions that Aquinas was reaching in the Summa Theologica were intelligible enough. They were clear and concise. Such things included whether God exists, and the nature of God, the nature of the intellect, and all sorts of other things that set-up the Christian belief. But what was quite new to me was that this Aquinas fellow was claiming to reach those conclusions not from any God-given revelation (though it was always consistent with those) but from pure reasoning of fact and common sense. I didn’t know that the two were related. I thought the faith had nothing to do with reason. But uniquely the Christian religion claims reason as emanating from the same God and that was Aquinas’ real contribution to Christian theology. And so, here I was confronted with an encyclopaedic book of three volumes that claimed to prove many of the truths of Christian religion, such as whether Mary had other children besides Christ, but also more fundamental truths such as whether God exists, from material already available to all of us (ie, not God-given revelation) but in order to understand it, I needed to learn a new language or science which Aquinas was using, which was the science of metaphysics as propounded by Aristotle.

But as fascinated as I was about it as a child, it was impossible for a child to learn it for themselves. For one thing, I had no teacher. But for another, it is immensely profound and deep. This was quite a new way of looking at things. I thought it interesting, but I had reached an impasse and was content to simply move on in life. But there were two things in particular that I stumbled across in science as a schoolkid that brought me back to the writings of Aquinas. The first was a biology class I think in Year eight. The science teacher was about to give us the scientific definition of, “life”. I immediately had recollections back to Aquinas and remembered that Aquinas had defined it in the Summa Theologica, and it had something to do with an entity determining for itself the course of its own movement. I had thought that that was a strange esoteric definition that had a meaning for the 11th century philosopher but surely had no real application in modern-day science. And then quite amazingly, the science teacher started to use the word “movement” and “change” in his scientific definition of life, and I naturally started to ask myself whether Aquinas was on to something after all that was not outdated.

The next time I was brought back to Aquinas was probably year nine physics. We were studying the concept of, "potential energy". I remember coming across that word, "potential" when I was reading Aquinas' first-way demonstration for the existence of God. But the physics equation of, "potential energy" was quite strange to me. It was defined to be 'mgh' where m is the mass, g is the gravitational pull and h was the height. I had no problem with the m and the g. But I had a big problem with the h. That was because the h could change in a relative way, not by movement of the object itself, but by movement of the earth or other mass that you are measuring the object from. So, I was asking myself the questions, "How can you possibly change the potential energy of a thing by simply changing the thing that you are measuring it from? How can the potential energy of a ball be different when measured from a certain height to the surface of the earth, but be different if you were to dig a hole at the surface of the earth and measure from inside the hole? I mean digging the hole did not in any way touch the ball. So how the hell could it give the ball more energy?" And the only way I could rationally answer these questions to myself was to investigate the concept of "potentiality" and that just brought me back to Aquinas. Truth be told, I had come across many things thereafter that kept bringing me back to it. When I entered university, I discovered that many scientists were grappling with philosophical terms such as, "causation" and, "phenomenology". Also, biological science spoke about a, "function" of a thing, and I was asking myself, "why would an unintelligent biological organ or thing have any function?" A human has an intellect and a will and can choose to act in a certain way. But, for example, a red blood cell does not have those things and yet people were talking about it as if the red blood cell has a function in the body and acts in a certain, almost, pre-defined way in nature. And so, this reminded me again of Aquinas whose writing had sort-of bridged-the-gulf between observable and manifest things to the senses, but yet reaching conclusions that were more profound and abstract, as if related to God and God-given things.

Ultimately, I finished university and became a lawyer and only after many years as a lawyer I stumbled across the "Centre for Thomistic Studies". I had seen my father's philosophy notes from that great metaphysician and lecturer, "Dr Woodbury" but I had not understood them. I had bought a book from Professor Peter Kreeft from the USA that attempted to add footnotes to an abridged version of the Summa Theologica but my understanding from that was still very, very basic. But now the syllabus of the Centre for Thomistic Studies included "Ontology" and "Defensive Metaphysics". They were the subjects I really wanted taught to me. That was the language that Aquinas had used in the Summa. I was not interested in the philosophy degree that that Centre could confirm on you – so I did not bother enrolling in any of the other subjects, just to get that degree. But I enrolled in Ontology and Defensive Metaphysics and finally got the education that I had been longing for as a child. Well wow! That was the third most fascinating thing that I had ever come across in my education as a human, and I regret to say that many, many humans never attain it. But it opened my eyes to a reality of the world (as seen by Aquinas and Aristotle) and has profoundly affected me ever since. It would be like forever having seen squiggles in the world around you and thinking they were just random things that existed in the world, only to learn later the English language, and then see the squiggles in a whole new light, as words comprising the Shakespearian plays, the laws of man and God, texts books, fantasy books, poetry – a whole new reality was now laid bare before me and it fulfilled my intellectual yearning and has ever since.

www.ingramcontent.com/pod-product-compliance
Lightning Source LLC
Chambersburg PA
CBHW030813310726
48980CB00006B/481/J

* 9 7 8 0 6 4 6 8 5 2 5 5 3 *